Brilliant blue shards of lightning rippled across the rain-swept sky. There was a resounding crack as a bolt struck a tree somewhere close, and the smell of brimstone was strong. Thunder had become continuous, each rising crescendo sounding like an echo of the last.

There was nothing they could do except wait. Then, when the storm seemed to reach the very peak of its fury, lightning struck in their midst. The concussion was so severe that it robbed McQuade of his hearing for a few seconds, but his horrified eyes saw one of the wagons disappear in a blinding flash. There was the quick smell of brimstone, of burning flesh. Then his hearing returned. A woman screamed. McQuade was out of his wagon, running . . .

ACROSS
THE RIO
COLORADO

Ralph Compton

St. Martin's Paperbacks

ACROSS THE RIO COLORADO

Trail map design by L. A. Hensley.

Copyright © 1997 by Ralph Compton.

ISBN: 0-312-96102-2

Printed in the United States of America

St. Martin's Paperbacks edition/March 1997

St. Martin's Paperbacks are published by St. Martin's Press, 175 Fifth Avenue, New York, NY 10010.

10 9 8 7 6 5 4 3

AUTHOR'S FOREWORD

*W*hile Texas statehood was many bloody years away, there were Mexican land grants available along the Brazos and Colorado Rivers. Through the efforts of Stephen Austin—a Missourian—a farmer could claim 277 acres, while a rancher was eligible for 4,615 acres. In the land-hungry east, land prices had reached an unheard-of dollar and twenty-five cents an acre. Thus many Americans became Mexican citizens, immigrating to south central Texas, where land was available for only a few cents an acre.

But it was perilous times. Traveling from St. Joseph or St. Louis, the trail led right through Indian Territory, a haven for hostile Indians and renegades of every stripe. Texas itself was little better, for it was the home of the dreaded Comanche Indians. But nothing slowed the quest for Texas land, and men drawn to the frontier surged forth to meet its demands.

While the immigrants themselves were whang-leather-tough, an even hardier breed was necessary to freight in goods over the treacherous trails, supplying the needs of these early settlers. Early caravans consisted of pack mules, but as the demand increased, there were trains of lumbering freight wagons. Teamsters riding the high boxes were armed with several revolvers, a long knife, and a Sharps .50 caliber rifle. These men fought Indians, outlaws, and occasionally, one another.

Wherever men went—to Colorado, Montana, or California to dig for gold, or to the Republic of Texas to farm or raise cattle—the traders with their pack mules or wagons always followed. These buccaneers who rode the high boxes took commerce to the western plains, because the potential rewards seemed worth the risk, but there had to be more. It was a time, in a changing land, that called forth men of courage. Some earned fame, some an unmarked grave beside a lonely trail, but all shared an epic American frontier that once was, but now lives only in the pages of American history.

PROLOGUE

❧

St. Louis, Missouri. April 11, 1837.

"*D* raw, damn you!"
    John Burke was just nineteen, and had spent the afternoon in the Emerald Dragon, a dive on the St. Louis waterfront.

"Put the gun away, John," said Chance McQuade.

There had been bad blood between the Burkes and the McQuades since that day in St. Joe, when Andy—Andrew Burke's eldest son—had drawn on Chance McQuade. Chance had been forced to kill Andy to save his own life, but the Burkes hadn't forgotten.

"You're a coward," Burke shouted, his voice trembling.

"You know better," said Chance quietly. "I'll draw against you only if I have to."

"By God, you got to," Burke shouted, clawing at his gun.

He was quick, but not quick enough. McQuade waited until he had the weapon clear of the holster. He then drew and fired once. Burke stumbled back against the batwing doors and fell into the saloon. Men had quickly gathered from several other saloons, all shouting questions. McQuade said nothing, waiting for the sheriff. When the lawman arrived, he had a shotgun under his arm and a wad of plug in his jaw. He was dressed like a farmer, in a red flannel shirt, overalls, and rough-out boots.

"Who drawed first?" he demanded.

"The dead man," somebody said.

"Anybody see it any different?" the sheriff asked.

When there was no response, he turned to McQuade.

"I'm rulin' it self-defense. I'm Isaac Seaborn. Who are you?"

"Chance McQuade."

"You ever see this hombre before he drawed on you?"

"Yes," said McQuade. "We're both from St. Joe. Three years ago, one of his brothers drew on me, and I was forced to kill him."

"I'd take it as a favor if you'd move on," the sheriff said. "Nothin' personal."

"Yes," McQuade said, "I understand. I'm looking for a job as a teamster or guide, and then I'll be leaving."

Before the sheriff or the men who had gathered could question him further, McQuade continued along the boardwalk. While he was sure his encounter with John Burke had been nothing more than a stroke of bad luck, he suspected the rest of the Burkes, including old Andrew, were somewhere in town.

Chance McQuade was thirty-two years old, with black hair and gray eyes, and had grown up in St. Joseph, Missouri. In 1821, William Becknell had opened a trade route into Santa Fe, New Mexico Territory, and twenty-year-old McQuade had ridden with him. In the years that had followed, Chance McQuade had become a seasoned frontiersman. He had ridden the high box, freighting goods through Indian Territory into Texas, and from Kansas City to trading posts in Kansas, Colorado, and Wyoming.

In this year, the spring of 1837, McQuade had come to St. Louis in response to a story in a Kansas City newspaper. Rufus Hook, a wealthy businessman, had received a grant to build a town in south central Texas. For a fee, Hook had offered to secure grants for individuals, and had

already signed a hundred families who would settle along
the Rio Colorado. Hook needed a wagon boss and guide.
The man he chose would receive a grant of his own, as
well as five hundred dollars. Chance McQuade knew the
freighting business backwards, forwards, and upside
down. He was quick with a pistol and deadly with a big
Sharps .50 caliber. His body bore the evidence of many
knife fights, and a large, ugly scar from a Comanche
lance. He had bossed many wagon trains where the teamsters had been older than himself. Now he wanted a rancher's grant in Texas—4,615 acres—and the five hundred
dollars Hook was willing to pay a wagon boss. Reaching
the address given in the newspaper, he was amazed to
find it no more than a hole in the wall, with a sign on the
door that read *Hook Enterprises*. When he opened the
door, a pale woman dressed in black looked at him from
the desk where she sat.

"I'm here to see Rufus Hook," said McQuade. "Is he
here?"

"Perhaps," she replied. "Who are you, and what do
you want?"

"I'm Chance McQuade, and I'm here to become his
wagon boss, taking that expedition into Texas."

Before she could respond, a door to the next office
opened. A heavy man—probably in his fifties—stepped
out. He was dressed in a dark suit, boiled shirt, and string
tie. But for a fringe above his ears, he was bald, and a
cigar was clenched in his teeth.

"Get back to your work, Emma," he said. He then
turned to face McQuade. "I am Rufus Hook."

He nodded toward the open door, and McQuade entered. He stood with his back to the wall, facing the desk.
His trousers were dark homespun, his shirt red flannel,
while his boots and Stetson were pure cowboy. On his
left hip, butt-forward, he carried one of the first Colt revolvers manufactured in America. He said nothing, waiting for Hook to speak. There was no chair other than the

one behind Hook's desk. Hook sat down, discovered his cigar had gone out, and dropped it into a mug that sat on the desk.

"So you're my wagon boss," he said. "In what ways are you qualified?"

"In every way that matters," said McQuade.

"I heard a shot a few minutes ago. Did you have anything to do with that?"

"I did," McQuade admitted, but volunteered nothing more.

"You don't talk much, do you?"

"Hook," said McQuade, "if a man measures up, he don't have to talk. If he can't or won't stand tall, then nothin' he's got to say will ever make any difference. Is that land grant you're offerin' me a farmer's grant, or a rancher's grant?"

"I haven't offered you anything, yet," Hook growled, "and if I do, it'll be my choice, not yours. You take a hell of a lot for granted, my friend."

"I take nothing for granted," said McQuade. "Whatever needs doin' with wagons and the teams, I can do, and I can do it better than anybody else. Now when I get your damned wagons to Texas, I want a rancher's grant. Do I get it or not? You have ten seconds."

"Get the hell out of my office, McQuade," Hook bawled. "Get out."

McQuade stepped out, closing the door, but that was as far as he went. Emma stared at him in awe. In a matter of seconds, the door opened. Hook was about to shout after McQuade, when he became aware of McQuade standing there, a grin on his weathered face.

"Your ten seconds have run out," said McQuade cheerfully.

Furious, Hook nodded toward his open office door, and McQuade again entered, closing it behind him. Hook wasted no time.

"I don't like pushy, smart-mouth men, McQuade, but time is short, and I'm forced to make an exception. There is a wagon camp five miles west of town, on the south bank of the Missouri. Eventually there will be a hundred wagons. Your initial duty is to go there and inspect the wagons and the teams, doing whatever you must to make them trail-worthy. I want mules pulling the wagons. Any oxen must be led or driven. The journey is to begin on May first. At that time, you will acquire an additional twenty-one wagons. These and their contents belong to me.''

''And their contents will be exactly what?''

''You'll know soon enough,'' said Hook. ''For now, I believe you have your hands quite full.''

''What about my rancher's land grant and the five hundred dollars?''

''You'll receive both when you have taken these wagons safely to the Rio Colorado,'' Hook replied. ''I am supplying a cook and food for the journey. When you take the trail, you may take your meals with my teamsters. I have also engaged a dozen fighting men to assist you with sentry duty and the fighting of Indians. For anything I have overlooked, I have a line of credit at Stallworth's mercantile.''

McQuade closed the door behind him, tipped his hat to Emma, and left the building. He didn't like Rufus Hook, but he relied on a philosophy that had served him well over the years. When a man hired on, he was being paid for his services, not necessarily to like the job or the man who had hired him. But putting likes and dislikes aside, there was a falseness about Rufus Hook, something that didn't ring true. The only thing about Hook that seemed honest was his obvious dislike for McQuade, and the only thing they were likely to have in common was their dislike for one another. McQuade decided he hadn't been told all he should know, that Hook was purposely keeping him in the dark, and he recalled a bit of scripture that suited the situation perfectly: *Men love darkness, for their deeds are evil.*

All Chance McQuade had to show for a dozen years

of riding the high boxes was a bay horse, his saddle, bed-roll, pistol, .50 caliber Sharps, and the clothes that he wore. He had no money for a night in a St. Louis hotel, so he rode along the river until he reached what had to be the wagon camp Rufus Hook had spoken of. He reined up, staggered by a veritable sea of humanity that revolved around what he estimated to be near the hundred wagons of which Rufus Hook had spoken. Most of the wagon canvas had weathered to varying shades of gray, and even from a distance, he could see where it had been patched. God only knew what might be the condition of the wagons themselves. Wheels ungreased for months—or never greased at all—invited broken axles, while improperly fitted iron tires would come loose, leading to splintered wheels. Dogs barked, cows bawled, children shouted, mules brayed, and above it all there was the roar of a big fifty. Half a dozen fires bloomed along the river bank, as women took advantage of the shallows to wash their clothing and blankets. A blanket had been spread on the ground, and men hunkered about it, shooting craps. Somewhere a rooster crowed. It reminded McQuade of a Green River rendezvous, without the trappers. Some of the men gathered as McQuade rode in. Mostly, their eyes were full of questions, but four of them regarded McQuade with open hostility.

"What'n hell are you doin' here, McQuade?"

Andrew Burke stood with his hands on his hips, sided by his three remaining sons, Matthew, Mark, and Luke.

"I'm the wagon boss, Burke," said McQuade. "All the way to the Rio Colorado."

"You'll never live to see it," Matthew Burke snarled.

"I likely won't, if I turn my back on you Burkes," said McQuade. "None of you are handy at pullin' a gun against a man facing you, and that leaves just one way for you to go."

"We've had a peaceful camp, up to now," said a bearded man with a revolver stuck under his belt. "What's behind all this bull-of-the-woods talk?"

"This varmint, Chance McQuade, has shot and killed two of my sons," Andrew Burke shouted. "He gunned down John, my youngest, not more'n two hours ago."

"John wouldn't have it any other way," said McQuade, "and he drew first."

"He sure as hell did," one of the onlookers said. "I was there. He was spoilin' for a fight."

"For the record," McQuade said, "three years ago in St. Joe, I shot Andy Burke when he drew on me. He was stinking drunk and slapping a woman around, which is the Burke style. I slapped him, givin' him a dose of his own medicine. He started the gunplay."

A dozen men had gathered, most of them accompanied by their wives and children, and they looked unfavorably upon the Burkes. The bearded man with the pistol under his belt spoke again.

"I'm Ike Peyton, McQuade. You say you been hired as wagon boss?"

"I have," said McQuade. "I've been ridin' the high box for twelve years, hauling goods into Texas, Kansas, Colorado, and Wyoming. I've fought Indians, outlaws, grizzlies, wolves, and some no-account varmints I thought was sidin' me. Between now and May first, I'll be helping you ready your wagons for the trail, and helping you to prepare for what's ahead."

"Big talk," Andrew Burke sneered. "McQuade's sold old Hook a bill of goods. There's not a thing he can do for us that we can't do for ourselves."

"Let me remind all of you of something," said McQuade, "especially you Burkes. I'm not costing any of you a thing. Nothing is at stake here except the Burkes' grudge against me. Are any of you wantin' to throw in with them, disliking me because I defended myself against a pair of damn fools who wouldn't have it any other way?"

"Hell, no," a man shouted. "We likely got enough ahead of us, without fightin' among ourselves."

There were shouts of approval, but McQuade's eyes

were on the Burkes. Their very manner told him it wasn't over. If he won the confidence of the rest of these people, that might prevent the Burkes from shooting him in the back. He could expect no more.

In the days that followed, more wagons drifted in, some of them bringing families from Indiana, Illinois, and Ohio. Chance McQuade quickly learned that he couldn't inspect every wagon. He must enlist the help of other men he could trust. He had become friends with Ike Peyton, and it was to Ike that he spoke.

"Most of these wagons need work, Ike. I won't have time to personally inspect them all. Do you know some of these men well enough to ask them to help? A chain is only as strong as its weakest link. If any wagon breaks down, the entire train grinds to a halt."

"Let me talk to some of them," said Peyton. "I'm sure we can count on a few of them to help. I'll see that they understand it in that light, that one breakdown hurts us all."

Ike Peyton was as good as his word, speaking to Gunter Warnell, Eli Bibb, Cal Tabor, and Will Haymes. With Ike leading them, they agreed to assist in preparing the wagons for the trail, and to help with any breakdowns that might occur along the way. The Burkes kept their silence, and there was no trouble from the rest of the camp. However, McQuade was in for some unpleasant surprises, beginning when Rufus Hook's wagons began rolling in. The first was the cook and supply wagon, driven by an old Negro with gray hair. Reining up his teams, he eased himself down from the wagon box. He wasted no time.

"I be Ampersand," he said. "Call me Amp or Sand, but not greasy belly, dirty apron, or biscuit shooter. I answer to Mr. Hook, an' nobody else."

"I'm wagon boss," said Chance. "Name's Chance McQuade. On the trail, everybody will answer to me."

"Wal, now," Amp said, "Mr. Hook be ridin' with me. I answer to him, not you."

Nobody—including McQuade—had an answer to that. Clearly, none of the men in the camp had been told Rufus Hook would be traveling to Texas with the train. With that in mind, McQuade prepared himself for more surprises, and they weren't long in coming. Hiram Savage and Snakehead Presnall arrived, and they had the look of tinhorn gamblers, a look that was further emphasized by the contents of the wagons they drove. Savage made no secret of the fact that his wagon was loaded with saloon equipment, including chairs, tables, an upright piano, and a roulette wheel. While Presnall's wagon was empty, it had been ingeniously equipped with six bunks, and two days after Presnall's arrival, he drove the wagon to town and returned with six women. Brash, young painted women.

"Whores," said Gunter Warnell. "I seen some of them in a saloon in town."

The next wagon that showed up brought two men in town clothes and derby hats.

"My God," Eli Bibb said, "this is startin' to look like a Sunday tea social."

"This is a wagon train, bound for Texas," said McQuade, as the men stepped down.

"We are quite aware of that," said the elder of the two. "I am Doctor Horace Puckett, and this is Attorney Xavier Hedgepith. We have been engaged to practice in a new town in Texas. We will be accompanying you."

"Derby hats, boiled shirts, clawhammer coats, and Sunday britches," said Cal Tabor in disgust. "Who you reckon will be replacin' their busted axles and broken wheels?"

"Not me, by God," Will Haymes said.

"I reckon it can't get much worse," said Ike Peyton.

But it could and did. The Reverend Miles Flanagan, an old zealot whose only sermon was fire, brimstone, and damnation, arrived.

"I am the Reverend Miles Flanagan," he said, by way of introduction, "and this is my daughter, Mary. Should any man of you look at her with lust in your hearts, I shall command Almighty God to strike you dead.''

Mary, with blond hair and blue eyes, looked to be maybe twenty-five, and she kept her eyes on her clasped hands. Chance McQuade regarded the girl with interest, wondering if she were about to expire with shame. Flanagan had brought a tent, and while the girl struggled to erect it, the Reverend sat on the wagon seat, studying his bible.

''Here,'' said McQuade, ''let me help you with that.''

''Please,'' she said, her eyes on Flanagan, ''I can manage.''

But McQuade helped her erect the tent, under the watchful eyes of the Reverend Flanagan. He glared at Chance as though he might order God to strike him dead at any time, and McQuade returned his gaze with all the venom he could muster.

''Thank you,'' the girl whispered.

''You're welcome,'' McQuade replied. ''My pleasure, when I can be helpful.''

''McQuade,'' said Ike Peyton, ''if he *can* send anybody to hell, you're goin' to get your tail feathers burnt off to the roots.''

''That old varmint don't speak for the God I believe in,'' McQuade said.

Finally, a dozen men rode in, each on a good horse and armed to the teeth. McQuade walked out to meet them, and they reined up. The lead rider spoke.

''You McQuade, the wagon boss?''

''I am,'' said McQuade. ''Who are you, and the pack ridin' with you?''

''I'm Creeker. Eventually you'll meet the rest of the boys, but for now, their names won't mean nothin'. Mr. Hook's hired us to shoot Injuns an' anybody else that gits too troublesome. You take care of the wagons, an' we'll git along.''

McQuade said nothing. The dozen riders unsaddled near the river, allowing their horses to roll.

"My God," said Gunter Warnell, "that's got to be a bunch of killers."

"I expect you're right," McQuade said. "I'm startin' to wonder what kind of town this is goin' to be, considerin' the kind of materials Hook's usin' to build it."

"I aim to talk to some of the other families," said Ike Peyton. "From what I've seen, we ought to organize. I don't like the looks of some of the folks that'll be goin' with us."

"Hell, I'd pull out and go back to Indiana," Eli Babb said, "but Hook made it clear he wasn't refundin' anybody's money. I ain't givin' the old buzzard two hundred dollars, and I want that grant I been promised."

In the days that followed, sixteen more wagons arrived, increasing the total to a hundred and twenty. The teamsters, hired by Rufus Hook, were all close-mouthed, but it wasn't difficult for McQuade to learn what the wagons contained. There was barrel after barrel of flour, sugar, and molasses. There were hundred-pound sacks of beans, whole hams, sides of bacon, bags of roasted coffee beans, clothing, boots, hats, kegs of coal oil, black powder, rifles, revolvers, knives, smoking tobacco, and plug. Two entire wagons had been devoted to barreled whiskey. There were even a few books and a chalk board for the proposed school.

"We ain't seen the school marm yet," Cal Tabor said.

"But I got an idea we will," said Will Haymes.

And they did. The last day of April, Rufus Hook showed up in the last wagon, and he had with him a girl who didn't look a day past eighteen. When Hook reined up, almost all the families were represented. Many intended to complain about the less-than-desirable individuals with whom they would be traveling. But before anybody could say anything, Rufus Hook spoke.

"I'm sure some of you will be surprised to find me

traveling with you, but I am not the kind to take your money and send you away, into unknown circumstances. While I have bargained in good faith with the Stephen Austin estate, I intend to be there, assuring myself that each of you receive the land you have been promised. I am sure enough of the future of the proposed town of Hookville, that I have personally funded a young lady who will teach school there. This is Lora Kirby.''

"By God," said Eli Bibb, loud enough for everybody to hear, "that gal's been doin' all her educatin' in a saloon, and she ain't been usin' books."

There was a roar of laughter, and Hook pounded his fist on the wagon seat. When he had them silenced, he spoke again, angrily.

"For every dollar each of you have paid, I am investing thousands, and I won't have any of you speaking ill of those who are working for me. I have gone to great lengths to see that this journey is as pleasant and as safe as possible. If any one of you—man, woman, or child— interferes with my destiny, the consequences will be severe."

Flicking the reins, he drove on toward the river. There he reined up, helping Lora Kirby down. Unbidden, Creeker and another of the hired guns unloaded yet another tent from Hook's wagon, and began erecting it.

"That's an almighty big tent, for one gent," said Cal Tabor.

"But just about right for one old buzzard and a saloon woman turned school marm," Eli Bibb said.

"My woman ain't likin' none of this," said Cal Tabor, "and she says most of the other women don't like it either. But what are we goin' to do about it?"

"Them of us that feels that way ought to draw up some rules," Ike Peyton said. "You got any ideas, McQuade?"

"Yeah," said McQuade. "Do what I aim to do. Those of you who can't stomach this bunch that Hook's bringin' along, keep away from them. Plan your supper fires together. Me, I got no choice. I'll be taking my meals from the cook wagon. But aside from that, I aim to mind my own business to the extent that I can.''

"You're sayin' if there's trouble, we can't count on you?'' Ike Peyton asked.

"Get together as many as you can of like mind,'' said McQuade, "and I'll side you, if it comes to that. Mind you, I'm just the wagon boss and guide. I can't tell Hook not to spend his nights in that tent with his school marm, just to please your women. But I'll do everything I can to keep your wagons rolling, and if anybody—including Hook—does anything harmful to the train, they'll answer to me. I'll stand up to them with a gun, if I have to.''

"That's what I wanted to hear,'' Ike Peyton said. "I'll line up some others who'll side you, if it comes to that.''

"Do that,'' said McQuade. "Remember, we take the trail tomorrow, and I look for some things to change, *pronto*, once we leave here.''

The trail to Texas. May 1, 1837.

"Wagons, ho,'' McQuade shouted.

The wagons took the trail three abreast. McQuade had made no arrangements with Rufus Hook as to where his wagons were to fit into the scheme of things, and as a result, Hook's twenty-one wagons ended up at the very end of the train. McQuade rode ahead of the wagons, guiding them south and slightly to the west. Once the wagons were moving, McQuade rode back down the line, looking for potential trouble. He found it immediately, for Rufus Hook was beckoning to him.

"McQuade,'' said Hook, "I don't like my wagons following the others. Some of my teamsters are falling behind.''

"Mr. Hook,'' McQuade said, not bothering to conceal his disgust, "some of your men are not teamsters, and that's your problem, not mine. Your wagons have dribbled in over the past two weeks. You and your men have ignored me. I made it a point to work with these people who are ahead of you, they know where they're supposed to be, and they're not falling behind. I'd suggest that you tighten your ranks and pace your teams to ours. Hostile Indians like nothing better than to find a train split, with a few wagons lagging behind. I have my wagons organized, and I'd suggest you organize yours."

McQuade rode on to the tag end of the train, circled it and started back. He grinned at Creeker and his heavily armed companions, as they followed Hook's wagons, eating dust. Most of the emigrants had horses and cows trailing their wagons on lead ropes, and they, in addition to the wagons, stirred up enormous clouds of dust. McQuade rode alongside Ike Peyton's wagon, and Peyton spoke.

"How're they makin' it back yonder?"

McQuade laughed. "If this was a cattle drive, they'd all be ridin' drag. Hook wants his wagons to take the lead. I told him no."

"Thanks," said Peyton. "I reckon it'll get rough before we reach Texas."

"I reckon," McQuade agreed. "I've been down some hard trails, but I have a feeling this one will be the granddaddy of them all."

Chance McQuade didn't know just how right he was.

Chapter 1

⌀

*W*ithout Rufus Hook being aware of it, Chance McQuade had quietly singled out every man among the hundred families he believed he could trust. Thus more than sixty men within the train were prepared to assist McQuade in any way they could. While it would be impossible for McQuade to be aware of everything that took place within the ranks, word could be relayed to him rapidly. Almost every wagon had at least one good horse trailing on a lead rope, a definite advantage in case of outlaw or Indian attack. Once the train was moving, McQuade rode alongside Ike Peyton's wagon.

"Ike, I'm scouting ahead to find water for the night. If there's trouble, fire three shots."

Peyton nodded. Maggie, his wife, sat stiffly beside him. She didn't yet share his dreams of a Texas land grant. As he rode, McQuade sorted out the families, studying strengths and weaknesses. While there were just a hundred emigrant wagons, there were more than four hundred emigrants, for a good four-fifths of the men had wives, sons, and daughters. The rest were single men who had teamed up, with as many as four to a wagon. McQuade saw them as potential trouble, for there had been fistfights over various women, before the train had taken the trail. Some of these single men had bought whiskey in St. Louis, and when boredom overtook them, McQuade reck-

oned he would have to crack some heads. Eventually he
came upon a creek with sufficient graze to supplement the
grain carried in each of the wagons.

"About twelve miles, hoss. About all we can expect
out of 'em, the first day. You get yourself a drink, and
we'll ride on back."

Estimating the distance at nine miles, McQuade met the
wagons. There was something he must settle with Rufus
Hook, and he decided to be done with it. Hailing the leaders, he waited until the wagons were near enough for him
to be heard.

"Rein up, when you cross that ridge yonder. Give your
teams a rest."

McQuade rode on, noting that other wagons had begun
to slow as the leaders followed his orders to rest the
teams. It would provide an opportunity for McQuade to
speak to Rufus Hook. By the time McQuade reached
Hook's wagon, it and the rest of his entourage had ground
to a halt. Hands on his knees, chewing an unlit cigar,
Hook sat like a nervous toad. He said nothing while Lora
Kirby eyed McQuade with interest.

"It's customary to circle the wagons at the end of the
day," said McQuade, without any greeting. "Do you
want to circle your wagons with the rest, or will you have
a circle of your own? I suppose I should tell you that
most of your emigrants don't favor mixing with whores,
gamblers, and gunslingers."

Hook laughed, and it was ugly without humor. "Is that
their terminology or yours, McQuade?"

"Mine," said McQuade bluntly.

"We have enough wagons for our own circle," said
Hook. "Never let it be said that Rufus Hook corrupted
any righteous man who was unwilling. For those who *are*
willing, you may spread the word that after supper, there
will be gambling, whiskey, and other entertainment available at the Hooktown Saloon tent."

Lora Kirby laughed, and McQuade said nothing. Words
failed him, and he rode away. From the seat of his wagon,

Miles Flanagan was watching. Mary sat beside him, and
again Chance McQuade was drawn to her. For an instant
her eyes met his, and she quickly looked away. On impulse, McQuade reined up next to their wagon.

"Preacher," said McQuade, "when we circle the wagons for the night, Rufus Hook aims to have a circle of his
own. Within that circle, there'll be a saloon tent, with
whiskey, gambling, and . . . women. You're welcome to
join our circle."

"Mr. Hook has promised to build me a church when
we reach Texas," Flanagan said stiffly. "I must assume
he is an honorable man, until he convinces me otherwise."

"I reckon he's about to do that," said McQuade. "I'm
told the devil quotes scripture when it suits his purpose."

"Don't talk down to me, you young fool," Flanagan
roared.

McQuade said no more. Wheeling his horse, he rode
back to the head of the caravan.

"Father," said the girl timidly, "suppose he is telling
the truth?"

"We shall see," Flanagan said shortly.

Reaching the head of the caravan, McQuade waved his
hat. "Move 'em out," he shouted.

The big wagons rumbled on. A cow got loose from a
lead rope and went loping away, pursued by a young girl
and her mother. McQuade rode ahead, reining up when
he reached the creek where they would circle the wagons
for the night. He guided Ike Peyton's and Gunter Warnell's wagons into position, one beside the other. The others, using the first two as a guide, formed a rough circle
two abreast. The huge circle crossed the creek at two
points, allowing water for the stock and for cooking.

"All the horses, mules, and other livestock goes into
the circle," McQuade shouted.

"I like that," said Eli Bibb, "all the stock bein' in the
circle."

"Not often I've been able to do it," McQuade said.

"You have to have lots of wagons. This is about the only way to avoid having Indians or renegades stampede the horses and mules."

Supper fires blazed at every wagon. It was time for Chance McQuade to take his first meal at Rufus Hook's cook wagon, and he found himself reluctant to go there. What was wrong with him? He put his mind to it, and almost immediately came up with the answer. His confidence lay with the emigrants who squatted around their supper fires, who likely had sold everything they owned, for teams and wagons to take them to the Rio Colorado. That, he concluded, was why he felt like a bull in a sheep pen when he was near Rufus Hook's camp. With misgivings, his dismounted near the cook wagon, nodding to the aged cook, Ampersand. Being there ahead of the others, he accepted the tin plate of food and the tin cup of coffee offered him. There was steak, beans, boiled potatoes, hot biscuits, and dried apple pie. While he couldn't fault the food, he had little appetite. He watched as some of Hook's hired guns erected a large tent. When they had it up, one of them backed a wagon to the entrance. They unloaded tables, chairs, and a roulette wheel. From a second wagon, two men manhandled a barrel of whiskey to the ground. It was rolled into the newly erected tent. The canvas was removed from the first wagon, revealing an upright piano. The rear of the wagon was then backed into the tent. One of the women was helped into the wagon, and taking her seat on a stool, began playing the piano. Even as McQuade watched, men from the farthest circle of wagons, men without wives, wandered into the saloon tent where a makeshift bar had been set up. Four of the men were the Burkes—old Andrew, Matthew, Mark, and Luke. They eyed McQuade, daring him to challenge them. But McQuade said nothing, finishing his supper. The woman at the piano struck up a lively tune, and the rest of the women quickly found partners for a rollicking dance. Men had brought tin cups, and the whiskey flowed freely. Snakehead Presnall sat at one of the tables, shuffling a deck of cards. Hook's gun-throwers had begun filing by the wagon, having their plates served. Doctor Horace Puckett and Attorney Xavier Hedgepith sat at one of the tables in the saloon tent, a bottle between them. There was no sign of Rufus Hook or Lora Kirby, but that seemed about to change. As the revelry in the saloon tent increased, the Reverend Miles Flanagan stepped down from his wagon box. For a horrified moment, he fixed his eyes on the saloon tent. Mary Flanagan sat on the wagon seat, her face pale, expecting the worst. It wasn't long in coming. Flanagan stalked to the big tent which had been erected for Rufus Hook and Lora Kirby. Standing there with hands on his hips, he issued a challenge.

"Mr. Hook, this is the Reverend Flanagan. I would have a word with you."

"Later," Hook shouted.

"Now," Flanagan shouted back.

Flanagan said no more. Seizing a tent post to the left of the tent, he wrenched it out of the ground. Quickly he repeated his performance with the tent post to the right, and the front of the tent collapsed. Hook fought his way free and stood facing Flanagan. Trying mightily to control his temper, he spoke.

"Reverend Flanagan, I will excuse a man an occasional mistake. This time, I'm making allowances for you being a preacher. I won't do it again. Now tell me what you want, and then get out of my sight."

"What I want," said Flanagan, "is for you to shut down this Sodom and Gomorrah in our midst. When I agreed to accompany you to this proposed town in Texas, I wasn't told of your intention to create dens of iniquity such as this. I won't tolerate it, sir."

"Preacher," Hook replied, "my inviting you to Texas don't give you a license to run my business. We ain't that far from St. Louis. You're welcome to hitch up your teams and return there."

With that, he turned away, beckoning to his hired guns, who were eating supper. Four of them put down their plates. While two seized the tent stakes and drew the ropes tight, the others took sledges and drove the stakes back into the ground. Miles Flanagan looked around, and the only friendly face he saw was that of Chance McQuade. It was to McQuade that he spoke.

"Mr. McQuade, it appears that I have been misled. Is there room for me and my wagon within your circle?"

"There will be by the time you harness your teams and drive there," said McQuade. He nodded to Mary Flanagan, and this time, she didn't turn away.

McQuade returned to the circled wagons. When he beckoned to Ike Peyton, Gunter Warnell and Eli Bibb answered his summons, as well as Ike.

"Gents," McQuade said, "Rufus Hook has his saloon tent open. Preacher Flanagan has seen the light, and wants to join our wagon circle. Will some of you make room for him?"

"We will," said Ike, "and I'd say there's hope for him. I wish I could say the same for some of them from our own circle, that's gone over there."

"When you've made a place for Flanagan's wagon," McQuade said, "get back to me. I have somethin' to ask of you."

By moving the Peyton and Warnell wagons, Flanagan was able to drive into the wagon circle, where he unharnessed his teams. The Peyton, Warnell, and Bibb women immediately welcomed Mary Flanagan.

"I don't believe the Flanagans have had supper," said McQuade. "Can some of you see to feeding them?"

Quickly the Flanagans were welcomed to a supper fire where the meal was still in progress. Having gotten their wagons back in line, Ike Peyton, Gunter Warnell, and some of the other men sought out McQuade.

"Now," said Ike, "what do you want us to do?"

"Hook included my meals from here to Texas," McQuade said, "but my appetite just ain't comfortable around that bunch he's trailin' with. I'd like to take my meals with some of you folks."

"We can't feed as well as Hook," said Warnell, "but you're welcome to what there is."

"I don't aim for you to feed me for nothing," McQuade said. "I'm not rich, but I'm not broke. Tomorrow, if one of you will loan me a horse for a pack animal, I'll ride back to St. Louis for a load of grub. All of you talk to your women and see what you're most in need of, and you can share what I'll add to your supplies. I expect the Reverend was to take his meals at Hook's wagon, which he won't be doing, so I'll buy enough to include him and his daughter."

"That's damn decent of you, McQuade," said Will Haymes, "and I promise you won't be sorry. Except for some of the young hell-raisers who have flocked to Hook's saloon, you'll have us all on your side. When we signed on for this journey to Texas, we had no idea that Hook would be going with us, or that we'd be surrounded with whiskey, whores, gamblers, and gunmen."

"Neither did I," McQuade said, "and I can't help wondering if Hook will keep his word on the land grants. It's been my experience that if you can't trust a man completely, he'll sell you out at the first opportunity."

"My God," said Cal Tabor, "most of us got nothin' to go back to. If we get to Texas and find we've been cheated—if there are no grants—what are we goin' to do?"

"Hook must have given you some written proof when you joined the train," McQuade said, "something to back up his promise."

"Just a receipt for what we paid," said Gunter Warnell. "Stephen Austin died last year and there's to be another overseer appointed. From what I was told, Rufus Hook has been assigned near a million acres, to be deeded to those of us in this train."

"I've been thinkin' about that," Eli Bibb said. "Hook's brought his own lawyer. Him, the doc, them two gamblers, and the dozen gunmen, that's sixteen men.

What's to stop Hook from assignin' rancher grants to all those men, and then buyin' 'em back?''

"Likely, not a thing," said McQuade. "Texas is a republic, owned by Mexico, and the nearest authority is in Mexico City. Long before we arrive, I reckon we'd better lay some plans of our own, and prepare for a fight.''

"It's somethin' everybody in this outfit needs to know," Ike Peyton said. "Even them that's over yonder, swillin' rotgut in Hook's saloon.''

"I agree," said McQuade, "but for starters, speak of it only to those you know we can depend on. There's goin' to be enough trouble, without stirrin' up any more. When we are nearer the end of this trail, we'll try and pull everybody together, before we have to face up to a showdown with Hook.''

Suddenly there was a shot from somewhere in the vicinity of Hook's wagon circle.

"Should some of us investigate that?'' Ike Peyton asked.

"No," said McQuade. "I reckon this is just a sample of what's ahead. With some of the people from our circle drinking Hook's whiskey, we'll be on the outs with him pronto. Let's shy clear of him for as long as we can.''

"Some of our bunch may get hurt or killed," Will Haymes said.

"Their choice," said McQuade. "You can't save a man from his own foolishness, unless he has the brains to see the danger.''

McQuade found the Flanagans near the Peyton wagon. Maggie Peyton and Ellen Warnell had served them their supper. McQuade said nothing, uncertain as to how he might approach the short-tempered preacher. But Flanagan set his plate down and got to his feet.

"Mr. McQuade, I owe you an apology. Like most men, I have been selfish, beholding things and men as I wish they were, rather than the way they are. When sin is so great that mortals cannot overcome it, we must flee from it. I have done that.''

"So have I," said McQuade. "I'm supposed to take my meals in Hook's camp, but I've decided against it. I've spoken to Peyton, Warnell, Bibb, Tabor, and Haymes about eating with them, and they've agreed. Tomorrow, I'm borrowing a pack horse and riding back to St. Louis for provisions. I'll see that there's enough to include you and your daughter, if that suits you."

"While I appreciate your generosity," said Flanagan, "I would feel awkward, accepting it. My circumstances have changed, and I will have no means of repaying you."

"I don't expect to be paid for everything I do," McQuade said. "The frontier's a hard land, and there's likely not a man among us who won't need help, somewhere between here and the Rio Colorado."

"He's right," said Maggie Peyton. "I believe we'll need you a lot more often than you'll be needing us, Reverend."

"Perhaps you're right," Flanagan said. "Very well, Mr. McQuade. I will accept your generosity, and I offer my heartfelt thanks."

Some of the men, seeking to make Flanagan more welcome, included him in their conversation. Maggie Peyton and Ellen Warnell began clearing away the pots and pans from supper, leaving Chance McQuade alone with Mary Flanagan. She blushed, and McQuade realized he had been staring at her. Embarrassed, he couldn't think of any logical way out, so he boldly spoke the truth.

"You are even more beautiful than I at first thought. Will you forgive me for staring at you?"

"Thank you," she said, her eyes on her clasped hands. "There is nothing to forgive."

"I'm glad your father saw fit to join our camp," said McQuade, "but I'm sorry he's had to give up his dream of a church."

"I'm not," she said hotly. "I hate Rufus Hook. He had his eyes on me, and he planned on me paying for anything he promised my father."

"I'm not surprised," said McQuade, "but it looks like Hook has his hands full, with his school marm."

"Surely you don't believe that," she cried. "That . . . that woman is no more a teacher than one of those mules out there."

McQuade laughed, enjoying her anger. "No," said McQuade. "I think she's doing what she does best, serving the purpose for which he brought her along."

"Those other women," she said, "look like they stepped right out of a . . . a . . ."

"Whorehouse," McQuade finished.

She laughed nervously. "Father won't allow me to use that term, but that's . . . that's what I meant."

"They did," said McQuade. "Some of the men recognized them. But they're only part of the problem. With the gambling and the whiskey, I'm looking for men to be killed."

"Isn't there something you can do, before it happens?"

"No," McQuade said. "These are grown men, and if they choose to play with Hook's fire, then they'll get burned. Maybe after a couple have been hurt or killed, the rest will get the message, but I wouldn't count on it."

"I want to thank you for being kind to my father, after he was so ugly to you," she said. "We've just wandered, since mother died, living from hand to mouth. I believe he saw this church in Texas as a last opportunity to build a home for me. Now it seems to have gone the way of everything else."

"Maybe not," said McQuade. "I heard a preacher once that said the Lord never closes one door without opening another. I've been ridin' the high box all over the frontier, fightin' Indians and outlaws, since I was seventeen. All I have to show for it is my horse, saddle, and my weapons. I'm thirty-two years old, and I think if I don't take a rancher's grant and make something of myself in Texas, that I never will. I'll die on some lonesome trail, with nobody knowin' but the coyotes and buzzards."

Without thinking, she had taken his hand in hers, and

when she tried to remove it, he held it tight. She said nothing, and he spoke.

"Mary—if I can call you that—I'd like to talk to you again. Startin' as a friend, and as . . . somethin' more, if you don't mind."

"I don't mind," she said softly, "if my father . . ."

"You're of age, aren't you?"

She laughed. "Lord, yes. I'll be twenty-seven, come June. An old maid, in anybody's book."

"Not in mine," he said. "I don't believe your daddy will object to me seeing you, and if he does, then I'll talk to him. It's time you were thinking of a life of your own."

"I'll talk to him," she replied. "He's thinking more kindly of you."

Flanagan had started back toward the wagon, and McQuade reluctantly released Mary's hand. He spread his bedroll near the Peyton wagon, and he heard Maggie laugh. He had an idea she might be telling Ike of his— Chance McQuade's—spending so much time with Mary Flanagan, and he decided he didn't care. There were younger men than he who might take an interest in the girl, and he didn't even want to think of that. Since they were downwind from Hook's saloon tent, he could hear the rinky-tink of the piano, and the laughter of the women. Let them raise hell as late as they wished, he thought grimly. He would take the trail with his wagons at dawn, leaving Hook's bunch to catch up or lag behind, as they chose. Most of the camp had already bedded down, with only the occasional wink of a cigarette from one of the men on watch. Suddenly a gun roared twice, and the piano became silent. Men shouted and cursed. McQuade rolled out of his blankets and got to his feet. Ike Payton and Will Haymes were up, staring toward the distant lanterns that marked the Hook wagon circle.

"I'd bet a team of mules one of our bunch was involved in that," said Ike.

"No bet," Will replied.

It was only a matter of minutes until three shadowy

forms worked their way through the circled wagons. Two of them carried a third man.

"That's far enough," said McQuade. "Identify yourselves."

"The Burkes," came the sullen voice of old Andrew. "They shot Matthew."

"Dead?" McQuade asked.

"No," said Burke, "but bad hurt. What do you aim to do about it?"

"Not a damn thing," McQuade said. "Patch him up as best you can, and let this be a lesson to the rest of you."

Cursing him, they carried Matthew on to their wagon, and soon there was a fire going, as they boiled water. Others, awakened by the conversation, stood within the wagon circle.

"You bein' wagon boss, they'll fault you," said Ike Peyton.

"My responsibilities as wagon boss don't include Hook's wagons," McQuade said. "I'll take a hand in whatever happens here, within our circle, but those with a hankering for Hook's gambling, whiskey, and women go there at their own risk."

"I reckon you'd better call all of 'em together and tell 'em that," said Ike.

"I aim to, in the morning before breakfast," McQuade said.

Again they lay down and tried to sleep. By the stars, McQuade judged it was well past midnight before the roar subsided and the lanterns went out.

When the first light of dawn grayed the eastern sky, McQuade had his horse saddled for the ride back to St. Louis. Ike Peyton had brought his bay for use as a pack animal.

"All of you gather around," McQuade shouted. "I have something to say."

They came together quickly. The Burkes—Andrew,

Mark, and Luke—were the last to arrive, looking as surly as ever.

"I'm about to tell you this morning what I should have told you last night," said McQuade, "but I had hoped most of you had better sense than to do what the Burkes did last night. They went to Rufus Hook's saloon tent, and Matthew Burke was shot."

"They was cheatin' him at cards," Andrew Burke shouted.

"He was there by his own choice," said McQuade, "and that makes it his fault. Though I'm the wagon boss, I have no say as to what happens in Hook's camp. I'm serving notice on all of you that if you go to Hook's saloon, it's at your own risk. Do any of you not understand what I'm saying?"

"I understand you're wagon boss," somebody shouted, "but I don't understand why you ain't boss over all the wagons."

"I'm doing what Hook hired me to do," said McQuade shortly. "I'm responsible for the emigrant wagons, none of which are in Hook's camp. If you go there and get shot, cut, or cheated, then don't come whining to me. I'm not the law."

A dozen of the younger men began to grumble and curse, but they became silent as more than sixty men with wives and families joined McQuade in silent opposition. It was Ike Peyton who spoke for them all.

"There ain't none of us approves of Hook's saloon, with whiskey, gambling, and women, but all we can do is stay away from it. Them of you as can't leave it alone, we're askin' you to take your wagons and join Hook's outfit."

No more was said, and those to whom the ultimatum was addressed, were a sober lot. The Burkes kept their hard eyes on McQuade, and he returned as good as he got. When breakfast was over, the women washed and loaded cooking utensils while the men began harnessing their teams. McQuade spoke to Ike Peyton.

"I'll wait until the wagons are lined out, on the trail, Ike, and then I'll ride back to St. Louis. I'll be back as soon as I can."

Ike nodded. When his teams were harnessed, and the Warnell wagon was ready, the two of them led out. The others rumbled into place behind them, and the train was on its way. McQuade, leading the pack horse, set out the way they had come. He wasn't in the least surprised to find that Hook's outfit hadn't broken camp. There wasn't a sign of a breakfast fire, nor was there anybody on watch. The wagons had traveled a little more than fifteen miles, and with his horses at a slow gallop, McQuade was soon there. Lacking a packsaddle, he had the supplies loaded into large burlap sacks. He was able to balance all four of them by tying their necks together in pairs, allowing each pair to straddle the horse in a manner that was comfortable for the animal. Leaving the mercantile, counting his money, he found that he had a little more than fifty dollars. With Mary Flanagan on his mind, he reined up before a particular store that he had passed on his way to the mercantile. Looping the reins of his horse about the hitch rail, he went inside. He quickly found what he was seeking in a glass display case on the counter.

"Good morning, sir," said the clerk. "Do you know the lady's size?"

"No," McQuade said, "and I have only fifty dollars."

"This one is fifty-dollars," said the clerk, "and I have some less expensive ones."

"The fifty-dollar one," McQuade said. "I'll gamble on the size. Make it a large one."

McQuade left the store with only some change in his pocket, but in his saddlebag was a little white box with a gold band. In the wilds of south central Texas, such things would be out of the question. Now that he had taken this expensive, and perhaps useless, step, he was beset with doubt. He knew Mary Flanagan liked him, but suppose it never went beyond that? Suppose old Miles Flanagan did an about-face, deciding he didn't approve of Chance McQuade, after all?

McQuade rode on, lost in his thoughts, and before he knew it, the moving wagons were in sight. Rufus Hook's wagons. McQuade could swing wide, avoiding them, but there was a stubborn streak in him that wouldn't allow him to dodge Rufus Hook. He continued, and by the time he reached the wagons, someone had alerted Hook of his coming. Pulling his wagon out of formation, Hook waited, Lora Kirby beside him. McQuade reined up.

"Where the hell have you been, McQuade? Fine wagon boss you are."

"I rode back to get some grub for me and the Flanagans," said McQuade. "I got the wagons on the trail before I left, and they're somewhere ahead of you."

"I'm well aware of that. Why didn't you wait for us?"

"We roll at first light, with or without you," McQuade said. "Your choice."

Without another word, Chance McQuade rode away.

CHAPTER 2

McQuade found that his wagons had made good time, and were a good five miles or more ahead of the Rufus Hook wagons. McQuade trotted his horses alongside Ike Peyton's wagon until the train stopped to rest the teams.

"I'll split this up among some of the other wagons," McQuade said, "if you don't have room for it."

"I got room," said Ike. "We didn't have much that was worth bringin' with us."

Many of the other men had gathered, obviously expecting some word of Rufus Hook's position. McQuade didn't disappoint them.

"Hook's maybe five miles behind us," McQuade said. "I told him if he aims to travel with us, we move out at first light."

There was shouting and applause, with grins on many faces. Keeping his saloon open until past midnight, Hook and his bunch would be ill-prepared to take the trail at first light. Ike and several other men helped McQuade load the supplies into Ike's wagon.

"I bought extra coffee and sugar," said McQuade. "If any of you run short, come and talk to Ike."

It was a truly unselfish act to which every man and woman could relate, and McQuade became one of them, for better or worse. There now was a solidarity among

them that had been absent, a bond that Chance McQuade
knew he must have, if they were ever to each the Rio
Colorado. In his own mind, he was sure of one thing:
reaching this Promised Land in Texas might be the easy
part. McQuade's mind harbored a growing suspicion that
Rufus Hook had a far bigger stake than just establishing
a new town. He had within his reach, thousands of acres
of Texas land, for almost nothing. When Texas became a
state, which someday it must, Rufus Hook could become
the wealthiest man in North America.*

"I'm riding ahead to look for water," said McQuade,
as the train prepared to take the trail again. As McQuade
rode past the Flanagan wagon, he tipped his hat to Mary,
and she smiled. It was enough to banish from his mind
all thought of Rufus Hook and the dangers which might
lie ahead. Riding along, he thought ahead. The train was
a little less than three hundred miles from the Neosho
River, where they would cross into Indian Territory.
While there were outlaws in southern Missouri, he expected little danger from them or from Indians, until they
reached the Territory. It would allow some time for his
teamsters to gain some confidence, and accustom them to
standing watch at night. While these people had little
wealth to attract thieves, their livestock was sufficient to
interest outlaws as well as Indians. When McQuade had
located water for the night's camp, he returned to meet
the wagons. Reining up on a ridge, he could see them
coming. There he waited, expecting to see the Hook wagons following at a distance, but there was no sign of them.
He doubted Hook would stop short of the McQuade camp,
for there wouldn't be sufficient water without going out
of the way to find it. When the Peyton and Warnell wagons drew near, he rode ahead of them to the creek he had
chosen. There was still an hour of daylight, and as the
men began unharnessing their teams, McQuade sought out
the Burke wagon. While old Andrew Burke and his trou-

*Texas was admitted to the Union in 1845.

blesome sons had made it hard on McQuade, they were part of the train, and his sense of responsibility told him he should at least inquire about Matthew. He found Mark and Luke unharnessing the teams, and old Andrew greeted him in silence, without enthusiasm.

"How's Matthew?" McQuade asked.

"Alive," said Andrew.

"I brought back some laudanum from town this morning," McQuade said. "If there's a need, you're welcome to some of it."

"We're obliged," said Burke grudgingly. "We'll keep it in mind."

McQuade turned away. Matthew Burke would need whiskey to break his fever and fight off infection, but let them get their own. Rufus Hook had an abundance of it. Reaching the Peyton wagon, he found that Maggie Peyton, Ellen Gunter, Minerva Haymes, Lucy Tabor, and Odessa Bibb had begun sharing the preparation of meals, and instead of five supper fires, there now were just two.

"Ladies," said McQuade, "that's a downright smart move. I won't be surprised if it's quick to catch on."

"It already has," Maggie Peyton said. "The others are followin' our lead. We was all killin' ourselves findin' wood for a fire of our own. With six of us sharin' the work, it's easier on us all."

"Six?" McQuade looked around and saw Mary Flanagan coming from the creek, a big two-gallon granite coffee pot in each hand.

When supper was ready, McQuade thoroughly enjoyed it, for the sharing further drew the families together. When Miles Flanagan had eaten, he went from one group of families to the other, spending some time with them all. Everybody seemed to enjoy the closeness, except some of the single men. The Burkes had their own fire, refusing to participate. It was well after dark before they heard the rattle of wagons and the jingle of harness, marking the arrival of Rufus Hook's wagons.

"I reckon the saloon will be openin' late tonight," said Ike Peyton.

"Yeah," Will Haymes said, "and closin' earlier."

It brought a round of laughter, for they all knew what Ike and Will meant. While they could do nothing about Hook's saloon, they could continue taking the trail at first light, leaving Hook and his late-night outfit behind. McQuade had already assigned the first watch, and some of the women had taken to their blankets, when the stillness of the night was shattered by a rollicking refrain from Hook's piano.

"Damn it," Ike Peyton grumbled, "I used to like the piano."

"There's hot coffee on the coals," said Maggie, "if you need it."

"I need it," McQuade said, and went to fill his cup. There was no moon, and he saw a shadowy form on the seat of the Flanagan wagon. When he drew near it, he spoke softly.

"Mary?"

"Here," she replied.

"Would you like some coffee?" he asked.

"Yes, please."

He reached the Peyton wagon, and without a word, Maggie handed him a cup. Quickly he filled it from the coffee pot, returned to the Flanagan wagon, and passed the cup to the girl. He then climbed up on the box beside her.

Ike Peyton laughed. "He don't waste no time, does he?"

"No," said Maggie, "and he shouldn't. She's a good girl, and she needs somebody like Chance McQuade."

For a while McQuade said nothing, content to sit there beside Mary Flanagan. When he did speak, he pleased her more than he knew.

"I'm glad you pitched in with the supper. Not that they couldn't have managed, but I want you to have friends, to become one of these folks."

"I'm already one of them," she said. "I discovered that tonight, when I was made to feel welcome."

She set the tin cup down, leaned her head on his shoulder, and he discovered she was weeping softly. It was a while before she trusted herself to speak again.

"It . . . means a lot to me, but . . . did you see my father? Do you know what he said to me, before he turned in for the night?"

"What?" McQuade asked, interested.

"He said, 'Daughter, I don't need Rufus Hook to build me a church. I've found it.' "

"I can believe that," said McQuade. "Some of the best preaching I've ever heard, was when all I had over my head was trees and sky."

It was a pleasant interlude. But then came the roar of a Sharps .50, in the direction of the Hook camp. There was a distant scream, and the piano jangled to silence.

"Dear Lord," said Mary, "what's happened now?"

"I don't know," McQuade said, "but I have an idea we soon will. Wait here, and I'll be back. They may try to suck us into this."

McQuade joined a dozen other men who stood looking toward the lights of the distant Hood wagons. Nobody said anything, and after the time it would have taken a man to saddle a horse, they heard riders coming. His Sharps in the crook of his arm, McQuade made his way through the circled wagons until he stood in the open. While he had given no order, he sensed the men behind him. Three riders loomed up in the darkness.

"That'll be far enough," said McQuade. "Who are you, and what do you want?"

"This is Rufus Hook," a grim voice replied, "and you got some answering to do."

"You ask the questions," McQuade said, "and if I can answer them, I will."

"A while ago, somebody shot one of my gamblers, Snakehead Presnall. He's hurt bad, and somebody from your camp fired that shot. Who was it?"

"You don't know who did it, yet you're accusing somebody from my camp," McQuade said coldly. "That's a fool question I won't take serious, unless you got some proof."

"One of your pumpkin rollers was shot last night, after he drew on Presnall. Now I'm tellin' you him or one of his kin got even by shootin' down Presnall from the dark. Now I want you to drag that bunch out here where I can question them and have a look at their long guns."

"No," said McQuade. "It's your saloon, your women, your gamblers, and your booze. Maintaining order is your responsibility, and I don't aim to dance when you come fiddling around. Now mount up and get out of here."

"Hold it, McQuade," Andrew Burke said. "Mark, Luke, an' me, we got our long guns, and Mister Hook is welcome to have a look at 'em. We ain't about to have him spoutin' off what he can't prove."

Unbidden, Ike Peyton brought a lighted lantern, as the Burkes came forth with their rifles.

"Creeker, Ellis," said Hook, "examine those rifles."

The two men accompanying Hook sniffed the muzzles of the long guns and checked the loads. Without a word, they passed them back to the Burkes.

"Well?" Hook said, impatiently.

"Loaded, an' no sign of havin' been fired," said Creeker. "But they've had plenty of time to reload."

"Where's the rifle belongin' to the *hombre* Presnall shot last night?" Ellis asked.

"Matthew's got no long gun," said Andrew Burke. "All he has is the pistol the was wearin' when he was shot."

"I guess we're supposed to take your word for that," Rufus Hook said.

"You're damn well going to," said McQuade. "You stomp in here without a shred of proof, with your demands. Now mount up and ride, all of you."

Wordlessly they mounted and rode back the way they

had come. The Burkes departed in silence, and nobody spoke until they had gone.

"Ungrateful varmints," Gunter Warnell said. "I wish you hadn't stood up for 'em."

"I can't side any of you without sidin' all of you," said McQuade. "Tomorrow, it may be any one of the rest of you. Rufus Hook's a man accustomed to having his own way, and the more you give, the more he'll take."

It was a truth they all understood, and they made their way back to the wagons and their blankets. The piano had resumed its seemingly endless attack on the silence of the plains. Now very much awake, McQuade returned to the Flanagan wagon, and was elated to find Mary still there.

"Hand me the cups," he said softly, "and I'll heat up our coffee."

She passed him the cups and he refilled them from the coffee pot. Handing the cups to her, he climbed back to the wagon box and sat down beside her.

"I heard most of it," she said. "What's going to happen now?"

"I have no idea," he replied. "Mostly, it depends on whether or not these young hell-raisers in our midst have learned anything. If there's more trouble, we'll be seeing Rufus Hook again. Or he may just have his gunmen take a few shots into our camp, after dark."

"But that's so unfair," she cried, "making all of us pay for the sins of a few."

"I couldn't agree more," said McQuade, "but that's the way of the frontier. Many a man with a grudge just wants somebody to pay, often not caring if he harms the innocent along with the guilty."

"Chance McQuade," she said softly, "you are a compassionate and understanding man."

"Coming from you," said McQuade, "I take that as a compliment."

"I wish I could take credit for having said that," she replied, "but I'm just quoting my father. I asked him . . . what you wanted me to, and he gave his blessing."

"I'm glad," said McQuade. "Otherwise, I reckon I'd be taking my life in my hands, out here with you, and him likely under the wagon."

She laughed softly. "Not really. Since I'm helping with the cooking, he insists on doing his share. He's out there with the first watch. He's taken to these people, and they seem to like him. I expect he'll be out there every night."

"Then I'll take my turn after he calls it a night," said McQuade. "While he's away, don't be surprised if I show up here, lookin' out for you. There's all manner of coyotes, wolves, and catamounts out here on the plains."

"I'm flattered," she said. "I'm practically an old woman, and I've never had a man so concerned about me. I realize it's the first week in May, but there's a chill in the wind. Do you have a remedy for that?"

"As a matter of fact, I do," he replied. He slid closer to her, and in so doing, spilled the rest of his coffee in her lap.

"Don't mind that," she said. "It'll dry."

He took her advice, drew her close, and they were still there when the Reverend Miles Flanagan came looking for his blankets.

McQuade's people were up and about well before first light, and when the golden rays of the rising sun fanned out across the eastern horizon, the wagons were again on the trail. During breakfast, Ike Peyton had summed up their dedication.

"We'll see just how long they can take it, raisin' hell till the small hours, and havin' us move out at dawn, without 'em."

"There'll be Indians and outlaws," said McQuade. "Maybe not until we reach Indian Territory, but they'll be coming."

McQuade rode ahead, seeking water. Reaching a creek, he decided to ride to a distant ridge beyond, so that he might see what lay ahead. There he was in for a surprise. Miles to the southwest was a rising cloud of dust.

"We need to know what in tarnation is stirrin' up that much dust," McQuade said to his horse.

McQuade rode on, eventually reaching the crest of a ridge that allowed him to determine the cause of the dust. Several hundred longhorn cows trudged along, bawling their displeasure. McQuade counted ten riders, four of them riding drag. He was now only a few minutes away, and he trotted his horse down the slope to meet them. Nearing the herd, he could see four pack mules running with the drag steers. The point rider saw him coming, and waving his hat, signaled the riders to mill the herd. The point man then rode ahead to meet McQuade.

"Hello, the herd," McQuade shouted. "I'm friendly."

"I'm Chad Guthrie," the rider replied. "This is my outfit. We're bound for St. Louis."

"I'm Chance McQuade, wagon boss for a hundred wagons bound for Texas. I rode on ahead, looking for water for the night."

"Find any?"

"Nice creek," said McQuade, "maybe half a dozen miles ahead of you. That's where I'll be circling the wagons for the night. Why don't you gents have supper with us, and tell us about all the interesting things we can expect between here and Texas? That is, if you *are* from Texas."

Guthrie laughed. "Pardner, where else you goin' to find longhorned varmints such as them you're lookin' at? I reckon we'll accept that invite to supper."

"We'll look forward to it," said McQuade. "I'll see you at the creek."

McQuade rode back the way he had come. It would be worth feeding these cowboys, for surely they had come through Indian Territory, and could share any difficulties they had experienced. He reached the wagons while they were resting the teams and told of his meeting the oncoming herd.

"That's something we hadn't counted on," said Will

Haymes. "I'll feel better, hearin' about what's ahead, from somebody that's been there."

"Texas can't be all that uncivilized," Gunter Warnell said, "if there are ranchers drivin' their herds to market."

"Has there been any sign of Hook's outfit?" McQuade asked.

"We ain't seen 'em," said Ike Peyton. "Of course, we ain't been lookin' for 'em."

The wagons took the trail again, every man eager to reach the creek and hear what the Texans had to say. Not surprisingly, the Texas herd reached the creek well ahead of the wagons, and the cattle had been taken downstream to graze. McQuade guided his teamsters upstream, well beyond the cowboy camp, and there they circled the wagons. The cowboys gave them time to unhitch their teams and turn them out to graze. The women got the fires going and put the coffee on. The cowboys rode up, looped their reins to the wagon wheels, and entered the wagon circle.

"Folks," said McQuade, "this here's Chad Guthrie. I'll let him introduce his cowboys, while we're waitin' for supper."

"We're obliged for the supper invite," Guthrie said. "I reckon the most godawful part of a drive, is us havin' to eat our own cooking."

They laughed, and he introduced his cowboys. They were a cheerful lot, enjoying the coffee and the women who brought it to them.

"We're bound for the Austin land grant, along the Rio Colorado," said McQuade.

"We're from east Texas," Guthrie replied, "but we've heard of the Austin grant. Been some trouble down there, folks sellin' their grants to speculators. Steve Austin kind of held things together, and when he died, some crooked dealin' took place."

"I reckon we'll have some fightin' to do, once we get there," said McQuade, "but for now, we're a mite concerned with what's ahead of us, between here and there. Indians and outlaws."

"It's the Kiowa while you're in Indian Territory and the Comanche when you cross the Red into Texas," Guthrie said. "We had to shoot some Comanches before we left Texas, and we had two brushes with the Kiowa while we was crossin' Indian Territory. We give the Kiowa some cows, hopin' they'd leave us alone, but the varmints come back durin' the night and stampeded the herd. We found their camp, shot it all to hell, and ran off all their horses. Next mornin', we rounded up our cows, includin' what we give them. There was a second bunch layin' for us, but we'd scouted ahead and found their tracks. Circlin' around, we caught 'em off guard, and purely discouraged 'em. Outlaws didn't bother us, but we crossed a days-old trail of nearly two dozen horses, all of 'em shod."

"We'd do well to scout far ahead of the wagons, then," said McQuade.

"That's what's kept us alive," Guthrie replied. "Know what's ahead of you, and be prepared for it."

The cowboys thoroughly enjoyed the food, accepting the second helpings offered them. More coffee was put on to boil, and when the first watch had to return to the herd, the others—including Guthrie—remained for a while. Preoccupied with their guests, none of McQuade's people noticed the arrival of Rufus Hook's wagons. Not until the piano jangled into action.

"My God," said one of the cowboys, "what's that?"

McQuade laughed. "That's Rufus Hook's piano."

With some help from some of the other men, McQuade told the Texans about Hook and his grandiose plans for building a town.

"I never heard of such," Guthrie said. "You mean he's got a saloon out here on the plains, with women, whiskey, and gambling?"

"That he has," said McQuade, "and since you was kind enough to warn us about the Kiowa and the Comanche, I'm warning you gents about Rufus Hook's saloon."

Guthrie laughed. "There ain't a saloon between New

Orleans and San Francisco Texans can't tame. I reckon we'd best ride over there and have a look at Hook's rolling medicine show. If he aims to set up a saloon in Texas, he'll have to get used to us. We'll give him a head start.''

They mounted and rode away, and after they had gone, Ike Peyton spoke.

"They're a likable bunch, and I hate to see 'em ride over to Hook's place. If they got any money, Hook will get it, and then have them shot if they protest.''

"I wouldn't be too sure of that,'' said McQuade. "They're all armed, and they've been fighting the Comanche and the Kiowa.''

There was no further conversation, for McQuade and his people were listening for some sign the Texans had arrived. It took less than half an hour, and then there were no gunshots. There was shouting, cursing, and the sound of glass breaking. The piano became silent, and what obviously was a brawl in progress continued for some minutes. Finally there was the sound of walking horses, and when they were near enough, McQuade called out a challenge.

"That's far enough. Identify yourselves.''

"Guthrie and friends. What's left of us.''

"Come on,'' said McQuade.

Guthrie and two of his cowboys were mounted. The other two were slung over their saddles.

"Dead?'' McQuade inquired.

"Not quite,'' said Guthrie. "They jumped us, two to one, and just pistol-whipped the hell out of us. I don't know how bad Pete and Juno's hurt.''

"Ike, Gunter, and Eli, help me get these men off their horses and into the wagon circle,'' McQuade said. "Guthrie, you and your amigos come along. We have medicine and bandages.''

A fire had been kept so that men on watch would have coffee. Maggie Peyton set the coffee pot aside and hung a pot of water to boil. Ellen Warnell and Odessa Bibb brought medicine kits. Mary Flanagan was there, offering her help, if needed. While Guthrie and two of his cowboys were on their feet, they had lost blood, having been cut with knives or broken bottles. Their heads had been bloodied, but they weren't hurt nearly as bad as the two men who were unconscious. Their scalp wounds were serious to the extent that Lucy Tabor and Minerva Haymes had to sew the lacerated scalp together with needle and thread.

"These men need rest," said Maggie Peyton. "Why don't you leave them here for the night, so we can look after them?"

"That's kind of you, ma'am," Guthrie said, "but I reckon it's our own fault we got all busted up. We wouldn't want to be a burden."

"It's no burden," said Ike. "The rest of you can stay, if you want."

"I reckon not," Guthrie said. "Somebody's got to take over the watch at midnight. If you will look after Pete and Juno, I'd be obliged. We'll leave their horses, and some of us will be here in the morning, early."

Unsteadily they mounted their horses and rode away.

"I'm sorry they went to Hook's saloon," said Maggie Peyton. "We don't even know why they were beaten."

"They didn't talk much," McQuade said, "but I'd say Hook's in for a surprise. While these Texas hombres are polite and quiet, they don't take to being pushed around. It's not over."

And it wasn't. An hour before first light, all hell broke loose. There was the roar of guns, the bawling of cattle, the thunder of hooves. Men shouted and whooped, and there were shrieks of terror from women within the Hook wagons. Glass shattered, and there was a thud as a wagon was toppled. Horses nickered, mules brayed, and suddenly it was over.

"My God," said Cal Tabor, in awe, "what happened?"

McQuade laughed. "I'd say that herd of Texas longhorns stampeded right through Mr. Hook's camp."

"The Lord works in mysterious ways," the Reverend Flanagan said.

"Some of us ought to ride up there and have a look," Gunter Warnell said.

"Saddle up and come along," said McQuade. "We wouldn't want Mr. Hook to get the idea we don't care."

Ike, Gunter, Eli, Cal, and Will saddled their horses, and not to be outdone, Reverend Flanagan rode one of his mules. While the devastation wasn't as great as McQuade expected, it was serious enough. The thud they had heard was the piano striking the ground, for the wagon in which it had sat lay on its side. Ampersand's cook wagon had been toppled, and the saloon tent was no more. It had been trampled into the ground, along with a pair of barrels that had contained whiskey. Tables and chairs had been reduced to firewood, while six near-naked women stood looking at their wagon, which lay on its side. Most gratifying of all, however, was the sight of Rufus Hook and Lora Kirby standing where their tent had once stood. The women looked at McQuade and his companions, and Chance tipped his hat. He wheeled his horse, and with the others following, rode back to their wagon circle. They had been there only a few minutes, when Chad Guthrie and his seven men rode in.

"How's Pete and Juno?" Guthrie inquired, as though nothing else had happened.

"They're awake and hungry," said Maggie Peyton. "All of you are invited to eat with us, if you like."

"Ma'am," Guthrie said, "you just don't know how welcome that invite is. We just had us a bad night. Somethin' spooked them cows, and they're scattered from here to yonder. We'll be all day and tomorrow, roundin' 'em up, and we're two men shy."

"That'll give Pete and Juno time to rest and heal," said Ellen Warnell.

"Your cows wrecked Hook's camp," Cal Tabor said. "He may come looking for you, expecting damages."

"Let him come," said Guthrie. "Considerin' what he

done to us last night, after one of his slick-dealin' gamblers cheated us, I reckon we'll just call it even. We're as peaceful as we're allowed to be, but we purely ain't opposed to shootin' no-account coyotes that won't have it no other way.''

CHAPTER 3

Chad Guthrie and his cowboys had breakfast within McQuade's wagon circle. Pete and Juno got unsteadily to their feet, declaring themselves able to ride.

"We'll be here at least another day," Guthrie said. "Maybe longer. We can't afford to lose any of the herd, this close to market."

"I reckon Rufus Hook and his bunch will be leaving, after they've picked up all the pieces," said McQuade, "but they're not the forgiving kind. Be sure you post a guard."

"We're obliged for your kindness," Guthrie said. "It's the way folks ought to be, and you'll make good Texans. If you're ever in east Texas, along the Trinity, look for my brand, the C-G Connected. You'll be welcome."

McQuade's wagons took the trail without seeing anybody from Hook's camp. McQuade had learned something of the trail ahead from Guthrie and his cowboys, but he wanted to see for himself, so he rode ahead of the wagons, as usual. While good water was essential, he wasn't nearly as concerned with that as with the possible presence of outlaws. Indian Territory had long been the refuge for hostile Indians, but it had also become a haven for renegade whites. Villages in southern Kansas, southwestern Missouri, and western Arkansas were looted by renegades who immediately disappeared into the wilds of

Indian Territory. McQuade doubted that these outlaws would hesitate to attack a wagon train, if only for the livestock. When McQuade eventually found water, he also found the remnants of a fire, not more than a few hours old, and a profusion of tracks. He back-trailed them to the northwest for more than two miles, primarily to determine the number of riders. He decided there were at least twenty-four. They had been following a stream, and before leaving it, had built a supper fire. McQuade followed the tracks far enough to establish a direction. The riders had circled to the southwest, telling McQuade what he wished to know. All the horses were shod, and that many white men bound for Indian Territory meant they almost had to be outlaws. He rode back to meet the oncoming wagons. He would wait until the wagons were circled and supper was done, before telling them of the tracks he had seen and his suspicions regarding them. Reaching the wagons, McQuade rode back along the line, speaking to the men and their wives, atop the wagon boxes. He tipped his hat to Mary Flanagan, and when he reached Hardy Kilgore's wagon, Hardy hailed him. McQuade turned his horse, riding alongside the wagon.

"My boy Jason saddled his horse a while ago, and rode down the back-trail," said Kilgore. "He wanted to see what Hook's bunch was doin'. The piano didn't survive the stampede, and they left it behind. But they got the rest of it together, and are followin', maybe half a dozen miles back."

"Thanks, Hardy," McQuade said. Obviously, Hook wasn't going to challenge Guthrie's outfit, although some of Hook's gunmen could ride back and attack the camp after dark.

There was no sign of the Hook wagons until after dark, when they circled half a mile upstream, and their supper fires were visible. Within Hook's patched-up tent, a lighted lantern hung from the ridge pole. Seated at a table, papers before them, sat Rufus Hook and his attorney, Xavier Hedgepith.

"Damn it," said Hedgepith, "why don't you just give up the saloon on the trail?"

"No," Hook said. "We're less than fifty miles out of St. Louis. Tomorrow, I'm sending Nall and Groat back to town for another tent."

"All you've done is turn that bunch of settlers against you. Hell, by the time we reach Texas, they'll be sold on McQuade and hating your guts," said Hedgepith.

"That's exactly what I'm aiming to do," Hook replied. "I want them relying entirely on McQuade, until we reach Texas. Then McQuade will die, and without a leader, they'll give in without a fight."

"Hook," said Hedgepith, "you're not the first with plans to build an empire at somebody else's expense, and there's always some element that can't be controlled. This bunch has seen McQuade spit in your face and get away with it. Before dawn this morning, your camp was flattened by a herd of longhorn cows, and you took it. By the time these people reach the Rio Colorado, they'll be so set against you, they'll have to be slaughtered to the last man."

"Hedgepith," said Hook, "you just see to it that the papers for individual grants have been drawn up accordin' to my instructions. All you got to do is be sure the grant reverts to me, when they fail to live up to their end of the deal. You sure you got papers on all of them?"

"You know damned well I have," Hedgepith said shortly. "I got papers on everybody in McQuade's train, includin' McQuade. I got papers on everybody in this camp, except for your whores and old Ampersand. If, by some miracle, this works out, you'll control near two million acres."

"It's goin' to work," said Hook savagely. "I've fought too hard, come too far to see it fail. I'll kill any man—or any number of men—gettin' in my way."

McQuade was pleased to see that all the families, more than eighty, had arranged themselves into groups of five or more, and were sharing their cooking. The others—in a total of seventeen wagons—were single men, some of whom were accompanied by women of questionable reputation. The Burkes were part of this group, and they all kept to themselves, becoming part of the train only when the wagons were on the trail. McQuade began to wonder if the Reverend Flanagan hadn't taken a permanent position on the first watch, to allow Mary some privacy. For the third night in a row, McQuade found Mary alone on the wagon box.

"I'm glad your daddy's comfortable on the first watch," he said, taking his place next to the girl.

"So am I," said Mary. "I think he's more concerned with the single men who brought women than he is with me. I'm afraid he's about to try and show them the error of their ways, and that might mean trouble for you."

"I don't see how it could," McQuade said. "Most of our folks have come together in a way that can't be anything but helpful. I can't see anything worse than this bunch of young hell-raisers fighting among themselves, and with Hook supplying plenty of whiskey, there's not much we can do. As for their women, I've known plenty of men who have kept one, although they're usually squaws."

"Have you ever . . . kept a woman?"

"No," said McQuade. "I've had some experiences, but no woman's ever been interested in me for more than a few hours. Usually until my money ran out."

"I didn't know you had money," she said.

"I don't," said McQuade. "I blew it all in St. Louis, when I went back for grub. Do you want me to get lost?"

"No," she said. "You've been here beside me for three nights, and I'd miss you if you went away. Besides, you were nice to my father when he didn't deserve it."

"This is our fourth night together," said McQuade. "Maybe we should celebrate. Do you want me to bring you some hot coffee?"

"No," she said, "I'm sick of coffee. Can't you think of something better?"

"As a matter of fact, I can," he said. Drawing her to him, he kissed her on the lips, long and hard.

"If that was coffee," she gasped, "I'd have a second cup."

"Anything to please a lady," he said, repeating his performance.

Suddenly the silence was shattered by the scream of a woman, followed by a man's cursing. The woman screamed again, and there was a shot. McQuade leaped from the wagon box, his revolver in his hand. There was a full moon, and stumbling around in the wagon circle was a stark naked woman. A man lay on the ground before one of the wagons, while another stood over him with a pistol.

"Drop the gun," McQuade shouted, "or I'll kill you where you stand."

The pistol clattered against a wagon wheel and fell to the ground. McQuade recognized the man as Trent Putnam, who had a woman with him. She cowered fearfully against one of the wagons. Hardy Kilgore came running with a lighted lantern, and while McQuade held his pistol on Putnam, Kilgore brought the lantern close enough for them to identify Luke, the youngest of the Burkes. Ike Peyton knelt beside him.

"He's alive," said Ike. "Maggie, stir up the fire and put on some water to boil."

"I'm goin' to string the bastard up," Andrew Burke shouted. "He shot Luke."

"You're not stringin' anybody up," said McQuade grimly. "Putnam, why did you shoot Burke?"

"He was with my woman," Putnam bawled. "Look at her standin' over yonder, naked."

"With your woman, in your wagon," said McQuade. "Where were you?"

"Gone to Hook's saloon, after whiskey," the naked

woman cried. "He was gone near an hour, and come back drunk."

Putnam stumbled and would have fallen, if he hadn't steadied himself against a wagon wheel. It was a touchy situation, and McQuade sought a solution. His voice slurred, the drunken Putnam spoke.

"Selma, I . . . I didn't mean to hurt you."

"One of you bring Selma a blanket," said McQuade. "We'll have to separate her from this varmint, until we decide what to do with him."

"No," Selma cried. "I'll go back to the wagon. He'll be all right, when he's sober."

"Go on back to the wagon, then, unless you're hurt. Are you?"

"No," she said. "He tried to . . . strangle me."

Two of the men carried the wounded Luke to the fire where Maggie Peyton had water boiling. While Ike raised him up, Maggie unbuttoned and removed his shirt. The wound was high up, sparing bones and vitals.

"Some of you tie Putnam to a wagon wheel," McQuade said. "We'll decide what to do with him when he's sober."

"By God," Andrew Burke snarled, "he ain't gettin' off, after shootin' Luke."

"I'd say one's as guilty as the other," said McQuade, "so punishment ought to be the same. Maybe I'll just boot the both of them out of this train."

"Luke's my boy," Burke shouted. "You can't do that to him."

"The hell I can't," said McQuade. "What do you say, people?"

There was a roar of approval, and some of the men cursed Burke.

"In the morning, before breakfast, we'll take a vote," McQuade said. "Putnam should be sober by then, and Burke should be conscious. He wasn't hit that hard. Some of us will keep an eye on Burke and Putnam the rest of the night. I'll need four men, each standing a two-hour watch. The rest of you Burkes go back to your wagon and stay there. Putnam will stay tied to that wagon wheel, and he'd better be safe and sound, come the morning.''

When Luke Burke's wound had been dressed, Maggie Peyton covered him with a wool blanket, and except for Eli Bibb on watch, the others returned to their wagons. The hour was late, but McQuade found Mary Flanagan waiting for him.

"Sorry," he said, as he climbed up beside her. "I reckon you saw and heard it all."

"Yes," she replied. "It's the first time I've ever seen a naked woman standing before so many people. What's going to become of her?"

"I have no idea," said McQuade. "Hopefully we can put the fear of God into Trent Putnam, as well as Luke Burke. As far as I'm concerned, they're three of a kind. Selma whatever-her-name-is ought to be horsewhipped for whoring around with Burke behind Putnam's back, while Burke's a damn fool for fooling around with another man's woman. It's unlikely Putnam would have been trying to strangle the woman if he hadn't been drunk, and he wouldn't have been drunk if he hadn't been to Rufus Hook's saloon.''

"So it all comes back to Hook's saloon," said Mary.

"It does, as far as I'm concerned," McQuade said. "I'm not one to excuse a man just because he's drunk. I don't drink, because I know what whiskey does to a man. Should I get drunk and kill a man, he's just as dead as if I'd been cold sober. So none of these people have any excuse for what happened, least of all, Trent Putnam.''

"Let's not talk about them anymore," said Mary. "When all this started, you were about to heat up my coffee. It's cold again.''

McQuade laughed. "You're in luck. I have a fresh pot.'' Drawing her close, he kissed her long and hard, and whatever difficulty awaited them at dawn faded into oblivion.

*   *   *

Well before dawn, Trent Putnam was stone sober, cursing anyone who came near. But Chance McQuade was one of the men on the last watch of the night, and with just a few words he silenced Putnam. The camp was up and about well before first light, and so that they might get the unpleasant duty behind them, McQuade called for a vote as to what should be done with Luke Burke and Trent Putnam. Now conscious, Luke Burke was brought out into the wagon circle on blankets. Trent Putnam had been freed from the wagon wheel and allowed to restore the circulation to his arms and legs. McQuade wasted no time.

"Burke, you're accused of fooling around with Putnam's woman, while he was gone to Hook's saloon for whiskey. Putnam, you're accused of shooting Burke, when you returned, drunk. I have the authority to expel both of you from this wagon train, as well as the woman who's been fooling around with the two of you. Do any of you have anything to say?"

"I was drunk," Putnam said. "I didn't know what I was doin'."

"No excuse," said McQuade. "You were sober when you decided to get drunk."

"The woman's been makin' eyes at me," Luke Burke said weakly. "I didn't take nothin' but what was offered."

"I didn't do anything wrong," Selma cried. "I was just makin' Trent jealous, so's he'd marry me, like he promised."

"We have a decision to make," said McQuade. "Do we allow this trio another chance, or do we expel them from this wagon train?"

Before anybody could respond, the Reverend Flanagan got to his feet, raised his hand, and cleared his throat. Greeted by silence, he spoke.

"Friends, I'm a believer in repentance. All of us are sinners saved by grace. I propose that these three sinners be forgiven, with provisions for punishment if they backslide. I'm prepared to perform a marriage ceremony,

which will fulfill Mr. Putnam's promise to this woman,
Selma. Unfortunately, assuming that Mr. Putnam agrees
to leave the whiskey alone, we have only his word. Likewise, we will have only Mr. Burke's promise that he will
stay away from Selma, who will be a married woman. I
propose that these two men take an oath before us all to
forgo the evil in which they engaged last night. Should
either violate that oath, they will then be expelled from
this community.''

"What about the woman, preacher?" somebody
shouted.

"Should the woman, Selma, be found in violation of
her vows, she too will be driven out of our midst," said
Flanagan. "Now, Mr. Burke and Mr. Putnam, do you
agree to take this proposed oath and abide by it?"

"Yeah," Burke said. "I'll take it."

"Mr. Putnam?" said Flanagan.

"I'll take it," Putnam growled.

"Now, young lady," said Flanagan, turning to Selma,
"if you'll stand here next to Mr. Putnam, I'll make an
honest woman of you."

"I ain't tyin' myself to that whore," Putnam shouted.

"If I'm a whore, you made me one," Selma cried.

"I was about to make that same observation," said the
Reverend Flanagan. "If you are unwilling to fulfill your
promise to this young woman, Mr. Putnam, I'm going to
suggest to these good people that you be driven from their
midst."

"I'll do it, damn it," Putnam bawled. "Get it over
with."

Putnam stood there with an expression on his face like
he'd been eating sour pickles, grunting out his vows,
while the women of the company smiled in satisfaction.
When the brief ceremony ended, the Reverend Flanagan
had some further advice for Trent Putnam.

"If you threaten or physically harm this woman as you
did last night, then I believe a good horsewhipping or
public hanging might be in order."

It became Miles Flanagan's finest hour, as he was cheered and applauded. Many of the men and women had their eyes on the young men of Putnam's caliber, and McQuade felt it was a good time to speak his mind.

"Let this be a lesson to the rest of you who are tempted to visit Hook's saloon. While we can't keep you away, when you show up drunk and raising hell, we can make you almighty sorry you went. Now let's get breakfast and get these wagons on the trail."

It was a crisis averted, and none of them were concerned with breakfast until they had spoken to McQuade and Flanagan. The Burkes glared at McQuade, but other men and some of the women stared them down, and they retreated to their wagon, helping Luke.

"I'm so glad that's over," said Mary, bringing McQuade a tin cup of coffee.

"I'm glad the Reverend Flanagan was here," McQuade replied. "I thought maybe they should have another chance, but not without some rules. Solomon himself couldn't have laid it out any better. Forcing Putnam to marry Selma was pure genius."

"I thought it was sad. He didn't want her. How could she be happy, knowing that?"

"I don't know," said McQuade, uncomfortable, "but he had used her, and he owed her something, didn't he?"

"No," she said. "If I'd been in her place—if I'd been used by a man, and he didn't want me—I'd kill myself before I'd marry him."

McQuade was on dangerous ground, and he said nothing, sipping his coffee. One of the other women spoke to Mary, drawing her attention from him. "Somewhere, somehow, those Burkes are going to cause trouble," said Maggie, as the big wagon rumbled along. "Did you see how they looked at McQuade?"

"Yeah," Ike replied, "but Chance McQuade can take care of himself. Them Burkes has had it in for him, long before he joined us as wagon boss. It's just his damn hard luck to have 'em show up on this ride to Texas."

"Well, I hope nothing happens to him," said Maggie, "if only for Mary Flanagan's sake. Have you noticed how she looks at him?"

"As a matter of fact, I ain't," Ike said. "Her daddy's took a permanent place on the first watch, leavin' 'em alone on that wagon box. I don't have to look at the gal to know she'd like to share his blankets."

"Ike Peyton, you should be ashamed of yourself. She's a nice girl."

"Didn't say she wasn't," said Ike, "but she's female. You was a nice girl, too, but I didn't have no problem gettin' you in my blankets."

She colored, but Ike leaned over, forcing her eyes to meet his, and she laughed.

The day after Hook's saloon tent had been trampled beyond use, two men leading a pack horse had ridden back to St. Louis for another tent. They brought some lanterns to replace those that had been broken, and shortly after Hook's wagons had been circled for the night, the new saloon tent had been erected. The dozen gunmen Hook had hired were already tired of the inactivity. Following the stampede that had demolished much of the camp, they had wanted to go gunning for the cowboys, but Hook had restrained them. Now they squatted beneath a lantern in the evenings, playing cards and grousing among themselves.

"Fifty dollars a month ain't all that much money," said Dirk, "when you consider we got no hope of ever raisin' the limit."

"Yeah," Mook agreed, "seein' as how he aims to file for grants in our names, and then take the land for himself. That just rubs me the wrong damn way."

"You all knew what the deal was, when we hired on," said Creeker. "It's a mite late to complain, 'cause none of us is gettin' more than we been promised. Fifty a month ain't bad pay for settin' on our hunkers until we're told to fight."

"I don't mind settin' on my hunkers," Slack said, "if the money's right, and what I mean by right, is us gettin' a better share when we're about to be used to build Rufus Hook a damned empire."

"I'd favor takin' us a bigger share—maybe all of it," said Rucker, "if there was a way we could do it. We could take over these wagons and maybe sell all this freight, once we get to Texas, but the real money's in the taking over of the grants. Hook's got all the land sewed up in some legal jumble we'd never be able to figure out."

"It's all been done by that shyster lawyer, Hedgepith," Groat said. "Suppose we was to throw in with him, gettin' rid of Hook? Then, once it's all tied down and legal, we just shoot Hedgepith and take it all."

"I heard Hedgepith's already in for half, once it's settled," Drum said. "Just why in tarnation would he join us in a double-cross when he'll be a rich man, anyhow?"

"Or he could have it all," said Porto. "Hell, he don't need us to double-cross Hook."

"You're wasting your time, all of you," said Creeker. "Between Hook and Hedgepith, they got this thing nailed down so tight, we couldn't loosen it with blasting powder."

McQuade rode out well ahead of the wagons. He estimated they had traveled at least fifteen miles a day. It was good time, but there had been no breakdowns. He had seen to it that every wagon's wheel hubs had been well greased. The weather had been favorable, much of the spring rain diminishing by the end of April. But from experience, he knew the mighty mountains far to the west wore halos of white, that when conditions were right, a veritable wall of rain would sweep across the Kansas plains, creating oceans of mud. As he squinted his eyes in the blue of the early morning sky, he could see a faint haze that crept up to the edge of the western horizon. He had seen that cloud band before, and whatever it brought to Colorado, Wyoming, and Montana Territories, it meant rain in Kansas, Nebraska, Missouri, and Indian Territory. McQuade believed they had one more good day on the trail. Eventually he found water for the night's camp, and rode back to meet the wagons.

"We had to pour some whiskey down Luke Burke," Ike Peyton said. "Fever's got a holt of him. Putnam and his woman's been at it again. She can out-cuss him, when she gets goin'."

McQuade shook his head and rode on down the string of wagons, speaking to all the families as he went. He only nodded to the Burkes. Putnam and his less-than-happy bride eyed him in silence. Reaching the last wagon, McQuade lagged behind, watching the back-trail. There was no sign of Hook's wagons, but that wasn't surprising. He wondered how they would fare after a drenching rain, when the prairie was wheel-hub deep in mud. Riding back to the head of the train, he jogged his horse alongside the Flanagan wagon for a ways, enjoying Mary's presence.

When the wagons had been circled for the night and the teams unharnessed, McQuade spoke to the men.

"There's rain on the way, probably by tomorrow night. While we wait for supper, we'd do well to load as much dry wood into the wagons as there's room for. Those of you with a cowhide, or a big enough piece of canvas, I'll show you how to stretch it beneath your wagon, makin' a 'possum belly.''*

Once it became dark enough, they could see lightning dancing along the far western horizon, and the wind had a moist feel to it.

"There'll be rain before dark," Gunter Warnell predicted, as they gathered around the breakfast fire. "We been havin' it too good."

"I wish you hadn't said that," said Will Haymes. "That's temptin' fate."

*The " 'possum belly'' or "cooney'' was slung beneath the wagon to carry dry firewood.

His words gained considerable credibility when one of their horses nickered and one of the sentries sounded the alarm.

"Riders comin'."

McQuade and half a dozen men stepped outside the wagon circle, waiting as a group of men rode in from the northwest.

"That's far enough," McQuade shouted. "Who are you, and what do you want?"

The men reined up and one of them spoke.

"Now that's just damned inhospitable talk. Wouldn't you say so, boys?"

There were growls of agreement. In the predawn darkness, McQuade counted two dozen men.

"I've always believed when a man asks you a question, you owe him some kind of an answer," said McQuade.

"Let's just say we're ridin' the way you're headed," said the stranger, "and for grub, we'd be willin' to see that you ain't bothered by Injuns or outlaws."

"Sorry," McQuade said, "but we can't take on anybody else to feed. As for Indians or outlaws, we have more than a hundred armed men. Ride on."

"We aim to," said the stranger. "We'll be seein' you."

"We'll be ready," McQuade said grimly.

They rode away, taking the same general direction the wagons must go.

"That sounded mighty like a threat," said Cal Tabor.

"It was," McQuade said. "They would have ridden with us long enough to figure some way to steal our stock, killing as many of us as necessary. We'll keep our eyes open from now on, especially after we reach Indian Territory."

Once the wagons had taken the trail, McQuade rode ahead, not nearly as interested in finding water for the night's camp, as in learning in what direction the mysterious riders had gone. True to their word, the horsemen had ridden the way the wagons must go. When McQuade reached suitable water which the wagons could reach before dark, he rode on for another ten miles, studying the tracks. That these men were outlaws, he had little doubt, and their appearing to ride on didn't fool McQuade. While they might strike at any time, he expected them to wait until the wagons entered Indian Territory. He rode back to meet the wagons, and when the train stopped to rest the teams, some of the men gathered, wishing to know what McQuade had learned.

"They're riding on," said McQuade, "but we can't count on that. Starting tonight, we double our watch, and I'll be ridin' careful while I'm scoutin' ahead."

CHAPTER 4

Springfield, Missouri. May 12, 1837.

*M*cQuade circled the wagons five miles south of the little village of Springfield, the last link with civilization before entering Indian Territory.*

"You won't have the mercantiles of St. Louis, with their river commerce," McQuade said, "but there ought to be some goods for those of you in need. This is likely our last chance to buy anything, unless we trade with Hook. We'll lay over here an extra day, so a few of you at a time can ride into town."

"I am not so poor that I cannot contribute to the rations," said Reverend Flanagan. "Those of you who so kindly fed me and my daughter, I want you to prepare a list that I may take to town. I will see that you do not run out of foodstuffs."

Realizing that Flanagan was sincere, the women of the families with whom Flanagan and Mary had been taking their meals prepared a modest list. It being a last opportunity to visit a store, some of the women elected to go along with their men, which involved taking some wagons. Mary would be going with her father, and McQuade saddled his horse and rode along with them.

*Springfield, Missouri was founded in 1835.

"It's no St. Louis," said Flanagan, as they approached the village.

There were two mercantiles, however, with a saloon and livery in between. The hotel, a single-story affair, sat next to a cafe. There were no public buildings, no jail, and no law. There were many horses at hitch rails before the saloon, the hotel, and the cafe, but no cause for alarm. But Chance McQuade was wary. Certainly, the way they had come, there wasn't another mercantile, saloon, cafe, or hotel closer than St. Louis. He knew of no other village in eastern Kansas or western Missouri, and certainly nothing in northern Arkansas except the brakes along the White River. What occasion had brought so many riders to this small town? Then he thought of the men who had appeared before dawn, offering to escort the wagons through Indian Territory for food.

"Mary," said McQuade, "stay near your father. There are entirely too many men here, to suit me. I'll be around, if you need me."

Mary smiled, and while Flanagan said nothing, McQuade saw relief in his eyes. Reining up before the largest of the mercantiles, Flanagan took his time getting down, allowing McQuade to help Mary. Half a dozen men emerged from the saloon, pausing to eye the men and women entering the mercantiles. McQuade followed the Flanagans into the store, and it proved to have a better stock of merchandise than McQuade had expected. The probable reason, of course, was the nearness of Indian Territory and the absence of law. Obeying an impulse, McQuade stepped behind a display, where he could observe the door without being seen. Six men entered the store and stood there looking around. All were armed, with pistols thonged down on their right hips. Without hesitation, they headed in the direction the Flanagans had gone. McQuade followed, in time to see one of the men seize Mary and begin forcing her toward the door.

"Take your hands off her," Flanagan shouted.

One of the men had drawn his pistol and was about to

hit Flanagan, when he stopped, frozen by the cold voice of Chance McQuade.

"Drop that gun, or you're a dead man. You with the lady, turn her loose, and the lot of you get out of here."

The man who had seized Mary laughed. "You shoot me, it'll be through her, bucko."

"Let her go," said McQuade, "or I'll kill all five of your friends."

One of the five made the mistake of reaching for his gun, and died with his hand on the butt of it. Mary Flanagan suddenly went limp and slid to the floor. Sullenly, the five men raised their hands.

"Now," McQuade said, "get out, and take that dead coyote with you."

Wordlessly, two of them gathered up the dead man, and they left the store. Mary got to her feet, her eyes on McQuade. Ignoring her father and the storekeeper, she came to him, and McQuade drew her to him.

"My God," said the storekeeper, "you'd better ride out and keep goin'. Even then, they might ride you down."

"You know them, I reckon?" McQuade said.

"Only when I see them," the man said cautiously. "They ride out of the Territory ever so often, if you know what I mean."

"I know what you mean," said McQuade. "Mary, you and your father go ahead and round up what you need. I'll wait for you."

McQuade turned back toward the door. Men had been drawn by the shot, arriving in time to see the dead man carried out. Some, including the Peytons and Warnells, were from McQuade's camp.

"There's more of 'em in the saloon," Ike said. "I reckon we'd best light a shuck away from here."

"Come on in and get what you came after," said McQuade. "The fat's already in the fire, and if we have to fight, I'd as soon do it here. Otherwise, they're likely to follow and shoot some of us in the back."

Ike and Maggie entered the store, followed by a dozen others from the wagon train. McQuade lingered near the front door, where he could see through a front window. Before anybody was ready to leave the mercantile, McQuade saw the five men he had driven away enter the saloon. Within a few minutes they emerged, hunkering near the door and lighting cigarettes. McQuade had seen their kind before, and he thought he knew what was coming. From his pocket he took an oilskin pouch, and removing a load, shoved it into the empty chamber in his revolver. Eventually, when the emigrants were ready to leave the store, McQuade stepped out ahead of them. The five waiting men stood up, hooking their thumbs in their pistol belts.

"My God," said Ike Peyton, "we got a fight on our hands."

"No," McQuade said, "they're after me."

"Not five agin one," said Ike. "You got Gunter, Eli, Cal, and me here to side you. If all five of 'em draw on you, they'll be drawin' agin us, too."

"We'll see how it stacks up," McQuade said. "This is my fight."

"Is there no other way?" Mary Flanagan asked anxiously.

"None that I know of," said McQuade.

McQuade walked toward the waiting men, and when he was within pistol range, he halted. When he spoke, he seemed totally relaxed.

"You started somethin' in the store, and I finished it. I shot your friend only after he drew first, and there's no sense in any more of you dying for his mistake."

"It was you made the mistake, shootin' him," said the man who had seized Mary. "He was my brother, an' there ain't nothin' you can say to change that. It's you an' me, damn you."

"You'd best keep it that way," Ike Peyton shouted. "There's five of us, and we'll kill any one or all four of your friends, if they don't stay out of it."

The four of them took Ike seriously, backing away and out of the line of fire. Chance McQuade remained where he was. Flanagan had his arm around Mary, and she stood there white-faced and trembling. A crow cawed nearby, and the man facing McQuade spoke.

"When that crow sings again, I aim to kill you."

McQuade said nothing, and in the minds of McQuade's companions, it seemed that a deadly clock was ticking off the remaining seconds of a man's life. McQuade stood with his left hip swiveled toward his adversary, his pistol butt-forward for a cross-hand draw. To those who watched, it seemed incredibly awkward. Suddenly the crow cawed again, and the gunman facing McQuade drew. He was fast—unbelievably fast—but McQuade was faster. None of them saw his hand move, but suddenly his pistol was spitting lead. His adversary blasted a single shot into the ground, and then McQuade's slugs slammed into him. Like an empty sack he folded, striking the ground on his back. A playful wind from the approaching storm snatched his hat and blew it away. The remaining gunmen stared at McQuade, not believing their eyes. He had fired twice, and he stood there with his gun leveled until the four turned away. Only then did McQuade walk back to the store where his friends waited. The men were white-faced and silent, while Mary Flanagan was weeping.

"We'd better be gettin' back," McQuade said. "That storm won't hold off more than a few hours."

McQuade helped them load their purchases, and then helped Mary up to the wagon box. The rest of the men helped their women up, then mounted their boxes and turned their teams back the way they had come. McQuade rode alongside the Flanagan wagon. The men from the saloon seemed to have all come out to witness the departure of the wagons.

"Damn," said one of the outlaws, "I never seen any hombre pull a gun that quick."

"There's a cure for his kind," another of the outlaws

said. "Shoot the varmint in the back, and he'll bleed just like anybody else."

"Time enough for that, when they git to the Territory," said a third outlaw. "Maybe they ain't rich, but they got money to come here an' buy. Farmers, an' I'm bettin' they've sold ever'thing they had. They's got to be money in some of them wagons."

McQuade and his companions reached their camp, and while McQuade issued no warnings, the men who had witnessed the gunfight and knew the cause of it, quickly spread the word to those who hadn't yet gone to the village. Well before dark, the rain began, and only because most of the families had brought extra canvas for shelter were they able to cook and eat their evening meal out of the rain. The wind was chill, and only because the back of the Flanagan wagon was facing the storm were McQuade and Mary able to remain dry, as they spent their usual evening on the wagon box. There was some lightning, none of it striking, and the night was peaceful enough. Mary had said little, and McQuade had an idea her mind was on the trouble that had taken place in town. She confirmed all his suspicions when she finally spoke.

"If you had been killed, I don't know what I'd have done. I think perhaps I would have died too."

"Do I mean that much to you?" he asked, speaking lightly.

"Yes," she replied, dead serious. "I was hoping that . . . perhaps you care for me. But if you do, how could you have taken such a risk?"

He was struck dumb, for a reprimand was the last thing he had ever expected. For a moment he said nothing, not trusting himself to speak. When he finally did, he struggled mightily to control his temper.

"Mary, this is the frontier. A man does what he has to do. Would you have had me stand there in the store and see you carried away by renegades?"

"No," she replied without hesitation, "but after that, why couldn't you have simply refused to fight?"

"Because, damn it, I would have been branded a coward, and I wouldn't have lived out the rest of this year. You'd have hated me, like everybody else."

"But I want you alive," she persisted. "Is that so wrong?"

"Up to a point, no," said McQuade. "I don't enjoy killing a man, but when it's him or me, what kind of choice do I have? If I'd backed down after I'd been called out, there's a good chance none of us would have left there alive. Is that so difficult to understand?"

"No," she said, "but it's difficult to accept. How can you be so . . . gentle with me, and then before my eyes, become a . . . a . . ."

"Killer," said McQuade.

"I wasn't going to say that," she almost whispered, "but I suppose it's what . . . what I mean."

"Mary Flanagan," said McQuade, "you mean a lot to me, but I don't aim to spend all my time with you apologizin' for what I am. I reckon you need to spend some time alone, thinkin' about what happened today and what might have happened if I'd backed down. Then I want you to think about what we've talked about tonight. If there comes a time when you can accept me for what I am, for doing what I must do, then I'll have somethin' to ask you. Until then—because I don't want to hurt you— I'll stay away."

He stepped down from the wagon box and vanished into the rain-swept darkness. The Peytons peered through the canvas pucker of their wagon, and it was Ike who spoke.

"I reckon they had words. My God, what does the woman expect? He kilt two men because of her."

"Ike Peyton," said Maggie, "you'll never understand women, if you live to a hundred. She wants him, but she's afraid of losing him in some senseless gunfight. It's the fear of every woman, that she'll give herself to a man, and he'll get his fool self killed."

"Maybe I don't understand women," Ike said, "but I

understand men, and until that little Flanagan gal knows at least as much as I do, she won't be sharin' McQuade's bed, and it'll be his choice. If he hadn't stood up to that shootout, they might have gunned us all down. By God, Chance McQuade's a man with the bark on, and Mary Flanagan's a fool if she throws him down. Why don't you talk to that woman, before McQuade washes his hands of her?''

"Maybe I will," said Maggie.

The rain continued all night and most of the next day, and when the skies finally were clear, it was too late for the sun to suck up any of the moisture. Even where they sat, some of the wagons had mired down.

"I think we'll be spending one more day here," McQuade said. "It'll take some time for this mud to dry up. There's no point in leaving here, only to get bogged down a mile or two along the way. Here, there's plenty of water."

"Hell, there's plenty of water everywhere," said Hardy Kilgore. "Just a little muddy, I reckon."

"I don't like the thought of laying over another day," Gunter Warnell said. "We're too close to town and that bunch at the saloon."

"It won't make any difference whether we're here or fifty miles south," said McQuade, "because those outlaws ride in and out of Indian Territory. When they decide to come after us, they'll find us."

"You think they'll come, then," Warnell said.

"Yes," said McQuade, "and they'll wait until we're deep enough into the Territory, so there'll be no witnesses."

McQuade was aware that Mary Flanagan had heard his exchange with Warnell, and she quickly turned away, before McQuade's eyes could meet hers. There was little to do, as they waited for a day of sun to dry up enough of the mud for them to continue. Despite all the trouble that had resulted directly from Hook's tent saloon, some of the single men from McQuade's train continued to go there. This included the Burkes, for Matthew and Luke were well enough to be up and about, and they made no secret of their visits to the Hook saloon. Miles Flanagan spoke of it to McQuade.

"Let them go," said McQuade. "The next time they get in trouble, they're on their own. They've been warned."

Indian Territory. May 16, 1837.

McQuade circled the wagons on the east bank of the Neosho River, estimating they were a little more than five hundred miles from their destination. Rufus Hook's wagons were upstream, within sight of McQuade's camp. During supper, Mary Flanagan surprised McQuade, when she spoke to him.

"I must talk to you tonight."

McQuade nodded. Everybody seemed to know they had been on the outs. Some of the other women observed Mary's action and smiled knowingly. As soon as the first watch, including Miles Flanagan, took its positions, the area around the Flanagan wagon became deserted.

"My God," said Ike Peyton, "when a bunch of females gang up on a man, he purely ain't got a prayer."

"We haven't ganged up on McQuade," Maggie said. "We've done the man more of a favor than he'll ever know."

When McQuade reached the wagon, he mounted the box without a word. Since Mary had invited him, he would allow her to set the tone of their meeting. She wasted no time.

"I've been miserable since I . . . since you . . . stopped talking to me, and I want you to know I'm sorry for what I said."

"You told me what you believed," McQuade replied.

"You're a grown woman, and you are entitled to your opinion."

"That's all it was," she said, "and I was being selfish. I realize that, now."

"So now you won't hold it against me if I get myself shot dead."

"Not if it's something you must do," she said. "Please, you must understand that I've had no experience with men. All I could see was . . . you lying there dead, leaving me alone."

"I can't promise you that won't happen someday," said McQuade.

"I don't expect such a promise," she said. "I've never had anything that lasted, and I wanted us . . . to be different."

"Mary," said McQuade, "I'm thirty-two years old, and I wouldn't have lived this long, if I wasn't careful. If I became anything less than what I am, you'd end up hating me, and I'd hate myself. All a man can do is play out the hand he's been dealt, and I don't know as he's got the right to ask a woman to share that."

"A woman takes a man for better or worse. I allowed my own selfishness to stand in the way of that, and I have two things to tell you. I was wrong, and I'm sorry."

"Mary," said McQuade, "this is the frontier. We may have a lot of time, or we may only have tomorrow. In either case, let's not waste any of it, hassling over the right and the wrong of things. If you'll have me, once we get to Texas, I'm asking you to share my life. What there is left of it."

"I'm accepting, Chance McQuade. If we have a day, a year, or ten years, let us make the most of it."

They made their peace in silence, two shadows coming together on the wagon box in the stillness of the night.

McQuade rode out ahead of the wagons, as they began their journey through the wilds of Indian Territory. Strong

on his mind was the advice of Chad Guthrie, warning him
of the importance of scouting ahead. Almost immediately
after crossing the Neosho River, he discovered the tracks
of many shod horses. They had crossed the river somewhere to the north, following the storm, for the tracks
were plain. He followed the tracks, expecting them to veer
to the southwest, which they soon did. McQuade sighed,
having no doubt it was the same bothersome outlaws, and
they now had a grudge against Chance McQuade. He rode
on, having little choice, knowing he had practically no
defense against an ambush. Even as he followed their
tracks, having doubled back, they could be lying in wait
for him. But he saw nobody, and eventually he reached
the stream where the outlaws had spent the night. It would
be suitable for the wagons at the end of the day, but instead of immediately riding back, he continued to follow
the trail. When the renegades had ridden away, they
hadn't deviated from their southwesterly direction.
McQuade reined up and rode back to meet the wagons,
his mind on the men ahead. From the tracks he had
learned two things: apparently they intended to remain
just ahead of the wagons, and their number had grown
after he had killed two of them. Both factors were dis-
turbing, for he now had every reason to believe that—
whatever their original motive had been—they were concerned now with vengeance. Reaching the wagons,
McQuade said nothing about the tracks, and his suspicions
of what lay ahead. There was a possibility, however slim,
that within the next several days the outlaws would
change direction, making his fears groundless. But there
was no hiding the numerous tracks, and long before reaching the creek where they would circle the wagons for the
night, the men in the lead wagons—Ike Peyton and Gunter Warnell—realized there was something McQuade
hadn't told them. They wasted no time in questioning him.

"I followed them a ways, beyond here," McQuade admitted, "and I'm hoping this may be just a coincidence,
that they'll continue on."

"You've killed two of their number," said Warnell. "It seems more likely to me that they're planning to wait until we're deep into Indian Territory, and then shoot you."

"I'm considering that," McQuade said, "but it's a problem I've created for myself. I've no right to alarm everybody in the outfit, when we're just dealing with suspicions."

"Chance," said Ike Peyton, "you're too damn generous for your own good. If these men are planning to kill you, it's of concern to every one of us. What you done was in our behalf, and it's unfair, you shoulderin' all the blame."

"Ike," McQuade replied, "I appreciate your concern, but there's nothing any of you can do. You remember what Chad Guthrie told us about scouting ahead. We must know who or what is lying in wait for us."

"Then you take the reins to one of the wagons, and let one of us scout ahead. Surely these varmints won't shoot one of us, just because they got a mad on for you."

"I'm obliged for the offer, Ike," said McQuade, "but from a distance, one man may look like another. Besides, a man alone is vulnerable. If they're vengeance-minded, any one of us might be gunned down."

So McQuade continued scouting ahead, taking all the precautions he could, but on the morning of their fourth day in Indian Territory, the renegades came after him. The tracks he had been following continued on, but he rode wide of them half a mile or more, north or south. They still might lay an ambush for him, but he wouldn't make it easy for them. The water he chose for day's end was roughly twelve miles ahead of the wagons, and prior to riding back to meet them, McQuade had watered his horse and was himself bellied-down for a drink. The stillness of the morning was suddenly shattered by a gunshot, and the lead slammed into the creek bank, just inches from McQuade's head. He rolled away as more lead plowed into the bank where he had been lying, and as slugs screamed after him, he ran for his horse. They were after him with long guns, and one slug from a Sharps .50 could cut a man in half. But reloading time and a galloping horse made use of the Sharps near impossible, and once he was in the saddle, they would be forced to pursue him with revolvers. Mounting on the run, he kicked the bay into a fast gallop back the way he had come. As he had expected, the long guns became silent. That meant they were coming, with the intention of riding him down. When he eventually reached a clearing, he looked back and saw them. Fanning out in a rough horseshoe formation, their intentions were to flank him, and with lead coming from three directions, they could scarcely miss. He had but one chance, and that was to outride them, but the distance was too great. Long before he reached the oncoming wagons, the bay would be lathered and heaving. But the valiant horse never had a chance. It screamed when the first slug struck it, and he felt it falter as it broke stride. The pursuing riders were within range and gaining, and lead whined around McQuade like angry bees. He was hit in the back, above his pistol belt, and again, high up, in his left shoulder. The hoofbeats of the faltering horse were as a ticking clock, for time was fast running out. He could only take cover, holding out as long as his ammunition lasted . . .

The sound of the big fifties carried, and ten miles back, Ike Peyton heard and understood. Gunter Warnell had already reined up his teams and was off the wagon box, going for his horse, secured to the rear of the wagon by a lead rope.

"What is it?" Maggie cried.

"McQuade's in trouble," said Ike. "Big trouble."

"Eli, Cal, Will," Gunter Warnell shouted, "those of you with horses, saddle up and ride. They're after McQuade."

Within seconds, twenty men rode out at a fast gallop. The only assurance they had that Chance McQuade still lived was the distant rattle of gunfire.

* * *

McQuade had little time to choose adequate cover. There was only an enormous waist-deep hole that been left when a mighty oak had long since been uprooted by high winds. Dragging his Sharps from the boot, McQuade left the saddle. Rolling, he plummeted headfirst into the hole, which was full of dead leaves. While he knew not what manner of reptile might have gotten there ahead of him, it couldn't be any more deadly than the lead that tore into the ground just seconds behind him. He could feel the blood soaking the back of his shirt from his two wounds, but they were the least of his worries. Suddenly the shooting stopped, an almost certain indication they were circling his position. When he was surrounded, his refuge would become indefensible, and they could rush him. Grimly, he contemplated his situation. He had the single load in his Sharps .50, the six loads in his revolver, with an additional dozen loads in an oilskin pouch. With them closing in, he was limited to the loads within his weapons. There would be no time to reload. Suddenly a voice boomed out.

"McQuade, we got you surrounded. I'm Gid Sutton, and you gunned down two of my riders. Now, you come out of that hole and face me like a man. Even break. If you can best me, you're off the hook."

"Sutton," McQuade shouted, "you're a lying, yellow coyote, tempting me with an even break after you and your varmints tried to ambush me. Come and get me, if you have the sand."

"By God, we got the sand and we got the guns. You'll die like a trapped rat."

As McQuade had feared, he was surrounded and they were well within pistol range. Guns roared as they neared his refuge, lead slamming into the banks above his head and showering him with dirt. He waited, hoping for a lull so that he might take some of them with him, but something struck the side of his head like a club and he knew no more . . . .

"Yonder they are," Ike Peyton shouted. "Dismount and use your pistols."

Peyton left his saddle while his horse was on the run. His companions followed his example, and with their revolvers, they cut down on the retreating outlaws. Outnumbered, Sutton and his followers ran for their horses and rode away.

"No," Will Haymes shouted, as some of the men were about to mount and pursue the outlaws. "Our hosses is spent, and McQuade's around here, bad hurt or maybe dead."

As gently as they could, they lifted McQuade from the hole. The back of his shirt was bloody from neck to waist, while blood welled from a terrible wound above his left ear.

"My God," said Ike Peyton, "his pulse almost ain't there. We got to get the bleedin' stopped, if we ain't already too late."

CHAPTER 5

ᴄⱳᴏ

R emoving McQuade's shirt, they found that besides his head wound, he had been hit four times.

"This is no place to work on him," said Will Haymes. "We got to get him back to the wagons."

"Will's right," Ike agreed, "but we'll need water, so we'll bring the wagons to him. There's a creek three or four miles back. Will and me will take him there. Take McQuade's saddle from his dead hoss, and then the rest of you light out for the wagons."

"What about yours and Will's wagons?" someone asked.

"Maggie and Minerva can handle them as far as the creek," said Ike. "Now ride."

Given the extent of his wounds, there was no good way to handle Chance McQuade. He was wrapped in blankets and Will Haymes hoisted him up to Ike, who steadied him as best he could. Their ride back to the creek seemed agonizingly slow, and when they finally reached it, they eased McQuade to the ground. Will felt for the pulse, and while it was weak, it was there. While they would need hot water to cleanse the wounds, that could come later. Ike sought just the right kind of soil, and mixing it with water, created a mass of mud. This he and Will spread over McQuade's terrible back wounds. Blood from his head wound had crusted on his head and the side of his face, but the bleeding had stopped.

"My God," said Will, "it's a miracle, him bein' hit three times, without puncturin' a lung."

"Yeah," Ike said, "but a lung ain't the only worry. If a slug strikes bone, it can mess up a man's vitals."

Long before they heard the rattle of the approaching wagons, there came a patter of hoofbeats. Mary Flanagan had borrowed a horse and came at a gallop, tears streaking her face as she rode. Her long dress hadn't been suitable for riding, and while it was hiked embarrassingly high, she neither noticed nor cared. She all but fell from the saddle, and by the time she knelt beside McQuade, she was so winded she couldn't speak. But Ike Peyton knew what was on her mind, and he spoke as reassuringly as he could.

"He's alive, Mary. We had to get mud on him to stop the bleeding."

She nodded. There was little more to be done until the wagons arrived. The wounds could then be cleansed and bandaged. Not wishing them to observe her trembling hands or her continued weeping, Mary got up, clenched her hands behind her back, and stood staring into the creek.

"Somethin' we ain't considered, Ike," said Will. "If that lead didn't go on through, he may be needin' a doc, an' you know where the nearest doc is."

"I know," Ike sighed, "and I know who he takes orders from."

When the first two wagons came in sight, Maggie Peyton and Minerva Haymes were at the reins. Not only had they handled the teams well, they were ahead of the rest of the wagons. Nobody bothered trying to circle the wagons until they learned how McQuade was. Within minutes the women had a fire going, and water on to boil. Miles Flanagan went to examine the wounded McQuade, where he knelt with his head down. He then went to Mary without speaking a word, for none was necessary. When the girl's fresh tears had ceased, Flanagan spoke to Ike Peyton.

"Our worldly possessions are few. There's room for him in our wagon."

As was usually the case, when there were women to see to a wounded man, they were allowed to do so. The men went about circling the wagons and unharnessing the teams for the night. Maggie Peyton had removed McQuade's boots, and with others lifting him up, she unbuttoned and removed his trousers. Looking up into Mary Flanagan's stricken face, she spoke.

"Mary, this won't be pleasant and perhaps not proper."

"I don't care," she cried, "I'm staying. He said . . . we might have just . . . one day."

They had no idea what she was talking about, but she was allowed to stay. Having had some medical training, Maggie took charge.

"We must turn him on his back," said Maggie. "Some of you hold that blanket tight, so the mud doesn't flake off. Mary, you're going to help me turn him over."

Mary did so, coloring at the sight of the naked McQuade, but she recovered quickly, for none of the other women were in the slightest perturbed.

"Ah," Maggie said, with satisfaction, "the wounds are clean. There's no lead to be dug out of him. We can disinfect and bandage him."

"Then he'll be all right," said Mary eagerly.

"We won't know for a day or two," Maggie said. "The good news is there's no lead in him. The bad news could be, there's some internal damage we don't know about, something the lead did on its way through. If he's hurt inside, there may be nothing we can do for him. We should know by this time tomorrow."

"Take him to our wagon," said Mary. "I'll stay with him until he's better, or . . ."

Her words trailed off, but they all understood what she had meant to say. McQuade was taken to the Flanagan wagon, and Mary never left him, even to eat. Food was brought to her at supper time. She was nodding with weariness when McQuade suddenly spoke.

"Mary?" His voice was weak, and she had to lean close to hear him.

"I'm here, Chance. I'm here."

"I . . . have a question . . . I was goin' to ask . . . in Texas," he said, "but there . . . may not . . . be time. Remember I . . . told you we might . . . have just . . . one day?"

"I remember," she cried, her voice breaking.

"Mary, will you . . . marry me . . . now?"

"Yes," she said, through tears.

"Get your father," McQuade said. "Must . . . talk to . . . him . . . while I can."

"I'll get him," said Mary.

The girl found Flanagan at his customary place during the first watch. She told him only that McQuade was conscious and wanted to talk to him. Because of the limited space within the wagon, she waited outside while Flanagan entered.

"Is that . . . you . . . preacher?" McQuade asked weakly.

"It is, my boy," said Flanagan. "What do you want of me?"

"Your . . . permission. Mary has . . . promised . . . to marry . . . me."

"You have my permission," said Flanagan. "Just as soon as you're able, I'll perform the ceremony."

"No," McQuade whispered. "Tonight, while . . . I'm conscious."

"Mary has agreed to this?"

"Yes," said McQuade. "In my saddlebag . . . there's a little . . . white box. Bring it."

Flanagan left the wagon, and having seen him enter, many of the train's men and their women had gathered. Flanagan told them as quickly and as simply as he could of Chance McQuade's strange request.

"I brought his saddle in," Gunter Warnell said. "I'll check his saddlebags."

Quickly he returned with the little white box and passed it to Flanagan. He opened it, and they all crowded close. Lantern light winked off the little gold band, and some of the women wept. They all knew that McQuade must have bought the ring when he had ridden back to St. Louis, only a day or two after meeting Mary Flanagan.

"Mary," said Flanagan, "there's so little room in the wagon, you get in and I'll stand outside. Chance, we're ready. Are you awake?"

"Yes," McQuade said, and they could barely hear him.

"Then we must get on with the ceremony," said Flanagan. "Mr. Peyton, will you hold the ring until the proper moment?"

With Cal Tabor holding the lantern so Flanagan could read from his bible, he quickly performed the ceremony. McQuade did his best to speak loud enough for them to hear his responses. Being unable to place the ring on Mary's finger, Flanagan did it for him. She leaned down, kissing Chance long and hard.

"God," said Eli Bibb, under his breath, "that's enough to finish him."

"Mr. McQuade needs his rest," Flanagan said. "We should leave him alone."

They quickly moved away, leaving Mary Flanagan McQuade beside the wounded Chance. She became aware that he was trying to speak, and she leaned closer.

"You're mine," he said softly, "if just . . . for a . . . day . . ."

He said no more, the only sound being his ragged breathing. She felt his forehead and it was hot and dry to the touch. Covering him with a blanket, she stretched out beside him, but not to sleep. Moments later, there was a sound outside the wagon.

"Mary?" It was the soft voice of Maggie Peyton.

"Yes, Maggie?"

"Here's a bottle of whiskey," said Maggie. "I thought it best not to give you this, with your daddy here, but McQuade's going to need it. Before morning he should have a raging fever. Whatever it takes, get half of this down him, saving the rest. He'll need it all and maybe more, to sweat that fever out."

"Thank you, Maggie," Mary said. "I'll see that he takes it."

Maggie Peyton knew what she was talking about, for McQuade began talking out of his head, as the night wore on. Mary found him burning with fever, and when she finally got the prescribed whiskey down him, she was exhausted. With the first gray light of dawn she again felt his forehead and found the fever hadn't subsided. She was about to force more of the whiskey down McQuade, when Maggie spoke.

"Is this the first or second dose?"

"The second," said Mary. "I gave him the first maybe four hours ago, and his fever's no better."

"Here's some water," Maggie replied. "Let's give him a little of that before he takes any more whiskey. Sometimes the cure's worse than the ailment. Why don't you come out of there for some breakfast and hot coffee?"

"I think I'll have to," said Mary.

With McQuade severely wounded, many of the emigrants were in a quandary as to what they should do. Ike Peyton chose to speak to them.

"I can't see jouncin' McQuade around in a wagon before his fever's broke. I believe we should stay here for a day or two. Does anybody object to that?"

Strangely enough, nobody did, perhaps because they realized that with McQuade unable to scout the trail ahead, one of them would have to replace him. Mary managed to get the rest of the whiskey down McQuade. Suddenly there was the sound of a shot, and lead screamed off the iron tire of a wagon wheel. Men scrambled for their guns, but there were no more shots. Instead, there was a challenge shouted by a voice they all had heard before.

"This is Gid Sutton, and that *segundo* of yours salted down two of my men. We got some lead into him yesterday, but we know he's alive. One way or another, I aim to have him. Are you givin' him up, or do we have to take him?"

"You'll have to take him," Ike Peyton shouted.

"About what I expected," said Sutton. "That bein' the case, the ante goes up. I figure them two men that died was worth five thousand apiece. I want McQuade and ten thousand in gold. Until you come across, I'll kill one of you every day. Male or female, it don't make no difference to me."

"That's an insane demand," Miles Flanagan said. "I'll talk to him."

Before any of them could stop him, Flanagan had left the safety of the wagon circle and stood in the open.

"No, preacher," a dozen men shouted, but Flanagan might not have heard.

"Mr. Sutton," said Flanagan, "I am a minister of the Lord, speaking for God-fearing people. In the name of common decency, I am asking you to withdraw your demands."

"One a day, preacher," Sutton shouted, "and you get to be the first."

Half a dozen rifles roared, and Flanagan was slammed to the ground on his back, all but cut in half by the lead from the big Sharps rifles.

"No!" Mary screamed, seeking to break out of the wagon circle. Maggie Peyton and Ellen Warnell restrained her.

But there were no more shots. Men and women alike stood in stunned silence, the only sound being the weeping of Mary Flanagan. Finally Ike Peyton, Will Haymes, Gunter Warnell, and Cal Tabor took blankets and recovered Flanagan's riddled body. Sutton had driven home his threat in a manner that left no doubt as to his intentions. There must be a decision made before the dawn of another day, or someone else would die. Aware that many of them were looking to him, Ike Peyton spoke.

"Gunter, enlist some help and begin digging a grave over yonder by the creek. We'll lay the preacher to rest before we do anything else. Maggie, will you talk to Mary and see if there's anything special we ought to do?"

But before the grave had been dug, there was more trouble. Rufus Hook and three of his gunmen rode up, dismounted, and entered the wagon circle. Hook wasted no time in making known the purpose of the visit.

"What is the reason for this delay? Where is Mc-Quade?"

As calmly as he could, Ike Peyton explained what had happened, up to and including the killing of Miles Flanagan.

"Since McQuade got himself and the rest of you into this predicament," said Hook, "I see no reason why I should concern myself with how or whether any of you get out of it. All I have to say is that I have the authority to appoint a new wagon boss, which I intend to do if these wagons aren't on the trail by this time tomorrow. Do all of you understand that?"

"We understand it," somebody shouted, "but we ain't abidin' by it."

"Then I suppose this is a good time to inform you that if you do not reach Texas in time to claim your grants by July fifth, they revert to me. It's in your contracts."

"Somehow that don't surprise me," said Gunter Warnell.

"Mount up and get the hell out of here," Ike Peyton said angrily. "We'll be there, by God, and Chance McQuade will be with us."

Without another word, Hook and his companions rode away. A little embarrassed, Ike spoke to the people around him.

"Maybe I was out of line, speakin' for all of us, but

I've had about all I can stomach of that slimy varmint.''

"So have I," said Gunter Warnell. "Let's hear it for Ike.''

They shouted their agreement, even the women, and it even brought a smile to the wan face of Mary Flanagan. When the grave was finished, they gathered sadly around as the body of Miles Flanagan was lowered into it.

"Mary," Ike Peyton asked, "what would you have us do that's fittin' and proper?''

"Here's his bible," said Mary. "Take it and read the Twenty-third Psalm, and one other passage that I've marked.''

Ike took the old bible and in a not-too-steady voice, read the Psalm. He then turned to the second passage, and from the thirteenth verse of the fifteenth chapter of St. John, read:

> *Greater love hath no man than this, that a man lay down his life for his friends.*

Mary turned away, weeping, leaving them to fill in the grave. More than two hours had elapsed since McQuade had been given a second dose of whiskey, and feeling his forehead, Mary found he was sweating. She sat down beside him, took one of his leathery hands in hers, and bowed her head.

One by one, men came to Ike, expressing their appreciation for his having stood up to Rufus Hook. They seemed to look to him for an answer to the ultimatum laid down by Gid Sutton and his band of outlaws.

"Damn it, Maggie," said Ike, "we're trapped between the devil and the deep blue sea. If I had all the money in the world, I wouldn't pay them blood-suckin' bastards what they're demanding, and I sure don't aim to hand McQuade over to 'em. That don't leave but one way out. We got to fight. But they're killers, and some of us will die.''

"Maybe not," Maggie said. "I've overheard some of McQuade's talk, about fighting on your own terms, attacking instead of waiting to be attacked. Why don't you ask yourself what he would do, and then do it?"

"God bless you, Maggie," said Ike, giving her an unexpected kiss. "I got some talking to do."

They were a somber lot as they gathered at Ike Peyton's request. Before he spoke a word, they knew the problem he was about to address.

"Friends," Ike said, "this mornin' we had a threat laid on us, along with demands that are impossible. I can only speak for myself, but if I had all the money in the world I'd not pay one red cent toward them varmints McQuade gunned down. As for them taking him, I got to say, they'll do it over my dead body."

There were shouts and cheers, and Ike waited until they subsided before continuing.

"With that settled," said Ike, "I reckon you're all wonderin' what we'll be doin' in the mornin', when they come gunnin' for us again. We're goin' to do exactly what Chance McQuade would do, if he was able. Come daylight, we're goin' to be staked out with our guns, waitin' for Sutton and his outlaws. The women will be in the wagons. When that bunch rides in, we're goin' to just purely shoot the hell out of them, before they even get a shot at any of us. Now who can I count on?"

To a man they rose up with shouts of agreement. When the uproar had died, Andrew Burke took it upon himself to speak.

"They ain't been no love lost between us Burkes and Chance McQuade, but by God, he's a man with the bark on. He done right, standin' up to Sutton's gunmen, and you can count on us tomorrow. We don't like bein' shook down by thieves and killers."

"We'll surround this camp before daylight," said Ike, "and we want them all within range before we open fire. We'll give them the same chance they give Reverend Flanagan."

* * *

Mary Flanagan spent her second night in the wagon with the wounded McQuade. She had a bucket of water and a tin cup, expecting him to be thirsty, and he was. The first time he awoke, it was only long enough to swallow half a cup of water. The second time, he seemed stronger. Taking her left hand, he felt the ring.

"It . . . wasn't a dream, then," he said.

"No," said Mary. "You're not having second thoughts, are you?"

"You should know better," he said weakly. "I . . . thought . . . on an *hombre*'s . . . marryin' day, he'd be busier than . . . this."

She laughed. "When you're able, I'll make it all up to you."

"Where are we?"

"At a creek near where you were shot," said Mary. "Nobody wanted to move on, with you feverish and sick."

She said no more, not wishing to burden him with all that had happened since he had been shot. She had no idea what he might do, if he knew that Ike Peyton and every man in the outfit would be waiting at dawn, prepared for a showdown with Gid Sutton and his outlaws. That he would be proud of them, she had no doubt, for not only were they about to rid themselves of Sutton and his renegades, they had defied Rufus Hook. McQuade was again asleep, and she lay down beside him. While she still wept bitter tears for her father, the old man had died knowing McQuade would care for her, and she took comfort in that.

Without a sound, Ike Peyton assembled a hundred and twenty-five men an hour ahead of first light. Besides their rifles, every man carried a fully loaded revolver. Lest the outlaws become suspicious, every horse and mule was left within the wagon circle. Men moved out afoot, and since Rufus Hook's camp was within sight to the north, Ike's

defenders all took positions in a skirmish line half a mile
long, facing southwest. It was from the same direction the
outlaws had appeared the day before, from the wilds of
Indian Territory. They had two powerful advantages: Sutton and his outlaws didn't believe they would fight for
the wounded Chance McQuade, and they had enough
guns to empty every outlaw's saddle. Impatiently they
waited. There was no sound except that of birds, and occasionally a nicker from a horse or the bray of a mule
from within the wagon circle. Just when it seemed they
weren't going to try and make good their threat, they rode
in from the southwest. As they rode through a clearing,
Ike Peyton counted thirty men, each with his rifle across
the saddle in front of him. They were strung out, well out
of revolver range, but Ike had instructed his men to rely
on the Sharps .50, making the first shot good. They reined
up, and Sutton again shouted his ultimatum.

"You farmers, this is Gid Sutton and his band. You
just ran out of time."

"Wrong, Sutton," Ike shouted. "*You* just ran out of
time."

It was the signal they had agreed upon, and rifles roared
in succession, each sounding like an echo of the last. Men
fell all around Sutton, and all that saved him was his horse
spooking and rearing. Head down, hugging the neck of
his horse, the outlaw rode for his life. Others tried to follow, and were blown from their saddles. It was over in
seconds, and only when Ike called them out did the defenders appear.

"We'll take a body count," Ike said. "Take weapons,
ammunition, anything we might be able to use."

"Look what I got," said Gunter Warnell, who was
leading a bay horse. "They killed McQuade's bay, and I
think it's only fair they replace him."

"We'll round up any other loose horses," Ike said.
"We'll tie 'em behind the wagons, on lead ropes. They'll
be useful in Texas."

After taking a body count, they looked at one another

in awe. They had gunned down no less than twenty-five of the outlaws. Will Haymes summed it up.

"Gents, at five thousand dollars a head, I reckon we done run up a pretty good tab."

They made their way back to the wagon circle, triumphant, not having lost a man, and with nobody wounded. Within the Flanagan wagon, Chance McQuade had heard all the shooting, and Mary Flanagan could no longer remain silent. Quickly she told him of the demands of the outlaws, and of the cold-blooded murder of Miles Flanagan.

"What you just heard," she said proudly, "was Ike Peyton and his men answering those impossible demands, and taking vengeance for my father's death."

"My God," said McQuade, "how many . . . how many stood up?"

"Every last one of them, Chance. A hundred and twenty men."

"Bring them here," McQuade said.

"Are you sure you're strong enough?" Mary asked anxiously.

"I'm strong enough," said McQuade.

They came, gathering as close as they could, Gunter Warnell leading McQuade's bay. Mary had let down the wagon's tailgate and McQuade lay on his belly, covered only with a blanket.

"You're one *bueno* outfit," McQuade said, as forcefully as he could. "It's been damn near worth gettin' shot, to have you stand beside one another against a common enemy. I believe it's this kind of solidarity that will bring Texas into the Union and make it a land of which we can all be proud. Now, if it's God's will, we'll beat Hook's deadline, whether we go ahead of him, around him, or ride right over him."

Their shouting was heard in Hook's camp, as Hook's men harnessed the teams, preparing to move out. They drove wide of McQuade's wagon circle, and every teamster had a fight on his hands, as the horses and mules shied at the dead men scattered along their path. Creeker, one of the hired guns, rode alongside Hook's wagon, and he laughed at the expression on Hook's face.

"It looks like McQuade's pussycats is turned into wampus kitties with claws a yard long, don't it?"

Hook gritted his teeth and said nothing. With Chance McQuade alive, his dream of taking the Texas land grants for himself seemed less and less like a sure thing.

In the Flanagan wagon, McQuade was again soaked with sweat and breathing hard from exertion.

"You shouldn't have done that," Mary scolded.

"I had to," said McQuade. "They stood up for me when I was unable to stand up for myself, and I couldn't let it pass. Anyhow, I have to get out of this wagon and clean up myself. I'm a mess, and these blankets are ruined."

"The blankets can be washed," Mary said, "and so can you. Your bandages must be changed again. I'll bring soap and water and take care of you."

"Who stripped me after I'd been shot? You?"

"No," said Mary. "Some of the other women. I was in such a state of shock, I wasn't of much use."

"I reckon Hook's right about one thing," McQuade said. "Me gettin' myself ventilated has got us all neck-deep in trouble. With Hook's wagons ahead of us, we'll have to take the trail tomorrow."

"You did what you had to," said Mary, "and you have the support of every man in this outfit. I know father was proud of you, and he'd be prouder still of the way they all stood up for you this morning."

"He was a man in every sense of the word," McQuade said, "and what's bothering me is the fact that I'm indirectly responsible for his death. I gunned down two of them, and from there on, it was vengeance."

"Your killing two of them might have rushed them some, but everybody—Ike and all the others—believe they would have come after us, and that many more than my father might have died. In his own way, he died for us, forcing us to take a stand. Ike and the others did what they believed you would have done.''

''I couldn't be more pleased with them,'' said McQuade. ''I want you to bind these wounds as tight as you can, so I can get up and out of this wagon.''

''I'll bind the wounds, but if you try to get up, you're going to fall on your face. You are just three days from being shot, of us not knowing whether you would live or die, and I think you should rest another day or two.''

His wounds cleansed and bound, McQuade tried to rise and found himself unable to do so. He lay back, breathing hard.

''You lost a lot of blood,'' said Mary, ''and you need several more days of rest and good food. Ike and some of the others want to talk to you, but you don't have to get up for that. We'll let down the wagon's tailgate, and they'll come to you.''

''Yes, ma'am,'' McQuade said.

CHAPTER 6

❧

Despite McQuade's protests, the train remained where it was for two more days, and on the sixth day following the ambush, they moved out. McQuade's newly acquired bay trotted behind the Flanagan wagon. McQuade lay on blankets, while Mary drove.

"I didn't know you could handle a team," said McQuade. "Can you cook too?"

"Not a lick," she said, with a straight face. "You should have asked some questions before you bought the farm."

"I reckon," said McQuade, "but I was just too struck with the looks of the farm. How much longer until we can get some plowing done?"

'Until I know you're able to stand the shock. I don't want you to have a relapse and die, just when I'm getting used to you."

"Well, for your sake, I hope it's worth the wait," McQuade said. "Who's doing the scouting for water, while I'm piled up in here?"

"Ike Peyton and Will Haymes, mostly."

"What about their wagons?"

"Maggie and Minerva are driving them," said Mary.

"The *lead* wagons?"

"Of course," Mary said. "Why not? They handle the teams as well as Ike and Will."

"Some of those outlaws escaped," said McQuade. "Suppose they belly-down with their Sharps fifties and blast Maggie and Minerva off those wagon boxes?"

"Ike and Will thought of that," Mary said, "but Maggie and Minerva wouldn't have it any other way. They want to know, when we're all in this together, why only the men are allowed to be shot. Why is that?"

"We're selfish brutes, set in our ways," said McQuade.

After supper, Ike and Will—accompanied by some of the other men, spent an hour with McQuade discussing the trail ahead.

"Looks like Hook's wagons are a day or more ahead of us," Ike said. "There appears to be plenty of springs, creeks, and rivers in Indian Territory, so water ain't a problem. But we ain't forgot what Chad Guthrie said, about knowin' the trail ahead. What surprises me is Hook bein' so damned anxious to run on ahead of us. Don't he know there's Kiowa in Indian Territory?"

"But for the stampede that flattened his camp, Hook's had virtually no trouble since leaving St. Louis," McQuade said. "Maybe he's got a mite too much self-confidence. You're right to continue scouting ahead. We must know, firsthand, what we're up against. About all we can expect from Hook is that he'll take some of the edge off the hostile Indians and outlaws ahead of us."

"Forgot to tell you," said Will Haymes, "but besides that bay of yours, we rounded up the rest of the hosses belongin' to them dead outlaws. There's twenty-four of them, trottin' along on lead ropes behind our wagons."

"A job well done," McQuade said. "What did you do with all those dead *hombres*?"

"Just what we figured they'd of done with us," said Will. "We left 'em all where they fell, and when we was ready to move out, we drove around 'em, so's not to spook the teams."

Taking the lead had wrought some drastic changes in the Hook camp. The saloon tent remained packed in a wagon, the lanterns and the cook fires were put out well before dark, and the night watch had been doubled. Each morning, Hook sent two riders scouting ahead for water and possible Indian sign. But while his men were quick with their guns, Indian Territory was new to them, and they were uneasy. The second day after Hook's caravan had taken the lead, his advance riders failed to return.

"Creeker," said Hook, "take Slack with you and see what's happened to Byron and Mook. They should have been back hours ago."

"I ain't likin' the looks of this," Slack said, as he and Creeker rode out. "Byron and Mook wasn't afraid of the devil hisself. If something's happened to them . . ."

Something *had* happened to the two gunmen. Creeker and Slack found them facedown on the bank of a creek, their scalps gone and their backs shot full of arrows.

"Damn," said Slack, "what are we goin' to do with 'em?"

"Leave 'em where they lay," Creeker said. "This is something I want Hook and all the others to see."

"I got me a gut-feelin' this scouting ahead is about to become damned unpopular," said Slack. "Let's get the hell out of here. I'm gettin' some nervous twitches betwixt my shoulder blades."

They took the back-trail at a fast gallop, while the Kiowa who had been observing them mounted his horse and rode away toward the southwest.

"Dead?" Hook shouted. "How could that have happened? I hired you men for your fast guns."

"Shoot a man in the back," said Creeker, "and a fast gun don't mean doodly squat."

"Damn it," Hook said, "we must have a place to circle the wagons for the night, with water. Why didn't you ride on?"

"No need to," said Slack. "Byron and Mook had already found us a creek. I reckon we'll have to drag 'em away, so's they don't pollute it."

Hook's wagons had stopped so that the teams might be

watered, and most of the men had come forth to hear what Creeker and Slack had to report. Now their eyes were on Rufus Hook, and he could see potential rebellion.

"Back to your wagons," Hook shouted.

Reluctantly the men climbed to their wagon boxes and clucked to their teams, every man with a long gun at his feet and a loaded revolver under his belt. When eventually they reached the fatal creek, they stared unbelievingly at the arrow-riddled bodies of Byron and Mook.

"Groat, Porto, Dirk, and Nall, get shovels from the cook wagon and bury those men," said Hook, "and be quick about it."

The four men chosen deliberately took their time performing the grim task, allowing the rest of Hook's company to get full benefit from the grisly objects bristling with Kiowa arrows. The women, including Hook's Lora Kirby, all huddled in a single wagon, some of them weeping. Xavier Hedgepith looked over his glasses at the furious Hook.

"I believe," said Hedgepith, "I advised you against taking the lead. In McQuade's wagons there are well over a hundred armed men. Including yourself, you had thirty-five, now shy Byron and Mook. McQuade, despite the fact you hate his guts, has experience you and your hired guns are lacking, and he has men who will fight for him. Take away your money, and who in this outfit cares a tinker's damn for you?"

"Shut up," Hook roared. "Damn you, shut up."

But with the exception of the four men digging graves, most of Hook's outfit had heard Hedgepith's words, and in their eyes, Hook saw the truth of what Hedgepith had said. Creeker was the first to speak.

"I reckon you've about played out your string, Hook. You ain't payin' near enough for a man to risk what happened to them gents layin' over yonder shot full of arrows. I'm of a mind to ride back to St. Louis, takin' with me anybody that's wantin' to go."

"I'll double every man's wages," Hook shouted.

"Hook," said Hedgepith pityingly, "you don't buy off a man with money, when he's afraid for his life. Why don't you swallow your pride, back off up this creek, and wait for McQuade's wagons to take the lead?"

"No," Hook snarled. "Hedgepith . . ."

But Rufus Hook's angry voice was lost among the shouts and curses of his men. The uproar finally died down enough for individual voices to be heard, and Creeker spoke up.

"Hook, the lawyer's got a handle on it. Hangin' on to McQuade's shirt tail you got a chance. On your own, that's exactly where you're goin' to be. On your own. What good is a hundred a month or five hundred a month to a man who's been shot full of arrows and scalped? Now you back off, allowin' McQuade's bunch to go ahead, or by God, you'll be all by yourself, this time tomorrow. Are the rest of you with me?"

"Hell, yes," they shouted in a single voice.

"Very well," said Hook, with poor grace, "take the wagons upstream and circle them. We will remain here until McQuade's wagons take the lead."

"Double wages?" Slack inquired. "You ain't backin' down on that."

Hook hesitated, and when his eyes met Hedgepith's, the lawyer shook his head.

"Double wages from here on to Texas," said Hook with a sigh.

"If we ain't included in them double wages," said one of Hook's seventeen teamsters, "I got me a hoss, and I'm makin' tracks for St. Louis."

There were shouts of agreement, and again Rufus Hook found himself uncomfortably caught up in circumstances of his own making.

"Double wages for everybody," Hook said wearily.

On the seventh day after he had been shot, despite Mary's misgivings, McQuade again rode out ahead of the wagons on his newly-acquired bay. Reaching a suitable creek, he was immediately intrigued by a pair of fresh graves, and then by the fact that instead of the Hook wagons continuing toward the southwest, they had all been driven upstream. It was enough to warrant some investigation, and McQuade crossed the creek. Circling wide, so as not to be seen, McQuade rode upstream. There, from concealing brush, he observed the Hook wagons. Mounting, he rode back to the newly made graves and continued toward the southwest. Soon he discovered the faint tracks of four unshod horses, and less than a mile beyond, they were joined by a fifth rider. He reined up, it all coming together in his mind. Turning his horse, he rode back to meet the oncoming wagons.

"So Chad Guthrie was right about the Kiowa," Ike said, when McQuade returned to find the men resting their teams. "What do you make of Hook's outfit just settin' there on the creek?"

"I think they've changed their minds about wantin' to take the lead," McQuade replied. "From the graves, I'd say the Kiowa got a couple of Hook's advance riders, and it brought on a rebellion among the others."

"So Hook's waitin' for us to keep the Kiowa busy, while he rides our shirt tails," said Gunter Warnell. "After all that big talk about us not makin' his deadline, are we goin' to just take this layin' down?"

"Not much else we can do," McQuade said, "but riding our back-trail in Kiowa country is no assurance of being left alone. The Kiowa aren't fools. They may well pass us by because of our large numbers, while worrying the hell out of Hook's outfit from behind. I don't aim for the Kiowa to take us by surprise, and I'll be out there every day, seeing that they don't."

McQuade's outfit went on to the creek, and ignoring the Hook camp a mile or so upstream, circled their wagons for the night.

"I think we'll triple our guard from now on," said McQuade. "We have more than enough men, and enough horses and mules to drive Indians mad. I want all the animals inside the wagon circle at night. We'll try to end our day while there's still enough light for them to graze for an hour or two before dark. Mostly, we'll have to depend on the grain we're hauling, especially for the mules.''

Supper was mostly a silent affair, everybody painfully aware of the nearby graves, and of the possibility of trouble from the Kiowa. Mary refilled McQuade's coffee cup, and he winked at her. She colored a little, and some of the other women smiled, aware that if he was well enough to ride a horse, we was ready to take his marriage seriously. Supper done and the cleanup completed, McQuade rode out to help the men haze the horses and mules into the wagon circle. When the animals had been secured, the first watch posted, and the wagons brought back into formation, McQuade returned to the wagon where Mary waited on the box, and climbed up beside her. It wasn't good dark, and she smiled at him, turning the ring round and round on her finger.

"We don't have to sit on the wagon box anymore," she said.

"Don't you reckon they're all goin' to know what we're up to, if we start spendin' all our time in the wagon?" McQuade asked.

"I reckon they will," said Mary. "I've worn this ring for almost two weeks, and all you've seen of me is . . . what you saw that first day we met."

"You mean there's more?"

"Chance McQuade, will you stop playing games? Is a wife useful only to worry herself silly that her man's about to be shot dead, to clean his wounds, and pour whiskey down him when he's feverish?"

"No," said McQuade, "there's more. After the hunt, the Indians allow the squaws to scrape the buffalo hides. I'm part Indian, you know."

"No," she said, "I didn't know. Do I have to shoot you, and then go get Maggie to take your britches off?"

"I reckon not," said McQuade. "Get in the wagon, woman. You can scrape the buffalo hides in the morning before breakfast."

McQuade rode out at first light, aware that he was probably being watched by the Kiowa. If they had killed two of Hook's men, certainly they wouldn't hesitate to extend to Chance McQuade the same fate. But McQuade found a suitable place to circle the wagons for the night, and returned to meet the train.

"Maybe," said Ike during supper, "the Kiowa will leave us alone."

"We can't count on that," McQuade said. "We'll continue with a tripled watch. They're up to something, but it may not necessarily involve us."

"The men have settled down," said Hedgepith with satisfaction. "With McQuade's outfit ahead of us, I believe our troubles are over."

"They'd better not settle down too much," Hook replied. "Havin' McQuade's bunch just ahead of us don't mean they'll help us."

"It sure as hell don't," said Hedgepith. "We have you and your damned deadline talk to thank for that."

"Hedgepith," Hook said, "you'd better watch your mouth. One day you'll go too far."

Sometime during the night, the Kiowa slipped into Hook's camp, stampeding every last horse and mule into the darkness. Some of the animals flattened Hook's tent, leaving him bruised, barefoot, and wearing only his drawers.

"Damn it," Hook bawled in frustration, "damn it."

"My goodness," Hedgepith said mildly, "how are we going to move these wagons, with all our horses and mules gone?"

"Mr. Hook," said Snakehead Presnall, "they turned over the saloon wagon and busted the roulette wheel."

"After them," Hook shouted. "Every man of you take your guns and go after them."

"Beggin' your pardon, suh," said Creeker with all the contempt he could muster, "but are you referrin' to the Indians or the horses and mules?"

"All of them, damn it," Hook snarled. "What the hell am I paying you for?"

"Not to drift around in the dark afoot, huntin' horses, mules, and Indians," said Dirk. "By God, I ain't movin' till daylight, and then just far enough to find my hoss."

There was shouted agreement so near unanimous that Hook swallowed his curses and bore his frustration in silence. Whatever his other problems, the lack of vigilance wasn't one of them, for every man was awake the rest of the night, his gun ready. Strong on the minds of them all were the arrow-riddled bodies of Byron and Mook.

The uproar was heard in McQuade's camp. McQuade sat up, listening.

"What is it?" Mary asked.

"It sounds almighty like all of Hook's horses and mules have stampeded," McQuade said. "I reckon I'd better get up for a while, and maybe join the men on watch. Where's my britches and shirt?"

She laughed. "Somewhere in the wagon, I think."

"You're a hell of a lot of help," he grumbled. "On the frontier, a man's a fool to take off anything more than his hat, when he sleeps."

McQuade found the missing articles, got dressed, and tugged on his boots.

"When will you be back?" Mary asked.

"I don't know," said McQuade. "Get some sleep. You still have to scrape those buffalo hides before breakfast."

She laughed, enjoying his strange sense of humor, as he climbed over the wagon's tailgate. In the moonlight he could see many of the other men gathered near Ike Peyton's wagon. Obviously they were waiting for McQuade to arrive.

"Sounds like Hook's bunch is all goin' to be afoot, come morning," Cal Tabor said.

"Yeah," said Hardy Kilgore, "and I'm so sorry for 'em, I could just break down and bawl like a baby."

"I feel the same way," Eli Bibb said. "I reckon we ought to all ride over there, come daylight, and offer our help."

"Don't worry, Eli," said Ike. "After somebody gut-shoots you, we'll put you up a nice headstone and look after Odessa."

They all laughed uproariously.

"Don't get too excited," McQuade said. "While they can't stampede our stock from the wagon circle, they can come after them while they're out to graze, or they can attack us while we're strung out for a mile."

That brought them back to the reality of their own danger, and they became quiet.

"There's something else I should have told you," said McQuade, "which I'm about to tell you now. There'll be no smoking while you're on watch. Nothing gives away your position in the dark more quickly than a lighted quirly or a pipe. Always stand your watch in pairs, never separated. A pair of Kiowa with knives can pick you off one man at a time, without the rest of us being aware of it, until we find your dead bodies."

"I reckon we shouldn't talk, neither," Hardy Kilgore said.

"I reckon you shouldn't, if you want to go on living," said McQuade. "Don't do anything to draw attention to yourselves. An Indian can find you by the creak of the leather in your boots, the shifting of your gunbelt, or while you're fanning yourself with your hat."

"God Almighty," somebody said, "maybe I'll hold my breath too."

"Good idea," said McQuade. "I overlooked that. Just remember that sound carries for a great distance at night, and that can work for you, as well as against you. Listen for any sound that seems out of place or unnatural."

McQuade's watch was still more than four hours away, so he went back to the wagon and climbed in.

"Are you still awake?" he asked softly.

"No," she said. "You told me to get some sleep."

"That's a disappointment. I don't have to stand watch for another four hours."

"I wouldn't want you lying here disappointed," she replied. "Why don't you gently wake me?"

"No use, I reckon. I'm wearin' everything except my hat."

It was all completely foolish. They laughed until there were tears in their eyes, and the men on watch got a totally false impression as to what was going on . . .

After the stampede, nobody in Hook's camp slept. They all sat there with their guns ready, any occasional conversation being answered by a grunt or total silence. In the dark, in his trampled tent, Hook had been unable to find his clothing and boots. As a result, he spent the rest of the night in his drawers, his teeth chattering in a chill wind. Even he had enough Indian savvy not to suggest a fire. The moment it was light enough to see, the men prepared to go looking for the scattered stock.

"First priority is the mules," said Hook.

"First priority is my damn horse," Creeker replied.

"And mine," said half a dozen of his companions.

Hook swallowed his fury and began looking for his clothing and boots. His position was precarious, because without the mules, he was stranded. The remaining ten men upon whom he depended for protection, however, could find their horses and simply ride away, if they chose. Despite all the cursing and commotion, Ampersand started his fire and got breakfast underway. Whatever their troubles, men had to eat. The old Negro looked at Rufus Hook and said exactly the wrong thing.

"How we move this wagon, without no mules?"

"I don't intend to move it," Hook said savagely. "I'm going to leave it set right here, with you in it, until Judgment Day, or until the Indians get you, whichever comes first.''

Ampersand had been with Hook for years, and thought he had endured all the man's ugly moods, but this was Hook at his worst. The old man silently vowed that if he was able to return to St. Louis alive, he would build himself a shack alongside the Mississippi, and for his remaining years, watch the steamboats go by.

''Damn it,'' said Slack, as he and his companions followed the trail of the stampeded horses and mules, ''we could beat the bushes for a week, without findin' one horse or mule.''

''Let them that's dependin' on mules look for 'em,'' Rucker replied.

All seventeen of the teamsters were following the same trail, and while none of them had anything to say, they were rankled by the crude remarks of Hook's hired gunmen. Odd as it seemed, the first animals to be recovered were mules, and the men who had lost horses were beginning to panic.

''I never cared for ridin' a mule,'' Porto growled, ''but if that's what it takes to git me out of this godforsaken country, I'm willin' to learn.''

''As I recall,'' said one of the teamsters, ''wasn't nobody ridin' mules. All of them was drawin' wagons.''

''That could all change,'' Ellis snarled, ''if we don't soon find some hosses.''

''I got a gun that says it ain't likely,'' one of the teamsters replied.

They stumbled on, the search growing longer and tempers growing shorter. The wind being from the southwest, they could hear the creak and the rattle of wagons, as McQuade and his outfit again took the trail. For a while they all were silent, as the implications of their predicament sank in. With McQuade and his much larger party gone, they would again be on their own. On their own, afoot.

*　　*　　*

McQuade rode out ahead of the wagons, wary, not knowing what to expect. He had an idea, however, that the Kiowa would be busy rounding up the stock they had run off from Hook's camp the night before. He wondered if Hook had sense enough to find just enough horses and mules to mount his men and send them after the Kiowa and the rest of the stampeded stock. He suspected the Kiowa would be concerned with the mules only as food. They would be interested in the horses. Including the animals taken from the Sutton gang, there were now more than a hundred horses in McQuade's own outfit, reason enough for a heavy guard. Finding a suitable camp for the night, he rode back to meet the wagons.

There was jubilation among Hook's teamsters as they began finding grazing mules, and gloom among Creeker and his companions, as they found no horses.

"It's lookin' like there'll be some *hombres* beggin' to ride on our wagon boxes," one of the teamsters observed.

"I'd have to think on it some," said another. "I ain't sure I can stand the stink."

By the end of the day, only five mules were missing, while not a single horse had been found, forcing Hook to make a decision.

"If we must, we can leave one wagon, spreading its goods among the others. But I'm not without sympathy for those of you whose horses haven't been found. I'm willing to lay over for another day, allowing you the use of mules to seek and recover your mounts. If you are interested in doing so, of course."

"What the hell choice do we have?" Creeker growled. "I ain't too proud to straddle a mule, if my only other choice is walking."

There was reluctant agreement from Creeker's companions.

"Just tonight, tomorrow, and tomorrow night," said Hook. "Obviously your horses have been taken by the

Indians. We shall see if you're man enough to recover them.''

Tracking hostile Indians, even to recover their mounts, was a task none of them relished, but they had little choice. The rest of them looked at Creeker, and he remained silent.

''Still no sign of Hook's wagons,'' Ike said, as they gathered around the supper fire. ''How does a man go about findin' his horse after it's been stole by Indians?''

''If he's smart,'' said McQuade, ''he'll find a trail and track the Indians, rather than tromp around lookin' for horses he ain't likely to find. I reckon Hook's bunch has all been horse and mule huntin' all day, and I'd bet they haven't found a single horse. The Kiowa split up, each man chasing a horse. They'll all come together some distance away, instead of close by, where Hook's bunch will be looking for tracks.''

''You've had considerable experience with Indians, I reckon,'' said Gunter Warnell.

''Enough not to take them for granted,'' McQuade said. ''Most Indians have cause for their hostility toward whites, but that has nothing to do with them stealing our horses. One tribe steals from another, so why would they hesitate to steal from us?''

''I think we should add to our watch,'' said Will Haymes. ''We have the men.''

''Any increase should be from midnight till dawn,'' McQuade said. ''If a man's going to nod off, it's usually during the small hours of the morning. I'm going to be with you each night during those hours, at least until we're through Indian Territory.''

''Hell, after that, it's the Comanches,'' said Eli Bibb.

''One thing at a time,'' McQuade said.

The first stars were out as McQuade and Mary made their way to the wagon.

''You'd better get some sleep, if you're going on watch at midnight,'' said Mary.

"I aim to keep you awake until I go on watch,"
McQuade said.

"You're going to take off more than just your hat,
then."

"Considerably more," said McQuade.

CHAPTER 7

❧

*A*t first light, Creeker and his nine companions rode out, unsure as to where to start searching for their lost mounts.

"We'll ride a five-mile circle," said Creeker, "lookin' for shod tracks. Any one of you findin' tracks, foller 'em. Somewhere these damn Indians had to come together. From there we ought to have some kind of trail leadin' us to their camp."

The stock had stampeded toward the east, and it soon became apparent that the Kiowa had been driving the horses. While the mules had slowed and fanned out, the horses had continued considerably farther than spooked animals would have run on their own. Finally the horses had been allowed to scatter, with the intention of discouraging pursuit.

"Each of us will track one horse," said Creeker, "but we don't know that bunch didn't take a roundabout way, so one of us could reach that camp ahead of the others. Watch what you're doin', and don't stumble into the midst of 'em."

They separated, and within a mile, Creeker realized they had done the right thing, for he found a set of unshod tracks pursuing the shod ones. Both horses had slowed from a gallop, to a trot, to a walk. Creeker followed the tracks eastward for half a dozen miles, reining up on a rise, aware that he might be approaching the camp. Suddenly there was the bray of a mule, and Creeker's animal answered. Creeker dismounted, and taking his rifle, crept to the top of the rise. Below him were Groat, Porto, Dirk, and Nall. Besides the mules they rode, there were the five missing animals needed to draw the wagons. Leading his mule, Creeker descended the rise.

"Reckon what these varmints are worth to Rufus Hook?" Nall asked. "By God, way he talked to us, we oughta hold 'em for ransom."

"Never mind them," said Creeker. "Did the trails you were followin' lead here?"

"Yeah," Nall replied. "We reckoned the others would, too, so we waited. Looks like them Indians all left here together."

They waited less than an hour for their five companions. There being a spring, they watered their mules and took the trail of the Indians and their stolen horses.

"They ain't but one thing botherin' me," said Dirk. "When we find that Indian camp, how do we go about gettin' our horses without bein' shot full of arrows?"

"It depends on how many Indians are in that camp," Creeker replied. "If there's just a few, maybe we can ambush the varmints. If there's a hundred, we'll have to come up with somethin' else."

"Let's do them like they done us," said Rucker, "and stampede all the horses. Then all we got to do is round 'em up."

"Damn, Rucker, why don't we just ride in and ask for 'em back?" Groat suggested.

Slack laughed. "Groat's right. Them Indians ain't gonna be settin' there shaking in their teepees, while we gather up our horses."

"Shut up, the lot of you," said Creeker. "They'll hear us comin', five miles off."

The trail they were following had begun to veer toward the northwest. Half a mile to the north, an Indian observed them, while his companion had taken a similar position less than a mile to the south. As though by prearranged signal, each Kiowa mounted his horse and galloped away to the northwest. The Kiowa camp boasted more than fifty warriors, and they came alive as their sentries rode in. Within minutes, they were mounted and riding toward the southeast. Eventually they divided, half of them continuing toward the southeast, while the rest rode toward the northeast.

"I got the feelin' we're almighty close to them Indians," said Ellis. "Maybe one of us ought to ride ahead . . ."

His voice trailed off, as a ridge to their right suddenly blossomed with hard-riding, screeching Indians.

"Take cover!" Creeker shouted.

Wheeling their mules toward the south, preparing to ride for their lives, they reined up, for coming at them was an equal force of whooping Indians. The mules spooked, and in the mass confusion that followed, not a shot was fired. Men were clubbed from their saddles, and when they came to their senses, they were mounted, with their feet bound and their hands tied behind them with rawhide thongs. They were alive, but nothing more. Each had a bloodied head and had been relieved of his weapons. Each mule was secured by a lead rope, an Indian riding behind, and the captives looked at one another in hopeless despair. They were riding toward the northwest, toward the Kiowa camp, and not a man of them had any doubt as to what would become of them there . . .

Chance McQuade had ridden out ahead of the wagons, and as was his custom, he took cover in a thicket, when he stopped to rest his horse. It was from there that he saw the Kiowa and their captives crossing his trail, half a mile ahead.

"Well, by God, horse," said McQuade, "some of Hook's bunch has got their tails caught in an almighty deep crack."

McQuade waited until the procession was out of sight.

He then rode on until he found suitable water a little more than five miles ahead. After resting and watering his horse, he returned the way he had come. Reaching the point where the Kiowa had crossed with their hapless captives, McQuade reined up. Common sense told him it was none of his business what became of Hook's men, but compassion won out. He rode cautiously the way the Kiowa had gone. Obviously, the Indians had satisfied themselves their captives had been alone, and they had no fear of pursuit. Fortunately, McQuade was downwind from the camp, and long before reaching it, he smelled wood smoke. A dog barked nearby, and he reined up. It was time to leave his horse, lest it nicker and betray his presence. Carefully, quietly, he crept forward until he reached a slight rise. From the crest of it, he could see at least part of the camp below. He counted a dozen teepees, and he wasn't able to see them all, because of trees and obscuring brush. But he could see enough to cause his blood to run cold, for the Kiowa were placing a line of wooden stakes in the ground. McQuade counted ten, equaling the number of captives. After the evening meal, after some satisfying torture, the ten captives would be burned at the stake. McQuade had seen enough. Quickly he returned to his horse, mounted, and rode away. When he met the wagons, he judged they would reach water well before dark. He waited until the teams were being rested, to tell his companions of the capture of Hook's men and their probable fate.

"If it was anybody else," Will Haymes said, "I'd be all for going to their rescue, but I ain't forgot the nasty way Hook treated us, while you was laid up, near dead."

"That was Hook's doing," said McQuade. "These men haven't done anything to us, and for our sake as much as theirs, we can't allow them to be murdered. If the Kiowa manage to get by with this, they'll believe their medicine is almighty strong, and they'll give us hell from now on."

"I reckon I understand your thinkin'," Ike said, "but

I don't favor gettin' some of us shot full of arrows, savin' Hook's bunch. With that many Kiowa, how do you aim to get us into that camp and get them captives out?''

''We'll create a diversion, takin' their minds off the captives,'' said McQuade. ''Nothin' is more important to an Indian than his horse. We can ride in just after dark. Some of us will stampede their horses, and that should rid the camp of most of them. We'll assign men to shoot any who try to prevent us from completing the rescue. Ten men, each leading an extra horse, will free the captives.''

''There ought to be at least sixty of us,'' said Cal Tabor. ''With ten men going after the captives, that would allow twenty-five to stampede the horses, and an equal number to shoot any Indians that decide to stand and fight.''

''That's a hell of a lot of men, just to stampede the horses,'' Hardy Kilgore said.

''I don't want them just stampeded out of the camp,'' said McQuade. ''I want them run far enough to keep those Indians afoot for two or three days. The longer they're without horses, the less likely they are to come after us with revenge on their minds. We'll kill as many Kiowa as we must, and no more. I want only to free those men, and to convince the Kiowa that we're bad medicine. That's how I feel. Do any of you object?''

''I do,'' said Andrew Burke. ''Us Burkes wouldn't carry a drop of water to Hook to save his soul from hell. And that goes for anybody that's cozied up to him.''

''You Burkes are out of it, then,'' McQuade said. ''Anybody else?''

''Yeah,'' said Trent Putnam. ''Leave me out of it.''

Quickly, a dozen others—single men—refused to participate. They were looked upon with contempt by other men, but McQuade said nothing to them. Instead, he spoke to the majority.

''We have more than enough men. I'll be leading the party, and I'll start by asking for volunteers. Fifty-nine of you. Stand over here beside me, if you're willing to ride with me tonight.''

Quickly they stepped forward, many disappointed because they hadn't moved quickly enough. McQuade spoke to them.

''We can't all go, but I'm thanking each of you who offered. I won't forget. Those of you who are left behind, I'll feel better with you here to defend the camp.''

Though McQuade's voice was calm, it was a deliberate slap at those who had rebuked him, and they all eyed him in sullen disfavor. Several hours of daylight remained, and the women started supper so the men would have time to eat before riding out. When the men had eaten, McQuade walked back to the wagon with Mary.

''You will be careful, won't you?'' she asked.

''Not me,'' said McQuade, a twinkle in his eye. ''It's always been my ambition to be shot full of Kiowa arrows.''

''That's one habit of yours I don't like,'' she said. ''You're always laughing at death.''

''Sooner or later, he comes for us all,'' said McQuade. ''Crying won't keep him away.''

She said nothing, looking away from him, biting her lip. Immediately he was sorry, and sought to make her smile, but she refused.

''You don't have to put on an act for me,'' she said. ''If you want to risk getting yourself killed, I can't stop you, but don't expect me to laugh about it.''

Instead of spending some time with her as he had intended, he left her at the wagon and returned to join the men who had congregated around the supper fire.

''In what order to you aim for us to ride?'' Ike asked.

''I want you and Gunter with me in the freeing of the captives,'' said McQuade. ''Pick seven men to ride with us. Eli, I want you and Cal to choose twenty-three men to side you in stampeding the horses and mules. Will, you and Hardy will choose another twenty-three men to defend us against any Indians choosing to stand and fight.

When you have all your men assigned to one of the three groups, we'll go over our plan of attack.''

McQuade had total confidence in them, and while they went about organizing for the attack, he poured himself another cup of coffee and kept out of the way. He was counting on Ike to choose the more accurate marksmen for those who would be charged with the defense of the attackers. In less than half an hour, Ike was ready.

''Our first move will be to stampede the horses and mules,'' said McQuade. ''Eli, you and Cal will decide how best to begin, but I'd suggest a west-to-east run. The camp is at the foot of a ridge, and from what I could see, the stock is to the west. Get them on the run and keep them running, right through the camp. Don't let up. We want that bunch left afoot for as long as possible, so that we can put them behind us. Will, you, Hardy, and your men hold your fire until the stampede clears the Indian camp, so there's no chance of you hitting our riders. Any Indians failing to follow the stampede will be your responsibility.''

''Where do you aim for us to find these captives?'' Warnell asked.

''They'll be tied to stakes,'' said McQuade. ''Every man of us will need a sharp knife. We'll ride in right on the heels of the stampede. When you've cut your man loose, he'll be stiff from bein' tied up. Get him up on the extra horse and ride like hell wouldn't have it, back the way you come. We'll group to the northwest. Those of you who have stampeded the horses and mules, keep them running. When you've run them at least ten miles, ride back to our camp. The defenders—those of you riding with Will and Hardy—cease firing just as soon as we've freed the captives. Swing wide, toward the northwest, and return to camp. Are there any questions?''

There were none. They rode out at dark, McQuade in the lead. Later there would be a moon, but by then, the attack would be over.

Mary watched them go, regretting her harsh words to

McQuade. Suppose he died in the attack? Assailed by loneliness, she made her way to what remained of the supper fire and poured herself some coffee. The Peyton wagon was nearby, and Maggie spoke from the darkness.

"Why don't you come set with the rest of us?"

"Thank you," said Mary, "I will."

"It's a woman's lot to worry," Odessa Bibb said. "They get themselves cut or shot, and we doctor them as best we can, so they can ride out and do it all over again."

Mary laughed, despite herself, and immediately felt guilty. Just as she had so recently accused McQuade of doing, she was making light of potential tragedy.

"Ike thinks McQuade's plan will work," said Maggie. "Chance is a careful man, Mary. A thinking man."

Creeker and his companions had been marched to a teepee and shoved inside. There they had remained, uncertain as to their fate.

"Damn it," Slack complained, "it'll be dark in another hour. What in tarnation are they goin' to do with us?"

"Was I you," said Rucker, "I wouldn't be in no hurry to find out. I got a gut feelin' this bunch has plans for us we ain't goin' to like."

He was more right than he knew. It began with the low throb of a tom-tom, growing in intensity until darkness shrouded the valley. At that time, the Kiowa came for them, and in the flickering light from a series of fires, they could see the line of stakes, each with a pile of brush at its base.

"My God," said Ellis. "My God."

Groat laughed. "You'd better call on somebody that knows you."

Each of the men was taken to a stake. They were backed up and their hands released long enough for them to be bound to the stakes. There they stood, as the tom-tom throbbed louder, each beat like the ticking of a deadly clock. Suddenly there was the drum of hoofbeats, shouting and shooting, and a veritable avalanche of horses and mules. Kiowa teepees were toppled, fires were scattered, and Indians scrambled to catch the wildly running horses. But when the shooting began, the horses were forgotten, as a dozen Kiowa fell dead or dying.

"It's our turn," McQuade shouted.

Leading the charge, McQuade rode to the farthest stake where Creeker stood, unable to believe his eyes. Bowie in his hand, McQuade was out of the saddle in an instant, slashing Creeker's bonds.

"Get on that horse and ride toward the northwest," said McQuade.

Creeker didn't have to be told twice. There was no saddle, but he kicked the animal into a fast gallop. A Kiowa came after McQuade with a lance, only to stumble and fall, as a distant marksman saw the danger. In seconds, McQuade and his companions had set the captives free, and all of them—saved and survivors—were in the clear. While the thunder of hooves had begun to recede, there were still distant shouts and the sound of gunfire, evidence that McQuade's men were doing their job well. The moon was rising, and when the devastated Kiowa camp was well behind them, McQuade and his companions reined up. Within seconds, Creeker and his companions joined them. It was an awkward moment, for not a man among the rescued doubted he had been given back his life. McQuade spoke.

"You men can keep the horses until you've recovered your own. We've stampeded the horses and mules far enough to allow you some time. I'd suggest you get at it as soon as it's light enough to see. You'll want to move on, before those Kiowa find their horses."

"McQuade," said Creeker, "you're the whitest man I ever met. We'll get these horses back to you. I'm givin' you my word."

McQuade said nothing. He rode away, his companions following. Creeker and his nine companions sat their horses, and it was Rucker who finally spoke.

"After what I been through, I ain't of a mind to take

any lip from Rufus Hook. We got a full moon for maybe
another four hours. I say let's catch up to that stampede
and get our horses and mules tonight. By God, I ain't
wantin' to be anywhere close, when that bunch of Indians
gather up their horses.''

"Rucker," said Slack, "that's the most sensible thing
you've said in all the years I've knowed you.''

Being of a single mind, circling the Kiowa camp to the
north, they rode away, seeking their horses and mules.
More than five miles east of the Indian camp, the three
factions of McQuade's outfit came together.

"Anybody hurt?" McQuade inquired.

"Not a man in my bunch," said Eli Bibb.

"Nor mine," Will Haymes said.

"The captives are free," said McQuade, "and we've
done all we can do. Let's ride.''

"You really think Hook's bunch will return our
horses?" Gunter Warnell asked.

"I do," said McQuade. "Anyway, they were horses
we took from Gid Sutton and his outlaws, and I wouldn't
begrudge any man a horse, here in Indian Territory.''

"I reckon it wouldn't have made any sense, cuttin'
them loose and leavin' 'em afoot," Ike Peyton said. "I
wouldn't want to see any man burnt at the stake, unless
it was maybe Rufus Hook himself.''

They all laughed grimly and rode on. Far to the east,
Creeker and his companions had caught up to the tag end
of the stampede, before the animals fanned out to graze.

"By God," Ellis said, "if we don't never have another
piece of luck, we can't complain. Would you look at
that?''

The mules Rufus Hook had grudgingly allowed them
to ride were there, and they still wore their saddles. With
them were the other five mules Hook would need to draw
his wagons.

"We'll take the varmints with us," said Creeker,
"while we look for the horses.''

They began finding the Indian mounts first, and they searched for another hour before locating their own horses. The animals had been together long enough to consider themselves part of a herd, and they all were grazing near the spring to which Creeker and his companions had followed the trail of the Kiowa and the stolen horses.

"Let's gather them up and get out of here," said Dirk. "After gettin' back them five mules for Hook, the least he can do is have the cook rustle us up some supper."

"That can wait," Creeker said. "We got somethin' else to do, first. Get your saddles off them mules and onto your horses. Then take your lariats and fashion some lead ropes for that bunch of mules and these borrowed horses."

Quickly they complied, but they didn't ride directly to Hook's camp, which was well beyond McQuade's. Instead, they rode on until they were challenged by one of McQuade's sentries. They reined up, and Creeker answered.

"This is Creeker and friends. We come to return ten horses McQuade loaned us."

"Stand where you are," the sentry replied. "I'll get McQuade."

Mary had been awake when McQuade had returned, and assuring herself that he was safe, she had gone to sleep, not concerning herself with him further. McQuade sat on the wagon's lowered tailgate, wide awake. He would begin his watch at midnight, and before he could get to sleep, he would have to get up again. He heard the sentry's challenge, and Creeker's response. But the sentry didn't have to leave his post, for most of the men who had participated in the rescue were still awake. By the time McQuade reached the sentry's position, Ike Peyton, Gunter Warnell, and a dozen others were already there.

"Ride on in, Creeker," McQuade said.

Creeker and his companions did so, reining up near the wagon circle.

"We took advantage of the full moon, and found our horses," said Creeker. "I ain't a man to forget. We're obliged."

Without another word, they rode away, and only when the hoofbeats had faded into the night did any of McQuade's outfit speak.

"McQuade," said Ike, "I've been around them that spoke from the Good Book, but I never knowed a man that lived it any better than you."

McQuade said nothing. He returned to the wagon to find Mary awake.

"What was that all about?" she asked.

"We loaned some horses to the men we took from the Kiowa," said McQuade. "They were returning them."

"I'm sorry I was cross with you before you rode out," she said. "Am I forgiven?"

"I reckon," said McQuade.

"I'm awake now. Why don't you join me?"

"Do I have to take off my hat, gunbelt, shirt, britches, and boots?"

"What do you think?" she asked.

"Damn," McQuade sighed, tugging at his boots.

There was considerable surprise within the Hook wagon circle, when Creeker and his companions rode in with all the stampeded mules and horses.

"I must say I am impressed," said Xavier Hedgepith. "I fully expected the lot of you to be murdered and scalped, leaving us short ten more mules."

"At least we got some hair to lose, Hedgepith," Groat said. "That's a hell of a lot more than can be said for you."

"Shut up, the lot of you," said Hook. "So you recovered the horses and the mules."

"Yeah," Dirk said, "but in escapin' the Kiowa, we lost our weapons. What do you aim to do about that?"

"Not a damn thing," said Hook.

"You ain't exactly bubblin' over with gratitude,"

Groat said. "Maybe we'll just take them five missin' mules back where we found 'em."

"I don't reward a man for doing his job," said Hook stiffly.

"We didn't hire on to wet-nurse your damn mules," Nall said. "Way we see it, we got five of your heehaws back, and they was the responsibility of your teamsters. Each of them mules ought to be worth a pair of pistols."

"What about you, Creeker?" Hook asked.

"That's the way I feel too," said Creeker. "We was captured by the Kiowa, and was lucky to escape with our lives. I speak for us all, when I say we don't ride another mile with this outfit, unarmed. You got all kinds of ammunition and weapons amongst the goods you're takin' to Texas. If you're that almighty cheap, then you can take the guns from our pay, but by God, we'll have weapons in the morning."

"Agreed," Hook said, "and you will pay for them."

"We'll pay, then," said Creeker, "and we'll remember your generosity."

McQuade rode out at dawn, intent on getting as much distance as possible between his outfit and the Kiowa. Hook's wagons were a day behind, meaning that he was three days away from any margin of safety. Pacing themselves, resting their horses, the Kiowa could easily ride seventy miles in a day. It was five times the distance a wagon could travel, on a good day. Reaching the water he sought for the night's camp, McQuade turned his horse and rode back to meet the wagons. It was then that he saw the distant smoke against the blue of the sky. It was likely bad news for Hook's outfit, and possibly for McQuade's, as well. Not only did they have Kiowa on their trail, the "talking smoke" was sending word of white man's presence to the Kiowa somewhere on the trail ahead.

Hook's wagons were on the move, and every man of them, Hook included, watched the back-trail. The puffs of smoke were even more evident to them, for they were closer. When they were forced to stop and rest the teams, Hook hailed Creeker.

"What do you think the smoke means?" Hook asked.

"I ain't got that much Indian-savvy," said Creeker, "but I'm guessin' these Indians has got friends somewhere ahead of us, and they're bein' told we're comin'."

"Why couldn't you have simply recovered your horses, without incurring the wrath of every Indian in the Territory?"

Creeker didn't consider that worthy of a reply. He looked at Hook with a mixture of disgust and pity, and rode away.

Chance McQuade's outfit had become seasoned enough, and his confidence in them had become such, that he believed they should be aware of what he suspected. When they next stopped to rest the teams, McQuade spoke to some of the men.

"We got off too easy last night. While we left the Kiowa afoot, and they may not find their horses in time to come after us, they're sending word ahead. Smoke signals have told other Indians we're coming."

"We don't know what to expect, then," Ike said. "They could strike while the wagons are all strung out on the trail, or after they're circled for the night."

"I'm sure they'll come up with something creative," said McQuade, "striking when we least expect it. We're most vulnerable while we're on the trail. They can swoop down on a few wagons, cut loose with arrow or lance, and then be gone before all of us can come together in defense. Ride with your pistols ready, with your children and wives keepin' their eyes open for an attack. When we take the trail tomorrow, we'll pull the wagons up three or four abreast, if the terrain permits. The shorter our line of wagons, the better our defense."

While McQuade was concerned with the Kiowa ahead, Hook's outfit had problems with the Kiowa from the raided camp, who had recovered their stampeded horses.

Lora Kirby, Hook's "school marm," hadn't slept with him in a week. Instead, she huddled in the wagon with the saloon women. Hiram Savage and Snakehead Presnall weren't much better, while old Ampersand, the cook, spent less and less time cooking. At supper time, the day after Creeker and his men had returned with the horses and mules, Hook called them together.

"Starting tonight," said Hook, "you're going to earn your money. The lot of you will be in charge of security. You now know something about Indians and their ways, which the rest of us do not."

"With responsibility, there's got to be some authority," Creeker replied. "Everybody—and that includes you—will accept any orders given for the safety of the camp. Without question. Agreed?"

"Agreed," said Hook. "Do what you must."

CHAPTER 8

❧

Despite the rough terrain, as a precaution against possible Indian attack, McQuade had the wagons traveling three abreast. Dead leaves concealed many obstacles, and the left rear wheel of Ab Henderson's wagon slid into a deep hole. The sudden shifting of the load to one side snapped the axle where the wheel joined, and the train ground to a halt. It took place while McQuade was scouting ahead, and he returned to find men fashioning a new axle from a fallen tree.

"Our luck just run out," said Henderson.

"We can't complain," McQuade said. "It's the first breakdown we've had, and there was no neglect involved. Throw enough weight on an axle, and it breaks."

He didn't mention the obvious, that they were in danger of Indian attack, and that any time lost only added to their peril. But the frantic pace at which they worked was evidence enough that every man understood the risk. They lost almost two hours, which eliminated the grazing time for the horses and mules at the end of the day. They had just taken the trail again, when the Kiowa struck. Two dozen strong, they charged the lead wagons while McQuade was near the end of the train. The men reined up, drawing their guns, but the Kiowa had the advantage. Ike Peyton, Gunter Warnell, and Eli Bibb drove the lead wagons, and they bore the brunt of the attack. While each of the men killed one of the attackers, some of the arrows found their marks. An arrow ripped through Ike's upper left arm, while another tore into Maggie's right thigh. While Gunter Warnell escaped injury, one of the arrows ripped into Ellen's right side. Eli Bibb caught one of the vicious barbs, just below his left collar bone. Men leaped from their wagon boxes, revolvers in their hands, and the Kiowa rode away, leaving six of their number dead or dying. When McQuade arrived at a fast gallop, no explanation was necessary.

"It'll be hard on those of you who have been hurt," said McQuade, "but we must get to water and circle the wagons, before we see to your wounds. Ike, are you able to handle your teams?"

"Yeah," Ike said. "I ain't hit that hard. Maggie . . ."

"I can hold out," said Maggie. "Best see to Ellen first."

"Eli took a bad one," McQuade said. "Odessa, can you handle the teams?"

"Yes," said Odessa, her face pale.

"Then let's get these wagons moving," McQuade said. "We must make up some time."

They took the trail, McQuade in the lead, each of them aware that their position had become more critical. Maggie Peyton, Ellen Warnell, and Eli Bibb had serious wounds, and the arrows would have to be driven on through. Any one or all three could be seriously ill for the next several days, with high fever. Worse, if the arrows had struck any vitals, Eli's and Ellen's wounds might be fatal. Very much aware of the wounded Maggie at his side, Ike pushed the teams as hard as he dared. Ellen Warnell lay back on the wagon box, her eyes closed, while Eli Bibb clenched his teeth. Odessa gripped the reins, keeping her teams neck-and-neck with Ike's. When they finally reached the creek, McQuade quickly got the wagons into formation for the night. Men unharnessed their teams, while the women got fires going. The wounded took priority over everything else. Mary quickly cleansed and bandaged Ike's wound. The others would be more difficult, for arrows had to be driven on through, before the wounds could be tended.

"Ike," said McQuade, "this is a mite touchy. That arrow in Maggie's thigh will have to be driven on through, and it's not a task for a woman. It's up to you to do it, unless you can't. I won't do it without your permission and Maggie's."

"Chance McQuade," Maggie said, "I tended your wounds. Now the least you can do is tend mine. Do what must be done, to get this wicked thing out of me."

"You heard her," said Ike.

"I'll do my best, then," McQuade said. "Gunter, you and Ellen have the same problem to face. That arrow has to come out of her. Can you remove it, or shall I?"

"If you're going to tend to Maggie," Ellen said, "then tend to me. God knows, none of us has had any experience with this."

"I'd be obliged, Chance," said Gunter. "I'll do it if I have to, but I trust your hand more than my own."

"Some of you help Mary get them into their wagons and get them ready," McQuade said. "Gunter, help Eli out of that shirt."

"Here's two quarts of whiskey," said Ike. "You're goin' to need it."

"Yes," McQuade said, "and that's just for Maggie. I'll need equal amounts for Ellen and Eli. They're all going to have to be dog-drunk before I can drive those arrows out."

McQuade went to the Peyton wagon and found Mary there. She had lit a lantern, and Maggie lay on her back, under a blanket.

"Maggie," said McQuade, "I want you to drink half of one of these quarts of whiskey. It's all we have to help you stand the pain."

"You're one in a million, Chance McQuade," Maggie said. "There ain't another man on this earth I'd trust, handin' me a bottle of whiskey and me jaybird naked under a blanket.''

Mary laughed and McQuade was thankful for the dimness of the lighted lantern. Odessa Bibb had taken it upon herself to see that Eli drank the prescribed whiskey, and he went on to Gunter Warnell's wagon. There he found Minerva Haymes and Lucy Tabor with Ellen Warnell. She too had been covered with a blanket.

"Ellen," said McQuade, "I want you to drink half this bottle of whiskey. This is going to be painful, and we have nothing else to see you through it. Minerva, I'll need you or Lucy to light me a lantern.''

"Do you want one of us here while you drive the arrow through?" Minerva asked.

"It's a grim thing to watch," said McQuade. "It's up to you."

"This is the frontier," Minerva said, "and I can't help feelin' that some of us ought to know about this kind of thing. I'll stay."

"So will I, if you need me," said Lucy.

"Thanks," McQuade said. "Give that whiskey an hour.''

With Ike wounded, McQuade went to see that the first watch had taken its position, and found Gunter Warnell had taken charge.

"Somebody else could have taken care of that, Gunter," said McQuade.

"I needed something to keep me busy," Warnell said. "We must secure our wagons at night. There's enough danger on the trail."

With Maggie and Ellen wounded, other women had taken it upon themselves to cook for McQuade, Warnell, and Ike Peyton. McQuade ate little. While he had removed arrows before, his patient had never been a female, and he was more nervous than he would have admitted. Returning to the Peyton wagon, he found Maggie deep in drunken slumber, snoring raggedly.

"I think she's ready," said Mary.

"I know," McQuade said. "I wish I didn't have to do this."

"You're not embarrassed, are you? Maggie wasn't."

"I'm not accustomed to doctoring naked women," said McQuade, "but I got it to do."

Mary removed the blanket and held the lighted lantern so that McQuade could see. He seized the shaft of the arrow and broke off all except what would be needed to drive the barb on through. Punching the loads out of his Colt, he took the weapon by the muzzle and began the grisly task. Even in her drunken stupor, Maggie grunted with pain. While holding the lantern, Mary had her eyes closed, unable to watch. When McQuade was finally finished, his shirt was soaked with sweat.

"Mary, there's hot water ready by now. Can you get one of the other women to help you cleanse, disinfect, and bandage her wound? I have to get to Ellen before the whiskey starts to wear off."

"Yes," said Mary.

McQuade went on to the Warnell wagon, where Minerva and Lucy waited with Ellen.

"She's asleep," Minerva said. "Has it been long enough?"

"I think so," said McQuade. "I'll only need one of you to hold the lantern. This is not an easy thing to watch."

"We're staying," Lucy said.

Lucy removed the blanket, while Minerva held the lantern. McQuade was relieved to see that while the arrow had pierced Ellen's side, it seemed to have struck a rib. There had been much bleeding, but the barb was driven out more easily than McQuade had expected.

"Will the two of you be able to cleanse, disinfect, and bandage her wound?" McQuade asked.

"Yes," said Minerva. "You're dripping. Go fetch yourself a dry shirt."

But McQuade's trial wasn't finished. He found Eli Bibb

in a deep sleep, and with his trembling hands slick with sweat, he drove the arrow on through. Odessa had insisted on holding the lantern, and when the ordeal was over, she stood there white-faced and silent. McQuade looked up and saw Mary at the wagon's tailgate, with the medicine chest.

"Could you take care of Eli?" McQuade asked. "I'm about done."

He sank down on the wagon's tailgate, and Mary climbed in. A silent Odessa still held the lantern. Hardy Kilgore brought him a tin cup of hot coffee, and McQuade accepted it with a nod of thanks. Finishing the coffee, he put the cup down. His head sagged with weariness, and the next thing he knew, Mary was speaking to him.

"I want you to go to the wagon and sleep. You've done more than your share. I'll be awake, looking in on Maggie, Ellen and Eli. Ike too, if he needs me. I'll see that they all get more whiskey if they become feverish."

"Thanks," he mumbled, making his way toward the wagon. He must go on watch at midnight. . . .

But McQuade was allowed to sleep, for they all realized what he had done. He awoke at dawn to the smell of brewing coffee. He was alone in the wagon, and he realized Mary had been up all night, seeing to the wounded. He got up and made his way to the breakfast fires, where Mary handed him a tin cup of hot coffee. She didn't wait for him to ask about the wounded, but volunteered the information.

"Ike got by without any fever. Ellen, Maggie, and Eli are on their second bottle of whiskey, and Maggie's starting to sweat. How do you feel?"

"Like I've been dipped in the creek and wrung out," said McQuade. "Why didn't some of you wake me for my watch?"

"Because any man of us can stand watch," Ike said. "You done your share and more, last night."

"We'll lay over here today," said McQuade. "When

Ellen, Maggie, and Eli are past the fever, we'll have to move on. These Kiowa have a real mad on, and as long as we're close by, they'll be tempted to come after us again.''

"The six we killed won't help our case any," Gunter Warnell said.

McQuade felt better after breakfast, and he looked in on the wounded. Only Maggie was awake. She looked at McQuade, a ghastly grin on her haggard face, and when she spoke, her voice was a little slurred.

"Answer me one thing, McQuade. What in thunder leads a man to get drunk? God, my head feels like it's been used for an anvil or a chop block, and I've sweated so much, I stink. Get this blanket off me.''

"The blanket stays until you stop sweating," said McQuade. "I'll have Mary bring you some water.''

Having survived an Indian attack, McQuade thought most of the outfit seemed just a little more confident. Some of them had questions.

"I can't understand why they didn't strike while we were replacing Henderson's axle," Will Haymes said.

"I can," said McQuade. "Everybody was on the ground, and could have acted much more quickly. As it was, with the wagons moving, you had to rein up your teams. I'd say it's a miracle none of you were killed.''

McQuade watched the sky for more smoke, but saw none. Time dragged, as they all waited for some improvement in the wounded. By noon, Maggie's fever had broken to the extent that she slept comfortably. Ellen and Eli had begun sweating, and by supper time, their condition had improved enough that McQuade believed they could travel. Only Eli was questionable, for his entire upper torso was swathed in bandages. But Odessa had an answer for that.

"I can handle the teams until Eli heals. The important thing is that we get these Kiowa behind us, before they decide to visit us again.''

"Bless you," said McQuade. "Does that suit you, Eli?"

"Hell, yes," Eli said. "Let's be on our way."

McQuade's outfit having lost a day allowed Hook's wagons to catch up. After losing all his stock to a stampede by Indians, Hook was in no hurry to move into the lead. He had his wagons circled upstream, within sight of McQuade's wagon circle, but as he was to learn, that didn't spare him the wrath of the Kiowa. The Indians struck at dawn, just as the men were harnessing their teams. Creeker and his companions fought valiantly, and it was they who drove the Kiowa away. Two of Hook's teamsters were killed, and three more seriously wounded. In the wake of it, Hook began shouting orders, most of which were directed at Dr. Horace Puckett.

"Don't just stand there, Puckett. I want these men seen to, and able to travel no later than tomorrow morning."

"I'm a doctor, not a magician," said Puckett, glaring at Hook. "I'll do what I can, but I can't promise you these men will be alive, come morning."

Two of the men had arrows driven into their shoulders, while the third had one of the deadly shafts buried in his side. Puckett found an arrow on the ground that had struck a wagon bow. His eyes on the barbed point, he shook his head.

"What's wrong?" Hook demanded.

"Barbed points," said Puckett. "They can't be drawn out."

"The hell they can't," Hook snarled. "They'll have to be."

"Then you draw them out," said Puckett, "and I'll doctor the wounds."

"Damn it, you're the doctor," Hook said. "Do what has to be done."

"This is beyond any training I've had," said Puckett. "Common sense tells me that if the shafts cannot be withdrawn, they'll have to be driven on through. The pain would be unbearable, and the shock could kill a man.''

"If you don't remove the arrows, they're dead men anyway," Hook said. "I'm ordering you to remove those arrows by whatever means you must."

"Order be damned," said Puckett. "I won't do it."

"Hook," Creeker said, speaking for the first time, "there're wagonloads of pain killer in front of you. Give these men enough whiskey to get them dog-drunk. While they're out, those arrows can be pushed on through."

Hook said nothing, his doubtful eyes on Puckett.

"It might work," said Puckett. "It's the only chance they have."

"Then dose them with as much whiskey as it takes," Hook said. He looked at Creeker, and the gunman's eyes never wavered. Hook saw rebellion there, and he realized that he must rid himself of Creeker, and probably the others, as well.

With the help of Savage and Presnall, Puckett tapped a keg for the necessary whiskey. Even then they could hear McQuade's outfit moving out, leaving them with wounded men, not knowing when the Kiowa might return. While Creeker and his men had managed to repel the attack, none of the Indians had been hit. But there had been many shots fired, and the attack hadn't gone unnoticed in McQuade's camp.

"They've discovered Hook's bunch," said Ike. "Maybe they'll leave us alone."

"Maybe," McQuade said, "but keep your gun handy."

Maggie, Eli, and Ellen had been made as comfortable as possible, knowing they could not remain another day so near the troublesome Kiowa. Besides, there were more ahead. McQuade rode out, as much to look for Indian sign as for water. Before reaching suitable water for the night, he had to ride around a slough, where there was standing, stagnant water. Reaching a clear-running creek, he watered his horse and rode back to meet the oncoming wagons. When the wagons had been circled and supper done, McQuade and Mary retired to the wagon.

"This is one of them nights I don't aim to take off anything but my hat," McQuade said. "It's too hot for blankets, and them damn mosquitoes is big enough to go after with a gun."

"They're from all that standing water," said Mary. "But this is just for one night, and then they won't bother us."

But Mary couldn't have been more wrong. Thirty-six hours later, she was the first to be stricken with burning fever and bone-wracking chills. His watch over, McQuade returned to the wagon at dawn, to find Mary feverish and talking out of her head. Maggie had healed enough to be up and about, and McQuade went for her. She had once worked as an assistant to a doctor. By the time she reached the wagon, Mary was shaking with chill.

"My God, Chance," said Maggie, "she has all the symptoms of malaria, and if she has it, there may be others. Whatever got to her may have gotten to them."*

"If she has it," McQuade said, "you can count on others having it. I'll stay with her, while you make the rounds of the other wagons."

Maggie hurried away, while McQuade sat there with his arms around Mary, dreading what Maggie might discover. He knew within minutes, for Ike Peyton, Gunter Warnell, Cal Tabor, and Will Haymes brought the bad news.

"Maggie says it's almost got to be malaria," said Ike grimly. "A dozen families is sick with it, and they're all scared half to death. Agin Indians and outlaws we got a chance, but this could wipe us out, without a doctor and medicine."

"I know where there's both," McQuade said.

"You're thinking of Hook's doctor, Horace Puckett,"

*Malaria is an infectious febrile disease now known to be transmitted by the anopheles mosquito.

said Gunter Warnell. "Do you really expect him to help us?"

"Yes," McQuade replied. "If I have to hog-tie Rufus Hook and hold a pistol to his thick head for as long as necessary. Gunter, you and Will saddle your horses and come with me. The rest of you keep your guns handy against Indian attack, and tell those who are sick that we've gone for medicine and a doctor."

The trio rode out, uncertain as to how far behind Hook's wagons might be. To their surprise, they found the wagons remained circled where they had been at the time of the Indian attack.

"Hook's had some men wounded or killed," said McQuade, when they sighted the circle of wagons. It was still early, and smoke rose from breakfast fires. Even in daylight, Hook wisely had men on watch. McQuade was about to sing out, when Creeker saw them and waved them in.

"I must see Hook," McQuade said.

Creeker nodded. Dismounting, McQuade and his companions followed Creeker to the cook wagon. Hook sat on a stool, eating from a tin plate. He eyed McQuade without any friendliness. McQuade didn't beat around the bush.

"Hook, we need a doctor and medicine. We have a dozen families with chills and fever. It could be malaria."

"Get the hell out of here," Hook shouted, dropping his plate. "You'll infect us."

"I'm not leaving here without your Doctor Puckett," said McQuade.

Hook's shouting had gotten attention, including that of Dr. Horace Puckett. But Hook was furious. He turned to Creeker, Groat, Porto, and the others, with a direct order.

"I want these three out of here," Hook snarled. "If they don't go, shoot them."

"I'll kill the first man that pulls a gun," said McQuade.

"Nobody's going to pull a gun," Creeker said, his cold

eyes on Hook. "Dr. Puckett, I believe these men have need of you."

"We have a dozen families down with chills and fever, Doctor," said McQuade. "Could be malaria, we think."

"It can be treated with quinine," Puckett said, "and we have an adequate supply."

"I have an adequate supply," said Hook, "and it will be saved for our own use."

"Rufus," Puckett said, "this is contrary to everything you promised me, before leaving St. Louis. You told me these people were to become residents of your planned community, that I would see to their needs. Well, they need me now, and I'm going, and I'm taking with me the necessary medicine for treatment."

"You go, then by God, don't bother comin' back," Hook snarled.

"If that's the way you want it," said Puckett mildly. "But remember, nobody knows the probable cause of malaria. Whatever lies ahead—whatever infected Mr. McQuade's party—may infect yours as well. Mr. Creeker, will you have one of your men saddle my horse, while I get my personal effects, my bag, and the necessary medicine?"

"Groat," Creeker said.

Groat went to saddle the horse, while Creeker remained where he was, his hard eyes on Rufus Hook. Xavier Hedgepith, who had witnessed it all, spoke to Hook.

"Don't be a damn fool. You already have three wounded men, and the doc's right. We could all be needing him, before this is done. Now you talk to him, before he leaves."

Clearly, Rufus Hook didn't wish to retract any of his harsh words, but he was all but surrounded by hostile faces. When the doctor returned, prepared to mount the horse, Hook grudgingly spoke.

"I was wrong, Doc. Since you'll be seein' to these people in Texas, I suppose it's your duty to doctor them along the way. Take what you need, do what needs doin', and come on back as soon as you can. We got three men near dead.''

"You can pour whiskey down them as well as I can," said Puckett shortly. "If this is malaria, it could become an epidemic. I'll return when I have done my duty."

He mounted the horse and rode out, following Mc-Quade and his companions. Just for a moment, Mc-Quade's eyes met those of Creeker and his men, and no words were needed. There were sighs of relief when the four horsemen rode into the McQuade wagon circle. It took Doctor Puckett only a few minutes to diagnose the illness as malaria.

"There are several kinds," said Puckett. "The most common is the thirty-six-hour variety. The attacks come every three days, with an almost continuous feeling of exhaustion and an inability to function. I'm beginning treatment immediately of those who are ill, and I'll remain with you until we are sure the danger of epidemic has passed."

McQuade watched with relief as Mary and the others were dosed with quinine. Doctor Puckett was up all night, checking the condition of his patients every hour. Maggie Peyton was with him, watching, listening, learning. By dawn of the next day, there was a definite improvement in all those stricken. Mary sat up, eating her breakfast and drinking coffee.

"It's no less than a miracle, the doctor coming to take care of us," she said. "How did you manage it?"

"The doctor had something to say about that," said McQuade. "Thank God all Hook's people don't take his orders without question."

Doctor Puckett remained with them three days. Between visits to his patients, he asked countless questions about the frontier, which McQuade attempted to answer. Maggie went to great lengths, feeding the genial doctor, making fresh coffee, and seeing that he had a place to sleep when he finally found time for it.

"We'll hate to see you go," said McQuade.

"I won't be that far away," Puckett replied. "I expect Mr. Hook's wagons will be catching up to you. He's had three wounded teamsters sweating out infection, but he's an impatient man. He won't wait for that. Besides, I suspect that whatever infected your party with malaria won't spare his. It'll be a miracle, if by the time he catches up to you, some of his men aren't sick."

That same afternoon, they heard the rattle of wagons. Hook had arrived, and it was but a short time until Creeker rode in. Nodding to McQuade, he spoke directly to Doctor Puckett.

"The chickens has come home to roost, Doc. We got us some sick *hombres*, and the sickest of the lot is the big rooster himself. He's scared he's gonna die, and the rest of us is scared he won't."

"It's what I've been expecting," said Puckett. "Will one of you bring my horse?"

McQuade saddled the animal and brought it to him, handing him his bag after he had mounted. They all gathered around, wishing him well, inviting him back. Creeker tipped his hat and rode out, Puckett following.

"Even with Hook havin' control of these Texas grants," Ike said, "I feel better just knowin' Dr. Puckett will be there."

"So do I," said Maggie. "He knows his medicine, and he's promised to teach me just as much as I'm smart enough to learn, once we get to Texas."

"Speakin' of Texas," Will Haymes said, "I been keepin' track, and this is June tenth. We been on the trail six weeks."

"We're better than half way across Indian Territory," said McQuade, "and while we've seen no more smoke, I don't believe we're done with the Kiowa. I think we'll go on posting a double guard and trailing the wagons three abreast. Those of you in wagons one and three, from front to back, keep your eyes open. You'll have an opportunity to see attacking Indians first, and I want all of you to be especially watchful as we pass through brushy or wooded stretches where there's plenty of cover. Cut loose with your guns, even if you don't hit any of them, and don't let them get close enough to hurt any of us. Ask Ellen, Maggie, or Eli how it feels to have an arrow driven through you.''

Creeker slowed his horse until he and Doctor Puckett were riding side by side, and it was Creeker who spoke. "What do you think of McQuade's outfit, Doc?''

"They're good people," said Puckett, "and I believe I'm going to like being a part of this Texas colony. It's going to be a success in spite of Mr. Hook."

Creeker laughed, slapping his thigh with his hat.

CHAPTER 9

*W*ith three teamsters wounded, Rufus Hook had been in a precarious situation, unable to distance himself from the hostile Kiowa. While Creeker had little respect for Hook, he had persuaded three of his men—Dirk, Nall, and Rucker—to take on the three wagons until the teamsters were able to resume their duties. But by the time Hook's wagons had caught up to McQuade's party, the trio of make-do teamsters were fed up. With Hook and seven other teamsters ill with what almost had to be malaria, there was obviously going to be another delay, allowing McQuade's outfit to forge ahead.

"Damn it," said Rucker, "I didn't hire on as no teamster. I'm done as a wagon jockey for Hook."

"Me too," Dirk and Nall said in a single voice.

"I told you it was for just long enough to get us away from that bunch of Kiowa," Creeker said. "By the time Hook and the rest of these *hombres* is cured of malaria, them three gents that was wounded should be able to handle their teams again. I ain't cozyin' up to Rufus Hook, if that's what's botherin' you. Seein' how McQuade has pulled that bunch of his together, I got me a feelin' that things is goin' to be a hell of a lot different, once we reach Texas. Hook's goin' to be some surprised, and that's why I'm goin' easy on him now."

"We'll still be under his thumb, even in Texas," said

Groat. "Ain't you forgettin' he's got all our names down for land grants, with plans for us signin' it all over to him?"

"It's a long ways between what he's expectin' and what he's goin' to get," Creeker replied. "When I get that grant in my name, it's mine, and Hook can go to hell."

Ellis laughed. "I like the sound of that, but what's the good of fiddlefoot hombres like us owning land grants in Texas?"

"None, I reckon," said Creeker, "if you aim to go on selling your soul and your gun to varmints like Hook. Me, I got ambition for somethin' better, and the way to start is ownin' land with my name on it."

"By God," Ellis said, "you done changed your tune some, since leavin' St. Louis."

"I have," said Creeker, "and I got Rufus Hook to thank for that. I've sold my gun, but by God, I'm still a better man than he is. Someday, not that far off, there'll be law on the frontier, and when it comes, I don't aim to be on the wrong side of it, with a gun in my hand."

"Hell, Creeker," Dirk said, "when we get to Texas, we'll be lucky to have a thousand dollars amongst us. How far can we get with that?"

"Texas is owned by Mexico," said Creeker, "and they're almighty anxious to settle the land. Why do you reckon they're dealing with greedy varmints like Hook? Once we get our hands on a grant, we'll ride to Mexico for some horses, cows, and bulls. When we got the seed stock, the natural increase will do the rest."

"Creeker," Groat said, "you're either the smartest hombre I ever met, or the biggest damn fool."

"He's started usin' his head for something other than a place to hang his hat," said Ellis. "A damn fool is a hombre that hires out to an old buzzard like Hook, jumpin' ever' time he hollers froggy. I'm with you, Creeker."

To Creeker's satisfaction, they all sided him, agreeing

to split with Hook after reaching Texas. But Creeker had a word of warning.

"We'll have to play along with Hook, because we'll need the money he's paying us, so it'll mean resisting the urge to gut-shoot him when he's orderin' us around."

But Creeker found it increasingly hard to follow his own advice. When Hook had recovered from his bout with malaria, he became more the tyrant than ever. One night after supper, when Lora Kirby refused to accompany him to his tent, he knocked her to the ground. He was about to kick her, when Creeker seized him by his shirt front and flattened him with a punch to the jaw.

"Damn you," said Hook, "you're fired. Get on your horse and ride."

"You might want to think on it some," Groat said. "If he goes, we all go."

"Maybe I'll go with 'em," said one of the teamsters who had been wounded. "If it wasn't for them and their quick gun work, the Indians would of kilt us all."

"And we ain't even close to bein' out of Indian Territory," said another.

Again Hook was forced to swallow his rage or risk wholesale rebellion, and some of the teamsters eyed him with something less than respect.

On watch, Creeker suddenly became alert, his gun in his hand. There was no moon, and while the shadow had been fleeting, Creeker knew someone was there. He cocked the pistol, and it seemed loud in the stillness.

"No," came a desperate whisper. "It's me. Lora."

Creeker let the hammer down and holstered the weapon. She crept out of the shadows and he guided her to a distant pine that stood in a small clearing. From there, even in the dim starlight, he could see anybody approaching. She eased herself down next to the tree, and Creeker sat down beside her.

"I never got a chance to thank you for what you did," she said.

"I wasn't expecting any thanks," said Creeker. "Where I come from, however lowdown a man is, he don't slap a woman around."

"No decent woman," she said, "but he knows what I am, and so do you."

"We've all done things we ain't proud of," said Creeker, "but that don't mean we have to go on doing them."

"Easy for you to say," she replied, "but you know why he brought me along."

"You don't aim to teach school, then."

Her laugh was bitter. "I can barely read and write."

"Most of these folks goin' to Texas have pulled up roots and aim to make another start in a new land. Why not you?"

"Me?" Again she laughed, and it trailed off into a sob. "A whore in St. Louis is still a whore in Texas. I've been fooling myself. Hook promised me a better life than I could ever hope for in St. Louis, but the more I see of him, the more certain I am that I'm lost to anything good and decent. I was better off, being everybody's woman, than a slave to a brute like Rufus Hook."

"If you could free yourself of him," Creeker asked, "would you?"

"My God, yes," she cried, "but I'm committed. He'd kill me."

"Not while I'm around," said Creeker, "if you're bein' honest with me."

"I am," she said, her voice trembling. "I've never had any man interested in me, but for a roll in the hay. What do you want?"

"More than a roll in the hay," said Creeker. "I know what you've been, and now I'm lookin' to what you can be. From here on to Texas, if I stand up for you, will you stay out of Hook's bed?"

"What happens when we reach Texas?"

"Plenty," Creeker said. "Somewhere behind the paint, behind all that you have been, I've got a gut-feelin' there's an honest woman. Let me have a look at her. We'll talk again, any night of your choosing. But starting now— tonight—you're no longer Hook's woman. You are a school marm, and nothing more."

"He'll laugh in my face."

"Let him," said Creeker. "If he tries to force you, or to hurt you in any way, scream your head off. I'll beat hell out of him."

"I've never heard you called anything but Creeker," she said. "Do you have any other name?"

"Riley," he said. "Riley Creeker. Are you really Lora Kirby?"

"Yes. My daddy is a Methodist preacher in Illinois. Since I was a child, I've listened to him preach that people were going to hell. I hope he never knows just how right he's been."

"How old are you, Lora?"

"I'll be nineteen in August," she said. "And you?"

"I'm twenty-three. There's still time for us."

"You've given me hope," she said. "I'll talk to you again tomorrow night."

She faded into the shadows and Riley Creeker watched her go. Without the paint and the hopelessness in her eyes, she would be beautiful, he thought. But could she—would she—resist Rufus Hook's demands? He found himself hoping she would.

McQuade's party again took the trail, and he rode ahead, seeking water and looking for Indian sign. Water seemed abundant in Indian Territory, and he concerned himself with Indian sign. When he eventually found a creek that suited him, there were ashes from an old fire and days-old tracks of a dozen unshod horses. There had been no recent rain, so McQuade was able to determine that the Indians had ridden in from the west, and that they had departed to the southwest. McQuade rode back to meet the wagons. There was little to be done defensively, when they had no idea where the Kiowa were. When the wag-

ons had been circled for the night and supper was underway, McQuade told them of the tracks he had found,
ahead of their arrival.

"Maybe we ought to triple the guard, from here on,"
Ike suggested.

"I doubt that will help," said McQuade. "A night attack would appeal to them only if they could stampede
the stock. I think we'll strictly have to be on our guard
while we're on the trail."

"They took us by surprise, that first time," Gunter
Warnell said. "If we move quick, I believe we can drive
them away before they're able to hurt us."

"Just keep that in mind," said McQuade. "Let them
get too close, and some of you will die."

The showdown between Rufus Hook and Lora Kirby
came the night following Lora's meeting with Creeker.
Hook had left nothing to anybody's imagination regarding
his crude relationship with the girl.

"Into my tent," he growled.

"No," said Lora. "Never again."

"We had an agreement," Hook said, loud enough for
everybody to hear. "That's why I brought you from St.
Louis."

"Then I'm breaking it," said Lora. "Send me back to
St. Louis, if you don't like it."

"You know that's impossible," Hook roared. "Now
get in there, or I'll drag you."

"Hook," said Creeker, "the woman's had enough of
you. Leave her be."

"And I've had enough of you pokin' your nose in
where it don't belong," Hook said, his voice sinking to
a growl. "This is none of your business."

"I'm making it my business," said Creeker ominously.
"It becomes the business of us all, when you abuse a
woman. What do the rest of you say?"

The teamsters said nothing, but it was evident that all
nine of Creeker's companions would side him, if need be.

Their thumbs were hooked in their pistol belts, and their hard eyes were on Hook. Hiram Savage and Snakehead Presnall, Hook's gamblers, were careful to keep their hands away from their guns. While Doctor Horace Puckett had spoken not a word, his eyes were on Hook, and they said much. It became another standoff, as Hook stood his ground. As usual, it was Xavier Hedgepith who had to reason with Hook, and it was the lawyer who eventually spoke to Lora.

"There's obviously been a misunderstanding," said Hedgepith smoothly. "Mr. Hook has agreed that you have been enlisted to teach school upon your arrival in Texas, and that your . . . ah . . . relationship with him is strictly voluntary."

"I have no relationship with him, besides what he forced on me," Lora said, "and now that I have a choice, I don't want him near me."

It cast Rufus Hook in a bad light, and he turned hate-filled eyes on Creeker, whom he considered guilty of rank insubordination. Creeker glared right back at him, both of them knowing that one day they would clash. Neither could afford a personal struggle while they faced the hazards of Indian Territory. Creeker was elated when Lora again visited him late at night, the more so because of the change in her attitude.

"I never expected that," she said. "I didn't believe he'd agree to leave me alone. I owe that to you, because I was afraid to stand up to him. But he'll find a way to get back at you. I could see it in his eyes."

"He's had to swallow a lot of things that's rankled his gizzard," said Creeker, "because of our situation. With all of us on the watch for Indians, we can't afford to fight amongst ourselves. Whatever hell-raising Hook has in mind will have to wait until we reach Texas."

"He's applied for land grants in everybody's name. Even mine. He's counting on us all signing our grants over to him."

"Yes," said Creeker, "but there's usually a lot of difference between what a man wants or expects, and what he finally gets."

"You're saying that everybody won't sign their grants over to Hook?"

"I can't speak for everybody," Creeker said, "but if I'm able to get my hands on some Texas land, it's mine. I got nine hombres sidin' me that feel the same way."

"What will you do with so much land?"

"We aim to pool the money Hook owes us to buy seed stock from Mexico. Horses, cows, and bulls."

She grew excited just listening to him talk, and Creeker told her what he and his nine companions had agreed upon.

"In a few years, you can be rich," she cried, "if men like Hook will leave you alone."

"Men like Hook will have to be dealt with," said Creeker. "At supper time, I noticed you've washed off all the powder and paint. I like what's underneath a whole lot better."

"Thank you," she said. "You're the first man who ever asked me to do that."

"Would you have done it, if another had asked you to?" Creeker asked.

"No," she replied. "I did what I was paid to do. None of them had the right to ask anything more. We both know I've been a whore, but you've treated me like a lady. After I left you last night, I . . . I didn't sleep. I thought of what you had asked of me, and somehow I . . . I felt clean, like I was somebody."

"If what I say—what I think—means so much," said Creeker, "there's something I'm wantin' to ask you, when we reach Texas."

"Why must you wait?" she asked.

"Because we're both under Hook's authority until then," said Creeker, "and I want to be my own man, with something to offer a woman."

"You have more to offer than any man I've ever

known," she said. "You gave me the strength to take back my life, to stand up to Rufus Hook, because you cared."

It practically took Creeker's breath away, and during the silence, she placed her cheek next to his. She was trembling, and there was no mistaking her tears. He drew her to him, kissing her long and hard. They parted just long enough to catch their wind, and then went at it again. It was she who finally broke the silence.

"I suppose I acted like a brazen woman, but I . . . I wanted that. I needed it. I put my heart and soul into it. What I have given you, no other has ever had."

"You didn't have to tell me that," said Creeker. "I've been with a few women, but not one like you. Now, more than ever, I want to ask you that question when we finally get to Texas."

"I can answer it for you tonight," she said, "but if that's what you want, we'll wait. But when we get to Texas, if you still want me, the answer is yes."

"Then we won't wait," said Creeker. "I'll tell you now. Whatever there is in Texas, I want you to share it with me."

Having lost two teamsters to Indians, but refusing to abandon any of his goods, Hook had instead left two wagons, distributing their contents among the remaining fifteen. But the overloading took its toll. They were two days on the trail, following the delay with malaria, when two wagons were crippled with broken axles. Hook's solution to the problem infuriated the teamsters, when he spoke to Slaughter and Weatherly, drivers of the pair of disabled wagons.

"I want you men to unhitch your teams and go back for those two wagons we left behind," Hook said, "and don't waste any time."

"Hell," said Slaughter, "that's thirty miles or more. We can fell trees, hew new axles, and be gone in less time."

"I didn't ask your opinion," Hook said. "I told the

two of you to return for those two wagons. Now, by God."

"There's Indians," said Weatherly. "I ain't riskin' my neck for no damn wagons."

"Creeker and his men will ride with you," Hook said. "Creeker?"

Creeker said nothing, his eyes on the furious teamsters. Slowly they began unhitching their teams from the disabled wagons. Creeker and his companions saddled their horses, and the twelve men rode out, following the backtrail.

"We can get there 'fore dark," said Groat, "but can we get back?"

"Maybe, with empty wagons," Slaughter said, "but we'll have to push the teams."

They rode warily, seeing nobody, but when they reached the abandoned wagons, they reined up in dismay. Brush had been piled beneath the wagons, and they had been burned. Nothing remained but the metal parts. The men looked at one another, and Groat laughed.

"Let's ride," said Creeker. "We'll make it back before dark, for sure."

"Yeah," Slaughter said wearily, "but we'll have to listen to Hook bellow and paw the ground."

"Not for long," Creeker said. "Leaving the wagons was his idea. We done what he had us do, and I don't take no bawlin' and pawin' when I've done the best I could."

"Hell, no," shouted Groat, Slack, Ellis, and Rucker. "We'll stand together, and when he lays into us, we'll give as good as we get."

They returned to a predictable fit by Hook, but his cursing came to an abrupt halt when Creeker drew his pistol and put a slug through Hook's hat. He was about to direct a new string of obscenities at Creeker, when Creeker spoke. His voice was low, deadly.

"One more cuss word out of you, and I'll put a slug

through your leg, and I'll go on doin' it until you shut your mouth or run out of leg.''

Hook stood there in silent fury, taking Creeker at his word. The teamsters, playing off Creeker's stand, were equally defiant. Even Hedgepith and Puckett watched with some amusement. None of the women were in sight, and there was no sign of approval from Savage and Presnall. Swallowing hard, Hook spoke.

''Slaughter, you and Weatherly take axes and fell suitable trees for axles. Hansard, you and Baker help them. Some of the rest of you take wagon jacks and begin jacking up those two wagons.''

It was a sensible order, and the teamsters went about their duties with more than a little satisfaction. There were some grins of appreciation directed at Creeker, as he and his men began unsaddling their horses. The teamsters worked furiously, for they still had to reach water for the night's camp. It was almost dark when they were finally able to circle the wagons, and by the time they were able to eat, there were golden fingers of lightning probing the western sky.

''We'd better be findin' us some high ground,'' Slaughter said. ''There'll be rain before this time tomorrow, and mud aplenty.''

''Be a good time to bust some more axles,'' said Weatherly.

Creeker and his men laughed, but the teamsters did not, for Hook had overheard. But he continued on to Ampersand's cook wagon, saying nothing.

The significance of the lightning wasn't lost on McQuade's party. The intensity of the storm and the amount of rain would determine how much time was lost.

''We'd best cover as much ground tomorrow as we can,'' Ike observed.

The wind from the northwest had the feel and smell of rain, and there was some doubt that they would have another full day before the resulting mud made the land all but impassable for the wagons. Mary and McQuade retired to the wagon early.

"If it's raining in the morning," said Mary, "why don't we just spend the day in the wagon?"

"Because we can't be sure the Indians won't pick just such a time to work their way into our wagon circle. Just when we think they've given up on us, they'll strike."

"I'll be so glad when we reach Texas, and don't have to always be ready for an attack."

"That won't change," said McQuade. "Not for a while. From what Chad Guthrie told us, the Comanches are even worse than the Kiowa. While some Indians are superstitious and won't attack at night, the Comanches will attack any time. I hope Hook had the sense to group these grants in such a way that we can organize against Indian attacks. Us with a rancher's grant, the nearest neighbor might be miles away."

The dawn broke to a chill wind and an overcast sky. While water obviously wouldn't be a problem, McQuade wasn't satisfied to ignore the danger of Indian attack. So he rode ahead as usual, looking for sign. Once the rain came, there would be no sign, and the Kiowa might be just over the next ridge. But McQuade saw no Indian sign, and he found a suitable creek not more than eight miles distant. The day's drive would be short, but they needed time to circle the wagons, graze the stock, and lay in as much dry firewood as time permitted. The rain might last for several days. As McQuade was riding back to meet the wagons, he could hear the rumble of distant thunder. There would be lightning, one of the hazards most feared by a frontiersman. Most of the families in his party had wisely avoided overloading their wagons. A man and his wife might be crowded, but at least they could sleep dry. He thought of Mary, as he so often did, and the changes she had brought to his life. But she had changed as well, from those first days when she seemed afraid to speak, to a frontier woman with strength. Following the Indian attack, she had assisted him in the care of the wounded without a whimper.

"Maybe another five miles," McQuade shouted, upon reaching the wagons. They had all become trail-conscious to the extent that he no longer had to explain his reasoning. Not a one of them would question this short day's drive, because of the coming storm.

Quickly the wagons were circled, and the stock was taken to graze. They must all be brought in before the rain came, because there would be limited visibility, providing the Kiowa with a perfect opportunity for a stampede.

"It's mighty early for supper," said Gunter Warnell, "but I'd rather eat now than have to hunker under a wagon, later."

"Let's get the fires going, then," Ike said. "I reckon we'll get our share of eatin' in the rain for the next day or two."

The women soon had the meal started. Ike had brought a large square of canvas, and stretched between two wagons, it provided enough shelter for a continuous fire, even in the hardest rain. Thus on rainy nights, there was always hot coffee for the men on watch. A triple watch kept enough men on duty so that each of them could remain just inside his wagon, near the rear pucker. Unless there was trouble, they could remain dry, invisible in the shadow of the wagon canvas. It afforded safety to women and children against Indians slipping into the wagons with knives. Because of the impending storm, the first watch went on duty early, and with supper over, those who could do so retired to their wagons. The rain came with a roar of rushing wind, battering the wagon canvas, and thunder shook the earth. Mules brayed and horses nickered, but the wagons had been circled three-deep, and there was nowhere to run.

"It's so good to have you here beside me," said Mary. "I'm so afraid of storms."

"Nothing to fear except the lightning," McQuade said, "and so far, it's not striking."

But that quickly changed, and McQuade held the trembling Mary close, as brilliant blue shards of lightning rippled across the rain-swept sky. There was a resounding crack as a bolt struck a tree somewhere close, and the smell of brimstone was strong. Thunder had become continuous, each rising crescendo sounding like an echo of the last.

"Oh, God," Mary cried, her trembling hands covering her ears.

There was nothing they could do except wait, and the storm continued to grow in its intensity. Finally, when it seemed to reach the very peak of its fury, lightning struck in their very midst. The concussion was so severe that it robbed McQuade of his hearing for a few seconds, but his horrified eyes saw one of the wagons disappear in a blinding blue flash. There was the quick smell of burning flesh. Then his hearing returned. A woman screamed. Quickly McQuade was out of the wagon and running, unsure as to what he could do, but feeling the need to do something. Other men were there, none of them able to get close to the furiously burning wagon. A coal-oil lantern exploded, adding to the fury.

"The Henderson wagon," Ike shouted, barely audible above the roar of the storm.

The Henderson wagon was on the inside of the wagon circle, and only the driving rain saved the other nearby wagons. McQuade ran to the rear pucker of one of the wagons, and heard weeping. It was Lucy Tabor.

"Lucy," McQuade cried.

"Cal's dead," said Lucy, between sobs.

"Maybe not," McQuade said, climbing into the wagon. But Cal Tabor had no pulse, and McQuade felt for the large vein in the neck. There he felt a faint throb.

"He's alive, Lucy. Just unconscious, and maybe with a concussion. Wrap him in all the blankets you can get your hands on."

McQuade left the Tabor wagon he found other men investigating nearby wagons, for the driving rain had begun to diminish the fire. While the lightning continued to flash, it was no longer striking, and in its light, McQuade recognized Maggie Peyton. Beside her was Mary, and in their night clothes they looked like a pair of half-drowned sparrows.

"What about the Tabors?" Maggie shouted.

"Cal's unconscious," McQuade shouted back. "Have you looked in on any of the others in nearby wagons?"

"Some of them. They're in bad shape, but nobody's dead."

Slowly they came together in the rain, realizing that Ab and Flossie Henderson were gone, thankful that their loss had not been greater.

"Back to your wagons," said McQuade. "There's nothing more we can do tonight. In the morning, we'll see to them, doing what we must."

McQuade helped Mary into the wagon, helping her strip off the sodden gown. To his surprise, he realized he was barefooted, wearing only his drawers. Stripping them off, he used them to wipe the mud from his feet. Rolling in the blanket next to Mary, he found her weeping. He lay there holding her close until she finally slept, but for him, there was no rest. Strong on his mind was the Henderson wagon, and the charred remains within that awaited them, come the dawn.

CHAPTER 10

ᴏᐧᕓᴏ

M ost of Hook's camp, Creeker, his men, and the teamsters, had to weather the storm as best they could.
Mostly, they hunkered under wagons. There was one hi-
larious moment, however, when Hook lost his tent. Once
the ground had grown sodden from the torrential rain, the
storm-bred wind had gotten beneath the tent, ripping the
stakes loose. The tent was swept away into the sky, leaving Hook standing there cursing. Dawn broke without any
end of the rain in sight.

"Damn it," Groat moaned, "we'll be stuck here a
week, waitin' for the sun to dry up all this mud."

But the rain slacked to a drizzle, and by early afternoon
the sky had begun to clear. With help from some of the
teamsters, Hook rescued his wayward tent from a tree.
The men were in a better frame of mind by supper time,
for just a few hours of sun had begun to dry the ground.
After supper, Hook spoke to Hedgepith, and the two entered the tent, where Hook lighted a lantern.

"Hedgepith," said Hook, "I want you to destroy any
and all papers entitling Lora Kirby to a land grant in
Texas. Any other promises I may have made in writing,
I want voided and destroyed. Do you understand?"

"Yes," Hedgepith replied, "but I disagree with you.
The grant you have promised her depends on her proving
up. If she fails—which she will—then the grant reverts

to you. Excluding her will mean one less grant. I can't
see hurting us financially, just because your personal relationship with her has gone to hell.''

Hedgepith was caught totally off guard by Hook's reaction. His right fist smashed into the lawyer's chin, tipping over the stool and spilling Hedgepith to the ground.

''My relationships are none of your damn business,''
Hook snarled, ''and only through my generosity are you
sharing anything with me. I'm considering reducing your
share, and it's becoming a temptation not to cut you out
of it completely.''

''You'll never do that,'' said Hedgepith, sitting up and
wiping blood from the corner of his mouth. ''I gave up
my practice in St. Louis, just on your word, and you're
going to keep it. Perhaps I can't make you, but I can make
you wish you had.''

''Are you threating me, you damn fool?'' When Hook
laughed, it was evil and without humor. ''There'll *be* no
law in Texas, except what I allow. I can put an end to all
your legal hocus-pocus with a little piece of lead.''

Xavier Hedgepith said no more. He got to his feet and
left the tent, and nobody within the camp seemed aware
of the hard words between himself and Hook. And that
suited Hedgepith perfectly.

When the rain had ceased, McQuade and some of the
other men contemplated what remained of the Henderson
wagon.

''It's only fittin' and proper that we do somethin' for
them,'' said Ike, ''but I purely got no stomach for siftin'
through them ashes.''

''We have plenty of shovels,'' McQuade said. ''Why
don't we all pitch in and cover the remains with dirt? The
earth is soft from the rain, and we can still bury them
deep.''

''I believe that's best,'' said Will Haymes.

The others nodded their agreement, and they all took
turns with the shovels. Within two hours they had a

mound that would soon grass over, a grave more suitable than any of them had thought possible. Mary brought Miles Flanagan's bible, and Ike Peyton read appropriate passages from it.

"It was them that was taken and us that was spared," said Ike, in closing, "and this ought to be as much a giving of thanks as a memorial to the Hendersons."

Despite the clearing skies and sunshine, there was a sadness, a sense of loss, that had descended upon them like a shroud. Most of the men occupied their time by taking the horses and mules to graze, but there was little for the women to do until supper time.

"We need to leave this place as soon as we can," Gunter Warnell observed. "We can't forget what happened here, as long as we're right on top of it."

"I've been thinking the same thing," said McQuade. "Maybe we ought to keep to high ground as much as we can, and move on in the morning."

"Let's gamble on it," Cal Tabor said. "I'd rather be fightin' the mud than just sittin' here waiting."

Rufus Hook spent the day in his tent, even after the skies had cleared and the sun had come out. He appeared briefly at supper, ignoring everybody and being ignored in turn. As had become the custom in Indian Territory, supper fires were extinguished before dark, and Hook no longer used a lantern. There was no movement within the camp until far in the night, when Lora Kirby slipped away to her rendezvous with Riley Creeker. But while Creeker and the girl talked of the future in Texas, a shadow crept toward the tent where Rufus Hook slept. Ever so stealthily it moved, and in its right hand the starlight glinted off the blade of a long knife . . .

When everybody had eaten breakfast and Hook hadn't appeared, Ampersand went to the tent and called to Hook. When his appeals went unanswered, the elderly Negro opened the flap and looked inside. With a terrified shriek, he turned and ran.

"What the hell's goin' on?" Groat demanded.

Ampersand couldn't speak. He pointed toward the tent with a shaking hand. Creeker, Groat, and Ellis went to investigate. When they stepped out of the tent, everybody in the party had gathered, wondering what had happened.

"Hook's dead," said Creeker. "Somebody slit his throat from ear to ear."

"Them damn Indians," Hiram Savage said.

"I don't think so," said Creeker. "We had the wagons circled, with plenty of men on watch, and there ain't that much cover around us."

"You're sayin' it was one of us that done him in?" said Snakehead Presnall.

"That's exactly what I'm sayin'," Creeker replied.

"We got no law, no proof," said Slaughter, one of the teamsters, "and there's nothing we can do for Hook. What's to become of Hook's wagons and goods, and who's goin' to pay us, when we reach Texas?"

"Nothing has changed," Xavier Hedgepith said. "Hook and I had an agreement that if anything should happen to him, I would follow through with his plans."

"Damned convenient for you," said Creeker.

"Are you accusing me?" Hedgepith snarled.

"Take it any way you like," said Creeker.

"McQuade and his party should be told of Hook's death," Doctor Puckett said.

"No," Hedgepith said. "Insofar as the grants are concerned, nothing has changed. All the administrative work would have been done by me, not Hook. I will act on behalf of all, including McQuade's party. For the time being, what he doesn't know won't hurt him. We have a duty to see that Mr. Hook is properly buried. Will some of you be responsible for the digging of a grave?"

"Long as we're gettin' paid," said Slaughter. "Hansard, will you help?"

"Yeah," said Hansard. "I'll help."

Creeker began saddling his horse, getting Hedgepith's attention.

"Where are you going?" Hedgepith demanded.

"These Indians are gettin' so bold, I'm goin' to look around for some sign," Creeker replied.

The sarcasm wasn't lost on Hedgepith, but he said no more. With the mud, there was no possible way they could take the trail anytime soon, and Hedgepith wished to be rid of Creeker and his suspicions. Creeker rode north until he was well away from the wagons, and he then rode southwest, the direction they must later travel.

"I think we'll make this a short day, because of the wet ground," McQuade said, as he prepared to scout ahead. "When you take the trail, keep to the high ground as much as you can."

With that, McQuade rode out. The condition of the ground was such that if Indians had been near since the rain ended, there would be tracks. McQuade had been gone only a short time, when Ike Peyton, in one of the lead wagons, shouted the caravan to a halt. A hundred yards ahead of them, a rider had trotted his horse out of the brush. He sat facing them, his hands shoulder-high, and shouted a question.

"Where's McQuade?"

"Who wants him, and for what purpose?" Ike inquired.

"This is Creeker, and I have some information for him. I'm alone, and I'm peaceful."

"McQuade's scoutin' ahead," said Ike, "and he's been gone only a few minutes."

"I'll catch up to him, then," Creeker said. "I'm obliged." He quickly galloped away.

"What in tarnation is that all about?" Gunter Warnell wondered.

"I got an idea we'll know, after he talks to McQuade," said Ike. "It sure didn't hurt, us helpin' Creeker and his bunch escape them Indians. Makes me wonder if somethin' big ain't took place in Hook's camp that McQuade ought to know.''

Creeker rode on, expecting McQuade to challenge him, and McQuade did.

''That's far enough, until I know who you are. You're covered.''

''I'm Creeker, and I have some information for you.''

Leading his horse, McQuade stepped out of some brush and waited for Creeker to join him. Creeker dismounted, and quickly related to McQuade what had happened to Hook, and Hedgepith's intention of taking over.

''I reckon we've swapped the devil for a witch,'' said McQuade.

''You think there's goin' to be trouble with Hedgepith, once we reach Texas, then?'' Creeker said.

''Probably more than we'd have ever had with Hook,'' McQuade replied. ''What do you think?''

''I think you're dead right,'' said Creeker. ''Even before Hook was killed, me and my bunch was mostly mindin' our business, with plans of our own, when we get to Texas. Now, with Hedgepith in the saddle, that's all the more important.''

''Hook had plans for you there,'' McQuade said, ''and you're expecting Hedgepith to try and hold you to them.''

''Hook had plans, made legal by Hedgepith, to claim grants in the names of every man of us, and then, for little or nothing, have us sign the grants over to him. While I can't speak for Hook's teamsters and the rest of his followers, those of us you cut loose from the Indians are taking our grants. Without law any closer than Mexico, that lawyer stuff of Hedgepith's ain't worth the paper he wrote it on.''

''That's exactly the way the rest of us feel,'' said McQuade. ''We've all been expecting a showdown with Hook, once we reached Texas. Now it looks like the showdown may become a bigger fight than any of us expected. But I believe we should play our cards close until we get to Texas. We still have Kiowa ahead of us, and beyond them, the Comanches, so we're in no position to challenge Hedgepith. I aim to see that my party knows what I've just learned from you, but we'll say or do nothing to warn Hedgepith."

"That's the way we're goin' to play it," Creeker said. "If Hedgepith comes up with anything you should know, I'll get word to you."

"We're obliged," said McQuade. "If you need help on the trail, or after we finally get to Texas, we'll side you."

"I'm makin' you the same offer," Creeker said. "We don't forget who our friends are."

Impulsively, Creeker offered his hand and McQuade took it. Then, without a word, each mounted his horse. Creeker rode back the way he had come, while McQuade went on the way he had started. When McQuade found a suitable place to circle the wagons for the night, he rode back to meet the caravan. The sun bore down with a vengeance, drying the land. While the teams were being rested, McQuade took the opportunity to relate what he had learned from Creeker.

"I ain't trusted Hedgepith since I first laid eyes on the varmint," said Hardy Kilgore.

"Me neither," Eli Bibb said. "Sure as hell, he kilt Hook, or had it done."

Most of the others were suspicious of Hedgepith, and McQuade could see doubt in their eyes, a dread that their chance for a Texas land grant had died with Rufus Hook.

"Nothing's changed," McQuade assured them, "except that we'll be dealing with this lawyer, Hedgepith, instead of Hook. Creeker tells me that Hedgepith's responsible for all the legal papers. What we might have in our favor is that the Mexican government may not accept Hedgepith as a replacement for Hook."

"Meanin' that we might ask for our grants without Hedgepith havin' a hand in the pot," said Ike. "I like the sound of that. I always felt like Hook had more cards up his sleeve than was on the table."

"We have another advantage that Hedgepith won't know about," McQuade said. "We've got friends right under Hedgepith's nose. Creeker and his *amigos* aim to take and keep any grants assigned to them, and Creeker's promised to pass along anything he learns that we might need to know."

"The man's proven himself, as far as I'm concerned," said Gunter Warnell. "He didn't have to tell us Hook was dead."

The wagons again took the trail, and avoiding low places, were able to reach the area McQuade had chosen to circle the wagons for the night. While McQuade expected trouble from the Kiowa before crossing the Red, there had been no sign of them. Supper was over and McQuade had begun to breathe easy, when he was shaken by the sound of gunfire. It blossomed from behind the Burke wagon and was answered by a fusillade from the vicinity of Trent Putnam's wagon.

"Damn it, hold your fire!" McQuade shouted. "I'm within pistol range of both of you, and I'll kill the next man that fires a shot. Drop your guns, and come out where I can see you."

It was just dusky dark, and McQuade had no trouble identifying Trent Putnam, as he crawled from beneath his wagon. From behind the Burke wagon, Luke emerged, followed by Andrew, Matthew, and Mark.

"McQuade," said Andrew, "this is a private affair. Why the hell can't you mind your own business?"

"When lead begins to fly within the wagon circle, it is my business," McQuade said grimly. "Now what's this all about?"

"I caught that snake-eyed Burke lookin' in through the back of my wagon," shouted Putnam.

"No excuse," said McQuade. "There's a canvas flap that lets down over the pucker. If it wasn't down, that's your fault. What do you have to say, Burke?"

"The pucker was open," Luke said sullenly, "and I

didn't see nothin' but the two of 'em swilling whiskey from a bottle."

"Maggie," said McQuade, "take a look in the wagon and be sure Selma's all right."

Maggie did, returning with a look of disgust on her face.

"She's passed out, dog-drunk," Maggie said.

"Putnam," said McQuade, "you and Burke have gone out of your way to be a bother to the rest of us, and I think it's time we extracted some punishment. Obviously, you don't like one another, and with all guns and knives aside, I want the two of you to have it out with your fists. When one of you can't get up, it's over. There'll be no stomping or kicks to the head."

"That ain't fair," Andrew Burke shouted. "He out-weighs Luke thirty pounds."

"Too bad," said McQuade. "Luke will just have to fight harder."

"Maggie," Ike said, "this could get nasty. You women should go to your wagons."

"Mind your tongue, Ike Peyton," said Maggie. "I can't speak for the others, but I'll be here to the finish, if they strip one another naked."

"So will I," Ellen Warnell said, and her sentiments were echoed by other women who had overheard.

"Mary?" said McQuade.

"I'm staying," Mary said. "I don't like either of them, but I like Trent Putnam least. I want to see Luke beat the hell out of him."

"Shame," said McQuade, raising his eyebrows, "that's no way for a preacher's daughter to talk."

"Your fault," Mary said. "You've corrupted me."

Some of the women had added wood to the supper fires, and coffee was brewing, as the two men removed their shirts. Each eyed the other in grim satisfaction. It was better than they had expected from McQuade. Burke made the first move, charging Putnam, who stepped aside and tripped him. There was some laughter, as Burke went facedown in the dirt, for when he tried to get up, Putnam kicked him in the behind, flattening him again.

"Damn it, Luke," old Andrew shouted, "don't just lay there."

Luke rolled sideways, lest he be booted again, and got to his knees. But Putnam was waiting for him, and Burke was barely on his feet when the heavier man charged, driving his fist toward Luke's sweating face. But Burke seized the wrist, and taking advantage of the momentum, drove his right boot hard into Putnam's groin. Putnam screamed in agony, and as his feet left the ground, Burke released the captured fist. Putnam fell facedown in a cloud of dust, and lay there sobbing. Virtually falling from the wagon, the drunken Selma ran to him.

"Damn you," the woman cried, her eyes on Luke, "you've killed him."

"I reckon not," said Luke, "but he may never be a daddy."

The shocked silence McQuade had expected didn't happen. The women laughed along with the men. But Trent Putnam wasn't finished. He struggled to his knees, and finally to his feet. He stood there swaying like a tall pine in a high wind, until he finally had enough wind to speak. He then turned hard eyes on Luke Burke.

"I ain't never liked you, Burke. Poke your nose in the back of my wagon again, and I'll blow it off, along with your head."

"There'll be no more shooting, Putnam," said McQuade, "unless I do it. Pull a gun one more time, and I'll kill you myself. That goes for you Burkes, too."

"By God," Putnam said, "when we get to Texas, you won't be wagon boss no more. Then I aim to get me a gun and go after some Burke blood. You hear that, boy?"

"I hear it," said Burke, "and I'll be ready. Your carcass will be dog meat."

The Burkes returned to their wagon, while Putnam and Selma returned to theirs, taking the time to cast dirty looks at McQuade.

"Maybe you should of just let them shoot one another," Ike said.

"It was a temptation," said McQuade, "but the way they were throwing lead so recklessly, they might have shot someone else."

McQuade and Mary returned to their wagon, while the men on the first watch returned to their positions.

"It's not enough that we're plagued with Indians and outlaws," Mary said. "We have the Putnams and the Burkes in our own wagon circle. What I fear is that by stopping them from killing each other, you may have them both trying to kill you."

"I've been on the bad side of the Burkes ever since St. Joe," said McQuade. "Putnam can climb on the wagon, if he likes. One more coyote added to the pack won't make that much difference."

When Creeker returned from his meeting with McQuade, Hedgepith was waiting.

"See any Indians?" Hedgepith inquired.

"No," said Creeker shortly.

"See anybody from McQuade's party?"

"I rode wide of their wagons and went ahead of them," Creeker said.

"You didn't answer my question," Hedgepith persisted.

"I *told* you I rode wide of them," said Creeker, in a dangerously calm voice.

Hedgepith said no more, but the look in his eyes said he didn't believe Creeker. Without another word, he turned and went into the tent that had belonged to Hook. Creeker unsaddled his horse, while Groat and Slack looked at him and grinned.

"Now that he's tall dog in the brass collar, he just ain't trustin' at all," Dirk said. "I'd not be surprised if he took to doubtin' us all."

"Don't push him," said Creeker. "There's goin' to be a showdown in Texas, and we got trouble enough between here and there."

"I reckon you know somethin' we don't," Porto said. "You been talkin' to McQuade, ain't you?"

"I'm admittin' nothing that might get back to Hedgepith," said Creeker.

"Damn it," Porto said, "that's an insult. I ought to gut-shoot you."

Creeker laughed. "We got friends in McQuade's party. That's all you need to know for now. That and the fact that none of McQuade's people trust Hedgepith. They're looking for a fight in Texas, and McQuade knows where we stand."

Hedgepith sat in the tent going over sheaves of paper, seeking any loopholes he might have missed. He had his doubts about Creeker and the men who had hired on with him, but this was no time for a division within his limited forces. He must wait until he reached Texas and had assumed control of the grants for which Rufus Hook had applied. Only then could he purge himself of the likes of Creeker and others who might stand in his way.

After a full day of sun, the land had dried. McQuade rode out ahead of the wagons, and having ridden not more than ten miles, he reined up before the North Canadian River. It was a milestone in their trek, for when they crossed the North Canadian, the Canadian was only some fifteen miles beyond. That meant they were less than a hundred miles from the crossing of the Red, which would take them into Texas. Elated, McQuade rode back to meet the wagons. Once they reached the bank of the North Canadian, circled the wagons, and unhitched the teams, there was rejoicing. Whatever trials awaited them in Texas, they were almost free of Indian Territory. McQuade had gradually increased the number of men on watch until everybody felt secure, but they were still vulnerable when they were on the trail. But the next morning, while they were crossing the North Canadian, the Kiowa came galloping in from the northwest. McQuade shot the lead rider off his horse, but the Kiowa fanned out in a long line, several attacking a single wagon. Hardy Kilgore was thrown off his wagon box, a lance driven through his middle. Jason, his son, got off one shot, only to have an arrow driven deep in his chest. Terrified, the Kilgore teams veered away from the attacking Kiowa, toppling the Kilgore wagon in the swirling brown water. McQuade fired five more times, accounting for four more of the attackers. Men from wagons which were not under attack had reined up their teams and were taking careful aim. One after another, Kiowa horses galloped away riderless, and the attack ended as suddenly as it had begun. McQuade hardly knew where to begin. Women wept, men cursed, and mules brayed their terror.

"The Kilgores," Maggie Peyton cried.

"Too late for them," shouted Ike.

Starting with the lead wagons, McQuade worked his way back, seeking the wounded or the dead. Odessa Bibb had an arrow in her left side, while Lucy Tabor had a shaft in her left thigh. Andrew Burke had a bloody gash under his right arm, where a Kiowa lance had narrowly missed being driven through his chest. Four wagons had crossed the river, and had escaped the attack.

"We'll take the rest of the wagons across," McQuade shouted, "and circle them on the south bank. We'll be here a while."

Quickly they complied. The Kiowa would be returning for their dead, which numbered more than twenty. When the wagons had been circled and the men were unhitching their teams, the women were getting fires going and putting water on to boil. Minerva Haymes had taken mud and was smoothing it over Andrew Burke's wound, to stop the bleeding.

"Maggie," said McQuade, "you and Mary get the whiskey and see that Odessa and Lucy drink plenty of it. When it's had time to work, those arrows will have to come out."

"Don't I know," Maggie said. "We'll see they're proper drunk."

"Ike, you and Gunter saddle up and ride with me," said McQuade. "We have to find Hardy and Jason Kilgore, if we can. Will, I want you, Eli, and Cal to see that everybody who is assigned to the third watch take up positions surrounding the wagon circle. While I doubt the Kiowa will attack again, we can't afford to gamble."

McQuade saddled his horse, and followed by Ike and Gunter, rode off downstream. They had no trouble finding the wagon, for the unfortunate mules had drowned and were acting as a drag. McQuade rode into the river and with his knife, cut the harness. He then tied one end of his lariat to a rear wagon wheel and looped the other end around his saddle horn. But the burden was too much for one horse. Ike rode in and tied his lariat to the wagon's other rear wheel. Slowly they dragged the wagon out of the water, but there was no sign of the bodies of either of the Kilgores.

"My God," said Gunter, "they're lost in the river. We may never find them."

"Beyond a doubt they both died in the attack," McQuade said. "We'll ride downriver a ways and maybe find them in the shallows."

But they rode for more than five miles, and the North Canadian seemed to increase in depth and in force. Finally the banks became so steep and overgrown with brush and oak thickets that McQuade called off the search. The trio returned to the wagon circle with the grim news, and McQuade went to the Bibb wagon to look in on Odessa.

"I gave her half a bottle of whiskey," said Mary. "Maggie's seeing to Lucy."

When McQuade reached the Tabor wagon, he found Cal there with Maggie. Lucy was already asleep.

"Cal," McQuade said, "you know that arrow has to come out, and you know the procedure. I don't think it's proper, me workin' over another man's woman, with her all . . ."

"Stripped down," Maggie finished.

"Yes," said McQuade. "Cal, why don't you . . ."

"My God, no," Cal cried. "I . . . I'm so spooked, I . . . I couldn't."

"It's up to you, McQuade," said Maggie, "and don't go gettin' the whim-whams about doctorin' a woman. You stripped me down and drove an arrow out of my leg, and not one of these other females is built any different."

Despite the circumstances, Cal laughed. "Go ahead, McQuade. Lucy is expecting you to take care of her. I'm goin' to do the only decent thing, and stay the hell out of your way."

McQuade sighed and began punching the loads from the cylinder of his revolver . . .

CHAPTER 11

*M*cQuade spent more than an hour driving through and removing the arrows from Lucy Tabor and Odessa Bibb. Crowded as it was within the wagons, Maggie and Mary remained with him, cleansing and bandaging the wounds. As usual, the procedure took its toll, and wrung out, McQuade returned to the wagon. He had liked Hardy and Jason Kilgore, and their deaths had shaken him. Any man deserved a decent burial by his friends, and their bodies having been lost in the muddy North Canadian dragged him even deeper into the depths of despair. Returning to the wagon, Mary found him sitting on the tailgate, staring morosely at the ground.

"For a man who just spent an hour with two naked females, you're awfully grim," she said, seeking to cheer him.

"I'm almighty tired of removing arrows, especially from naked females," he said, without a trace of humor.

She was immediately sorry. Placing the medicine kit in the wagon, she boosted herself up on the tailgate beside him.

"It isn't the arrows, is it?" she asked.

"No," said McQuade. "At least Odessa and Lucy are alive."

"You're blaming yourself for what happened to the Kilgores."

"Mary, there's a reason, a cause, for everything."

"But you didn't know the Kiowa would attack while we were crossing the river."

"No," McQuade said wearily, "but I knew they'd take another swipe at us before we could get out of Indian Territory. The worst possible time for an Indian attack is during a river crossing. My God, why didn't I make allowances for that?"

"What more could you have done?"

"I could have stationed fifty men at the river," said McQuade, "protecting each of the wagons as they crossed. They struck where we were the most vulnerable."

"But if you had taken fifty men from their wagons, stationing them near the river, that would have left their wagons, their women and their children unprotected."

"Bless you, Mary," he said, putting an arm around her shoulders, "but I just can't help feeling that I could have—should have—done something differently."

Mary said nothing, for Will Haymes was approaching.

"Some of us would like to have a service for the Kilgores," said Will, "even though we ... they ... were lost. Would you and Mary join us?"

"Yes," McQuade said.

"I'll get the bible," said Mary.

It was a sad gathering, and it was done quickly, but somehow they all felt better for having participated. Afterward, there was nothing to do but wait for time and the whiskey to begin the healing process for Odessa and Lucy. While it seemed unlikely that the Kiowa would return, McQuade kept a double guard posted for the rest of the day, tripling it at sundown.

Half a mile upriver, the significance of the early morning attack by the Kiowa wasn't lost on Creeker and his men. In seconds, they had their weapons, and were prepared for an attack. The remaining fifteen teamsters were quick to follow their example.

"What's going on?" Hedgepith demanded, emerging from his tent.

"Indian attack downriver," said Creeker.

"If you're considering riding down there," Hedgepith said stiffly, "Don't."

"If I could get there in time to be of any help, I'd go," said Creeker. "It would be the decent thing to do, but you wouldn't understand that."

"I understand that you'd be wasting ammunition better spent defending your own camp," Hedgepith said. "Now put your weapons away and get these teams harnessed for the trail."

The men eyed Hedgepith in disgust as he returned to his tent. Slaughter, one of the teamsters, turned to Creeker with a question.

"Since they hit McQuade's camp this morning, when do you reckon they'll be comin' after us?"

"Late today or early tomorrow," Creeker replied. "We can't be more than a hundred miles north of the Red, and when we cross it, we'll be in Texas. If you aim to cross the Red with your hair in place, forget any orders you get from Hedgepith. Startin' tonight we better cut back to two watches, so's we got more men awake and ready. Today, when we take the trail, there'll be five of us ahead of the first wagon, and five behind the last. All of us will be watching for Indians. If you hear one of us sing out or fire a shot, rein up and hit the ground with your guns ready."

"That makes more sense than anything I've heard since we left St. Louis," Hansard said. "Suppose we elect you wagon boss an' tell Hedgepith to go to hell?"

"Leave Hedgepith alone, and let him think he's giving the orders," said Creeker. "I got no ambition to be wagon boss. I just want to get to Texas with all my hair, and without any arrows in my carcass. We all got to work together."

Quietly, without warning Hedgepith, they all vowed their support.

*   *   *

Nightly, when the camp was asleep, Lora Kirby slipped away to join Riley Creeker, and a few days after Hook's death, she had some truly astounding news.

"Hedgepith's in for a surprise, if he thinks Hook's saloon women are going to work in a Texas saloon," she said.

"What are they goin' to do?" Creeker asked.

Lora laughed. "It's what they've already done. They've been slipping away at night, meeting some of the teamsters. Every last one of them—Mabel, Reza, Eula, Sal, Nettie, and Cora—has been spoken for, once we get to Texas."

"I reckon them gamblers—Savage and Presnall—had better learn to dance," Creeker said. "I swear, the sweetest part of this whole thing is goin' to be watchin' it all collapse around Hedgepith's ears."

Creeker and his men split up, five riding ahead of the wagons, and five riding behind. They were trailing McQuade's party, which lessened the possibility the Kiowa might hit them from the southwest, but Creeker's eyes were constantly on the back-trail. But when the attack came, it was from the south.

"God Almighty," Ellis shouted, "yonder they come!"

Remembering what Creeker had told them, the teamsters reined up and hit the ground with their guns in their hands. Creeker and his men were out of their saddles, and twenty-five men formed a line of defense the length of the strung-out wagons. The Kiowa, riding bunched, fanned out. It proved their undoing, for the defenders singled out individual targets, and after the first volley, more than fifteen Kiowa horses galloped away riderless. The remaining Kiowa whirled their horses and retreated.

"Anybody hit?" Creeker shouted.

"Hell, no," said Slaughter. "We was ready for 'em, an' shot first."

Hedgepith stalked down the line of wagons, his eyes

on the jubilant teamsters. When he spoke, there was impatience in his voice.

"You men did your jobs, and there's no celebration in order for that. Now get back to your wagons and get them moving. Creeker, you and your men take your positions and keep your eyes open."

With that, he turned on his heel and walked back to the lead wagon. Slaughter and the other teamsters had their hands near their pistols, but Creeker laughed. It proved contagious, and the men soon had the wagons moving again. Quietly, Creeker rode alongside each wagon, commending the men for their valiant defense. It solidified his unofficial leadership of the party, leaving Hedgepith in an even more weakened position than he realized. Creeker and his men rode warily, but they reached the bank of the Canadian River half a mile upstream from McQuade's outfit, without incident.

McQuade and his party had heard the shooting along their back-trail, and there was little doubt in anybody's mind as to the reason behind it. There was talk among the men, during supper.

"From the shootin', I'd say they put up a good fight," Will Haymes observed.

"If they did," said Ike, "it was in spite of Hedgepith, and not because of him. The man don't strike me as havin' much common sense."

"Somehow I don't think they're depending on Hedgepith, when it comes to defense," McQuade said. "Creeker and his bunch may have hired on as gunmen with Hook, but they have become something more than that. The frontier has a way of taking a man through the fire. He'll come out of it bigger, stronger, and tougher, or he'll bend and break."

"This bein' the Canadian," said Ike, "you figure we're maybe a week away from the crossin' of the Red?"

"Not more than ninety miles," McQuade replied. "If nothing else happens to slow us down, we're not more than a week away. I believe if we can get another two days behind us, the Kiowa will back off.''

"Then all we got to worry us is the Comanches," said Gunter Warnell.

"Maybe," McQuade said, "but we can't afford to let down our guard. I can't shake the feeling that the Republic of Texas has some surprises in store for us, and that most of them won't be pleasant."

The night on the banks of the Canadian River was peaceful, and with all possible precautions, they crossed the river and rolled on toward the southwest. Another milestone would be the distant Red River, beyond which lay the land on which all their hopes and dreams rested.

In western Indian Territory, outlaw Gid Sutton and his five surviving men—Withers, Vance, Taylor, Paschal, and Byler—had established an outlaw stronghold. Following their devastating defeat by Chance McQuade's outfit, they had set about establishing another band of renegades more formidable than the first. Outlaws had come from Kansas, Indian Territory, Nebraska, north Texas, and from as far away as Colorado. After his ignominious defeat, Sutton had kept a man on the trail of the Hook and McQuade parties. Thus he had come up with a plan to enrich himself, and in so doing, get revenge. Sutton's companions were getting restless.

"Damn it, Sutton," said Withers, "how much longer you goin' to hold off? We already got sixty men, not countin' ourselves. That's more'n we ever had before."

"I wouldn't mind havin' a hundred," Sutton replied. "We made a mistake, last time, not goin' after them supply wagons trailin' McQuade. Hell, there's a fortune in goods, just for the taking. Once we take them wagons, McQuade and his bunch will come runnin' to the rescue. That's when we cut 'em down, and I want enough men to do it proper."

"This bunch ain't gonna set here on ready much longer," said Vance.

"There's some things you ain't told 'em," Paschal

said. "I was close enough to see them twenty-five *hombres* just shoot hell out of attacking Indians, without losin' a man. We ain't goin' up agin a bunch of short horns. Them teamsters and the gun-throwers with 'em is every bit as tough as McQuade's party."

"Just keep your mouth shut," said Sutton. "These *hombres* don't have to know everything. Byler, tomorrow I want you to scout both parties, lettin' us know where they are. I want 'em across the Red and in Texas, before we move in. Then we'll be free of Kiowa."

"But not of the Comanches," Taylor said.

"Hell, Taylor," said Sutton, "you want ever'thing handed to you on a silver plate? We git them wagons to Texas, we ain't all that far from them settlements along the Brazos an' the Rio Colorado. We ain't splittin' all the booty with these varmints for nothin'. They'll be ridin' shotgun, keepin' the Comanches off us, until we can convert them wagonloads of goods to cash."

"I like that better than goin' after McQuade's outfit, just for revenge," said Withers.

"Me too," Vance said. "Revenge don't put no gold in my pockets."

"Sutton's got the right idea," said Paschal. "Them supply wagons is never that far behind McQuade's outfit. Once we go after them wagons, we'll have to fight McQuade's party sure as hell, revenge or not."

"He's right," Taylor said. "I was watchin' that day one of the bunch from the supply train met McQuade on the trail. Whatever their reason for the two trains travelin' apart, they're friendly to one another. I saw McQuade an' this other hombre shake hands."

"Then don't let me hear any more complaints about waitin' for more men," said Sutton. "We'll be needin' 'em. Besides, we got plenty of time. Every day we wait, them wagons will be that much closer to the settlements. That'll be one day less we'll have to wrassle with them."

That quieted them. Sutton went to their supply wagon, and as he so often did, looked upon their arsenal of weapons and ammunition. There were two kegs of black powder, a wooden box of empty whiskey bottles for use as bombs, and coil after coil of fast-burning fuse.

"By God," said Withers, from behind Sutton, "it looks like we're goin' to war."

"Maybe we are," Sutton replied. "This time, we'll have some surprises."

McQuade had kept the wagons traveling three abreast, although the terrain had turned stoney and irregular. One day after crossing the Canadian River, Ike Peyton's wagon slid a left rear wheel into a rut with enough force to snap the axle.

"Damn," said McQuade, under his breath.

"I don't like suggestin' this," Ike said, "but we may have to go back to a column of twos, instead of threes. There's narrow places where it's hell keepin' three side-by-side wagons far enough apart so's the wheels don't hook one another. These damn jugheaded mules all wants to walk the same path."

McQuade laughed. "I know how they are, Ike. We'll have just about enough time to replace that axle and make it to the next water, before dark."

Reaching the area McQuade had chosen, they circled the wagons, unharnessed their teams, and took the stock to graze. The women got the supper fires going, and had supper ready when the stock was driven back within the wagon circle. The sun dipped behind a dirty gray bank of clouds on the western horizon, and as twilight fell, there were flares of lightning.

"Another storm comin'," said Ike Peyton. "Sometime tomorrow."

Strong on all their minds was the tragic night the Hendersons had gone to a flaming death after their wagon had been hit by lightning. While they were willing to take their chances with outlaws and hostile Indians, they had no control over the elements.

"I'm going to pray there won't be any lightning,"

Mary said, when she and McQuade had gone to their wagon.

"There can be lightning without it striking," said McQuade. "We have no control over it, and I think we'll be safer in the wagon than anywhere else."

"But there are so many iron parts to a wagon," Mary said.

"There are no iron parts to a tree," said McQuade, "and a lot more trees are hit than wagons. I been on the frontier for twelve years, and I've seen a wagon struck by lightning only once. God knows, that was enough."

When the wagons took the trail at dawn, the wind had risen. Coming out of the west, it brought the unmistakable smell of rain. McQuade rode ahead as usual, aware that there might not be much time before the storm reached them. On a good day, the wagons might travel as far as fifteen miles, but with a storm building, McQuade would settle for ten or less. Being caught on the move during a storm was bad enough, because of the lightning, but there was another more common danger. Severe thunder and lightning could stampede the teams. While mules were faster than oxen, they spooked at anything or nothing, and their being harnessed to a wagon wouldn't deter them. McQuade rode what he estimated was a little more than ten miles. While there was no fresh water, there was a dry *arroyo* which the rain would soon fill. McQuade rode back to meet the wagons, finding the teams moving at a gait faster than usual. The wind grew in intensity, rolling the big gray clouds in from the west. The sun was barely noon-high when clouds swept over its face and the first big rain drops splattered on wagon canvas.

"Keep going," McQuade shouted, as the lead wagons slowed. "Maybe three miles yet."

Thunder pealed closer, and while lightning wasn't striking, it flicked golden tongues of fire from low-hanging clouds. Each time thunder shook the earth, mules brayed in terror, but every man kept his teams on a tight rein. Just when McQuade believed they were going to make it, all hell broke loose. Lightning struck a tree a dozen yards to the left of the lead wagons. A flaming torch forty feet high, it terrified the teams nearest it, and the teams drawing all three of the lead wagons stampeded. They tore off to the northwest, as Ike Peyton, Gunter Warnell, and Will Haymes fought to rein them in. The teams drawing the next three wagons, finding nothing ahead of them, lit out straight ahead. The situation quickly worsened, as lightning struck again, somewhere close. Sheets of rain roared in on the wind, and the flaming tree sputtered out. Through valiant efforts of the men on their wagon boxes, the teams were held in check.

McQuade rode after the stampeding teams, and through the driving rain, saw the Peyton wagon jam a pine between the right rear wheel and the wagon box. The wheel was torn off and the wagon rolled on its right side. Maggie was thrown free, but McQuade saw no sign of Ike. The Warnell and Haymes wagons had met similar fates, the shuddering mules coming to a halt only when they could drag the disabled wagons no farther. Maggie was on her hands and knees when McQuade reached her. She had a gash over her left eye, and the rain was washing blood down over her face. Dismounting, McQuade took her arm and they ran through the mud and driving rain toward the wrecked wagon. They quickly found Ike, his right leg caught under a wagon wheel.

"Busted leg," Ike gritted.

"Some of us will be back for you," McQuade said. "Maggie, stay with him, while I see about the others."

"They'll need help," said Maggie.

"But not here in the rain and mud," McQuade said. "We'll have to get them to shelter in some of the other wagons."

Men who had managed to control their teams now left their wagons and ran to the aid of their less fortunate neighbors. Already half a dozen men had lifted the disabled wagon enough to free Ike Peyton. Gunter Warnell knelt over Ellen, his left arm bent at an awkward angle.

"How is she?" McQuade asked.

"I don't know," said Warnell. "Both of us were thrown off the box. She hit her head on something, and the wagon's front wheel ran over my arm."

"Stay with her," McQuade said. "Others are coming to help you back to shelter."

McQuade found the Haymes wagon upside down, and no sign of Will or Minerva.

"Will, Minerva," he shouted.

"We're under the wagon," Will answered.

"Are you hurt?"

"No, thank God," said Will. "We're bruised and skint up, but nothing worse."

"Help's on the way," McQuade said. "When some of the others get here, we'll lift the wagon off you."

Joel Handy, Tobe Rutledge, and Isaac McDaniel were the first to arrive, and the four of them were able to raise one side of the wagon enough for Will and Minerva to crawl out. Their faces were bloody from cuts.

"Joel," said McQuade, "help Will unharness his teams. We'll have to circle the rest of the wagons and secure all the stock. When the storm's done, we'll get to work on all the wagons that are disabled."

"How many others?" Haymes asked.

"Five more, that I know of," said McQuade. "The teams with the first six wagons all stampeded. Ike has a broken leg and Gunter a broken arm. I still don't know about Bud and Bess Jackman, Oscar and Winnie Odell, or Levi and Callie Phelps."

"They're all bein' seen to," Joel Handy said.

"Tobe," said McQuade, "unharness Gunter's teams and lead them back to the rest of the wagons. He won't be able, with a busted arm, and Isaac, I'd appreciate it if you'll do the same for Ike. I have to get the rest of the wagons circled so we can begin caring for the injured."

McQuade mounted his horse and rode back toward the column of wagons, just in time to meet Eli Bibb and Cal Tabor. They, among others, had followed the second trio of runaway teams, and quickly reported to McQuade what had happened.

"The women caught hell," said Cal. "Bess Jackman's got a busted ankle, Winnie Odell a broken arm, and Callie Phelps a broken hip. Bud, Oscar, and Levi got skint up some, but nothin' worse."

"The wagons is tore all to hell," Eli added.

"We're goin' to be here a while," said McQuade. "I'll need both of you to help me in circling the wagons."

When the wagons were circled, the injured brought to shelter, and the stock secured, those who were able gathered to hear what McQuade had to say.

"We have five people with broken bones. Somewhere, not too far behind us, is Doctor Puckett, with Hedgepith's outfit. I've set a bone or two, but I'm no doctor. For the sake of those who have broken bones, I'm going to ask Doctor Puckett to set them. Some of you stretch Ike's canvas between a couple of wagons, so we can have shelter for a fire. Puckett will need hot water. I'll return as soon as I can."

"You want a couple of us to ride with you?" Cal Tabor asked.

"No," said McQuade. "I don't look for any trouble from Hedgepith over this."

McQuade saddled up and rode along their back-trail, unsure as to how far behind his outfit Hedgepith's wagons were. The rain continued.

Hedgepith's party—not more than three miles behind McQuade's—had fallen victim to the fury of the storm. While nobody had been killed or injured, teams had stampeded, severely damaging two wagons. Worse, these wagons, driven by Slaughter and Hansard, had been loaded with barreled whiskey. Five barrels, three from Slaughter's wagon and two from Hansard's, had been smashed. Hedgepith was furious.

"Damn it, why didn't you rein in the teams? You call yourselves teamsters?"

"We rode out the stampede," said Hansard sullenly.

"Wasn't nothin' else we could do. We could of been killed."

"It would have been no great loss," Hedgepith snapped.

"You sayin' our lives ain't worth five barrels of whiskey?" Slaughter demanded.

"Not to me," said Hedgepith.

"Then, by God, when you get my wagon patched up—if you do—then drive it yourself," said Slaughter. "I want what you owe me, as of right now."

"Put me down for the same," Hansard said.

"Your deal with Hook was that you get paid when we reach the Rio Colorado," said Hedgepith, "and I'm holding you to that. Pull out now, and you get nothing. Continue on, and you'll be paid as promised. Minus the cost of the lost whiskey, of course."

But Hedgepith had gone too far, and Slaughter called him.

"Hear that, you mule whackers? You got to pay for lost goods. Are you goin' to take that?"

"Hell, no," they all shouted in a single voice.

"Well, now, Mr. Hedgepith," said Slaughter, "you ain't threatenin' just me an' Hansard no more. Pull in your horns, back off on chargin' us for losses, or every man of us will leave your wagons settin' where they are."

Hedgepith looked from one to another, finding only grim resolution in their eyes, and did what he had to.

"I suppose I spoke hastily. I'll absorb the losses. We have the necessary tools. Can the wagons be repaired?"

"Yeah," said Slaughter, "but it'll take some time, and we ain't even goin' to think of it in pouring rain."

"Then circle the rest of the wagons," Hedgepith said, "and we'll remain here until the wagons can be repaired."

Creeker and his companions had said nothing during Hedgepith's confrontation with the teamsters. Now Hedgepith glared at them, and they grinned at him in return.

"Rider comin'," Weatherly sang out.

McQuade reined up out of rifle range.

"Come on, McQuade," Creeker shouted.

Hedgepith said nothing, remaining where he was. McQuade rode in.

"We had some teams stampede," said McQuade, "and we have five people with broken bones. We have need of Doctor Puckett."

"We also had teams stampede," Hedgepith said, "and . . ."

Groat laughed, and before Hedgepith could say more, Creeker cut in.

"Come off it, Hedgepith. We got nobody injured, and you know it."

"If one of you will bring my horse," Doctor Puckett said, "I'll be on my way."

Nobody said anything as Puckett mounted his horse and rode out with McQuade. By the time they reached McQuade's wagon circle, a fire had been built beneath the canvas shelter and water was boiling. Skinned and bruised, Maggie Peyton had already given the injured massive doses of whiskey.

"Just a little longer," said Maggie, "and they'll be out of it. The women got theirs first, so they'll be ready before Ike and Gunter."

"Was anyone hurt in your party, Doctor?" Mary asked.

"No," said Puckett. "We had some teams stampede, two wagons were heavily damaged and five barrels of whiskey lost."

"Maggie," Mary said, "you've been through a lot. Why don't you rest, and let me help the doctor in whatever way I can?"

"You can help," said Maggie, "but I have to keep busy. If I just set and do nothing, I'll be so stiff and sore by mornin', I can't get up. I'd best look in on Ike. It takes a lot of whiskey to knock him out."

While the thunder and lightning had passed, the rain continued, as Doctor Puckett began setting the broken bones of the injured.

CHAPTER 12

⌘

Dr. Puckett spent more than three hours setting and splinting broken bones. The rain had continued and showed no sign of letting up any time soon.

"You're welcome to stay for supper, Doctor," Maggie said.

"Thank you," said Puckett, "but I should get back before dark. Just impress upon the people whose bones I have set that they're not to do anything foolish. Another break without allowing the bones to knit can be serious."

"I'll see that they take care of themselves," Maggie said. "We're beholden to you."

"I'll ride back with you, Doc," said McQuade.

They reached Hedgepith's wagons without incident, and with a friendly goodbye, the doctor and McQuade parted. Creeker and several of his men raised a hand in greeting, but McQuade saw no sign of Hedgepith. Reaching his own wagon circle, McQuade visited the wagons where those who had been injured had been taken. Only Ike and Gunter were awake. The three women still slept.

"This is one hell of a mess," Ike complained. "Doc told Maggie I wasn't to use this bum leg for a month, and there's a godawful lot of work to be done to that wagon."

"Not just your wagon," said McQuade. "Six teams stampeded, and five of the wagons were seriously damaged. The Haymes wagon was the only one to come out of it without a busted wheel or broken axle. There are plenty of us to repair the wagons. Just remember, had it been somebody else with a broken leg, you'd be helping repair his wagon. Just do as Maggie tells you, and don't hurt that leg again.''

"I always do what Maggie tells me, broken leg or not," said Ike. "I didn't know I had any choice."

"You don't worry about this old varmint," Maggie said. "I can handle the teams better than he can, and without all the swearing."

McQuade found Gunter Warnell with a splint on his arm, grimly watching the steadily falling rain.

"I don't know what's ahead of us in Texas," said Gunter, "but it can't be any worse than what we've run into in Indian Territory."

"That's kind of how I feel," McQuade said. "When this rain lets up, we'll all get busy and repair your wagon. It'll be a mite crowded until then."

"I won't be worth a damn, with this arm," said Gunter. "The Doc told Ellen it's a bad break, and if I put any strain on it before it knits, it could heal crooked."

"I'm tellin' you the same thing I told Ike," McQuade said. "It could have been someone else with a broken arm, and you helping to repair his wagon. We're all in this to the finish, and we're goin' to make it."

"You're a patient and determined man, McQuade, and I doubt any of us could survive on this frontier, without you. I didn't like Rufus Hook, but God rest his soul, he knew what he was doing, when he hired you."

McQuade said nothing, going on to the wagons where Bess Jackman, Winnie Odell, and Callie Phelps had been taken. He found Mary with Bess, who had awakened. After a word of reassurance, McQuade and Mary then visited the other two wagons. While Winnie and Callie had just awakened, they were in good spirits.

"Except for the wrecked wagons," said Mary, "we have a lot for which we should be thankful."

"Even *with* the broken wagons, we have plenty to be thankful for," McQuade said. "A wagon can be made good as new. Any one of those with broken bones could have been killed. We should offer our wagon to those who were hurt, whose wagons were wrecked."

"I already did," said Mary, "but others were ahead of me. These are generous people, and they realize one of the smashed-up wagons might have been their own."

They made do with the little shelter they had, preparing supper, feeding the injured, and sharing their wagons. McQuade posted a triple watch for the night, compensating for poor visibility caused by the continuing rain. The next morning, shortly after dawn, the rain slacked to a drizzle and eventually ceased.

"Let's get started on those wagons," said McQuade. "There's a chance we can repair them today, if we all pitch in."

Necessary repairs to the Haymes wagon were minor, although their personal belongings had suffered. All Minerva's treasured china had been broken. All five of the other wagons had one broken wheel, and three of them had broken rear axles. Wagon canvas had been ripped, bows snapped, and in several cases, the harness itself had been damaged by the terrified mules. McQuade kept them all busy, for he wanted the damaged wagons back within the wagon circle. The critical repairs— replacing broken wheels and axles—were done first. That done, the wagons were taken to their place within the wagon circle, where lesser repairs and cleanup would be done. Canvas was patched, while slender hickory saplings were bent into bows to replace those broken. Their most important tools were axes, and McQuade swung one until his hands were blistered, hewing axles to replace the broken ones. Fortunately, every wagon carried at least one spare wheel, and with many hands laid to the task, all those whose wagons had been damaged saw them repaired and back within the wagon circle by suppertime.

"I have never seen a more neighborly bunch of folks

in my life,'' said Ike, when he had been helped into his own restored wagon.

Hedgepith's teamsters set to work as soon as the rain ceased; and by early afternoon, the two damaged wagons were again ready for the trail.

"With the wagons ready,'' said Hedgepith, "why are we not moving out?''

"Mud,'' Slaughter said. "You got an almighty short memory.''

Hedgepith said nothing. Wet-weather streams were running bank full, and water would not be a problem for at least another day or two. The repaired wagons were returned to the wagon circle and preparations were made for the night. Slaughter paused for a word with Creeker.

"You lookin' for more trouble with the Kiowa?'' Slaughter asked.

"I don't know, one way or the other,'' said Creeker. "We're close to enough to Texas that they should be backing off, but we can't risk it. We'd better stay with two watches until we cross the Red.''

Although the storm had ended the day before, McQuade decided to wait another day before taking the trail again. A full day of sun would lessen chances of wagons bogging down in mud, and it would allow those who had been injured to adapt to their situation. In the afternoon, McQuade went from wagon to wagon, assuring himself that all was well, and leaving word of his intention to take the trail the following morning. All seemed in order until he reached the Putnam wagon. The pucker was drawn tight and the curtains pulled down at front and back.

"Putnam,'' McQuade said, "are you in there?''

Selma lifted the curtain from the rear pucker, and McQuade saw enough to assure himself that she was totally undressed. She was also very nervous, for her voice was little more than a squeak.

"Trent's not here,'' she said.

"Then where is he?'' McQuade demanded.

"I promised not to tell," said Selma.

"You might as well," McQuade said. "I'll get it out of him when he returns, and I'll not forget that you covered for him. The Kiowa could be scalping him this very minute. Now where is he?"

"Oh, I don't care what you do to him, or what the Indians do to him," she said. "He went to the other wagon camp, for more whiskey."

"How long has he been gone?" McQuade asked.

"Maybe an hour," said Selma. "He's afoot. He thought you wouldn't know, if he didn't take his horse."

"Damn it," McQuade said. If the Kiowa discovered Putnam afoot, he wouldn't have a prayer. Quickly McQuade visited the other wagons. Reaching the Burke wagon, he confirmed what he already suspected. Only old Andrew, Matthew, and Mark were there.

"Where's Luke?" McQuade asked.

"Around here somewhere," said Andrew cautiously.

"In the Putnam wagon, by any chance?"

"I don't know," Burke said. "Why don't you go find out for yourself?"

But McQuade had his answer, and it wasn't Luke who was in danger. McQuade found Cal Tabor and Will Haymes, and quickly explained the situation.

"Saddle up," said McQuade, "and bring an extra horse. We'll try to save the damn fool, if we can."

McQuade rode by the wagon and told Mary where he was going, and why. She was less than sympathetic.

"Why don't you just let the Indians have him?"

"It's a temptation," said McQuade, "but given that small victory, their medicine men might talk them into trying for a larger one. We'll be back as soon as we can."

The trio rode out, McQuade in the lead.

"Even without the Indian threat, goin' afoot was a fool thing to do," Will said. "He's got no way of knowin' how far back Hedgepith's wagons are."

"I doubt they're more than three or four miles behind us," said McQuade. "The storm must have caught them, just as it did us. But that's distance enough for a rider to catch a man on foot, and one Kiowa would be more than a match for Putnam.''

"Hedgepith's outfit could have driven wide of us and be somewhere ahead," Cal said.

"Not likely," said McQuade. "Trailing us, they feel some measure of safety from the Kiowa. I expect for them to wait until we take the trail again, and they'll follow."

They had no trouble finding Putnam's tracks in the muddy ground, and within less than a mile, his stride increased mightily.

"He's runnin' like hell wouldn't have it," said Will.

They quickly discovered the reason for Putnam's haste. Tracks of two unshod horses led in from the northwest and galloped after the fleeing Putnam. Suddenly his tracks were gone, and only those of the side-by-side galloping horses remained.

"Caught him up between them," McQuade said. "We're too late."

Almost immediately the horses had changed direction, galloping back the way they had come. Within a matter of minutes, McQuade and his companions found Trent Putnam. He lay belly-down, and four arrows had been driven deep into his back. His scalp and pistol belt were missing.

"God," said Will, "what a grisly sight. We should have brought a shovel and buried him here, so the others won't have to look at him."

"I want the others to have a damned good look at him," McQuade said. "We'll bury him outside the wagon circle. While he was a damn fool, he was a human being, and we'll do what's fittin' and proper."

"You're right," said Cal. "I just hope the Almighty thinks more highly of him than I did. I wonder how Selma's goin' to take this?"

"Not too well," McQuade said, "but she'll attend the burying, if I have to personally hog-tie and drag her there."

"What about Putnam's wagon?" Will asked. "There was just him and Selma, and I got my doubts that she knows one end of a mule from another."

"I share those doubts," said McQuade, "but I won't be surprised if Andrew Burke's youngest ends up with that wagon."

"And with Selma," Cal added. "By God, the two deserve one another. I hope she deals him the same busted flush she handed old Putnam."

McQuade broke off the shafts of the arrows, and they hoisted Putnam belly-down upon the unwilling horse. They reined up some fifty yards from the wagon circle, and the body was removed from the horse.

"Stay here with him, Will," McQuade said. "Cal, get Joel or Tobe, and the two of you bring shovels. While you're digging a grave, I'll tell the others, including the widow."

Mary had told others, and most of the party was awaiting McQuade's return. Selma, of course, wasn't there. Quickly he told them of the unfortunate Putnam's fate.

"A grave is being dug," said McQuade. "We'll hold services in an hour. Maggie, Ellen, Mary, Minerva, I'll want some of you to help prepare the widow Putnam. Do what you feel you must."

"She'll be there," Maggie said grimly. Reaching into her wagon, she came up with one of Ike's wide leather belts.

McQuade led the way to the Putnam wagon, followed by Maggie, Mary, Ellen, Lucy, Minerva, and many other women.

"Selma," said McQuade, "I have bad news. Trent Putnam's dead, killed by Indians. A grave is being dug. We'll have services within the hour. Some of the ladies have come to help you prepare yourself."

"No," Selma wailed, "I don't want to see him. I'm not going. Leave me alone."

McQuade sighed. "That's what I expected. Maggie, it's up to you and as many others as it takes."

From somewhere on her person, Maggie produced a sharp knife. Slashing the pucker string, she opened the rear of the wagon. Wearing only his hat, Luke Burke leaped out and hit the ground running. Selma wore nothing but a look of fury, and began cursing the startled women. But they rose to the occasion. They seized Selma, dragged her out of the wagon, and flopped her belly-down in the mud. With four of them holding her, Maggie began using the belt. The leather on bare skin sounded like gunfire. One, two, three, four times the strap fell, and when McQuade expected Maggie to let up, she did not. Only after a dozen blows did she let up, and then only after Selma's cursing had been replaced with genuine cries of anguish.

"Mary, you and Lucy get in the wagon," Maggie said, "while Ellen, Minerva, and me boost her up to you."

But after Maggie let up with the belt, the weeping Selma became as uncooperative as ever. Allowing her body to go limp, she made it as difficult as possible for the women as they tried to get her back into the wagon. Once they had her in, they dropped her among whatever personal effects happened to be in the way.

"Mary," said Maggie, "take that big wooden bucket from my wagon, fill it with water, and bring it."

"Cold water?"

"The colder the better," Maggie said. "We'll cool this little catamount down some, as we're washing the mud off her."

"No," Selma shouted, thrashing and kicking.

"We'll either wash you or drown you," said Maggie. "Your choice."

McQuade went with Mary, and since the bucket was large, he took it to one of the wet-weather streams and filled it. Mary following, he returned to the Putnam wagon.

"Here's the water, Maggie," said McQuade. "Where do you want it?"

Before Maggie could respond, Selma came up off the

wagon floor, kicking, scratching, and clawing. Maggie stunned her with a knee to her stomach and slammed a fist into her jaw. She sat down abruptly. There was nobody else in the wagon except Maggie, and she seized the bucket of water McQuade was offering. She then drenched Selma from head to toe.

"There," said Maggie, with satisfaction, "you're clean enough for the burying. Then if you want to go back to being a pig, see if I care."

None of them had ever seen anything like it, and their curiosity overcame any sense of impropriety. Somehow, the determined women managed to get a long dress on the troublesome Selma, although she wore nothing else. Maggie had scratches on her arms and face, and was wet and muddy. McQuade helped her down from the wagon's tailgate, and she spoke to the other women.

"Now I have to make myself presentable. Some of you stay here and see that she don't take off that dress. God knows, we've all seen enough of her without it."

"I'll go and see if the grave's ready," said McQuade.

Ike sat on the wagon box, grinning as Maggie approached.

"What are you grinnin' at, you old varmint?"

"You," said Ike. "You look like you been wrasslin' a pig in a briar patch."

"I have," Maggie said, "but for the briar patch. This pig has claws."

"That woman don't even come close to bein' worth the trouble she's caused," said Ike. "Why'n hell didn't you just leave her be, and bury Putnam without her?"

"It's not the proper thing to do," Maggie said. "I was tempted to march her down to the grave jaybird naked, but we got to show some respect for the dead."

McQuade found the grave almost ready. He took a shovel and finished it.

"I covered Putnam with a blanket," said Will. "With his scalp gone, he was startin' to draw flies."

"Go ahead and wrap him in the blanket," McQuade

said. "I doubt Selma cares a damn, one way or the other, and there's no use exposing the other women to such a grisly sight, when it serves no good purpose."

McQuade returned to the wagon circle, spreading the word that the service could begin at any time. Maggie emerged from the wagon in a clean dress.

"Ike," said McQuade, "I'll help you, if you want to go."

"Much obliged," Ike replied, "but he wasn't one of my favorite people, and there's no hypocrite in me."

McQuade took the bible from Mary and read the Word over Trent Putnam. Some of the women wept, but Selma wasn't one of them. She stood there in silence, unrepentant, glaring at anyone who chose to look at her. When the short service was concluded, she was the first to leave. None of the Burkes had been present, which in no way surprised McQuade. While Luke Burke's unsavory relationship with Selma Putnam had been anything but proper, there was no law to condemn him. If anybody was to be censured, it had to be Selma, and Maggie Peyton had seen to that. But McQuade wasn't satisfied to have Luke Burke get off scot free, and he wasted no time in visiting the Burke wagon.

"Well, by God," said Andrew, in mock surprise, "two visits from McQuade in a single day. Now that beats a goose a-gobblin'."

"You know why I'm here, Andrew," McQuade said, "and you don't have to cover for Luke. Everybody saw him leave the Putnam wagon, wearin' only his hat."

Andrew laughed. "You purely got to admire that boy. There's just somethin' about him the women can't leave alone. Takes after his daddy."

"Too bad his daddy didn't have the brains to teach him not to trifle with a married woman," said McQuade.

"Watch your mouth, McQuade. I could take offense. Besides, I hear the woman in question ain't married no more. She's anybody's game, and I expect old Luke will be callin' on her regular, so don't go gettin' your nose out of joint."

McQuade turned away in disgust. What was the point in hounding the old devil about his wayward sons, when he obviously was proud of having taught them all they knew? All he had gained during this trying day was the knowledge that the Kiowa were still within striking distance. With that in mind, he made an announcement just before supper.

"I don't believe that was a coincidence, those Kiowa being there to grab Putnam. They obviously have scouts keeping an eye on us, so this is no time to let down our guard. We will continue with a double watch until we're out of Indian Territory."

"Then we'll be in Comanche territory," said Will Haymes.

"If the Comanches prove as troublesome as the Kiowa," McQuade said, "then we'll stay with our double watch all the way to the Rio Colorado."

Supper over, McQuade and Mary had reached their wagon, before she found a private moment to speak to him.

"Luke Burke is back in Selma Putnam's wagon," she confided.

"How do you know?"

"Ellen Warnell saw him," said Mary, "and he didn't come out. The pucker string has been replaced, so nobody can see in."

"Damn it," McQuade said, "I've had enough of that woman. Putnam's dead, and if she wants to wallow around with Luke Burke, I don't care. I've known whores who were more respectable than she is."

"Really? Tell me about them."

"Oh, hell," said McQuade, "don't take everything I say literally. I said I've known some. I didn't say I'd known them professionally."

She laughed, and he relaxed.

*   *   *

At breakfast, there was no sign of anyone around the Putnam wagon, and McQuade was reminded of something. With Putnam dead, who was going to handle the teams? There was virtually no possibility that Selma Putnam could, and with that in mind, McQuade went to the wagon and slapped the canvas.

"Leave me alone," Selma shouted.

"This is McQuade, and we'll be taking the trail in a few minutes. Are you coming with us, or staying here with this wagon?"

"The wagon will be ready to go when you are," she said. "Now leave me alone."

McQuade said no more, and when it was time to take the trail, Luke Burke held the reins of the team, while Selma sat beside him on the box of the Putnam wagon. Some of the other women eyed her in disgust, including Mary, who handled her own teams with the best of the men. McQuade rode ahead, looking for sign, for the ground was still soft from the recent rain. Maggie Peyton handled her teams expertly. Ike sat beside her, his splinted leg stretched out, a Sharps .50 beside him. Although Gunter Warnell's left arm had been splinted, he managed the reins with his right hand. McQuade rode past the Jackman, Odell, and Phelps wagons, tipping his hat. Bess, Winnie, and Callie rode the wagon boxes with their splinted arms and legs. They must move on.

Hedgepith's wagons followed, every eye on the newly made grave, as they passed the place where McQuade's wagon circle had been the night before.

"Somebody got busted up pretty bad," Slack observed.

"I doubt that happened during the stampede," said Creeker. "I'd not be surprised if we're bein' stalked by the Kiowa."

Hedgepith had given no conflicting orders, and while Creeker and four men rode ahead of the wagons, the other five riders followed, their eyes on the back-trail. While Doctor Puckett still shared a wagon with Hedgepith, the two communicated less and less. Savage and Presnall had been strangely quiet, while the seven women had kept strictly to themselves. Ampersand, the cook, had said virtually nothing to anyone since Hook's murder. A bond of sorts had been forged between Creeker, his companions and the teamsters, after their successful defense against the attacking Kiowa. They no longer looked to Hedgepith, but relied upon themselves, while all Hook's fallen women had forsaken whorehouses and saloons for a new life in Texas.

McQuade rode cautiously, but found no Indian sign. Most of the wet-weather streams had dried up, and it became necessary to seek water, where there was graze, and a suitable place to circle the wagons for the night. They had lost time, and McQuade wanted to cover as many miles as possible, so he stretched his ride to what he believed was fifteen miles. There was a deep, clear creek, good graze, and a suitable clearing for the wagons. After searching the surrounding area for Indian sign, McQuade watered his horse and rode back to meet the wagons.

Gid Sutton had sent Withers to report on the progress of McQuade's wagons and the nearness of Hedgepith's supply train. Withers rode in at suppertime, and after unsaddling his horse, went to Sutton's tent.

"They must of had some teams stampede durin' the storm," said Withers. "They been patchin' up wagons and people."

"But they're movin' again?" Sutton asked.

"Yeah," said Withers. "They'll make a good fifteen miles today."

"Five more days," Sutton predicted, "and they'll be crossin' the Red. With the wagon we got, it'll take us maybe four days to catch up to them. We'll pull out tomorrow."

"Any more men show up while I was gone?"

"Yeah," said Sutton. "There'll be eighty-five of us.

I'll give 'em all the word right after supper.''

Sutton waited until the outlaws were down to final cups of coffee before telling them of his plans.

"There's two wagon trains," Sutton said, "and they'll be crossin' the Red maybe five days from now. The smallest one—fifteen wagons—is the one we want. There's a fortune in trade goods, with only twenty-five fighting men, includin' the teamsters.''

"What about the other train?'' a newcomer shouted.

"They're usually a day ahead,'' said Sutton. "We'll take the wagons we want, and if the bunch that's ahead is fool enough to buy in, we'll pay 'em off in lead.''

"Just how many wagons is in this bigger train?'' somebody asked.

"More than a hundred,'' said Sutton, "and there's pretty women, too.''

"Hell,'' one of the new arrivals bawled, "let's take all the damn wagons, the women, and any gold we can find.''

There was a roar of approval that was near unanimous, and Gid Sutton grinned at his five surviving friends. When the shouting had diminished, he spoke.

"You're gettin' ahead of me,'' he said. "We'll take the supply wagons first. When them that's in the wagons ahead hears the shootin', at least some of 'em will ride like hell along the back-trail. Half of us will be waitin' for 'em, while the rest rides on ahead and guns down them that's stayed with the wagons that's ahead.''

Again they roared their approval, and Sutton said no more. Not only was revenge within his grasp, but untold riches as well.

CHAPTER 13

McQuade again chose a creek with graze, and the teams were being unhitched when a wagon topped a ridge half a mile to the southwest. They watched in amazement as eleven more wagons followed.

"Where'n hell are they goin'?" Will Haymes wondered.

"Back the way we've come," said McQuade. "The question is, why?"

"We'll soon know," Levi Phelps said. "They've seen us."

McQuade and many of the other men waited outside the wagon circle as the wagons came on. Reining up their teams, the first two men stepped down from their wagon boxes and came to meet McQuade and his companions.

"I'm Grady Stern," said one of the men, "and this is Tom Shadley."

"I'm Chance McQuade, wagon boss for this outfit. Why don't you folks have supper with us? We're bound for the Rio Colorado, and we'd like to talk to you about the trail ahead."

"Yeah," said Gunter Warnell, "are you familiar with the land grants there?"

"I reckon," Shadley replied. "We just give ours up, and we're goin' back to where we come from."

"Save it until after supper," said McQuade. "You folks must be hungry."

"God, you can't imagine how hungry," Stern said. "Ever'thing comin' into Texas has to be wagoned in from New Orleans, and the damn Comanches is thick as fleas on a dog's behind. We ain't had flour, sugar, coffee, or bacon in a year, and our stock is near starved for grain."

"Circle your wagons and join us for supper," said McQuade.

McQuade returned to the wagon circle and found the rest of the party waiting. "We have a dozen families for supper," McQuade announced, "and they're going to tell us what we can expect on the Rio Colorado."

"From what I've heard," said Isaac McDaniel, "we might want to follow 'em back to St. Louis."

"Isaac," McQuade said, "let's wait until we've heard the rest of the story before we make any decisions."

Seven of the newly arrived families had children in their teens, and there were entirely too many in Mc-Quade's party for introductions. The heads of the twelve families stood and gave their family names, and without further delay, they had supper. Some of the women wept when they saw the food, the hot coffee, the sugar. When supper was over, Grady Stern stood up.

"I reckon me and Tom can talk for everybody. What would you all be wantin' to know?"

"First," said McQuade, "we'd be mighty interested in knowin' why you gave up your land grants, after enduring so much just to claim them."

"There's war comin'," Stern said. "War with Mexico."

"How would that have affected you?" Will Haymes asked.

"We all had to take an oath of allegiance to Mexico," said Stern. "When war comes, we would be expected to join the Mexican army."

"Against who?" McQuade asked.

"Against Sam Houston's militia," said Stern. "There's

thousands of Texans who refuse to bow to the Mexican government. They've claimed land since Spain claimed Texas, and after the Alamo, they stomped hell out of Santa Anna's soldiers at San Jacinto. Houston and his bunch is plannin' a town in the bend of the Colorado, and they aim for it to become the capital of the Republic of Texas.''*

"Instead of deserting your grants," said McQuade, "why didn't you tell the Mexicans what they wanted to hear, and then join forces with Sam Houston? The future of Texas is with the United States, not Mexico.''

"Maybe so," said Tom Shadley, "but the Mexicans are in control. Miguel Monclova and fifty fighting men have been dispatched by Santa Anna himself. They made life hell for us. They took away my boy and Grady's, and we don't know if they're alive or dead.''

"These are Mexican soldiers?'' McQuade asked.

"Not so's you'd know it," said Shadley. "They dress like renegades and outlaws, but Monclova claims they have the power of the Mexican government behind them, and we had no way of knowing if they spoke the truth.''

"They mistreated our women and dared us to stand up to them," Stern said. "They ruined Andy Snider's daughter, and when Andy called their hand, they rode in one night and gunned down Andy and his woman. That's when the rest of us decided to quit while we was ahead.''

"Is everybody in the Texas Colony of the same mind?'' McQuade asked.

"No," said Stern, "but them that's left ain't workin' their grants. They've all set up camp near that town that's bein' laid out in the bend of the Rio Colorado. They've sworn to keep their grants, even if they have to fight Mexico, and Sam Houston's promised them they can, when Texas is granted statehood.''

---

*The town, originally named Waterloo, was founded in 1838. The name was changed to honor Stephen Austin, Father of Texas. Austin became the state capital in 1850.

"But you didn't want to wait for that," McQuade said.

"No," said Shadley, "because we don't know when it's comin', if ever, and neither does old Sam. What good is land, if a man can't work it? Them that ain't givin' up is all settin' on their hunkers half-starved, not knowin' if it'll be a month, a year, or ten years."

"The important thing," McQuade said, "is that there is organized opposition to these men who claim to represent the Mexican government. If Houston is successful in this fight against Mexico, what's going to become of the Texas Colony, of the land grants?"

"Houston believes he has the answer to that," said Stern. "When Texas is granted statehood—if that ever happens—Sam has promised to go to Washington on behalf of all who have received Mexican grants. He claims the State of Texas will recognize every one of the grants."

"That's a strong promise," said Gunter Warnell. "How many of those who have taken Mexican grants have remained with Houston?"

"Near two hundred," Stern replied.

"You folks stayed with your grants, then," said McQuade, "instead of joining Houston and the rest."

"Why, hell, yes," Shadley said angrily. "We took oaths of loyalty to the Mexican government. We played by their rules, and then Monclova and his bunch treated us like dogs."

"When they made life intolerable for you," said Will Haymes, "why didn't all of you join Houston's militia and fight?"

"None of us are young men," Stern said, "and we don't have the years it might take to own our grants free and clear of the Mexican government. Miguel Monclova has already threatened Mexican soldiers, if families don't desert Sam Houston's camp and return to their grants. We wasn't told when we went to Texas we'd have our families torn apart, that we might have to fight Mexico, that we might die for a piece of ground."

"We all decided the price was more than we was willin' to pay," said Shadley.

"There's another party behind us," McQuade said. "They have plans to build a town on the Rio Colorado, and have the goods necessary to stock a trading post. I hope you'll tell them what you've told us."

Shadley laughed bitterly. "They'll play hell buildin' anything, least of all a tradin' post. Monclova and his bunch will strip them like locusts. Maybe we can trade 'em some advice for some grub."

Stern, Shadley and the others returned to their wagons, leaving McQuade's camp in a somber, doubtful mood.

"It appears there's just a hell of a lot we wasn't told, when we signed on with Rufus Hook," said Ike Peyton. "Question is, where do we go from here?"

"We go on to Texas," McQuade said. "What I told them, I believe. The future of Texas lies not with Mexico, but with the United States of America. All of you heard what they said. They stuck with their grants, trying to work the land, when they should have followed the others, joining Houston's militia."

"You believe we shouldn't try to claim the grants, then," said Tobe Rutledge, "but go on and throw in with Sam Houston."

"That's exactly what I believe," McQuade replied. "If there's going to be trouble with Mexico, there won't be any peace for any of us until Texas comes into its own. And that must come by overthrowing Mexican rule. I realize all we've heard has been secondhand, but I don't doubt what these people have told us. This is the frontier, and there's more at stake here than these promised land grants. Not only do we have the opportunity to make a place for ourselves, but to become a part of something grand, the building of the West."

"Hell, McQuade," said Oscar Odell, "we'll leave Sam Houston in Texas to fight the Mexicans and send *you* to Washington."

That drew laughter and they all got into the spirit of the thing.

"McQuade," said Cal Tabor, "suppose we all decided to turn around and go back to St. Louis. What would you do?"

"I'd go on to Texas, join Sam Houston's militia, and eventually claim my land grant," McQuade said. "Now that we're on the subject, how many of you aim to turn around and go back?"

"I got nothin' to go back to," said Ike Peyton. "The long shots are the ones that pay off big."

"That's how I see it," Gunter Warnell said. "I'm goin' on."

One by one, they vowed to go on. Even the Burkes were enthusiastic. When McQuade and Mary retired to their wagon, she spoke.

"I've never been more proud of you than I was tonight. These people were shocked at what they heard, they needed a sense of direction, and you gave it to them. Father would have loved it."

"I only told them what I believe," said McQuade. "Anything worth having is worth fighting for, and once Texas becomes a state, there's no reason the land grants shouldn't be honored. It's a big land, and somebody has to settle it. Why not those of us who fought for it?"

At first light, McQuade's wagons took the trail to the southwest, while the returning wagons rolled away to the northeast. Leading his own train, Hedgepith was the first to see the wagons coming. Reining up his team, he stepped down. The rest of his wagons came to a stop. Creeker, Groat, Porto, Dirk, and Nall—the outriders at the front of the train—all rode ahead and joined Hedgepith.

"Where are you people bound?" Hedgepith demanded.

"St. Louis," said Grady Stern. "We hear yours is a supply train. Can you spare us some grub?"

"No," Hedgepith said shortly.

"Take it on to Texas, then," said Shadley, "and let the Mexicans take it away from you."

"What are you talking about?" Hedgepith demanded.

"You'll find out when you get there," said Stern. "We'll be as generous to you as you been to us."

"Hedgepith," Creeker said, "swap these people some supplies in return for what they can tell us about the Texas Colony and the land grants."

"What *can* you tell us about the Texas Colony and the land grants?" Hedgepith asked suspiciously.

"Plenty," said Shadley. "We just come from there."

Hedgepith reached a decision. Most of the teamsters had come forward to see what was causing the delay, and it was to them that Hedgepith spoke.

"Slaughter, Hansard, Weatherly, and Baker, see that these people in the wagons ahead of us are given adequate portions of bacon, beans, and coffee."

"You got a wagonload of hams," said Groat helpfully.

"Some hams, as well," Hedgepith said, his hate-filled eyes on the grinning Groat.

Stern and Shadley were in no hurry, waiting until the teamsters brought the sacks of supplies from their wagons. By then, Creeker and all his men, as well as the teamsters, had gathered to hear what Stern and Shadley had to say. They told the same grim story that McQuade and his party had heard the night before.

"Why, that's . . . that's impossible," Hedgepith exploded. "I have papers, deeds . . ."

Shadley laughed. "So did we, but Miguel Monclova has fifty men, all armed to the teeth, and they got more comin'. The only chance you got is to throw in with Houston's militia and ride out the storm. God help you if Monclova finds out you got all these wagonloads of goods, before you reach Houston's camp."

"What else?" Hedgepith pleaded. "What else can you tell me?"

"Nothin'," said Stern. "That's the truth of it, just like

we told all them folks in the wagons ahead of you.''

"You told them?'' Hedgepith asked. "What are their plans?''

"They didn't tell us, and we didn't ask,'' said Shadley, "but as we was hitchin' up to come thisaway, they went on toward the Red, and Texas.''

Creeker, his men, and the teamsters laughed, appreciating the look on Hedgepith's face. Shadley, Stern, and their companions mounted their wagon boxes and guided their teams around Hedgepith's wagons. Hedgepith, suddenly aware that he apparently was the butt of a joke, turned on them in a fury.

"Damn it, you men get back to your wagons. Creeker, you and your men return to your positions behind and ahead of the train.''

"Five of us are already in position,'' said Creeker mildly.

"You know what I meant,'' Hedgepith shouted. "Don't get smart with me.''

"Yes, suh,'' said Creeker insolently. "I mean no, suh. Sorry, suh.''

The wagons took the trail again, Hedgepith not bothering to share whatever was on his mind. The most interesting thing Creeker had learned was that McQuade and his party had been told of the situation in Texas, but had continued on. Creeker again rode out well ahead of the wagons, and Hedgepith was so preoccupied, he didn't even notice. Obviously, he had no intention of telling them how this startling news might affect their own circumstances. As Creeker neared the tag end of McQuade's train, he circled wide, coming out ahead of the caravan. He wanted to talk to McQuade, to get his thoughts on the grim news from Texas.

McQuade had chosen a place with water and graze to circle the wagons for the night and had started back when he saw the horseman coming. He reined up, waiting for

Creeker to reach him. Creeker wasted no time.

"We got the word this morning from that bunch that pulled out, leavin' their grants. Mind you, I ain't askin' for Hedgepith. For the sake of the rest of us, I'd like to know how you see it, and what you aim to do."

"I don't care if Hedgepith knows," said McQuade. "We're going on to Texas, and we will join Sam Houston's bunch. These folks that pulled out made the mistake of trying to work their grants, when they should have joined the opposition until the fate of Texas has been resolved. I believe the future of Texas lies with the United States, not Mexico."

"I'm glad to hear you say that," Creeker replied. "I'm speakin' for twenty-five of us, when I say that we aim to throw in with Houston. Trouble is, I look for Hedgepith to tell us we got to claim our grants or forfeit them. For sure, we can't swear allegiance to the Mexican government if we join Houston and the opposition."

"Swearing allegiance to the Mexican government didn't help these folks that just pulled out," McQuade said, "and it wouldn't help us. While we have no proof these renegades in the company of Miguel Monclova represent the Mexican government, we can't be sure that they don't. I believe our only chance is to join Houston's rebellion and fight for statehood. Somebody's going to settle Texas, and after we've joined the fight for independence, I can't imagine our grants not being honored."

"That's kind of how I see it," said Creeker. "Hedgepith has papers entitling all of us to land, and after this fight with Mexico, who's to stop us from taking the land offered us in the original grants? We might have to kill Hedgepith to get the papers, but I reckon we can do that, if he won't have it any other way."

"He'll have no more authority than the rest of us," McQuade said. "I reckon you got no idea what he aims to do, once he gets there?"

"No," said Creeker. "We're goin' on, but he ain't said

a word about what's to be done when we arrive. Knowin'
him, I look for him to try and strike some kind of deal
with the Mexican government.''

"Then you'll have to break with him," McQuade replied. "I believe Monclova and his bunch will take
Hedgepith's wagons, and all of you will end up fighting
for your lives.''

"That's about what I expect," said Creeker. "I'll talk
to the men in Hedgepith's party, and get back to you. If
he insists on us claiming our grants in the face of trouble
with the Mexican government, we'll split with him and
join your outfit, if we're welcome.''

"You'll be welcome," McQuade replied. "If Hedgepith is smart enough to lay off these grants until Houston's
militia takes hold, we'll all be in a better position.''

Creeker and McQuade rode together until they met
McQuade's wagons. Creeker then rode on, returning to
his own party. Although Hedgepith hadn't seen him riding
away, he was fully aware of Creeker's return. When he
beckoned, Creeker turned his horse, riding alongside the
wagon.

"Where have you been?" Hedgepith demanded.

"Riding the trail ahead," said Creeker.

"Would your interest in the trail ahead have anything
to do with McQuade's party?''

"I don't consider that any of your business," Creeker
said.

"While you're working for me, anything you do is my
business," said Hedgepith.

"The situation in Texas bein' what it is," Creeker said,
"we got the right to know who you're goin' to deal with.
Will it be the Mexican government, or Sam Houston's
militia?''

"You were promised wages and a land grant," said
Hedgepith angrily, "and that in no way entitles you to
question my judgment.''

"Wrong," Creeker said, his eyes cold, his voice hard.
"Every man of us is entitled to question anything you say

or do, when there's a chance we'll be hung from the same limb as you. Now do you aim to join forces with Sam Houston's militia, or will you cozy up to Monclova and try to settle on those grants?''

''Why don't you just wait until we reach the Rio Colorado and find out?'' Hedgepith said, with a humorless smile.

''I don't have to wait,'' said Creeker. ''I already know.''

Hedgepith said nothing more, and Creeker rode on ahead of the wagons, catching up to Groat, Porto, Dirk, and Nall. They looked at him questioningly.

''McQuade's bunch is goin' on to Texas,'' Creeker said, ''but they're throwin' in with Houston's militia. They believe the Mexicans will pluck Hedgepith like a Christmas goose, and then gun us all down like dogs.''

''By God, they've got the straight of it,'' said Rucker. ''I know damn well Hedgepith is goin' to deal with them Mexicans. Run the Mexicans out, and we'll be dealin' with Texans. Hedgepith won't be the tall dog in the brass collar no more.''

''All the more reason to throw in with Houston,'' Groat said. ''I ain't never trusted that varmint, Hedgepith, and it's soundin' like him and them Mexicans is all of the same stripe.''

Most of McQuade's party was aware that Creeker had ridden ahead to meet McQuade, and when he returned, the men stopped to rest their teams. Obviously, they wished to know what news Creeker might have brought regarding Hedgepith's reaction to the dozen families who had forsaken their grants in Texas. McQuade didn't disappoint them.

''I was afraid of that,'' Ike Peyton said. ''Hedgepith won't care a damn about anything except gettin' his hands on them grants.''

''Yeah,'' said Isaac McDaniel. ''He'll waltz in amongst them Mexicans, and we'll end up in the same briar patch as them folks that give up and pulled out."

"No," McQuade said. "Before Hedgepith has a chance to involve us with the Mexican government, we'll make contact with Sam Houston's militia. The twenty-five men in Hedgepith's party are of the same mind, accordin' to Creeker. That means they'll quit Hedgepith cold, and go with us, leavin' Hedgepith's wagons without teamsters."

"Then you aim for some of us to ride south and talk to Sam Houston before we have to commit ourselves to anybody," said Will Haymes.

"That's what I have in mind," McQuade said. "While I'm not doubting the word of the families who pulled out, I want to know, firsthand, what lies ahead of us. After we cross the Red, we'll be maybe two hundred and seventy-five miles from the Rio Colorado. As I see it, we can circle the wagons a hundred miles out, and three or four of us can continue on horseback. We need to know where this Miguel Monclova and his bunch are roosting."

"Won't hurt none if we can get our wagons near Houston's camp, before that Mexican outfit knows what we're up to," said Tobe Rutledge.

"That's what I have in mind," McQuade replied. "We want those grants, but we can't allow Hedgepith—with Monclova's help—to force us to accept them under Mexican rule. Not with the possibility of a war with Mexico. Two weeks after we cross the Red, we'll circle the wagons and ride south to find Sam Houston's outfit."

"If Hedgepith goes ahead," said Bud Jackman, "he could have Monclova's bunch after us before we can join Sam Houston's opposition."

"I'll be talkin' to Creeker again," McQuade said. "We'll stop Hedgepith, if we have to hog-tie him and post a guard."

Gid Sutton listened as Taylor reported what he had seen while scouting the progress of the Hedgepith and McQuade parties.

"Twelve wagons, there was," Taylor said. "They was headed northeast, back the way them Texas-bound wagons just come. What do you make of that?"

"How should I know?" Sutton growled. "Maybe Texas wasn't all it's cracked up to be. What about McQuade's bunch, and that supply train follerin' him?"

"They're goin' on," said Taylor.

"That's all that concerns us," Sutton replied. "Once they're across the Red, they're our meat."

Many of the renegades had gathered around, and Doolin, one of the newcomers, said what was on the minds of many of them.

"We heard plenty of talk about takin' over this supply train, but we ain't heard much about how it's to be divvied up. What's in it fer me?"

"We won't know what's in it for any of us," said Sutton, "until we take it and learn what's there. Until then, you'll have to take my word that it'll be worth the risk."

"I don't like takin' anybody's word, when there's a chance of havin' my ears shot off," Doolin said. "If I'm goin' to shoot an' be shot at, then I got to know it's worth the risk before I jump in."

There were shouts of agreement from some of the others, and Sutton hauled them up short with an angry response.

"By God, any of you that wants out, get out. Saddle up and ride. I won't have any of you chowin' down on my grub or guzzlin' my coffee an' whiskey. Just don't forget there's law to the north, east, an' west, an' not a damn thing to the south but that wagon train."

"That law would welcome some of you with a rope," said Taylor, his eyes on Doolin.

"You got a point," said an outlaw who had sided with Doolin. "Reckon I'll stick."

"Me too," Doolin said sheepishly. "I just want to know I ain't riskin' bein' gunned down on a wild goose chase."

"Some of them wagons is loaded with barreled whiskey," said Sutton. "It's worth its weight in gold, to the Comanches."

"God," Doolin said, "you'd sell whiskey to the Comanches?"

"I'd sell my own mother to the Comanches, if the price was right, an' it was paid in gold," said Sutton. "It'd hurt my feelings somethin' fierce, if I thought you disapproved."

Doolin said nothing, but he and many of the newcomers eyed Gid Sutton with a new understanding. He would sell them out or double-cross them at the drop of a hat, and he would drop the hat himself.

Creeker and the twenty-four men who had thrown in with him had reached unanimous agreement. They would desert Hedgepith and join Sam Houston's militia, even at the risk of forfeiting the promised grants. The teamsters were particularly angered by Hedgepith's continued silence as to his intentions.

"Damn him," said Slaughter, "he'd lead us all right in amongst them Mexican coyotes, without us havin' a say. I reckon we'd better shanghai this outfit, long before we reach the Rio Colorado."

"Yeah," Weatherly said. "All we got to do is grab Hedgepith and them gamblin' slicks, Hiram Savage and Snakehead Presnall. Doctor Puckett won't stand in our way."

"We'll wait a while," said Creeker. "I aim to ride south with McQuade when he goes to meet with Sam Houston and the militia. If by then, Hedgepith ain't told us what he aims to do, we'll have to take over. For sure, while we're looking for Houston's militia, we can't risk having Hedgepith warn Miguel Monclova and his bunch. Grants or not, I reckon they'd gun us down, rather than have us join the Texas rebellion."

* * *

Chance McQuade had again ridden ahead, and he reined up on the north bank of a fast-flowing river. It had to be the Red, and when the wagons reached it, they would be within two hundred and seventy-five miles of their destination. Mentally, McQuade ticked off the days until he and some of the men would ride south, seeking Sam Houston's militia. Just twelve days, at fifteen miles a day, provided there were no delays. Elated, McQuade rode back to meet the oncoming wagons, to tell them they were about to enter the Republic of Texas . . .

CHAPTER 14

∽

Red River. July 2, 1837.

"*F*or sure, we ain't gonna make that deadline Hook set," said Gunter Warnell, when the wagons had been circled on the north bank of the river.

"I doubt Hedgepith will try to enforce any of Hook's rules," McQuade replied. "None of that will matter, if Texas declares and wins its freedom from Mexico."

"The sooner we can make contact with Houston, the better I'll like it," said Joel Hanby. "Way it is now, we got nothin' we can tie to. We're sure we can't trust Hedgepith and the Mexican government, and all we know about Sam Houston's militia is secondhand. I purely don't like not knowin' where I stand."

"Neither do I," McQuade said, "but I want to be a little closer before we ride south to find Houston's militia. I'm figurin' another twelve days at fifteen miles a day. Then we'll circle the wagons and go looking for Houston."

"Who you aimin' to take with you?" Bud Jackman asked.

"One man from our outfit, and maybe Creeker, from Hedgepith's," said McQuade.

"Hedgepith will know we're up to something," Cal Tabor said.

"He'll know anyway, when we circle the wagons and stay put," said McQuade. "I think by then it won't matter what Hedgepith knows or doesn't know. With all his men prepared to quit, what can he do?"

"He can track down this Miguel Monclova and his bunch, and bring them after us," Eli Bibb said.

"With the men Creeker's promised, there'll be more than a hundred and forty of us," said McQuade. "The odds are in our favor."

Despite all the uncertainty, enthusiasm ran high. On occasion, the Burkes actually spoke to McQuade without hostility.

"Everybody trusts you," Mary said, "and I'm proud of that, but I just wish it was all over, that we had our grants and there was no trouble with Mexico."

"So do I," said McQuade, "but if there's fighting to be done, I'm for gettin' on with it. The sooner this conflict with Mexico has been resolved, the sooner we can get on with our lives."

"We don't actually *know* there's trouble with the Mexican government," she said hopefully. "All we have is the word of those families who pulled out."

"I don't doubt them for a minute," said McQuade. "After all the hardships of reaching Texas, I can't believe they'd turn tail and run without a good reason."

"I suppose war with Mexico would be a good reason," she sighed.

McQuade laughed. "Come on, get in the wagon. We'll fight if and when we have to. I have other plans for tonight. At least, until I go on watch at midnight."

Hedgepith's wagons approached the Red half a mile west of McQuade's wagon circle, and Hedgepith still had said nothing about what he intended to do. During supper, Doctor Puckett approached Hedgepith, who looked at him questioningly.

"Mr. Hedgepith, in light of what we learned from those people who had given up their grants and left Texas, I believe we are entitled to know what you have in mind."

"In regard to what?" Hedgepith growled.

"You know what," said Puckett. "Do you still intend to claim those land grants from the Mexican government, even if it means taking up arms against the Republic of Texas?"

"Everybody who joined this expedition was told before leaving St. Louis that receiving a grant involved taking an oath of allegiance to the Mexican government," Hedgepith said, "and as far as I'm concerned, nothing has changed. Does that answer your question?"

"It does," said Puckett. Just for a moment, his eyes met those of some of the men who had heard Hedgepith's response, and the doctor saw rebellion. Later, when darkness had fallen, he was approached by Creeker.

"We need to talk, Doc," Creeker said. "After everybody beds down, I'll be on watch."

Puckett said nothing, and Creeker turned away, not wanting Hedgepith to observe his brief conversation with the doctor. Since Creeker didn't know when Puckett might contact him, he asked Lora to remain with the other women during that particular night. Puckett waited until well after midnight. There was moon- and starlight, and Creeker stepped from behind a tree as Puckett approached.

"Take a seat by the tree, Doc," said Creeker. "We can see anybody comin', long before they can see us."

Puckett sat down and Creeker hunkered beside him. Wasting no time, Puckett spoke.

"I get the impression most of you don't trust Mr. Hedgepith."

Creeker laughed softly. "We don't. Do you?"

"Frankly, no," said Puckett, "but he has the bit in his teeth. What do you intend to do about him?"

"Nothing," Creeker replied. "We just don't aim to follow him into a hole where we'll have to fight our way out."

"So you intend to break with him. When?"

"I've gone as far as I aim to, until I know where you stand," said Creeker. "I want your word that nothin' I say will get back to Hedgepith."

"You have it," Puckett said.

"We believe—and I'm speaking for twenty-five of us—that our chances are better with Sam Houston's militia and the Republic of Texas, than with the Mexican government," said Creeker.

"I'm inclined to agree," Puckett replied. "When will you make the break?"

"When McQuade and his party does," said Creeker. "Somewhere beyond the Red, they aim to circle their wagons. McQuade plans to ride south in search of Houston's militia, and I aim to ride with him. Once the problem with Mexico is settled, even if it's war, we're countin' on the Republic of Texas to honor our land grants."

"I see no reason why they wouldn't," said Puckett. "I can't see Texas forgetting those who help her fight for independence."

"That's how McQuade sees it," Creeker said. "He believes the future of Texas is with the United States, not Mexico. We feel the same way."

"Mr. McQuade is a far-sighted young man," said Puckett. "You may tell him that I'll be going with the rest of you, when the time comes. Have you thought of what is to become of these women?"

"We have," Creeker said. "They're all spoken for, and not one for the purpose Hook intended. Everybody will be accounted for except that pair of slick-dealing gamblers, old Ampersand, and Hedgepith himself."

"That will leave Hedgepith with fifteen wagons and no teamsters," said Puckett. "What can he do, except go along with the rest of us?"

"He can track down this Miguel Monclova," Creeker said, "if he's that big a fool. You know Monclova can provide the necessary teamsters. You should also know that as soon as he gets control of those wagons, Hedgepith is a dead man."

"I'd have to agree with you," said Puckett, "no more than I know. But if Monclova is the tyrant he appears to be, we still need more than secondhand information about Sam Houston's militia and the proposed rebellion. I suppose this is what McQuade has in mind."

"It is," Creeker replied. "He wants to know how solid Houston is, and that he'll stay with us to the finish. McQuade's careful, playin' his cards close, and I admire that."

"So do I," said Puckett, "and if Houston stands as tall as we think he does, then we'll do well to join forces with him. Imagine what these wagonloads of supplies would mean to those Texans, so far from civilization, forced to fight the Mexican army."

"I haven't thought that far ahead," Creeker replied, "but it could mean the difference between victory and defeat for Houston's bunch. It don't seem far-fetched, when you know that Monclova and his gang will kill Hedgepith and take it all."

"I believe McQuade should make Houston aware of these supplies," said Puckett. "I'd say this militia is hard-pressed to purchase anything, without a fight with Monclova. The nearest source of goods would be New Orleans, while we have fifteen wagonloads within perhaps three weeks of Houston's camp."

Creeker laughed softly. "You'll do, Doc. I'll speak to McQuade about this, telling him you suggested it. We'll talk again after we've crossed the Red."

In a bend of the Colorado River, some forty-five miles northwest of Sam Houston's camp, Miguel Monclova had established a headquarters. There he was involved in a heated discussion with his two trusted lieutenants, Pedro Mendez and Hidalgo Cortez.

"I do not believe we should have allowed the *americanos* to go," Mendez argued.

"Nor do I," said Cortez.

"They are of no use to us," Monclova said. "It is a simple thing to sit within the halls of government in Mexico City and devise oaths of allegiance, and quite another to enforce them, when the *Tejanos* and *Americanos* are hundreds of miles away. They take our oaths because they want our land, but when it comes to the saber and the *pistola*, they turn on us. Now tell me of the *Tejano*, the Señor Houston and his *milicia*."

Pedro Mendez laughed. "The *caravana* for which he waits does not come. Per'ap he and his *Tejanos*, they fight on empty bellies, no?"

"*Por Dios*, we have only to wait," said Monclova. "Time and hunger favor us."

"But Mexico City does not," said Cortez.

"It does not matter," Monclova said. "Our orders come from General Santa Ana himself, and he does not choose to honor the grants negotiated by the Señor Stephen Austin. The general sees the grants only as a means to an end. The *Tejanos* and *Americanos* swear allegiance to Mexico, and when their numbers are great enough, they make war with us for their independence. We will starve out as many as we can, and those who remain will be shot down like the dogs they are. We will rid ourselves of them before the falling of the leaves."

The third day of July, McQuade's wagons crossed the Red, into Texas. The Hedgepith wagons followed. At that point, McQuade rode almost due south. They were in Comanche country, and the trail ahead must be scouted carefully. McQuade wasn't that familiar with the water in Texas, and the distances between good water might have some bearing on the miles they must travel each day. When McQuade finally found a good stream, it was much farther than the wagons usually traveled. But they had no choice, and as McQuade returned to meet the wagons, a horseman rode out ahead of him. Recognizing Creeker, McQuade rode on.

"I reckoned it was time we talk again," Creeker said, "seein' as how we're in Texas. I spent some time with Doc Puckett, and he's goin' with us."

"I felt like he would," said McQuade.

"When do you aim to ride south, looking for Sam Houston's militia?"

"Two more weeks," McQuade said. "On a good day, we can cover fifteen miles. Some days, like today, will be longer, since we must have water. I figure we'll circle wagons a hundred miles shy of our destination. From there, we'll ride south. I'll want you with me, representing the men in Hedgepith's party. I think no more than three of us will go, since it's important that we don't attract the attention of Miguel Monclova. We don't know where he is, and we'll have to ride careful."

"With Hedgepith hell-bent on claiming those grants, he could very well find Monclova before we reach Houston's camp," said Creeker. "I think we got to buffalo the varmint with a pistol barrel, hog-tie him, and post a guard, until we're satisfied joining Houston's militia is the thing to do."

"We may be forced to do that," McQuade said, "and anybody else that's inclined to go along with Hedgepith. What about that pair of gamblers, and the cook?"

"I doubt Hiram Savage and Snakehead Presnall have enough guts between 'em to stand up to us. If they try anything foolish, we'll rope them to a tree, along with Hedgepith. As for Ampersand, he'll go along with us. Hedgepith talks down to him."

"We're of the same mind, then," McQuade said. "If anything changes, or if you need help, sound off."

"Thanks," said Creeker.

The two rode together until they could see the oncoming wagons of McQuade's outfit. Creeker then guided his horse into the brush and was gone. McQuade waited for the lead wagons, and then trotted his horse alongside them.

*   *   *

With Houston's militia on the Rio Colorado. July 3, 1837.

Sam Houston sat on the decaying trunk of a wind-blown tree, shifting his cane from one hand to the other. Three of his trusted men—Joshua Hamilton, Stockton Saunders, and Alonzo Holden—had brought unwelcome news regarding an expected wagon train with much-needed supplies.

"We rode all the way to the Red, where she leaves Texas and loops into Arkansas," said Hamilton, "and we waited three days. No sign of any wagons."

"I don't understand it," Houston replied. "I was told our goods would be shipped by steamboat to Little Rock, and wagoned from there."

"Don't make sense," said Saunders. "The whole idea was to avoid Indian Territory, and they still didn't show. What could have happened?"

"I hate to bring this up," Holden said, "but maybe certain parties in St. Louis haven't come through with the support they promised."

Houston sighed. "It's a possibility we must consider."

"Without it, where does that leave us?" Hamilton asked.

"In a perilous position," said Houston. "Ration-wise, we're down to river water and dried beef. In a serious fight with the Mexicans, we'll be using our weapons as clubs."

"One of us could ride to Little Rock, take a steamboat to St. Louis, and maybe learn what the problem is," Saunders said.

"If our backers in St. Louis have let us down, going there won't change anything," said Houston. "Besides, we don't have the time. Monclova has to know we have our backs to the wall."

"We have them outnumbered more than four to one," Hamilton said.

"But they have ammunition," said Holden, "and that gives them an edge."

"For the time being," Houston said, "do not discuss

this situation with the others. I'll speak to them after I've asked for help.''

"Help from who?" Holden asked.

"The Almighty," said Houston.

The day's drive to water was even longer than McQuade had expected. The first stars were twinkling silver in a purple sky, when they circled the wagons and unhitched the teams.

"This is Comanche country," McQuade warned. "Keep the supper fires small and douse them as soon as you can."

McQuade and most of the men took the horses and mules to graze by starlight. Their time would be limited to an hour, and McQuade had already ordered the watch doubled.

"You think the Comanches might attack at night?" Oscar Odell asked.

"It's possible," said McQuade. "I've had no experience with them, but I've known men who have. Some tribes are superstitious, believing that if they die in battle in darkness, their spirits will wander forever. From what I've heard, that's never bothered the Comanches, and we're goin' to take it as gospel."

The fires were doused as soon as the meal was done, and they ate supper by the light of stars. There was quiet jubilation among them, as they prepared to spend this first night in Texas.

Hedgepith's wagons were circled even later than McQuade's, and Creeker cautioned old Ampersand about his cook fire. Creeker turned to find Hedgepith staring at him. He said nothing, however, and Creeker turned away. Later, he saw Hedgepith speaking privately with Hiram Savage and Snakehead Presnall. It was enough to arouse Creeker's curiosity and his suspicion. While on watch, he usually stretched out, head on his saddle. Tonight, however, he dropped his saddle in the shadow of a wagon and positioned his hat in a manner that was deceptive from a distance. He then took cover beneath the wagon itself. An hour passed without any disturbance, and Creeker had begun to wonder if he'd guessed wrong. Suddenly, a dozen yards away, a pistol roared. Once, twice, three times. Two of the slugs slammed into Creeker's saddle, while the third sent his hat spinning. Creeker fired twice at the muzzle flashes, and there was a groan.

"What'n hell's goin' on?" Groat demanded. He was accompanied by most of the others on watch.

"Somebody tried to gun me down," said Creeker, "and I returned the favor."

"Perhaps you have been shooting at shadows," Hedgepith said. "For one who appears concerned about attracting hostile Indians, you are quite careless."

"That shadow took three shots at me," said Creeker. "Why don't we go see if it's got a name?"

Creeker led the way, and when they reached the body, both Groat and Rucker struck matches. Hiram Savage lay on his back, a revolver in his right hand. He had been hit twice in the chest, and was very, very dead.

"Well, now," said Creeker, "what possible reason could this varmint have for wantin' me dead? You got any ideas, Mr. Hedgepith?"

"Of course not," Hedgepith said stiffly. "You seem the kind to make enemies easily. I wouldn't be surprised if you provoked the fight."

Creeker laughed. "Hedgepith, if you're a lawyer, the devil's a mule. The man's pistol has been fired three times. A hombre ain't likely to do that, after takin' two slugs in the chest."

"Why, hell, no," Groat said. "I heard three shots, and then two more. Ellis, have a look at that varmint's pistol, and see how many times it's been fired."

"That won't be necessary," said Hedgepith. "What's done is done."

"Maybe it ain't necessary," Groat said, "but we're goin' to do it."

Several men lighted matches so that Ellis could examine the weapon. Others gathered close as Ellis broke out the cylinder. Two loads remained.

"Satisfied, Mr. Hedgepith?" Creeker asked.

Hedgepith stalked away in silence, furious at the laughter that followed.

"Back to your posts," said Creeker. "We'll bury the varmint in the morning."

They all turned away, nobody doubting that Hiram Savage had died attempting to do as Hedgepith had ordered. Creeker put on his ventilated hat and settled down to the rest of his watch. He saw a shadow flit across a clearing and drew his revolver, relaxing when he recognized Lora. Without a word, she came to him, trembling.

"What is it?" he asked softly.

"I was afraid . . . afraid you . . ."

"I take a lot of killing," he said.

"I hate that man," she said. "God, how I hate him. Can't we leave him?"

"Not yet," said Creeker, "but soon."

"He's trying to kill you, and I'm afraid he will. Please . . . don't wait too long."

"I'll be careful," Creeker said. "Like I was tonight."

The five shots had been heard in McQuade's camp, and the men on watch were contemplating the possible cause.

"Sounded like a hand gun," said Levi Phelps.

"It was," McQuade said, "Two hand guns."

"Five shots," said Cal Tabor. "How do you know they weren't all fired by the same gun?"

"The difference in time between the third and fourth shots," McQuade said. "The fourth shot was like an echo of the third. The fourth and fifth shots were return fire."

"Then it was an ambush that fell through," said Isaac McDaniel. "Ain't many men that could take two or three hits, and then get off two good shots."

"You've got the straight of it," McQuade said. "I'd bet my saddle the *hombre* that cut loose with those first three shots is dead."

"I hope it wasn't one of the gents sidin' with us," said Eli Bibb.

"I reckon we'll know, when Creeker and me talk again," McQuade said. "There has to be trouble brewing in that outfit, and I think what we've just heard is the start of it."

McQuade rode ahead of the wagons as usual, and he wasn't surprised when, as he returned, he was joined by Creeker.

"I reckon you heard the shots last night," Creeker said.

"We did," said McQuade. "Hedgepith's move?"

"After supper, I saw him talking to Savage and Presnall. Usin' my saddle and my hat, I laid a trap, and Savage walked into it."

He supplied no details, for he was alive, and none were necessary.

"Hedgepith sees you as a threat, then," McQuade said. "The leader of a rebellion. Do you think somebody from within your own ranks has been talking?"

"No," said Creeker. "I think Hedgepith is crooked as a shaved deck, but that don't make him stupid. He's seen me ride out often enough to guess I'm making contact with you, and he's got to suspect we have a plan. He knows all about Sam Houston's militia, and if we're going against Hedgepith, that tells him we're favoring Houston."

"You reckon he'll try to contact Miguel Monclova before we have a chance to join Sam Houston's militia?" McQuade asked.

"I'm not sure," Creeker replied. "If he does, that'll mean leaving the wagons and ridin' south, and Hedgepith has nobody to send. That means he'd have to personally go, and I've got my doubts that he's prepared to do that."

"So he tried to solve his problem by gunning down the leader of the opposition."

"That's how I see it," said Creeker, "and he's about run out of men he can count on to do his dirty work."

"There's nobody left but Snakehead Presnall and Hedgepith himself, then," McQuade said.

"That's it," said Creeker. "The rest of us believe Hedgepith aims to use us as pawns to take over those land grants, whatever the cost. If we cut loose from him, we'll lose the wages owed us from St. Louis, but a man's a damn fool to risk his neck for maybe a hundred dollars."

"Don't give up on the wages," McQuade replied. "Before you ride out, take whatever Hedgepith owes you, if you have to pull a gun."

"And have the varmint brand us all as thieves?"

"Small matter," said McQuade. "We'll all be branded a lot worse than that, if we don't take Texas from Mexico."

"You're right," Creeker said. "What we have to do is prevent Hedgepith from reaching Monclova, before we talk to Sam Houston."

"Yes," said McQuade, "and if Hedgepith makes his move before we're ready, it'll be up to you to see that he's stopped in his tracks. Buffalo him with a pistol and hog-tie him, if it's the only way. But if it comes to that, don't waste any time letting me know. We may be forced to contact Houston sooner than we've planned."

The two men parted company shortly before they reached the oncoming wagons. Most of McQuade's outfit sensed a change within Hedgepith's ranks, and they chose this time to rest their teams. Men gathered near the lead wagons, and McQuade didn't disappoint them.

"Hiram Savage is dead," said McQuade. "He went after Creeker last night, and Creeker was forced to shoot him."

"Follerin' Hedgepith's orders," Ike Peyton said.

"That's what Creeker thinks," said McQuade, "and it looks that way to me. Creeker is of a mind that Hedgepith will soon have to make some effort to reach Miguel Monclova, to involve us all with the Mexican government, before we can side with Sam Houston."

"Hell," said Will Haymes, "we can't have that. Let's make our move first."

"We don't have to worry about Hedgepith gettin' ahead of us," McQuade said. "None of the men in Hedgepith's outfit trusts him, and if he makes any move to ride out, he'll be stopped, if it means slugging him with a pistol and binding him hand-and-foot."

"Exceptin' for Hedgepith, I'm startin' to think more highly of that outfit every day," said Joel Hanby.

"Damn right," said a dozen other men.

Their confidence renewed, they mounted their wagon boxes and moved on.

Eighty-five strong, Gid Sutton and his gang reached the Red River.

"We're maybe two days behind 'em," Sutton said. "When we make camp tomorrow night, we'll find where they've bedded down. Then we'll hit 'em at daylight the next day."

"You still aim to take the smaller train first?" Paschal asked.

"I do," said Sutton. "While there may be gold, silver, and women to be had amongst that bigger bunch of wagons, there's fifteen wagonloads of trade goods in that supply train that's follerin' 'em. We'll grab the sure thing first, with the fewest defenders. Then, even if McQuade's bunch comes runnin', we ought to be ready for 'em. Any questions?"

"Yeah," said Withers. "I think we oughta know just how far ahead McQuade's bunch is, before we lay into that supply train. I've seen McQuade's outfit in action, without him, and they fight like the devil and all his angels."

"Withers," Sutton said, "leave the plannin' to me. We got a three-to-one edge agin that supply train. By God, if we can't wipe 'em out before McQuade's bunch can saddle their horses, then we're in the wrong business."

That drew some laughter. They crossed the Red before making camp, and while some of the men got supper underway, Sutton met with Taylor, Vance, and Paschal.

"After supper," said Sutton, "the four of us will ride ahead and find where that supply train is. We'll hit 'em at first light, before they're good awake."

CHAPTER 15

✧

*T*he attack came at dawn, as Creeker and his companions were saddling their horses, and the teamsters were harnessing their teams. The attackers had slipped in on foot from north, south, east, and west. The first shots brought Hedgepith from his tent, Snakehead Presnall at his heels. They became the first to die, allowing the rest of the defenders a few seconds to take cover. Creeker's defense against Indian attacks prevailed, as each man lay flat beneath a wagon and returned fire. Gid Sutton had led the attack from the north, and he quickly fell back, as the four men nearest him were cut down. The firing diminished elsewhere, and Sutton realized his mistake. While this had been a surprise attack, these men were no short horns, and the fight might be of longer duration than he had expected. That brought to mind Withers's suggestion that they determine how near McQuade's outfit was, and he silently cursed himself for not having done so. But it was too late for that. He had to overcome resistance and take this supply train before help could arrive.

"Rush them, damn it," Sutton bawled.

While they had withstood the first attack, the defenders had been hurt. Creeker's upper left arm was bloody. Porto, Quay, and Drum were down, unmoving. Much of the wagon canvas had been torn by lead, and Creeker anxiously eyed the distant wagon where the women were. But he could do nothing. They were surrounded, and it seemed only a matter of time until the attackers rushed them. He couldn't see the rest of his men, and only two or three of the teamsters, but he doubted they could resist another attack. While it seemed they had been under siege for hours, it had been only a few minutes. While he had no doubt McQuade's outfit would hear the gunfire and send help, he wondered if they would be in time. Lead whanged off wagon wheels and kicked up dirt all around him, all the evidence he needed that another attack—perhaps the last—had begun . . .

McQuade was saddling his horse, preparing to scout ahead, when he first heard the rattle of distant gunfire. Others had heard it too.

"Hedgepith's outfit is in trouble," McQuade shouted. "Fifty of you saddle up to ride with me. The rest of you stand fast with your guns ready."

There were more than fifty riders, but McQuade didn't take time to count. He led out at a fast gallop, and there was no longer any sound of gunfire. The Hedgepith outfit wasn't that far away, and McQuade reined up, unsure as to the position of the attackers. Suddenly the gunfire resumed, and McQuade raised his hand, getting the attention of his men.

"From the sound of it," said McQuade, "they're surrounded. Gunter, I want you, Cal, and Will to each choose a dozen men. Gunter, you'll circle around, comin' in from the north. Cal, you'll ride in from the east. Will, you'll come at them from the west. The rest of us will move in from the south. We'll move in close enough to use our revolvers. When you're in position, dismount and advance on foot. Make every shot count."

McQuade and his riders dismounted, moving ahead through underbrush. Again, the gunfire had diminished, but it soon flared up again. Finally McQuade could see the gray of wagon canvas ahead, and between his skirmish line and the wagons, puffs of smoke, as the attackers began another fusillade. McQuade drew his revolver, and his men following his lead, they began firing. Seventeen men died. The three remaining attackers threw down their guns and stumbled to their feet.

"Joel, Tobe, Isaac, hog-tie these varmints," McQuade ordered. "The rest of us will wait here. That bunch defending the camp won't know us from the attackers."

Gunter, Cal, and Will wasted no time. Closing in, they cut loose with their revolvers. The men within the wagon circle, realizing that help had arrived, began firing. It became a deadly crossfire, forcing the attackers who were still alive to surrender.

"Don't shoot no more," somebody shouted. "We're givin' up."

"Stand up, drop your guns, and walk toward the wagons," McQuade shouted.

Slowly they complied. There were ten of them, making a total of thirteen. His shirt sleeve bloody, Creeker left the wagon circle, a grin on his dirty face. Other men, some of them wounded, followed.

"We got here as fast as we could," said McQuade. "Who is this bunch of coyotes?"

"Nobody I recognize," Creeker said. "Maybe one of them that's still alive can tell us."

"Good idea," said McQuade. Cocking his pistol, he held its muzzle to the head of one of the captured men.

"I ain't talkin'," the surly outlaw said.

"You don't know just how right you are," said McQuade. "You have until the count of three to tell me who's responsible for this attack. One. Two—"

"I'll talk. It was Gid Sutton, damn him. He run out on us."

"He's right," Will Haymes said. "Gunter, Cal, and me took a look at the dead, and we didn't see a man we recognized. What are we goin' to do with these varmints that come out alive?"

"The only decent thing to do is to hang the lot of them," said McQuade. "Tie them good and tight. We need to see to the wounded. Where's Doctor Puckett?''

"Here," Puckett replied. "I've been at the cook wagon. Ampersand has cooked his last meal."

"Hedgepith and Presnall are dead," said Creeker. "They were the first to get it, and if it hadn't been for them drawin' most of the first volley, none of us would have made it."

It was Doctor Puckett who went to the wagon where the women were, and hearing his voice, they came out. Two of the teamsters were dead, as were Porto, Quay, and Drum, all Creeker's men. Among the teamsters, Slaughter, Hansard, Weatherly, and Baker had been wounded.

"With Hedgepith gone, we have to make some decisions," McQuade said. "But first, we ought to decide what to do with these captured varmints."

"I like your first suggestion," said Will Haymes. "Hanging's too good for them."

"No," shouted the outlaw who had identified Sutton as head of the gang. "It ain't fair to stretch our necks. You don't know it was our lead that done the damage."

"We don't know that it wasn't," McQuade said, "and you'd have gunned this bunch down to the last man, if we hadn't rode in. We know what your intentions were, and on the frontier, that gets you the rope."

Several of the outlaws wept, others cursed, but it availed them nothing. One by one, they were mounted on a horse, a noose about their necks. When the horse was slapped from beneath them, they kicked their lives away.

"I never seen anything like this," said Cal Tabor. "I know they deserved it, but God, it's hard to swallow."

"Get used to it, all of you," McQuade said. "Until law comes to the frontier, this is the best you're likely to get. Let's cut this bunch down and get on to other things."

"I've never seen so many dead men all at once," said Tobe Rutledge. "I hate to bring this up, but shouldn't we bury them?"

"Yes," McQuade said, "but not one at a time. Some of you look around and find us an *arroyo* that's deep enough to hold them all. Then we'll cover them well enough to keep the coyotes and buzzards away from them.''

''Hell,'' said Weatherly, ''they done their best to kill us, and if they had, they'd have let us lay and rot.''

''That's the difference between us and them,'' Creeker said.

''Those of you with wounds had better let Doctor Puckett see to them, before you do anything else,'' said McQuade. ''Then we'll have decisions to make.''

Slaughter, Hansard, Weatherly, and Baker took McQuade's advice.

''You'd better go with them, Creeker,'' Gunter Warnell said. ''You're bleeding.''

''Go on,'' said McQuade. ''Somewhere there's a hell of a lot of horses that might come in handy in Texas. Some of you come with me, and we'll look for them.''

''That bunch brought a wagon with 'em,'' Groat said. ''Might be somethin' in there we can use.''

''Why don't you take a couple of men and check it out?'' McQuade suggested.

Some of the men, including Creeker, had gone to the wagon where the women had emerged, and there was a reunion of sorts taking place.

Ike Peyton laughed. ''I reckon there won't be any saloon girls on the Rio Colorado for a while, and that'll make our women happy.''

Bud, Oscar, and Levi had reclaimed their horses and had found a suitable *arroyo* for the burial of the dead men.

''As many of you who have the stomach for it,'' said McQuade, ''rope one of those dead coyotes and drag him to that *arroyo*. When that's done, Doctor Puckett should have everybody patched up that's needin' it. Then we'll talk.''

''Shouldn't we search them dead varmints?'' Ike asked.

''Yes,'' said McQuade. ''Take gold or silver, and any weapons or ammunition you can use. By all means, search Hedgepith.''

Doctor Puckett bandaged Creeker's wound first, and he joined McQuade in searching Hedgepith's tent.

"I reckon his legal hocus-pocus won't mean anything to us," Creeker said, "but I'd say we ought to take it all with us. We'll need to prove we was once promised grants by the Mexican government, I reckon."

There wasn't much in Hedgepith's tent, but they struck pay dirt when they searched the wagon. Among all the legal papers was a strongbox. It was locked and it was heavy.

"Ike was goin' to search Hedgepith," said McQuade. "Maybe he'll find a key."

Eventually, Ike came to Hedgepith's wagon with his findings, which he presented to McQuade. There was a pocket watch, a hundred dollars in gold coins, and a key. It fit the strongbox, and McQuade opened it. There was five thousand dollars in double eagles.

"There's twenty of you left," McQuade said. "Divide this equally among you, and it'll take care of any wages owed."

"That's two hundred and fifty dollars each," said Creeker. "None of us was owed that much."

"Consider it a bonus," McQuade said. "It'll be that much more of a stake, when you get to Texas. The big question is, what do you aim to do with these fifteen wagonloads of grub, guns, and trade goods?"

"I don't consider it mine," said Creeker. "If it was up to me, I'd donate it to old Sam Houston's militia. They've got to be hurtin'."

"Creeker," McQuade said, "you're a man with a heart. Why in tarnation did you ever get tied in with a ruthless old buzzard like Rufus Hook?"

"Same reason you did, I reckon," said Creeker. "Every man's guilty of an occasional bad judgment."

Eventually they all came together. The dead had been buried, the wounded had their wounds tended, and Hedgepith's wagon had been searched. Besides McQuade, there were fifty-six men from his outfit. From Hedgepith's there was Creeker and six of his men, Doctor Puckett, thirteen teamsters, and the seven women who had been destined for a saloon on the Rio Colorado.

"We found a strongbox in Hedgepith's wagon," said Creeker. "There's five thousand in gold inside it. Mr. McQuade has suggested it be divided equally among the twenty of us that's left, considerin' it wages owed. I'd favor that, except we're forgettin' Doc Puckett."

"I wasn't promised wages," Puckett said. "You owe me nothing."

"I think we do," said Creeker.

"So do we," Ike Peyton said, "and I'm speakin' for McQuade's outfit. Why don't we give Doc the hundred we took off Hedgepith, and what we took from them dead outlaws?"

"No," Puckett protested. "I don't want it."

"We'll take a vote," said Creeker. "All in favor, sound off."

There was a mighty shout of approval that stunned the little doctor. McQuade laughed at the expression on his face.

"Come on, Doc," Creeker said. "This is somethin' we want to do for you."

"Very well," said Puckett. "I will accept."

"Now there's somethin' Creeker and me have discussed," McQuade said, "but we don't believe it's just our decision. What's going to become of these fifteen wagonloads of grub and supplies that Hedgepith inherited from Hook?"

"We don't know how long we'll be squattin' with Houston's militia, fighting the Mexicans," said Slaughter. "Maybe we'll need these goods ourselves."

"You're gettin' close to what McQuade and me was considerin'," Creeker said, "but we wasn't goin' to claim everything for ourselves. We kind of thought Sam Houston and his militia might be hurtin', and that what's in these wagons, which don't belong to us, anyhow—might help us all claim Texas for the United States."

"By God," Slaughter shouted, "let's do it. We unload all this in his lap, old Sam can't deny us our land grants."

Again there was a thunderous shout of approval, for while they helped Sam Houston's rebels, they would be helping themselves.

"That's settled, then," said Creeker, "but there's more. We got fifteen wagons, and only thirteen teamsters. Who's goin' to take the extra wagons?"

"Seein' as how we're bein' paid right handsome," Dirk said, "I'll take one of 'em. I can tie my horse in behind, and we ain't got that much farther to go."

"I'll take the other," said Nall.

"We'll take whatever that's usable from the cook wagon," Creeker said, "and leave it behind. Doc, if it's all right with you, we'll need you to take the wagon that Hedgepith was using. We'll need it to carry his legal papers, and whatever we can salvage from the cook wagon."

"I can do that," said Puckett.

"One more thing," Creeker said. "We have to make some arrangements for the ladies. With Hook and Hedgepith out of it, I reckon we don't have to hide the fact that all these girls has been spoken for. Instead of saloons and whorehouses, they'll be livin' on ranches and farms."

Creeker paused, interrupted by shouts of approval, which included the women.

"What I'm thinkin'," Creeker continued, "is that you teamsters that's claimin' one of these females can set her on the wagon box beside you, and we can leave this extra wagon behind. How about it?"

Again there were shouts of approval.

"Tull," said Creeker, "Mabel will be ridin' with you. Kendrick, you'll be takin' Reza. McLean, Eula rides with you. Rowden, Sal will go with you. Lemburg, you'll have Nettie, and Blackburn, you'll take Cora. Now does that suit everybody?"

"Not quite," McQuade said, his eyes on Lora Kirby.

"Since I won't have a wagon, I'll need somebody to

look after Lora for me," Creeker said. "Doc, will you let her ride with you?"

"Certainly," said Puckett. "You're welcome, Lora."

"If that's everything," McQuade said, "we're ready to move out. I believe, since we've lost so much of the day, we'll work your wagons into our circle, and stay where we are. Tomorrow, we'll get an early start. One thing more. If you men who are wounded don't feel up to it, some of my men can bring your wagons."

"Arm and leg wounds," said Slaughter, "and we've had 'em before. Let's be goin'."

It was almost noon when the extra wagons were worked into the circle. The rest of McQuade's outfit had no trouble accepting the decisions that had been made, and all were especially glad to have Doctor Puckett in their midst.

"Doctor," Maggie Peyton said, "you're welcome to take your meals with us."

"Thank you," said Puckett, "but there are plenty of provisions in my wagon that were taken from the abandoned cook wagon. This was intended to feed Hook's outfit, and since we're without a cook, I suppose we should continue to feed ourselves."

"Nonsense," Maggie said. "Split up those provisions among the rest of us, and we'll do the cooking for all of you, unless you prefer to do your own."

"My God, no," said Creeker, who had overheard Maggie's offer. "Take provisions from any of the wagons. Sam Houston gets what's left, when we reach the Rio Colorado."

The first night after the combining of the two outfits, some of the women in McQuade's outfit made an extra effort to welcome the former saloon women who had been with Hook's party.

"Those women aren't very friendly," Mary complained to McQuade.

"They'll have to get used to you," said McQuade. "This is a way of life none of them are used to. They expect other women to look down on them, because of

what they've been in the past. Don't go out of your way
to try and win them over. They'll be suspicious of you,
if you're too nice."

There were now a hundred and thirty-five wagons, and
their first day on the trail, the train had no trouble.
Creeker, his men, and the remaining teamsters were ap-
preciative of the women who had taken over the cooking
for them, and there were no real problems until the third
night after the joining of the two outfits. Ned Blackburn,
a teamster, was on the second watch, leaving Cora alone
at the wagon. Cora screamed loud enough to wake the
dead, and by the time McQuade reached the wagon, some
of the men from the second watch had Matthew Burke at
gun point.

"You Burkes are real lady killers," said McQuade in
disgust. "You know Cora is Ned Blackburn's woman.
Now what are you doing here?"

"She was a whore when she left St. Louis," Matthew
said, "an' there ain't no law that says one man can take
her all for himself."

"This woman has been chosen by a man who aims to
stand her before a preacher and have him read from the
Book," said McQuade. "Who she was and what she was
back in St. Louis is past and done."

"She was a whore then, and she's a whore now,"
Burke insisted.

Seizing the front of his shirt, McQuade slammed his
right fist into Burke's chin. He went limp and McQuade
turned him loose, allowing him to fall facedown in the
dirt.

"Damn you, McQuade," said Andrew Burke, "you
just won't leave us alone, will you?"

"Not as long as you Burkes continue to be troublesome," said McQuade. "This whelp of yours was bothering a woman who has a man. She wanted nothing to do
with him, but he wouldn't leave her alone. That's the
trouble with you Burkes. Nothing matters except what you

want. Now you drag this varmint back to your wagon and keep him there."

Ned Blackburn was there, his hand on the butt of his revolver, his hard eyes on the still unconscious Matthew Burke.

"Sorry, Blackburn," said McQuade. "We've had trouble with the Burkes before. I'll do what I can to keep them in line."

"It ain't your fight, McQuade," Blackburn said. "I appreciate your concern, but where I come from, a man stomps his own snakes. I hope you don't put too much store in this varmint on the ground, because next time he comes sneakin' around Cora, I aim to shoot him stone dead."

"You do, by God," Andrew Burke threatened, "and you'll have to shoot all four of us Burkes. I swear it."

"I can do that, too," said Blackburn calmly.

"You Burkes get the hell back to your wagon and stay there," McQuade said.

The Burkes stomped away, leading the half-conscious Matthew. The men on watch returned to their posts and McQuade returned to his wagon.

"The Burkes again?" Mary asked.

"Who else?" said McQuade. "How did you know?"

"Old Andrew has a voice like a bullfrog."

"And a brain to match," McQuade said. "I'm glad those women from Hedgepith's outfit have changed their ways, but my God, why couldn't they have done it another time and another place?"

Come the dawn, McQuade was saddling his horse to ride ahead, and Creeker led up his own horse.

"Mind if I ride with you?" Creeker asked.

"Come along," said McQuade.

"Sorry to have brought you extra problems with those women," Creeker said, as they rode along. "We didn't have all this foolishness before."

McQuade laughed. "You didn't have the Burkes. I'm

startin' to wonder if maybe the Lord ain't usin' 'em to punish me. I had to shoot one of them in St. Joe some years back, and another before we left St. Louis. Now I have the father, old Andrew, and three of the sons right under my nose.''

"Uh oh," said Creeker. "Look yonder."

On a rise half a mile ahead, an Indian sat his horse, staring at them. He finally kicked his horse into a lope, riding across the ridge and out of sight.

"Comanche," McQuade said, "and he won't be alone."

"I'm glad we've joined outfits," said Creeker. "The Kiowa were bad enough, but I hear the Comanches are worse."

"That they are," McQuade said, "and they'll attack at midnight as readily as they will at dawn. We'll dismount and lead our horses to the top of that rise. A man on horseback makes a substantial target."

Reaching the top of the rise, they paused, but there wasn't a rider in sight.

"Where the hell did he go?" Creeker wondered. "There's not enough cover for a man or a horse, and for certain not enough for both."

"I hear that Texas is shot full of *arroyos*," said McQuade, "some of 'em deep enough to conceal a whole tribe. I expect this is the kind of country we'll encounter from here on to the Rio Colorado."

"There won't be as many creeks and water holes as we found in Indian Territory," Creeker said. "That'll make it twice as dangerous when we find water."

"You're right about that," said McQuade. "From the few maps of Texas I've seen, where we're going, the only rivers I can recall before we reach the Rio Colorado is the Trinity and the Brazos. We'll just have to gamble on whatever lies between. When we do find good water, we'll have to begin filling our water barrels. Two barrels to a wagon, we can survive an occasional dry camp."

They rode on, and in the distance there appeared a little patch of green. It grew as they approached, becoming a respectable stand of willows lifting their leafy heads above the rims of a canyon.

"Water," said McQuade, "but we won't be able to get too close to it."

"Maybe there's a runoff," Creeker said.

"This is sandy country," said McQuade. "The runoff is usually swallowed up pronto."

That proved to be the case. While the upper end of the canyon was deep and the cool spring was overhung with willows, the runoff disappeared abruptly. There were tracks of deer and coyotes around the spring, and more recently, tracks of unshod horses.

"Three riders," Creeker said. "They could be passing through, or scouting for a larger party."

"You can't judge the number of Comanches or the nearness of the tribe just by horse tracks," said McQuade. "This three, for instance, might be the only three within a hundred miles. But they'll ride all night, kill their horses if they have to, and by tomorrow evening, there'll be a hundred Comanches ready to take scalps."

"That's damn scary," Creeker said. "You know them mighty well."

"I once knew a man who lived with them," said McQuade, "and he could tell some tales that would scare hell out of a brave man. That's why we won't take any chances. It's time we rode back to meet the wagons."

On the canyon rim overlooking the spring, they scanned the surrounding country as far as they could see, until shimmering heat waves robbed them of reality. Seeing nothing, they rode back the way they had come.

"Considerably more than fifteen miles," Creeker said.

"Yes," said McQuade, "and there may be more days like this. We may be circling the wagons by starlight, but it's better than dry camp."

"After what you've told me about the Comanches, I'm wondering if that one Indian we saw won't come back with enough friends to give us hell."

"He might do just that," McQuade said. "We're most vulnerable when the wagons are strung out. If we can limit their attacks to times when the wagons are circled, they can't hurt us that much. The only defense we have on the trail is to keep our eyes open and see them coming. With every man reining up, hitting the ground with his revolver in hand, we can defend ourselves. At night, we're going to have to depend on a heavy watch.''

"We have enough men," said Creeker.

"Starting tonight, we're going to make good use of them," McQuade said. "Having seen one Comanche, I look for him to bring plenty more. We'll go with two watches, with a change at midnight. You take half the men for the first watch, and I'll take the rest of them for the second watch."

"Suits me," said Creeker. "With that many men on watch, I won't have to worry about wakin' up to a Comanche standin' over me with a knife in his hand."

They met the wagons, and McQuade estimated they were a good dozen miles from the canyon with its spring.

"Let's ride to the back of the train," McQuade said. "I'll take one side and you take the other. Tell 'em we have a long day ahead of us, and there's Indian sign."

The wagons rolled on, McQuade and Creeker riding ahead. Dirk and Nall were on the boxes of two of the wagons, leaving Groat, Slack, Rucker, and Ellis riding behind the last wagons.

"We ain't gonna make it 'fore dark," Creeker said.

"No," said McQuade, "but it'll be close. We'll ride on ahead of the wagons and scout that spring. We must get the wagons circled before it gets too dark, because we'll have to lead the stock to water. That'll take a while."

The sun had already slipped beneath the western horizon, fanning out a glorious array of crimson fingers that reached toward the deepening purple of the distant sky.

"Ike," McQuade shouted, "keep 'em moving. Creeker and me are ridin' ahead to scout the spring."

McQuade kicked his horse into a fast gallop, and doing likewise, Creeker fell in beside him.

CHAPTER 16

True to McQuade's prediction, the wagons were circled by starlight, and considerable time was needed to lead the stock to and from water. Supper was late, and the second watch had to relieve the first so they could eat.

"Water won't be as plentiful here as it was in Indian Territory," McQuade told them, "and we may have to travel farther each day to reach the next water. The Comanches know we're here, and we'll be fighting them. A hundred and thirty-five wagons, three abreast, that's forty-five wagon lengths, strung out on the trail. Your only chance is to see them in time, rein up, grab your guns and fight. At night, we'll continue with two watches, half of us until midnight, the rest until dawn."

The night passed without incident, and when the wagons took the trail the following morning, Creeker again rode out with McQuade.

"You're askin' for it," said Creeker, "ridin' alone in Comanche country."

"I reckon you're right," McQuade said. "I'll feel a lot better if you get scalped along with me. By the way, I never did get around to learning what was in that wagon we took from the Sutton gang."

"Some ammunition," said Creeker, "but mostly fuse and black powder. Two kegs of it. We loaded it all into Doc Puckett's wagon, along with the weapons taken from those dead outlaws. I got a feeling Sam Houston's militia can use it all.''

"I reckon we should have tried to round up Sutton's horses, but we have about all the stock we can handle,'' McQuade said.

"It wouldn't have been easy,'' said Creeker. "Some of that bunch ran out, and as they took their own horses, they spooked the rest. They were a cut-throat lot.''

"Something tells me I'll be seeing Gid Sutton again,'' McQuade said. "He's a vindictive varmint, and he carries a grudge.''

McQuade and Creeker were more than ten miles ahead of the wagons, and still hadn't seen any sign of water.

"Filling the water barrels on each wagon is startin' to seem like a good idea,'' said Creeker. "We must have traveled eighteen miles yesterday. Any more than that won't be possible. I like to have the wagons circled before dark.''

"So do I,'' McQuade said. "We'll give it another five miles, and if we don't find decent water, we'll look for graze and plan on a dry camp.''

The first water they found was a stagnant pool in a box canyon. There was no spring, and no coyote or deer tracks.

"If it's not good enough for coyotes and deer, it's not good enough for us,'' McQuade said. "We'll ride on a ways.''

"Still no Indian sign,'' said Creeker. "I don't know which is worse, findin' it or not findin' it.''

"It can be bad news, either way,'' McQuade said. "They can come and go without any sign, if it suits their fancy.''

When they eventually reached water, it was beyond their wildest expectations, for it was a fast-flowing river.*

"I figure we're about thirty-five miles south of the

*In the vicinity of the present-day cities of Fort Worth and Dallas.

Red,'' said McQuade. ''This has to be the Trinity.''

''What's the next river beyond it?'' Creeker asked.

''The Brazos,'' said McQuade. ''As I recall, there are three major rivers in Texas, all of them emptying into the Gulf of Mexico. There's the Trinity, the Brazos, and the Rio Colorado.''

''How much farther to the Brazos?''

''A good twenty miles,'' McQuade said. ''That's about where we'll want to circle our wagons and ride south to find Sam Houston's militia. His camp, from what those returning emigrants told us, is at the crookedest part of the Rio Colorado.''

''Tomorrow's drive, however long it takes, should get us to the Brazos,'' said Creeker, ''and the day after, we'll go looking for Houston's militia. God, it'll feel good to reach some kind of destination, even if only to fight Mexicans.''

After watering their horses, they rode back to meet the oncoming wagons. They were less than half way, when off to their right, a single rider appeared. He galloped his horse until he was riding even with them.

''Bad news,'' said McQuade. ''Eventually there'll be another to our left, and maybe three or four taking up the slack behind us.''

''We can't be more than five or six miles ahead of the wagons,'' Creeker said. ''We can ride like hell.''

''They're counting on that,'' said McQuade. ''Our horses will be winded and blowing in half that distance. If we can find some cover, there's a chance we can hole up until help can reach us.''

Just as McQuade had predicted, a rider soon appeared to their left, and when Creeker turned in his saddle, there were three bobbing specks on their back-trail.

''Three of 'em behind us,'' said Creeker.

''The flankers will keep us from riding away to either side,'' McQuade said, ''while the three behind us will continue to close the gap. They're goin' to try and get close enough to put some arrows in us before we reach the wagons, and before help reaches us.''

Then McQuade did a strange thing. Drawing his revolver, spacing his shots, he fired three times into the air.

"You reckon they'll hear?" Creeker asked.

"I don't know," said McQuade. "It's a gamble, but we don't have a lot of cards on the table. Ike, Cal, and Will are in the lead wagons. Ease back to a slow gallop and spare your horse as much as you can."

Not quite five miles distant, the wagons rumbled along. Maggie was speaking, when Ike raised his hand for silence. Suddenly he reined up his teams, as Cal and Will already had done. As other wagons rumbled to a stop behind him, Ike grabbed his Sharps .50 and leaped off the wagon box. Cal and Will were saddling the horses that trotted behind their wagons.

"Gunter, Eli, Joel, Tobe," Ike shouted, "saddle your horses and let's ride. McQuade and Creeker are in trouble somewhere ahead."

The men moved quickly, and within minutes, seven riders galloped forth to meet whatever trouble lay ahead.

"They're closing in," Creeker shouted. He drew his revolver and fired twice, without effect.

"You might as well save your ammunition," said McQuade.

But the Comanches flanking them had ridden in close, and arrows began flying. One of them tore a gash across McQuade's left arm, above the elbow, and his horse screamed as it took an arrow in the throat. The valiant animal stumbled, took a second arrow and fell. McQuade kicked loose just in time, rolled free and came to his feet, his revolver in his hand. He shot one of the flanking Comanches off his horse, but the three galloped along the back-trail, coming closer. Hearing the roar of the revolver and seeing McQuade afoot, Creeker wheeled his horse, his gun blazing as he rode. The remaining Comanches were all close enough, and arrows whipped close. One ripped through Creeker's left side, while a second slammed into his shoulder. On he rode, his good arm outstretched to McQuade, who caught his hand. With

McQuade behind him, Creeker wheeled the horse, kicking it into a fast gallop. They could hear the pound of hooves as the Comanches gained on them.

"There's an *arroyo* ahead," McQuade shouted.

Creeker needed no urging. McQuade slid off the horse, and seconds later, Creeker all but fell out of the saddle. The arroyo was shallow. Neither man could stand without being exposed from the waist up. McQuade was on his knees, ready to fire, but the Comanches had slowed their horses, and with good reason. There was a shout, as seven riders came thundering from the north. Like smoke, the Comanches faded into the distance and were gone. Ike had caught Creeker's fleeing horse, and the seven men reined up.

"We got here as quick as we could," Ike said.

"Creeker took two bad ones," said McQuade. "Some of you help him mount his horse, and I'll double up with one of you."

"Hell," Creeker grunted, "I ain't dead yet." Seizing the horn, he mounted his horse.

They reached the wagons to find their companions anxiously awaiting them. Lora all but fell off the wagon box getting to Creeker.

"How far are we from water?" Doctor Puckett asked.

"Maybe six miles," said McQuade. "I just got a scratch, but Creeker took a couple of bad ones."

"Creeker," Puckett said, "we'll need water to tend those wounds. Can you make it six more miles?"

"I'll manage," said Creeker. "The important thing is that we get these wagons circled before dark."

McQuade was brought one of the extra horses. He rode it bareback until he reached his own dead animal. There he retrieved his saddle and bridle. He caught up to the lead wagons, joining Creeker, who rode with gritted teeth.

"I owe you one, *amigo*," said McQuade.

"I quit keepin' score after that fight with Sutton's gang," Creeker said. "What bothers me is that I may not be in shape to ride south with you to meet Houston."

"We'll wait a couple more days, if we have to," said McQuade.

They reached the bank of the Trinity without difficulty, and while the men circled the wagons and unharnessed the teams, the women started supper fires. Over one of them was a pot of water being heated to tend Creeker's wounds.

"Unfortunately, we have nothing for pain except whiskey," said Doctor Puckett, "but there's a blessed plenty of that. Creeker, we'll make room for you in one of the wagons. I want you to put down enough whiskey to take you out, while I remove those arrows."

"Doc," McQuade said, "you don't know how glad I am to hear you say that. All the way across Indian Territory, I had to drive arrows through."

"Take off your shirt," said Puckett, "and I'll bandage your wound while we're waiting for the whiskey to take effect on Creeker."

McQuade's wound was superficial but painful, and he could feel the arm beginning to stiffen. Puckett cleansed it with hot water, sloshed it full of whiskey, and applied a muslin bandage. Room had been made in the wagon Puckett drove, and Creeker had stretched out on blankets, waiting for the whiskey to work. During supper, McQuade told the rest of the party what he and Creeker had already discussed.

"Tomorrow may be another long day," said McQuade, "because we'll be going all the way to the Brazos. Unless I'm totally wrong, it'll be maybe eighteen miles to the south. At that point, we won't be more than a hundred miles from the Rio Colorado. We'll circle the wagons on the Brazos and ride south, looking for Houston's militia. We must find Houston without being seen by Monclova's bunch, and I don't see any need for more than two of us to ride out. The fewer of us, the less chance we'll be seen. I aim to take Creeker with me. Are there any questions or objections?"

"Seems to me you're gettin' mighty damn partial to

that bunch that follered Hook and Hedgepith," said Andrew Burke.

"Since you're making an issue of it," McQuade replied, "I'll give it to you straight. I aim to take a man with me I can trust, and that eliminates all you Burkes. Is that clear?"

"Plenty," said Andrew. "I reckon I just don't like the way you do things, McQuade. I been thinkin' about all these wagons loaded with guns, grub, an' all, an' I can't figger what makes this Sam Houston more worthy of 'em than us. Hell, I feel like I'm as deservin' as he is. We ain't started no fight with Mexico. He started it; let him finish it."

"People," McQuade said, trying mightily to control his temper, "you heard what Burke said. I think all of you know where I stand, so I'm not going to say a word. Give Burke his answer."

There was an angry roar of indignation, and when it died away, individual voices could be heard.

"Turn the no-account varmint out of this wagon train."

"Give him to the Comanches."

"String him up."

Burke turned his back on them and returned to his wagon. McQuade said nothing, and the uproar subsided. When Doctor Puckett had removed the arrows and tended Creeker's wounds, he spoke to McQuade.

"The wound to his shoulder is the most serious. While the arrow in his side looked bad, it had struck a rib and didn't go deep. He may come out of this without infection, since it was tended quickly."

Since Creeker would be in no condition to take charge of the first watch, McQuade sought out Gunter Warnell.

"Gunter, will you take over the first watch while Creeker's unable to?"

"Sure," said Warnell. "What do you aim to do about the Burkes?"

"Nothing," McQuade said, "unless they create trouble."

The Burkes wasted no time. Sometime before midnight, Mary screamed and McQuade awoke to find the wagon canvas in flames. He shoved Mary out of the wagon and tore at the canvas. Others came to his aid and the burning canvas was ripped away, saving the contents and the rest of the wagon.

"Now who do you reckon is responsible for that?" Ike Peyton said.

"I have my suspicions," said McQuade. "Some of you come with me. I'm going to pay a visit to the Burkes."

McQuade had purposely assigned the Burkes to the second watch, and he wasn't in the least surprised to find them all awake, for it was close to midnight. He was surprised, however, to find them all gloriously drunk. Luke and Selma were there, as well.

"Well, McQuade," said Andrew, "we was just about to mosey over there an' see what all the excitement was about. Hell of a time for a fire, with the Comanches gatherin'."

"Where did you get the whiskey, Burke?"

Burke laughed. "We ain't got a drop of whiskey. Drunk it all."

Selma giggled, and Luke caught her to keep her from falling. Foolish grins on their faces, Matthew and Mark leaned against the wagon. Andrew sat on the ground, his back against a wagon wheel, his old hat tipped down over his eyes. Not only had many of the men followed McQuade, but some of the women had, too. McQuade turned to them.

"We won't get anywhere with this bunch until they're sober," said McQuade. "There's a place in the river where we watered the stock, where the water's shallow."

McQuade seized Andrew Burke by the ankles, dragging him away from the wagon. Ike Peyton caught him under the arms, and they headed for the river. Burke cursed them every step of the way. With a heave, McQuade and Ike slung him off the bank and into the shallow water. Other men had seized Matthew, Mark, and Luke in a similar fashion, and they quickly joined their father. Not to be outdone, Maggie Peyton and Ellen Warnell brought Selma, kicking and screaming, to the river bank. She too was thrown in. The lot of them sat there cursing, and McQuade had an answer for that.

"The lot of you are going to sit there until you shut your mouths," said McQuade.

"Damn right," Ike said. "We'll stand here till daylight, if need be, throwin' the lot of you back in, for as long as it takes. When you're sober enough to come out of there, we'll talk about some rules for you varmints."

Everybody stood there in grim silence, and it was Selma who gave in first.

"I'm freezing. I want to come out."

"Come on," said McQuade, "and then I want you to return to your wagon."

She crawled out on hands and knees, nobody offering to help her. When she got to her feet, she stumbled off toward her wagon.

"By God, I'm comin' out," Matthew said, "and anybody tries to put me back, he comes in with me."

"I'll put you back," said McQuade, "if that's what it takes."

Matthew crawled out and sat on the bank, squeezing the water out of his hair. Mark, Luke, and Andrew followed.

"Now," McQuade said, "we're going to talk about my burned wagon canvas."

"You got no proof we burnt your damn wagon canvas," said Andrew sullenly.

"I don't know of another soul in this outfit who would have set fire to my wagon canvas," McQuade said. "Only you Burkes. But I don't have any proof. What do the rest of you think should be done?"

Without a word, a dozen men quickly stripped the canvas from the Burke wagon.

"We got no proof," said Ike, "but we know you Burkes pretty damn well. Consider it your own wagon canvas you burnt. We still got to deal with you for stealin' that whiskey, but we'll leave that up to McQuade."

"From now on," McQuade said, "at least one of the men on watch will be stationed at those wagons loaded with whiskey. Anybody breaking into these wagons is subject to being shot. Will, that will be your post for the rest of the night. You Burkes have played out your string. I've reached the point that I could shoot the whole damn lot of you, and still sleep with a clear conscience."

With that, McQuade turned away, and except for the Burkes, everybody followed. The men who had stripped the canvas from the Burke wagon quickly stretched it over the bows of McQuade's wagon and secured it to the wagon box.

"Come on, Mary," said McQuade, taking her arm, "and get what sleep you can. I'll be going on watch pretty soon, and I'll just wait until then."

"Do be careful," she cautioned. "One of them could shoot you in the back."

He said nothing, realizing the truth of it. He found Ike leaning against his wagon.

"Sooner or later," said Ike, "one of that bunch is goin' to try to kill you."

"They've tried before," McQuade said. "I've had to shoot two of them. That's why they're down on me."

"Don't turn your back on them," said Ike. "If they cause any more trouble, I believe we should cut their wagon out of the circle and let them shift for themselves."

"It's a temptation," McQuade said. He made the rounds, speaking to the other men on watch, finding most of them of the same mind as Ike. When he reached the Burke wagon; he found Andrew, Matthew, Mark, and Luke there. All had changed into dry clothes, for in the starlight, he could see the wet ones strung across the wagon bows to dry.

"The lot of you are on the second watch," said McQuade, "and it's in progress."

"We just ain't in the mood for it, McQuade," Andrew said. "Some other time."

"Your choice," said McQuade. "If you refuse to pull your weight, your wagon can be cut out of the circle. There's already been talk of that, and we'll vote on it tomorrow. I've made the rounds, and I haven't seen Luke. Pass the word along to him."

McQuade made the rounds of the guard posts at least once an hour. He had caught a few of the younger men sleeping—or worse—gathering to talk. He wasn't surprised when he again visited the various posts, when he found the Burkes where they were assigned. Even Luke was there. McQuade said nothing. He didn't doubt that any one or all four of them would back-shoot him if the opportunity presented itself, but there was a measure of safety in the fact that so many feared exactly that. While the Burkes hadn't been there for the hanging of the captured members of Gid Sutton's gang, they were very much aware of it. If McQuade were shot in the back and the guilty Burke couldn't be singled out, every one of them would face the swift justice of the rope. McQuade doubted any of them hated him that much. He made his way to Doctor Puckett's wagon, expecting the doctor to be awake, and he was. The man never slept when the wounded might become feverish and need whiskey to fight infection. It was a trait McQuade admired.

"How is he, Doc?" McQuade asked softly.

"Still no fever," said Puckett. "He's a strong man. He may pull through without fever or infection."

"I hope he does," McQuade said. "We should reach the Brazos tomorrow, and it's from there that Creeker and me will ride to Houston's camp."

"You could take someone else with you," said Puckett. "He won't be comfortable in a saddle for at least a week."

"From what I've seen of him, he won't wait that long," McQuade replied. "He's come a long way—he and his friends—since they hired on with Hook in St. Louis.''

"A lot of us have," said Puckett. "I must admit I wasn't proud of our outfit with Hook in control, and less so when it fell into Hedgepith's hands. Frankly, I had little confidence in Creeker and the men who accompanied him, but it was they who stood up to Hook, and later, Hedgepith. It was Creeker who pulled the teamsters together and set up a defense against Indian attacks. These are the kind of men Sam Houston will need, if he's to win Texas for the United States.''

"I fully agree, Doc," said McQuade. "God knows how many years we are away from law on the frontier. I hate being judge and jury, but we all have to be strong enough to tie a noose until something better comes along.''

"Speaking of a noose, what are we going to do about the Burkes? I thought of them when I saw your wagon canvas in flames.''

"So did everybody else, including me," said Mc-Quade. "We had no proof, but with all of us of the same mind, we may have taught them the error of their ways. Last time I was at their wagon, they had pulled in their horns and had taken their positions on watch.''

"They're a cowardly lot," Puckett said. "I suppose they had been at the whiskey.''

"I haven't checked out either of the wagons," said McQuade, "but I don't know where else they would have gotten it. From now on, there'll be a man near those wagons, with orders to shoot any and all thieves.''

"It's the devil's brew," said Puckett. "I'd suggest that it be destroyed, but it has its place as a medicine. I know of nothing better to combat a fever, or to drug a man, allowing him to sleep through pain.''

"I've been thinking of that," McQuade said, "and like everything else, it'll be in short supply. If the war with Mexico comes about as we expect, it'll be needed.''

"With that in mind," said Puckett. "I have a request. When you speak to Houston, tell him about the whiskey, suggest that it be set aside for use as medicine. Tell him a doctor recommends it.''

''Doc, I like the way you think,'' McQuade replied. ''I'll use your exact words.''

McQuade went on his way, somehow feeling better for the time spent with the doctor.

At dawn, McQuade returned to Doctor Puckett's wagon, wishing to know Creeker's condition before he made plans for the day.

''Still no fever,'' Doctor Puckett said. ''When he wakes, we'll see how he feels.''

''He's awake,'' said a voice from within the wagon, ''and he feels like breakfast. Where is Lora?''

''Under the wagon, where I slept,'' said Lora. ''I'll bring you breakfast.''

''Quick, woman,'' Creeker said. ''All I can taste is whiskey. I feel like somethin' sick just crawled down my throat and died.''

''I reckon that answers my question,'' said McQuade. ''We'll move on to the Brazos.''

''If you scout ahead,'' Creeker said, ''don't go alone. I won't be there to save your hide.''

''You can rest easy,'' said McQuade. ''I don't aim to ride out at all. I know we have to reach the Brazos today, no matter how far it is. We'll just make as good a time as we can, startin' after breakfast.''

McQuade climbed into one of the whiskey wagons, and since everything seemed intact, went on to the second one. It was the wagon from which some barrels had been lost when the teams had stampeded, and there was some room. One of the barrels had been tapped, for the smell of whiskey was strong. The bung hole was near the top, and finding the bung on the wagon floor, McQuade used the butt of his revolver to drive the wooden plug in tight. He then wrestled the barrel up next to the others.

''Doc,'' said McQuade under his breath, ''you've got

one hell of a lot of medicine here, if we can just keep the Burkes and their kind away from it.''

The wagons took the trail and all seemed secure. Since McQuade would be ahead of the lead wagons all day, he left Groat, Slack, Rucker, and Ellis behind the last wagons. The last few wagons were the most vulnerable during an Indian attack, but when the attack came, it was from a quarter least expected. The lead wagons were coming upon an *arroyo*, and with a mad whoop, mounted Indians came swarming out like angry bees. McQuade had his revolver out, but an arrow creased the rump of his horse, and the animal reared. Men reined up, leaping off their wagon boxes, prepared to fight. Guns roared, frightened mules brayed, as women on the wagon boxes fought to hold the teams. Many Indian ponies raced away riderless, and the attack ended as suddenly as it had begun. Despite his spooked horse, McQuade had accounted for two dead Comanches, but what concerned him was their wounded. The first six wagons had borne the brunt of the attack, and while a dozen deadly arrows had pierced arms and legs, only one man was down. McQuade leaped out of his saddle and ran to the fallen Ike Peyton. Maggie was already there, her face pale, her hands trembling. For all the doctoring she had done, helping others, there was nothing she could do for Ike. A Comanche arrow was buried deep in his chest and there was bloody froth on his lips. Doctor Puckett came on the run, elbowing his way through weeping women. Mary stood beside Maggie, who pushed her aside. She knelt beside Ike. His eyes had dimmed and as he recognized approaching death, he spoke.

''McQuade . . .''

It was little more than a whisper, and McQuade leaned close to hear any last words.

''Take care . . . of . . . Maggie . . .''

It was the end. McQuade stumbled to his feet, wiping streaming eyes on the sleeve of his shirt. Someone took his arm, and it was a moment before he could see well enough to recognize Mary. Maggie stood up, her weathered face a mask of pain, and when her knees gave way, it was Doctor Puckett who caught her.

"Take her to our wagon, Doc," said McQuade, "and Mary, you stay with her."

"That would be best," Puckett said. "We have many wounded."

When Puckett had taken Maggie away, all eyes were on McQuade. Will Haymes spoke.

"Should we bury Ike here, or take him with us?"

"We'll take him with us," said McQuade. "He deserves proper burying, when Maggie is able to be there. Make room for Ike in his wagon, and I'll take it the rest of the way to the Brazos."

CHAPTER 17

∾

"*I* gave Maggie a sedative that should allow her to sleep," said Doctor Puckett. "What would you have us do about Ike's burial?"

"We're taking him with us," McQuade said. "He'll be buried when Maggie is better able to accept it. Do you believe we should wait here until you can tend the wounded, or should we move on to the Brazos?"

"We'd best move on," said Puckett. "We'll need plenty of hot water, and for safety's sake, we ought to have the wagons circled. I'll talk to the wounded."

"Please do," McQuade said. "I believe they'll all agree to endure their pain for a while, rather than risk being stranded on the plains overnight, without water."

Gunter Warnell had a bloody gash across the back of his neck, while Ellen had taken an arrow in her right arm. Odessa Bibb, Lucy Tabor, and Minerva Haymes all had one of the deadly barbs in their thighs. Joel Hanby had an arrow driven all the way through the calf of his right leg.

"I can break this one and remove both halves," said Doctor Puckett. "We must move on to water."

"Go ahead, Doc," Joel said. "We don't know how far we got to go before sundown."

Before they again took the trail, McQuade took a count of the dead Comanches. There were thirteen.

"An unlucky number," said Doctor Puckett, who had followed.

"It's not near enough," McQuade said. "They cost us Ike, and it wouldn't be enough if we killed every damn Comanche in Texas."

With his horse tied behind the Peyton wagon, McQuade climbed to the box. With the Warnell and Bibb wagons flanking him, McQuade led out. They stopped only to rest their teams, and each time, Doctor Puckett looked in on Maggie. McQuade doubted they would reach the Brazos in time to bury Ike. It was a ritual he dreaded, and not just for Maggie's sake. He realized he hadn't fully appreciated the presence of Ike Peyton, until like a mighty oak hit by lightning, he had been struck down. But that wasn't the worst of it. Life on the frontier was hard on a woman, without a man at her side. Now Maggie would be alone, and Chance McQuade was haunted by Ike's last words. Maggie was not more than a year or two older than Mary. Dying, Ike had known he had only seconds left, and to McQuade it seemed that he had shown his concern for Maggie in the only way that he could. It was a burden he didn't want or need, something he must discuss with Mary, when he could. To his relief, the Brazos wasn't as far as he had believed, and thanks to their early start, they reached it before sundown. While the men circled the wagons and unhitched the teams, the women started supper fires. Over several of them hung pots of water, being heated for the cleansing of wounds. Doctor Puckett visited the wagons where arrows had to be removed, seeing that massive doses of whiskey were taken by the wounded, and leaving more for later. As soon as McQuade had the Peyton wagon in the circle and the teams unharnessed, he went to his own wagon, which Mary had positioned. She was unharnessing the teams, and he took over the chore.

"How is Maggie?" he asked.

"Awake," said Mary, "but she won't talk. She's just lying there, and her eyes aren't seeing anything."

"That tells me what I need to know," McQuade said.

"We can't bury Ike until she's able to be there, but there's a limit as to how long Ike can wait. That limit runs out first thing in the morning. Somebody has to talk to her."

"I've tried," said Mary, "and it might as well be the wind blowing."

"Do you know what Ike's last words were?"

"No," she said. "I was as bad off as Maggie."

"He asked me to take care of Maggie," said McQuade. "I'm honored by his trust, but scared to death of the responsibility. My God, she can't be much older than you."

"Two years older," Mary said, "and her shape makes me look like a drudge."

"It does not," said McQuade.

"It does so," she said. "You've seen most of it, Chance McQuade. Don't lie to me."

"Hell," said McQuade, "it wasn't my fault she got an arrow in her thigh. I wasn't the least bit interested in her carcass, beyond removing the arrow from it. Don't you think we are being disrespectful, Ike lying dead while we fight over Maggie's naked behind?"

"I'm sorry. Maggie's a beautiful woman, and I'm jealous of her, but there are far more important things to consider. She believes in you. Will you talk to her?"

"Yes," said McQuade with a sigh. "I'll talk to her. You want to stay close, just to be sure I don't look at anything I'm not supposed to see?"

Tears crept down her cheeks, and he knew he had gone too far. He gathered her up, as she struggled to get loose.

"Now I'm sorry," McQuade said. "That was uncalled for."

"Oh, but it wasn't," she said. "I deserved it."

But he refused to let her go, and finally she turned to face him.

"Go on and talk to her," said Mary. "Forget everything else except helping her make it through this. Later, we'll talk about . ... Ike's last words."

Reluctantly McQuade let down the wagon's tailgate and climbed in. Maggie Peyton lay on a blanket, her head on a folded blanket, facing the rear of the wagon. She was dressed as she had been the day before, with only her shoes removed.

"Maggie," said McQuade, "we have to talk."

There was a long silence, and when McQuade had decided she wasn't going to speak, she did.

"Ike's been my life since I was thirteen years old. Now he's gone. I only regret that one of the arrows didn't take me, so I could have gone with him."

"Maggie, you must carry on. It's what Ike wanted. He asked me to look after you, to help you, and I'm here to tell you I'll do all I can."

She tried to laugh, and it fell away to a sob. "Will you lay beside me on cold winter nights? Will you set across the breakfast table from me, tellin' me I'm pretty, when my hair ain't been combed, and I look like hell?"

"Maggie," said McQuade, "I can't be a husband to you, but I can be your friend. So can Mary. But only if you let us."

McQuade knelt beside her, taking her hands in his. On the tips of her fingers was dried blood where she had bitten the nails off. He had no more words, but when her swollen eyes met his, none were needed. She threw her arms around him and wept with great, heart-wrenching sobs. Her tears soaked his shirt, while he said nothing, allowing her to rid herself of a burden only tears could relieve. Finally she was silent, and when she let him go, she spoke quietly.

"Thank you, Chance McQuade. If you didn't have a wife I think the world of, I'd take you for myself."

McQuade laughed. "If I didn't have a wife, Maggie, I'd take you in a minute."

"When will Ike be buried?" she asked, becoming serious.

"In the morning," said McQuade. "We've reached the Brazos, and there's no hurry. When Creeker's able to ride, we'll head south, looking for Sam Houston. The wagons will remain here, until we know where Houston is."

"I'll be ready for the burying. There's one thing I . . . I don't think I can do. There's a trunk in the wagon, and in it, Ike's old blue suit. He bought it for the day we stood before the preacher, and he was proud he could still get in it. Could you . . . would you . . . see that he's laid out in it?"

"He'll be wearing it, Maggie," said McQuade. He left quickly before he became any more choked up than he already was, and the first man he saw was Will Haymes.

"How's Maggie?" Will asked.

"Better," said McQuade. "She's preparing herself for the burying tomorrow. There's something I promised Maggie we would do. In the wagon there's a trunk. In it there's an old blue suit of Ike's—"

"My God," Will cut in, "I couldn't bear that."

"I'm going to take care of that, myself," said Mc-Quade. "There's something else I want you to do, along with anybody you can get to help you. This is my idea."

"Anything but puttin' a suit on Ike," Will said, relieved.

"I want some kind of coffin for Ike, even if it's a hollow log. Can you manage it?"

"I can," said Will, "and I'll do it, if I have to take a plank from every damn wagon in this circle."

McQuade realized he had forgotten to ask Maggie if there was a particular place she wanted Ike buried, but he didn't have the nerve to face her again. Most of the men were gathered near the supper fires, awaiting the evening meal.

"We'll need to dig a grave for Ike," said McQuade. "I think beneath that big cypress tree, near the river. Will some of you volunteer?"

"We'll do it," Andrew Burke said.

Recalling only too well the Burkes' antics of the night before, some of the men turned hard eyes on them. McQuade thought some of them were about to deny the offer, and he was quick to speak.

"Go ahead," said McQuade, "and you should do it before dark."

The four of them went to their wagon, took shovels, and left the wagon circle.

"Sometimes tragedy brings out the best in people," Doctor Puckett said quietly.

"It seems to," said McQuade. "How are our wounded folks?"

"They'll all recover," Puckett said, "but there'll probably be some infection and fever."

"They'll have time to heal before we take the trail again," said McQuade. "We'll leave the wagons circled here until Creeker and me can find and talk to Sam Houston."

"I've been neglecting Maggie," Puckett said. "Do you think I should visit her?"

"I've talked to her," said McQuade, "and she's accepted Ike's death, but I don't think it would hurt if you spent some time with her, maybe after supper. She thinks highly of you. But before you do, I need to ask a favor of you, in doing what Maggie asked me to do. There's a suit in her trunk, and she wants Ike laid out in it. I'll need some help, and I don't like to ask anyone else. Some of these people knew Ike well, and they're . . ."

"A bit nervous," said Puckett. "I'll help you after supper, and then I'll visit Maggie."

"Thanks," McQuade said. "I'll have Mary take her some supper and after your visit, spend the rest of the night with her. I'll sleep under the wagon."

After supper, McQuade and Doctor Puckett began the unwelcome task of dressing Ike Peyton in his blue suit, as Maggie had requested. For a finishing touch, they added a red tie over a clean white shirt. True to his word, Will Haymes had somehow come up with material enough for a coffin, including a lid. Will, Tobe, Joel, and Isaac brought it to the back of the Peyton wagon.

"I don't know how you did it," said McQuade, "but

it's a magnificent piece of work. I know Maggie will be pleased.''

"This once was three cedar chiffoniers," Will said, "but some of the ladies thought Ike needed a coffin more than they needed their chests of drawers. Do you want to put him in it now?"

"I think we should," said McQuade. "Open it. Doc and me will put him in it, and then we'll lift it back into the wagon."

At that point, the Burkes returned from their grave-digging, watching McQuade and Doctor Puckett place Ike in the coffin. Only when the coffin had been lifted into the wagon did Andrew Burke speak.

"The grave's done. We made it good an' deep."

"We're obliged," said McQuade. "Go to the cook fire where the coffee pot's still on. The ladies have saved you some supper."

"I'm eatin' with Selma," Luke said.

"Well, the rest of us ain't," said Andrew, "an' we're hungry."

They turned away, and when they had gone, it was Will Haymes who said what they all were thinking.

"By God, somewhere under that hair, thick hide, and cussedness, there might be some *hombres* worth knowing."

"Doc," said McQuade, "while you're visiting with Maggie, I need to talk to Creeker."

"Go ahead," Puckett said. "I heard him telling Lora he's riding south with you in the morning, in search of Sam Houston."

"I'll talk him out of that," said McQuade, "if Lora hasn't already."

"She's in the wagon with him," Puckett said. "You'd better announce your arrival."

The rest of the men laughed, and it was a moment before it dawned on McQuade. He went on, but as he approached the wagon, he identified himself.

"Come on," said Creeker. "Lora brought me supper, and I'm just finishing it."

"He's not telling you the truth," Lora said. "This is a second helping."

McQuade laughed. "I'm glad he's feelin' better, but I don't believe he'll be riding south in the morning."

"That damn sawbones is a snitch," said Creeker.

"He's one more smart *hombre*," McQuade said, "and you're not going anywhere until he says you're ready."

When Doctor Puckett reached the wagon, he found Mary there, and she had managed to persuade Maggie to eat.

"I was about to take these dishes to be washed," said Mary. "Maggie, I'm going to stay with you tonight, and I'll be back."

"You needn't do that," Maggie said. "I must get used to being alone."

"You'll never be alone," said Mary. "You have friends. Now hush. You don't want the doctor thinking you're a fussbudget, do you?"

"That's what I am," Maggie said. "He might as well know now as later."

Puckett laughed, hoisting himself up to the wagon's tail-gate. Mary took the dishes and left them alone. After a long silence, it was Maggie who finally spoke.

"You were kind to come, Doctor, but I'll be all right. It was like . . . facing the end of the world, and I . . . I didn't believe I could."

"We are all stronger than we realize," said Puckett. "God gave us *all* that extra something that we can call forth at a time such as this. My mother always said He never closes one door that He doesn't open another. We must look for it with eyes of faith."

"Your mother taught you well," Maggie said softly. "I've heard many a preacher that didn't make as much sense as you. Mary has a bible. Would you . . . read the Word over Ike tomorrow?"

"Certainly," said Puckett, "if that's what you wish. Do you have a favorite passage?"

"No," Maggie said. "I wasn't brought up in the church, but I'm a believer. Do you . . . have a favorite passage?"

"Yes," said Puckett. "Several of them, in fact. Did Ike have the faith?"

"He did," Maggie said. "He swore a lot, but mostly at the mules. They're a bunch of jugheaded varmints that don't understand nothin' else."

"As long as he had the faith," Puckett said, "you don't have to concern yourself with where Ike is. When I read over him in the morning, I'll turn to one of my very favorite passages. You listen closely."

"I will," said Maggie. "I believe Ike's gone to a better place. Really, it's me that I . . . I'm concerned about. God knows, I got nothin' to go back to, and with Ike gone, there's nothin' ahead but a land grant I can't work by myself. I'm a selfish woman."

"In your position there's nothing selfish about concerning yourself with the future," Puckett said. "Maybe I can brighten that future a bit. I am not just flattering you when I say I have been impressed with your nursing ability. While I don't know what lies ahead for me in Texas, I don't expect to be working a land grant. As the West becomes settled, there will be a need for doctors, and doctors will need nurses. With just a little help, you can become a very capable nurse. Will you allow me to help you, to further develop your potential?"

"Lord, Doctor, I . . . I don't know what to say."

"Say you'll do it," Puckett said. "Anybody can work a land grant, but it takes special people to tend the sick."

Maggie had forgotten her misery, and caught up in what Puckett was proposing, had taken a seat beside him on the wagon's tailgate.

"I'll do it, Doctor, if you'll help me," she said. "God knows, I need something—some purpose—if I'm to go on living."

"You referred to yourself as a selfish woman," said Puckett, "when it's me that's the selfish one. I'm trying to begin my practice on the frontier with my own dedicated nurse."

"This has been the darkest day of my life," Maggie said, "and I'm thankin' you from the bottom of my heart for helpin' me to go on."

"Get what rest you can," said Puckett, "for we still have to say farewell to Ike in the morning. But through it all, remember you have friends here, not the least of which is me. Goodnight."

Then he was gone, a departing shadow in the starlight. Mary had been waiting in the darkness beside the wagon, a smile on her face. Waiting another minute or two, she spoke.

"Maggie, I brought you a fresh cup of coffee."

"Thank you," said Maggie. "Come sit with me for a little while."

"I'll stay until you finish your coffee. Then you need to get some rest."

So much had happened during the day, McQuade gave up any thought of sleep. There were hot coals and a fresh pot of coffee, and he spent much of the evening talking to the others who were as sleepless as he. When he took over the second watch at midnight, he was surprised to have Mary join him.

"I've been talking to Maggie since Doctor Puckett was there," said Mary, "and I'm so excited, I'm wide awake. You can put your mind at rest about Maggie. The doctor's got plans for her. He wants her to become his nurse, when we reach the Rio Colorado."

"She'll likely become much more than that," McQuade said. "I think Doc Puckett is a lonely man."

"Chance McQuade, what an outrageous thing to say. Ike's not even in the ground."

"Oh, hell," said McQuade, "don't lay that proper preacher's-daughter voice on me. I know Ike's yet to be buried, but this is the frontier, and a woman shouldn't be alone. I'd say before Maggie becomes a nurse, she'll become Mrs. Doc Puckett, and I don't care a damn if it's proper or not. It'll be good for them both.''

Mary laughed. ''I couldn't agree more.''

McQuade made his hourly rounds, stopping occasionally to speak to Doctor Puckett, who had taken up residence near the coffee pot.

''All those with serious wounds have fevers,'' said Puckett, ''and I'm expecting them all to break before morning.''

''That's good news,'' McQuade said. ''Seriously, when do you believe Creeker will be well enough to ride?''

''Give him another two days, and he should be able to manage without hurting himself. That is, if he doesn't overdo it.''

''I'll see that he doesn't,'' said McQuade. ''He's used to riding, and it won't be as hard on him as it might be on someone else. Besides, we need to get him out of your wagon.''

''I'm in no hurry,'' Puckett replied. ''I think he's been needing some time with Lora. He had to fight Rufus Hook for her, and they slipped around in the dark after Hedge-pith took over.''

The night wore on, and with the dawn, McQuade made preparations for Ike's burial. It was a duty he didn't relish, and while they owed it to Ike, he wanted it over and done before breakfast. He didn't know Maggie had asked Doctor Puckett to read the Word over Ike, until Mary handed him the bible. McQuade, with the help of Gunter Warnell, Eli Bibb, and Will Haymes, lifted Ike's coffin out of the wagon.

''Allow me a few minutes in the wagon,'' said Maggie. ''I must get my Sunday best from the trunk.''

Everybody had gathered for the burying except those who had been wounded the day before. Even Creeker was there, Lora by his side. Most of them—even the Burkes—wore the best they had. Doctor Puckett was dressed in a solid black suit, white ruffled shirt, and a flowing black string tie. McQuade thought he looked more like a preacher than a doctor. Maggie soon emerged from the wagon, dressed in black.

"We're going to open the coffin and hold the service here," said McQuade. "Those of you who want to follow it to the grave are welcome to do so."

McQuade lifted the cedar lid of the coffin and stood aside, allowing one and all to file past for a last look at Ike Peyton. McQuade stood next to Maggie, an arm around her shoulders. She would be the last to stand before the coffin. Finally it was time for her to be led to it, and while there were tears, she bore up well. Her tears had been shed the night before. Doctor Puckett stood at the head of the coffin and opened the bible.

"I am reading from chapter eight of the book of Romans," said Puckett.

> And we know that all things work together for good to them that love God, to them who are the called according to his purpose.
> For whom he did foreknow, he also did predestinate to be conformed to the image of his Son, that he might be the firstborn among many brethren.
> Moreover, whom he did predestinate, them he also called: and whom he called, them he also justified: and whom he justified, them he also glorified.
> What shall we say to these things? If God be for us, who can be against us?

"There is much more that I could read," said Puckett, closing the bible. "But Ike does not need it, and it is better for those of us left behind to read it for ourselves. For if we seek God, it is because we already have Him, for He has given us the faith to believe, for faith, like salvation, is a gift from God. We believe Ike had both, and that his immortal soul has returned to the God who claimed him before the foundation of the world. Let us pray."

The prayer was short. While many followed the coffin

to the grave, Maggie did not, nor did Mary and McQuade. Maggie was calm, McQuade eyed Puckett with new respect, and it was Mary who spoke.

"Doctor Puckett, I have heard my father preach many times, and he was an eloquent and dedicated man, but I've never heard anything more moving than what you just said."

"Thank you," said Puckett. "It's what I believe, what my ancestors have believed, and what Christ taught while here on earth."

"All Ike's tribulations are behind him," McQuade said. "It's those of us left behind who still have a long trail to ride."

"You can have your wagon, McQuade," said Maggie. "I'll return to my own, and when we take the trail again, I'll take the reins."

Doctor Puckett laughed. "Are you going to swear at the mules?"

"If the varmints need it, I can rise to the occasion," Maggie said, looking him in the eye.

"It's been a long night," said McQuade. "Let's have some hot coffee and breakfast."

On the Brazos. July 5, 1837.

Those who had been wounded in the Comanche attack were much improved, all threat of infection behind them. Creeker, following Ike's burial, hadn't returned to the wagon.

"The hard floor of the wagon was hurtin' me more than the wounds," he said.

"We'll wait two more days," said McQuade, "and then we'll ride south."

There was no further sign of the Comanches, and the only enemy was boredom, as the days dragged on. McQuade took advantage of the time, speaking to many of the men about the defense of the wagons while he and Creeker were away.

"I don't care how quiet and peaceful it seems," McQuade told them. "I've heard this before, and I'll swear to the truth of it: when you don't see Indians, it's time to worry."

But Mary seemed possessed of some premonition, and for the two days and nights before McQuade was to go, she worried constantly.

"My mother was like this," she said defensively. "That's all I remember about her, but just when it seemed everything was going well, she began to worry."

"Damn it," said McQuade, "when you go courting trouble, it always meets you more than half way. We must find Sam Houston's militia before we go any farther with all these wagons. Creeker and me can get ourselves and our horses out of sight in a hurry, but not these wagons. Once we near the Rio Colorado, we'll have to know exactly where we're going. We can't just pick up these wagons and put 'em in our pockets."

"I know," she sighed, "but I haven't forgotten the day you and Creeker were attacked by the Comanches. You were near enough for help to reach you. This time, you'll be far away from us, and Sam Houston's militia won't know you're there."

"It'll be up to us to find them before the Comanches and Miguel Monclova find us," said McQuade. "There's some risk involved, but not nearly as much as taking this wagon train with us before we know exactly where we're going."

"There's something I'm supposed to ask you," she said, "and I . . . I'm . . ."

"Afraid?"

"No," said Mary, "that's not the word for it."

"Then ask," McQuade said impatiently. "I promise not to hit you."

She laughed nervously. "Oh, I know you better than

that. Lora Kirby asked me if she can stay with me while you and Creeker are gone. I told her I'd ask you.''

"Why would you have to ask me?"

"Well," said Mary, "because of . . . of what she . . . was . . . before Creeker."

"Forget what she was," McQuade said. "By God, if the Burkes can change, anybody can. The woman needs friends, and she's never goin' to have them, if the rest of you all keep your noses out of joint because of what she once was. Didn't your daddy ever speak to you about such?"

"Yes," she admitted, "but sometimes it's not easy to practice what he preached. Don't you know that?"

"I know," said McQuade, relenting. "Take Lora in and be friends with her, if you can. I know Creeker will feel better. Not so much for his sake, but for hers.''

"I'll be as much a friend as she'll allow me to be," Mary said. "Maybe we can both worry about you and Creeker together."

"Yes," said McQuade, with a sigh. "That will be a great help to us."

CHAPTER 18

On the morning of the seventh of July, McQuade and Creeker prepared to ride south in search of Sam Houston's militia. Within his bedroll, each man packed a quart of whiskey and in a pack behind each saddle, there was food for two weeks. Before departing, Creeker spent a few minutes alone with Lora, while McQuade joined Mary in the wagon.

"I can't promise you I won't worry," said Mary. "The only answer my father ever had to my mother's worrying was to say some prayers. I'll do that."

"Thank you," McQuade said. "I believe that will do more good than the worrying."

Creeker was with Lora in Doctor Puckett's wagon, and her feelings were much the same as Mary's.

"I don't even want to think of what would become of me if you never came back," she said.

"Then don't think of that," said Creeker, "because I'm comin' back. You think, after I've drifted from pillar to post all my life, that I'm goin' to lose it all, just when I've found you and there's a future ahead?"

"I know you won't, if you can help it," she said. "The way I've lived my life, God has always seemed awfully far away. Mary says instead of worrying, we should talk to Him."

"That's good advice," said Creeker. "We'll be as careful as we can, and even taking our time, we should be back in six days.''

Everybody gathered to see them off and wish them well, and as the rising sun began building a glory on the eastern horizon, they crossed the Brazos and rode south. Riding at a slow, mile-eating gallop, they rested their horses once an hour. When they reached fresh water they took a longer rest, allowing their horses sufficient time before they drank. They saw no one.

''We're makin' good time,'' Creeker said. ''We could likely reach the Rio Colorado late today, if we tried.''

''We could,'' said McQuade, ''but I don't think that's wise. The river runs just about all the way across Texas, and we don't know where we'll find the Monclova camp or the Sam Houston camp. We don't want to stumble onto Monclova while we're looking for the militia, and I want to reach the Rio Colorado with some daylight ahead of us.''

''Those returning emigrants didn't tell us where Monclova's bunch is,'' said Creeker, ''and that's the one thing we most need to know. While we know Houston hopes to build a town on the river, how are we to know where we'll find Monclova's camp?''

''We don't know that he has a permanent camp,'' McQuade said. ''In fact, we don't even know where along the river those grants are located. If we can find Houston's militia, they should have some idea as to where Monclova's bunch is.''

''We also don't know that Monclova ain't had more men join him,'' said Creeker. ''If he had fifty men before, he could have a hundred by now.''

''Against fifty armed men, we'd be a pair of gone geese,'' McQuade replied, ''and any more wouldn't make much difference. We just have to avoid Monclova's bunch.''

''We can do it, just you and me,'' said Creeker, ''but not with the wagons. If these Mexicans don't have a permanent camp, and are just ridin' around, they'll spot us.''

"I'm considering asking Houston for as many out-riders as he can spare. Suppose we had fifty mounted men riding the length of the train, from the lead wagons to the last?"

"With enough ammunition, we could stand off an army," Creeker said, "and we have the ammunition. We even got that pile of guns we took from Sutton's gang."

"If we were told the truth, that Houston has at least two hundred men, then there is virtually no way Mon-clova can hurt us," said McQuade. "And that goes for the Comanches, too."

"This expedition has taken on a lot more promise since Hook and Hedgepith cashed in," Creeker said.

"Yes," said McQuade, "and what began as one man's greedy obsession may well change the course of history. The irony of it is, if both Hook and Hedgepith had lived to reach Texas, their dreams of a town would have been in vain. I believe the Mexican government would have seized the wagons and everything in them, using the am-munition and the weapons against Sam Houston's reb-els."

"It makes you wonder," Creeker said. "I heard a preacher once that said God uses the ungodly to perform miracles. I don't know if Sam Houston's a godly man, but he's about to witness a miracle."

To the south, along the Rio Colorado, Houston's battered forces had just beaten back an attack by Monclova's Mex-ican renegades. Houston himself had a bloody arm, while a dozen others had more serious wounds. Three men had died. Houston's lieutenants—Joshua Hamilton, Stockton Saunders, and Alonzo Holden—looked grim.

"There may not be enough ammunition to withstand another siege, sir," Hamilton said.

"We'll hold out as long as we can," Houston replied. "Have we medicine to treat the wounded?"

"Only alcohol for disinfectant," said Saunders. "Noth-ing for pain, nothing to fight the possible infection."

"The spirits of the men are pretty low," Holden said. "We no longer have ammunition for hunting, and the soup's gettin' damn thin."

"We've reached the end of the trail," said Hamilton. "We can no longer fight to save Texas, for there's nothing to fight with. We must save ourselves, if we can. You must soon make a decision or the men will desert."

"Tomorrow," Houston said, "I'll talk to them."

They left him then. Removing his battered hat, he knelt and bowed his head.

Miguel Monclova was pleased when his lieutenants, Pedro Mendez and Hidalgo Cortez, reported to him.

"We do as you say," Mendez exulted. "We attack at dawn, hit them hard, and then we ride away. Three die, many be wounded."

"*Excelente*," said Monclova. "There are yet too many of them and not enough of us, but that soon change. We have more men, more guns, more ammunition. *Por dios*, then we kill them all."

McQuade and Creeker found a secluded spring, cooked their supper, and doused their fire before dark.

"What about Comanches?" Creeker asked. "Do we dare sleep?"

"One at a time," said McQuade, "and then with one eye open. We'll move well away from the spring, and sleep near the picketed horses. They'll warn us if anybody tries to slip up on us."

"You sleep first," Creeker said, "and I'll wake you at midnight."

"Keeno," said McQuade. "I want to get an early start in the morning. I'd like to reach the Rio Colorado by noon. Then maybe we can find the militia's camp before dark."

McQuade arose at midnight. They had left the spring, picketing the horses on a wide plateau, with virtually no cover for potential enemies. McQuade looked at the twinkling stars in a purple velvet sky, at the barren plains, and thought of Mary. He had slept but little, already awake when Creeker had come to awaken him. He was eager to take the trail south, to meet with Houston, to relieve himself of the responsibility of the wagons and the multitude of people who depended on him. But would he ever truly be free, as long as the territory was in the clutches of Mexico? He got up and walked, restless, and well before first light, Creeker was awake.

"I haven't slept very well," said Creeker. "Maybe it's those Comanches, fresh on my mind. What say we conceal a small fire, stir up some breakfast, and hit the trail?"

McQuade laughed. "We're both of the same mind. I've been thinkin' of that very thing for the last hour or two."

They rode south, watchful but seeing nobody, and well before the sun was noon high, they came upon a river which they believed was the Rio Colorado. Almost immediately, the river widened into what became a small lake. They rode until the banks again narrowed and the river flowed on toward the southeast.*

"It's got to be the Rio Colorado," said McQuade. "The question is, do we ride up- or downstream to find Houston's militia?"

"Ever since we rode south, I've been wishing we'd gone through Hedgepith's papers," Creeker said. "It wouldn't hurt if we knew where along this river those grants lie."

"I've thought of that, myself," said McQuade, "but I've changed my mind. I believe if we went nosin' around those grants, we'd be more likely to run into Monclova's outfit. I'm thinkin' Sam Houston is in no way involved in these grants, beyond trying to recruit men to fight for Texas."

"You're likely right," Creeker said, "but I can't help wondering if Monclova's camp won't be somewhere to the south. With this river flowing into the Gulf, it would

---

*Lake Buchanan, near the present-day town of Lampasas, Texas.

be easy to bring men and supplies along the coast, from Mexico. Maybe by sailing ship, if we are up against the Mexican government.''

"By God," said McQuade, "you may be on to something. It's been a while since I've seen a map of the Texas coast, but it can't be more than three hundred miles from Matamoros to the point where the Colorado empties into the Gulf. We must discuss this with Sam Houston. My God, a sailing ship could drop hundreds of armed men right in his lap.''

"And ours," Creeker said. "That would give them a supply line all the way from Mexico City to the Rio Colorado. The best we can do is what we're doing now: wagoning in supplies from St. Louis, or New Orleans.''

"Houston ought to have men watching Matagorda Bay," said McQuade. "Any Mexican ship landing there will be bad news for all of us.''

They rode carefully, reining up when they saw the distant gray of smoke against the blue of the sky.

"Somebody's camp," said Creeker. "Downriver maybe two miles.''

"Well-manned, I'd say," McQuade replied. "That smoke can be seen a hundred miles in every direction. I believe we've found Sam Houston's militia, but we'll ride careful.''

Rounding a bend in the river, they reined up. Ahead was a log structure on the order of a barn, surrounded by a stockade constructed of upright logs. Beyond, along the river, a large number of horses grazed, while armed men stood watch. On a staff just above the stockade gate fluttered a flag with a single star.

"One thing I'm sure of," said McQuade. "That's not the Mexican flag. I once saw one on a sailing ship in the harbor at New Orleans. Now the trick is to be recognized without being shot.''

The crude fort was between them and the massive herd of grazing horses, so they rode around behind it, away from the river. Once they were within sight of the herd, but well out of rifle range, McQuade shouted to the riders.

"Hello, the fort. We're friends, come to see Sam Houston."

Four men kicked their horses into a gallop, reining up fifty yards shy of McQuade and Creeker. The lead rider shouted a question.

"Who are you, and what do you want?"

"McQuade and Creeker," McQuade shouted back, "and we want to talk to Houston. We have a wagon train five days north of here. Now do we see Houston or not?"

"Ride around to the gate and wait there. I'll tell him you're here."

McQuade and Creeker rode to the gate at the front of the stockade. The gate opened and the man who had challenged them went inside. His three comrades sat their horses and eyed McQuade and Creeker. Each man had a rifle under his arm and their eyes were full of suspicion and questions. The one who had gone to talk to Houston returned hurriedly.

"Mr. Houston will see you. Leave your horses here."

McQuade and Creeker dismounted, following their host through the gate. The fort was crude in the extreme, providing only shelter. Bedrolls and blankets littered the dirt floor, saddles lay in piles, and rifles leaned against the walls. A dozen half-naked men lay on blankets, bloody bandages covering their various wounds. X-frame tables lined one wall, and men—fifty or more—sat on rough-hewn benches. They got hastily to their feet, as McQuade and Creeker entered. There was no mistaking Sam Houston, as he came forth to meet them. His dress was rough, his old hat the worse for wear, and his boots muddy, but there was a certain eloquence about him, even in these rough surroundings. His voice was deep, his manner reserved, and he spoke courteously.

"Will you gentlemen be seated?"

"Not for a while," said McQuade. "We've been in the saddle for two days. We have a lot to tell you. The most important is that we have fifteen wagonloads of supplies, including guns, ammunition, and black powder, five days north of here.''

Every man within the building lost his reserve, surging forth, shouting questions, each seeking to drown out the other.

''Silence,'' Houston bawled, and it had the desired effect. ''These men have come to our rescue, God be praised, and the least we can do is show them some courtesy. Please continue, gentlemen.''

Taking turns, McQuade and Creeker told of the men and women who had signed on with Hook in St. Louis, seeking Mexican land grants. Without going into detail, they told of Hook's and Hedgepith's deaths, leaving the freight for the proposed town ownerless. The men cheered when told of the decision of the emigrants to not only join Houston's militia, but to contribute the fifteen wagonloads of supplies.

''The way we see it,'' McQuade concluded, ''is that the future of Texas lies not with Mexico, but with the United States. We've decided that if we have to fight the Mexicans, we'll fight them first, and then take a chance on our land grants.''

''By the Eternal,'' said Houston, ''if I live to see the stars and stripes raised over these Texas plains, you will all have those promised land grants. I swear it, before God.''

''What's your situation?'' Creeker asked.

''Until you gentlemen rode in, it couldn't have been worse,'' said Houston. ''Monclova's forces attacked yesterday at dawn, killing three men and wounding all those you see there on pallets. We used the last of the alcohol for disinfectant, and we have nothing for pain or fever. We don't have enough powder and shot to repel another attack.''

''How many men do you have?'' McQuade asked.

''More than two hundred, not counting the wounded,'' said Houston. ''You don't see them here, because they're standing watch out in the brush. We have the numbers, but we have so little ammunition, we dare not attack. The best we've been able to do is to defend ourselves, and after the attack yesterday, we're unable to do even that.''

"I figure the wagons are about eighty-five miles north of here,'' McQuade said. "Since we didn't know where you were, Creeker and me rode south to find you. If nothing goes wrong, the wagons are at least five days away, and you don't have that much time. Will you allow a hundred of your men to ride back with us, immediately?''

"A hundred and more,'' said Houston. "What do you have in mind?''

"Resting our horses, we can ride all night,'' McQuade said, "and we'll be there in the morning at dawn. Every man can carry fifty pounds behind his saddle, without it being too hard on his horse. We can send you whiskey for medicine, laudanum, food, powder, shot, and we have a pile of extra weapons we took from a band of outlaws. It should put you in a position to hold out until the wagons can get here with the rest of it. By the way, we'll be bringing a doctor with us.''

"The Almighty God didn't overlook a thing,'' Houston said, his voice breaking.

"One thing more, before we go,'' said McQuade. "Do you have a map of Texas, showing the coastline?''

"Yes,'' Houston replied. "I'll fetch it.''

He spread the map out on one of the crude tables. McQuade and Creeker studied it.

"Here's the fort, where we propose to build a town,'' said Houston, circling a bend in the river.

"Where do Monclova's attacks come from?'' McQuade asked.

"From downriver,'' said Houston, "and they retreat in that direction. But we have no idea where their permanent camp is, or if they have one.''

"It's somewhere downriver from here,'' McQuade said. "See how near we are to the Gulf of Mexico? Following the river, it can't be more than a hundred and fifty miles.''

"No more than that," said Houston.

"Unless we can stop them, they have a supply line, by water, directly from Mexico City," McQuade said. "A sailing ship can bring hundreds of armed men to Matagorda Bay, and they can march up the Colorado, right into your back door."

"My God," said Houston. "You're right. They can bring in anything they need. Even cannon."

"You need half a dozen men watching Matagorda Bay day and night," McQuade said. "I realize they need arms, ammunition, and food. The hundred riders you're sending with us can return here sometime tomorrow night. You should then deploy at least four men to watch for incoming ships, and others to locate Monclova's camp."

"But what are we to do about incoming ships?"

"We're going to sink them," said McQuade, "before they can unload armed men and supplies. We'll just have to hope that first ship doesn't arrive before I can get back here with the wagons."

"With powder and shot, we can hold our own," Houston said. "Once we're decently armed, we'll stage some attacks of our own."

"Try to avoid any conflict until we get here with the wagons," said McQuade. "Use the powder and shot we'll send just for defense. Monclova and his bunch are only a drop in the bucket compared to what we'll face, if Mexico City sends a ship to Matagorda Bay. The moment your riders return with powder, shot, and food we'll send you, order four men to Matagorda Bay. At first sight of a Mexican sailing ship, they're to get word to you immediately. We must intercept anything coming from Mexico City. If we can block their supply line, we can starve them out just like they've been starving you."

"By the Eternal," said Houston, "that's their weakness, just as it's been ours. Holden, Hamilton, Saunders—ride out and bring me fifty of those men on watch. Those of you in this room who are sound of limb, get your saddles and go for your horses. You will be riding north with these gentlemen for powder, shot, food, and medicine.''

Seizing saddles, whooping their joy, they practically ran over one another getting out the door.

"We have a couple of quarts of whiskey in our bedrolls,'' McQuade said. "We'll leave that with you for your wounded, and we'll send more with your returning riders.''

"It will be a blessing,'' said Houston. "The most difficult thing about asking these men to fight is the knowledge that the wounded will most surely die for lack of medicine. With food, powder, shot, medicine, and a doctor, the men will become more confident, and my burdened conscience can take a rest. I'll see that you have fresh horses.''

In a remarkably short time, the men had ridden in from sentry duty and had been told of their mission by those Sam Houston had sent forth from the fort. McQuade and Creeker followed Houston outside the fort, where the assigned men stood beside their horses. Quickly, Houston told them what was expected of them, and his voice was lost in their shouting. When they quieted, their eyes were on Creeker and McQuade.

"Mount up and let's ride,'' said McQuade. "With luck, we can be there by dawn.''

They rode north, with another four hours of daylight. They rested their horses every hour, and while the men who rode with them were enthusiastic, they talked little. Mostly they kept to themselves, and while resting the horses, Creeker and McQuade could talk.

"You forgot to ask Houston about using some of these men for a wagon escort,'' said Creeker.

"I didn't forget,'' McQuade replied, "I just thought better of it. We don't know that Monclova hasn't been sent more men, and if there's another attack, Houston will need all the men he has. We can bring the wagons along the way we rode in, and keeping to open country, we should be able to avoid the Comanches.''

"I hope so," said Creeker. "Those Indian attacks play hell when they take you totally by surprise. Where outriders are concerned, you might consider allowing women—those who are able and willing—to take the reins. That would free some of the men to ride shotgun, lessening the danger of surprise attacks."

"That may well be the solution to reaching the Rio Colorado without any more losses to the Comanches," said McQuade. "You can use your head and your gun, and that's what keeps a man alive on the frontier. If circumstances had been different, we could have been working together all the way from St. Louis. Damn Rufus Hook and his stubborn ways."

They rode on, and it soon became obvious they would reach the Brazos and the circle of wagons long before daylight. Once, while resting the horses, McQuade had a suggestion for Sam Houston's men.

"Gents, by resting the horses often, we'll reach the wagons sometime after midnight. I'd suggest that all of you sleep until dawn and have breakfast before returning to the Rio Colorado. We can load you up with supplies while you eat, and by pacing yourselves like we're doing, you can still reach Houston's fort by sundown tomorrow."*

"I'm fer that," said one of the men. "We been eatin' so poorly, it'll take a while fer my belly to git over the shock of honest-to-God grub."

There were growls of agreement and some laughter. It was a practical suggestion they could appreciate, for their horses would need rest for the ride back to Houston's fort. By the stars, McQuade judged it was less than an hour past midnight when they reached the south bank of the Brazos. There he again spoke to the men.

"Let Creeker and me ride in first. Because of the Co-

---

*A good horse, rested often, can cover as much as five miles in half an hour, over flat ground and lesser slopes. A slow gallop doesn't tire a horse as quickly.

manches, we've been posting triple sentries. We'll alert the men on watch that you're coming, and one of us will ride back for you."

They sat their horses and waited, as McQuade and Creeker crossed the river. Riding as near the circled wagons as they dared, but still out of gun range, McQuade called out a greeting just loud enough for the sentries to hear.

"Creeker and McQuade riding in. Hold your fire."

"Come on," a voice replied. "This is Will Haymes."

Creeker and McQuade dismounted, looping the reins of their horses around a wagon wheel. Climbing through the maze of wagons, they entered the circle. To their amazement, almost everybody was awake, prepared to greet them. Mary ran to McQuade, while Lora wasted no time in getting to Creeker. Questions flew thick and fast, and it was McQuade who spoke.

"We found Houston's militia, and they're in a bad way. He has two hundred men, and we brought a hundred of them back with us. They'll get what sleep they can, and then have breakfast with us. They'll be riding back, taking powder, shot, medicine, food, and whiskey for use as medicine. As soon as they're on their way, we'll take the trail with the wagons. We're about eighty-five miles away. If you have more questions, ask Creeker. I'm going out and signal those men to come on across the river. Will, you'll have to move three wagons, so they can bring their horses into the circle."

McQuade left the circle, returning to his horse. Oscar Odell had already unsaddled the horse Creeker had ridden, while Levi Phelps was unsaddling McQuade's horse.

"They looked give out," Oscar said, "and we reckoned you and Creeker was too."

"Thanks," said McQuade. "I'm going to the river and call in Houston's riders."

It wasn't that long a walk, and McQuade didn't mind it after so much time spent in the saddle. Reaching the bank of the Brazos, the starlight allowed him to see the mass of riders across the river.

"This is McQuade," he called, just loud enough for them to hear. "The sentries know you're coming, and we've opened a place for you to ride into the wagon circle. Come on."

"We're comin'," a voice answered.

McQuade walked on back toward the wagon circle, where Will Haymes had moved the three wagons. Prior to entering the circle, the riders reined up.

"Go on in and find a place to drop your saddles," said McQuade. "The wagons will be put back in place, and your horses will be safe from the Comanches. Get what sleep you can, and we'll have breakfast at first light. You'll meet all of us then."

They entered the circle, dismounted, and began unsaddling their horses. One at a time Will hitched the teams to the displaced wagons, filling the gap in the circle. All sentries had returned to their posts, and everybody else seemed to have gone back to their blankets or bedrolls. Only Mary and Lora were still awake, excited and relieved over the safe return of McQuade and Creeker. But Doctor Puckett had been waiting for Mary and Lora to finish their greeting. He spoke.

"Tomorrow, perhaps while we're resting the teams, I'd like to hear all about the Sam Houston Militia. For now, I think you weary travelers need sleep. Creeker, you and Lora can have the wagon. Warm as it's been, I'm sleeping outside."

"Doc," said McQuade, "I've made plans for us to take the trail tomorrow without asking you about those who were wounded the day Ike was killed. Will they be able to travel comfortably?"

"I think so," Puckett replied. "Everybody's tired of the inactivity."

Creeker and Lora accepted the offer of the wagon, while McQuade and Mary went on to their wagon.

"I missed you," said Mary, "but I don't think quite as

much as Lora missed Creeker. She's so afraid something's going to happen, that her chance for a decent life will somehow slip away.''

"She's more of a worrier than you are, then," McQuade said. "How is Maggie?''

"Sleeping in her own wagon and spending every waking minute picking the doctor's brain for medical learning. She's going to become either the best nurse, or the worst nag in all of Texas.''

McQuade laughed, and they drew the curtains at the front and back of the wagon.

"Just how tired are you?" Mary asked.

"Exhausted," said McQuade, "but I'd be willing to sacrifice my last remaining strength for a good cause.''

"I have one," she said. "Take off everything, including your hat.''

CHAPTER 19

∽

The camp came alive well before first light, since breakfast had to be prepared for the hundred extra men. McQuade, Creeker, and a dozen other men set about assembling the packs that would be taken to Houston's stronghold on the Rio Colorado. Some packs contained only food, others only powder and shot, and a few only bottled whiskey and the medical supplies Doctor Puckett had recommended. By the time Houston's riders had eaten, their packs were ready.

"We've had no time for introductions," said McQuade. "Except for Creeker and me, you know none of us, and none of us know any of you. But that can come later. For now we know that we're all together in this fight for Texas independence, and that will have to be enough. You men ride careful, and we'll be along with the wagons as soon as we can."

McQuade's outfit shouted good wishes, and one of Houston's men stepped forward, his hand up. When the uproar diminished, he spoke.

"I'm Anton Bickler, from Tennessee, an' for all of Houston's militia, I'm thankin' you. God only knows what we'd have done, if you hadn't come to our rescue. Keep an eye out for the Comanches and Monclova's bunch, an' we'll look forward to havin' you join us on the Rio Colorado."

With that, they mounted and rode out. McQuade's outfit watched them as they rode across the Brazos and were lost among the sagebrush and thickets to the south.

"I just hope Monclova's bunch didn't attack Houston and his men again this morning," said Creeker.

"So do I," McQuade said. "Now we have to get to our breakfast and begin this last few days of our journey."

But McQuade had something to say, and he said it before breakfast.

"Creeker's come up with an idea that could spare us attacks from Comanches as well as Monclova's bunch. We need as many men as possible to serve as outriders, to flank the wagons from one end of the train to the other. These men will be ready to recognize and repel any attack before the attackers can get close enough to hurt us. Trouble is, we don't have these men. Creeker believes—and I agree—that many of you women can take the reins, freeing the men to ride alongside the wagons. Creeker and me have ridden all the way to the Rio Colorado, and we know where the water is. There are no drop-offs, and the plain is mostly flat. How many of you ladies can and will take over your teams the rest of the way to the Rio Colorado?"

There were enthusiastic shouts, and after a show of hands, McQuade had sixty men to serve as a mounted escort the rest of the way. During breakfast, McQuade spoke to Cal Tabor about something he had been considering.

"Cal, Ike's has always been one of the three lead wagons, but now that Ike's gone, I'd like you to take his position. Maggie's capable, but the lead wagons call for a man with a quick gun."

"I'll do it," said Cal. "With the outriders prepared for an attack, that'll give us time to rein up, get off the box, and shoot back."

McQuade went looking for Maggie to tell her of the new arrangement, but was unable to find her. Mary was having breakfast with Creeker and Lora.

"I don't know where she is," Mary said, "unless she's in the wagon."

"My God," said Creeker, "she may have gone to Ike's grave. The Comanches . . ."

Creeker dropped his coffee cup and was one step behind McQuade. While the new-made grave could be seen from the wagon circle, it was far enough away that a watchful Comanche could have taken Maggie without difficulty. She was there, her head bowed, and McQuade and Creeker hurried to her.

"Maggie," McQuade scolded, "the Comanches could have stolen you away without any of us knowing you were gone."

"I didn't think of that," said Maggie. "I just wanted a little time alone with Ike before we had to go. I'm ready now."

McQuade positioned Maggie's wagon beside his own, with Mary at the reins. After the wagons crossed the Brazos and the train was strung out, three wagons abreast, McQuade assigned his sixty outriders. Front-to-back, thirty armed, mounted men flanked the train on either side. Groat, Slack, Rucker, and Ellis rode behind the last wagons, their eyes on the back-trail. McQuade and Creeker rode ahead of the lead wagons.

"This was a good move," said McQuade. "I just regret we didn't come up with it a lot sooner. Ike would still be alive."

"It works only to the extent that the women can handle the teams and wagons," Creeker replied. "We passed through some rough country in Indian Territory. It was hard on some of the men, and with sixty women at the reins, you might have been in some real trouble. We have an advantage from here on to the Rio Colorado, because you and me had a chance to ride it ahead of the wagons."

Their first day on the trail after leaving the Brazos was uneventful, and they circled the wagons near a spring where McQuade and Creeker had rested their horses.

"Easiest day we've ever had," said Isaac McDaniel.

"Them hundred riders that's ahead of us is leavin' a trail we could foller in the dark."

McQuade spoke to all the women who had taken the reins, allowing their men to ride alongside the wagons.

"If it means the difference between some of us living and dying," Ellen Warnell said, "it's worth it, and the very least we can do."

"That's what hurt us before," said Lucy Tabor. "By the time the men knew an attack was coming, the Indians were already on us. Now, the men are ready to fight, without the lost time it takes to rein in the team and get off the wagon box."

Every woman appreciated the opportunity to do her part, freeing the men to devote their time and attention to the protection of the wagon train. Many within the party, men and women alike, thanked Creeker for his plan which they believed would see them all to their destination alive.

Two days after their victory, Miguel Monclova announced their permanent camp was to be moved downriver, some twenty-five miles beyond Houston's fort. While his men were curious, none were in a position to question the move except Pedro Mendez and Hidalgo Cortez, and they remained silent. Monclova would reveal his purpose when he was ready. Half a dozen miles before they reached Houston's fort, they veered to the north, away from the river. While Monclova didn't fear Houston's forces, there was nothing to be gained by having them suspect Monclova's headquarters was being moved. Thus it was with some surprise that they came upon the trail left by Houston's men, as they had ridden north with Creeker and McQuade.

"Many riders," Pedro Mendez observed, "Where do they go?"

"*Madre de dios*," said Hidalgo Cortez, "per'ap we frighten them all away."

"Ortiz, Juan," Monclova said, summoning two men, "ride near enough to the *Tejano* fort to see if it is still inhabited, and report back to me. We will continue on."

Within the hour, Ortiz and Juan caught up to the rest of the band, and riding alongside Monclova, reported what they had seen.

"We see but a few *Tejanos*," said Ortiz, "and many *caballos* be gone."

"They do not run," Monclova said.

"But where do they go, and why?" Mendez asked.

"We do not concern ourselves with that," said Monclova. "When we have established our new camp, we ride back to the fort. Tomorrow at dawn, we attack. While so many of the *Tejanos* are away, we will kill those that remain, and burn their fort."

The sun had already slipped below the western horizon, and the first stars twinkled their silver majesty in a darkening sky, when Houston's men who had ridden north reined up on a ridge overlooking Sam Houston's fort. Kicking their tired horses into a trot, they rode on, unaware that they returned barely in time . . .

McQuade continued to take precautions against the Comanches, with half the men on watch until midnight, and the rest until dawn. They were unmolested, and with McQuade and Creeker knowing the distances to the next water, they had an edge. The Texas sun bore down on them unmercifully, and if they had an enemy, it was the heat. The third day after leaving the Brazos, McQuade had a decision to make.

"We're going to have to slow the gait and rest the teams more often, or the heat's going to be our undoing," he said.

While there was heat lightning far to the west, there was no sign of rain, and even at night, the heat became oppressive. Less than an hour until midnight, McQuade sat on the tailgate of the wagon, wearing only his drawers.

"Why don't you join me? It's a mite cooler," he said.

"No use," said Mary. "In here, I can wear nothing at all, and if I came out there, I'd have to get dressed."

"No, you wouldn't," McQuade said. "There's no moon."

"There's mosquitoes as big as turkey buzzards, and my hide's not as tough as yours. Besides, you'll be going on watch soon, and I'd be alone."

At midnight, McQuade took over for Creeker, and when he reached the Peyton wagon he found Doctor Puckett and Maggie on the wagon box, talking. He grinned in the dark, for it reminded him of those nights which now seemed so long ago, when he and Mary had spent their evenings in similar fashion. It worked out well, he thought, for that allowed Creeker and Lora the use of Puckett's wagon. He went on, speaking to the men. He had purposely separated the Burkes, and when he found Andrew slumped against a wagon wheel, he thought the old man was asleep.

"Burke," he said.

There was no response, and when McQuade felt for a pulse, there was none. He ran to the Peyton wagon.

"Doc," he said urgently, "you're needed. Andrew Burke's either dead or close to it."

The doctor came off the wagon box, Maggie following. He ran to his wagon for his bag, and McQuade led him to the inert Andrew. Puckett didn't bother seeking a pulse, but drew his stethoscope from his bag. He knelt, listening, repositioned the scope, and listened again. When he spoke, it was to Maggie.

"He's alive, but not by much. Maggie, bring me some blankets."

Maggie ran for the blankets, and Puckett got astraddle of Andrew Burke, his hands flat on Burke's chest. Once, twice, three times, he pressed down hard. He continued the process until Maggie returned. He then tried the pulse, had trouble finding it, and getting astraddle of Burke again, began pressing down on his chest. Breathing hard, sweating, he again listened through the stethoscope.

"Spread one of the blankets on the ground, Maggie. I'll need you to help lift him onto it, McQuade."

Maggie spread one of the blankets, and McQuade helped Puckett lift Burke onto it. Without being told, Maggie spread the other two blankets over Andrew.

"You'd better tell the other Burkes," Puckett told McQuade. "It's his heart. It had all but stopped. It's a bit more steady, but still weak. He may not last the night."

McQuade quickly found the three Burkes and led them back to Andrew. The doctor then told them what he had told McQuade.

"There's not much I can do," said Puckett. "Each time he has one of these attacks, his heart will become progressively weaker. He has no business harnessing, unharnessing, or driving the teams. Stress or strain of any kind could be the finish of him."

"But he wasn't doin' nothin' but leanin' agin a wagon wheel," Matthew said.

"That's the best advice I can give you," said Puckett. "He hasn't been taking care of himself, and it's caught up with him. Go on back to your posts. I'll keep an eye on him the rest of the night."

"I'll stay too," Maggie said. "I want to know what you did to save him."

McQuade continued his rounds, saying nothing about Andrew Burke's condition. There was nothing to be done that Doctor Puckett and Maggie couldn't do, and McQuade wanted nothing to delay an early start the next morning.

There was rejoicing at Houston's fort, on the Rio Colorado. There were hams, sides of bacon, beans, sugar, and best of all, coffee. There was whiskey to treat the wounded men who were feverish and suffering infection, and most of all, powder and shot for their weapons.

"It's a miracle from the Almighty God," Houston shouted.

"Sir," said one of the men, "you should know that a trail crossed ours up yonder to the north. Fifty or more horses, headin' downriver. They was far enough north so's not to be seen from here, and they looked to have passed through early this mornin'."

"That brings to mind what our friends McQuade and Creeker suggested," Houston said, "and that's the possibility Monclova has or will establish a headquarters closer to the Gulf in anticipation of a sailing ship from Mexico City."

"They also suggested you send men to watch Matagorda Bay," said Joshua Hamilton, "to report to you if and when a ship is sighted."

"That is precisely what I intend to do in the morning," Houston replied, "and now that we have adequate ammunition, I want no less than a hundred of you surrounding this encampment. If Monclova attempts another surprise attack, I want the surprise to be his."

After supper, directed by Joshua Hamilton, Stockton Saunders, and Alonzo Holden, the hundred men requested by Houston were supplied with ammunition and positioned in an enormous circle that surrounded the fort. Houston spoke to the hundred and more men who remained.

"I want all of you to supply yourselves with ammunition. Until we can locate the headquarters of Monclova and monitor his movements, we must be prepared for attack at all times."

Twenty-five miles downriver, Monclova set up his camp and made preparations for a dawn attack on Houston's fort.

"We will depart two hours before the dawn," said Monclova, "and we will attack when it is light enough to see. We will take no prisoners."

Several times during the night, McQuade had spoken to Doctor Puckett about Andrew Burke's condition. An hour before dawn, he again paused where the doctor and Maggie sat with the ailing man.

"Is he going to make it, Doc?" McQuade asked.

"I think so," said Puckett, "but if he fails to take care of himself, the next one will take him on out."

McQuade spoke to the other Burkes, and when their watch was done, they —with the help of Doctor Puckett— carried Andrew to the Burke wagon. It was still without canvas.

"There is an extra canvas in my wagon that was taken from the wagon captured from the Sutton gang," said Puckett. "You're welcome to it. You'll need it to protect Andrew from the direct sunlight."

"We're obliged," Matthew replied. "I'll go with you and fetch it."

The train took the trail, McQuade estimating that they were a little more than fifty miles north of the Rio Colorado.

Miguel Monclova and his entire command of fifty-two men rode upriver, preparing to attack Houston's fort at dawn. They were in good spirits, believing Houston's forces to be fewer than before, short on supplies and ammunition. Pedro Mendez and Hidalgo Cortez rode one on either side of Monclova, who discussed battle plans with them.

"The two of you will take half our forces upriver and attack from the west. I will be commanding the others from the east. When we have killed them all, we will meet at the fort and destroy it. *¿Comprendistéis?*"

"*Sí,*" said both men.

They rode on, readying their weapons, anticipating victory. Long before nearing the fort, Pedro Mendez and Hidalgo Cortez led half the forces to the north, so that they might bypass the fort and attack from the west. They were not aware that Houston's sentries had heard them coming, and dispersing, had allowed them to pass. Quietly, many of Houston's defenders came together, and one of them spoke.

"They're splittin' up, aimin' to come at us from two directions, like last time. Wilkes, you light a shuck to the fort and warn Mr. Sam. The rest of us will split up and ride the circle, spreadin' the word. All we got to do is let 'em through our lines and then surround the varmints."

They dispersed, and as dawn approached, the defenders prepared themselves for the coming attack. At the fort, Houston spoke quietly to the men who had remained there.

"Hold your fire until they're well within range. Divide equally into two forces. Force one will be positioned by the west wall, force two by the east wall. Force one will begin firing, reloading as force two opens fire. The sentries from the outer perimeter will move in, setting up a crossfire."

Monclova's divided forces crept nearer the fort, and to the west. Pedro Mendez and Hidalgo Cortez paused, uneasy.

"I do not like this," Mendez said. "Where are their sentries?"

Almost immediately he had his answer, as the defenders near the west wall cut loose a fusillade. It was signal enough for the sentries who had moved in behind the attackers, and they joined in, creating a deadly crossfire. The attackers could flee toward the river with little cover, or to the north. Without firing a shot, they ran for their lives, leaving behind their dead. Monclova, leading the rest of his men in from the east, encountered a crossfire of equal proportions.

"*¡Madre de dios!*" Monclova shouted. "Fire! Kill them!"

But the surprise had been total, and the attackers who lived through the first volley had no desire to experience a second. They broke for the north, and finding himself alone, Miguel Monclova had little choice but to follow.

"Hold your fire," Houston shouted, as it became obvious Monclova's forces had fled in ignominious defeat.

Tasting victory for the first time in many a day, the defenders shouted to one another as they surged toward the fort.

"Remember the Alamo!"

Hamilton, Saunders, and Holden were taking a count of the dead, and Houston waited for their report.

"Twenty of them dead," said Hamilton, when the three returned.

"Well done, men," Houston said. "Having lost so many, I don't look for them to try again until reinforcements arrive, but we can't take any chances. Those of you who were on sentry last night are relieved for the day. Joshua, you and Stockton position forty men on sentry duty until sundown. Alonzo, choose four men and send them downriver, where they are to watch Matagorda Bay. See that they have food and ammunition for a week, and at that time, they will be relieved. If there is any sign of a sailing ship, three are to remain on watch, while the fourth rides here to warn us."

With renewed spirit, the men hastened to do his bidding.

Miguel Monclova's battered forces came together along the river, a few miles east of Houston's fort. Monclova was furious.

"*Por Dios,*" he bawled, "*Cobardes, perros*, why you do not shoot? Why you run?"

"*Comandante,*" said Hidalgo Cortez, "we run because we do not wish to die as our comrades have. There are many more of them than before."

Monclova was forced to consider his decimated forces, for many of those who had survived had been wounded. He had no choice except to return to his camp and await the promised ship which would bring supplies and reinforcements.

McQuade removed Andrew Burke from sentry duty, and Matthew and Mark took over the teams. The next day following Burke's attack, when the wagons had been circled, Doctor Puckett again examined Andrew Burke. Later, Puckett reported to McQuade.

"He appears stronger," said Puckett, "and that's usually a man's undoing. Soon as he begins feeling better, he falls back into his old bad habits. He's flatly refusing to give up his pipe.''

"Do you think that's the cause of his heart condition?" McQuade asked.

"From an official standpoint, I have no proof," said Doctor Puckett, "but I personally think that's part of it."

"Keep him alive a little longer, Doc. A buryin' will cost us another day."

Puckett laughed. "You're about as long on compassion as patience."

Beginning their fourth day after leaving the Brazos, McQuade estimated they had come at least sixty of the remaining eighty-five miles. They had been on the trail only an hour when the Comanches struck, and the first warning McQuade and Creeker had was sudden gunfire somewhere behind them. Wheeling their horses, they fell in behind the outriders who had been nearest the lead wagons. The attack had come three-quarters of the length of the strung-out wagons, and the Comanches had already vanished. Will Haymes stood beside his horse, trying to calm the skittish animal. There was a bloody gash along its left flank.

"Anybody hurt?" McQuade asked.

"Only my horse," said Will. "We saw them coming, and shot three of them off their horses before they got close enough to hurt us. Some of us rode after them a ways, and that's how they nicked my horse."

"It worked out just grand," Bess Jackman said. "They were driven away before they ever got to us."

Bess had taken over the teams, allowing Bud to join the outriders.

"We didn't kill many of them," said Joel Hanby, "but thank God, they didn't git none of us."

"That's the important thing," McQuade said. "Let's move on."

The outriders returned to their positions, while McQuade and Creeker rode to the front of the train, answering questions as they passed the other wagons. The rest of the day was uneventful, and when they again circled the wagons, they were only about twenty-five miles from their destination.

Three days after Sam Houston had sent four men to watch Matagorda Bay, one of the four rode in on a lathered horse. One of the men took the weary horse, and its rider all but fell from the saddle. Houston didn't wait for him to report, but came to meet him.

"What is it, Watkins?" Houston asked anxiously.

"Mexicans, sir. Near a hundred, ridin' from the south."

"No ship, then," said Houston.

"No, sir," Watkins said. "They was ridin' in columns, like soldiers, but they was all in civilian clothes. We watched 'em ride upriver. I rode north, circlin' around 'em, to git the word to you."

"Rest a while," said Houston. "Then take a fresh horse and ride back to Matagorda Bay. The four of you remain there until you are relieved." He then turned to Stockton Saunders. "Stockton, there is a duty to which I am going to assign you and Alonzo. You are to select two men to ride with you, and the four of you are to seek out the location of Monclova's camp. The two men you will take with you are to remain there, watching for any activity. Now that reinforcements have arrived, we must be aware of their movement at all times. Once you know where the camp is, and the men have their orders and are secure, report back to me."

"A week's rations and ammunition for the men, sir?" Saunders asked.

"Yes," said Houston. "After a week, you will send men to relieve them. Make note of it, and remind me."

Houston sighed. It was all he could do. While his men were capable enough, he looked forward to the coming of the wagons, for he had been impressed with the manner in which McQuade and Creeker had foreseen his vulnerability by water. While initial reinforcements had arrived on horseback, that was no assurance that more men—with massive amounts of ammunition and supplies—wouldn't sail into Matagorda Bay. His men had ammunition, had scored a telling victory, and men were in strategic positions to observe enemy movement. For the first time since San Jacinto, Houston believed that the Republic of Texas—with or without statehood—would overcome Mexican rule.

Downriver, Miguel Monclova was jubilant when reinforcements arrived, and even more so when the *comandante* in charge, Antonio Hermosillo, handed him a bulky envelope from General Santa Anna himself. Monclova sighed with satisfaction, for had the general not lived up to his word? A sailing ship would soon arrive, with a plentiful supply of food, ammunition, and medical supplies. There would be a cannon with carriage, and what better use to be made of it than to knock down the walls of Sam Houston's foolish fort?

"Good news?" Mendez inquired.

"*Excelente*," said Monclova.

The Rio Colorado. July 12, 1837.

McQuade and Creeker topped a rise and looked down on the Rio Colorado. Instead of riding on down, they stepped their horses aside and shouted as the outriders and the line of wagons rumbled past. When the last wagon rolled down toward the river, McQuade and Creeker rode ahead of the lead wagons and trotted their horses downriver. The wagons followed, and as the sun sank toward the western horizon, its rays swept the uprights of the fort's stockade, where an evening breeze touched the Lone Star flag of the Republic of Texas. It was a moment to be remembered, and every team was reined up. Men and women lifted their voices in a shout that brought men running from the fort. Those who had been on sentry duty rode in behind the wagons, shouting a welcome. Sam Houston himself ran to greet them. McQuade and Creeker swung down from their saddles, taking his hand.

"Welcome," Houston shouted, loud enough for them all to hear. "Welcome to the Republic of Texas."

CHAPTER 20

*T*he wagons were circled near the fort, to the east, on the bank of the Rio Colorado. It became a festive occasion, the women preparing supper for everybody. There were more than twenty supper fires, every one with a coffee pot. Houston's men were from Kentucky, Tennessee, Georgia, Mississippi, Alabama, Louisiana, Kansas, Missouri, and Arkansas. They went from wagon to wagon, introducing themselves, delighted when they met emigrants who had come from these states or had friends and kin there. After supper, with sentries plentiful, Houston called a meeting of the emigrants and his own men. Coffee pots bubbled over beds of coals, while Houston told of events of the past several days. He was quick to give credit to the emigrants for their gifts of food, medicine, and ammunition.

"They attacked us at dawn," said Houston, "and with the ammunition you sent us, we caught them in a crossfire. Twenty of the attackers were killed. We didn't lose a man."

There were delighted shouts from the emigrants, who were hearing of the victory for the first time.

"Mr. McQuade and Mr. Creeker gave us some excellent advice," Houston said, "So we sent men to watch Matagorda Bay, in case the Mexican government sent a sailing ship with reinforcements, ammunition, and food.

Well, the ship hasn't come, but the reinforcements have, and we learned about them only because our men were near the Gulf, watching for the ship."

"They traveled overland?" McQuade asked.

"They did," said Houston. "Along the coast, on horseback, a hundred strong."

"That won't make much difference," Creeker said. "When we arrived, you gained more men than they did."

"I am aware of that, and most thankful," said Houston.

"That doesn't mean the ship won't come," McQuade said. "It's one thing for men on horseback to travel from Mexico City, but quite another for wagons to successfully follow the same route. I've never been to Mexico, but I've known men who have, and it's mostly rough country. I still believe a sailing ship will bring food, ammunition, and other things, such as medical supplies."

"I share that belief," said Houston. "Matagorda Bay is still being watched. It's such an obvious possibility, we can't afford to overlook it. We are to be notified immediately when a sail is sighted."

"Sometime soon," McQuade said, "I'd like for you to study these legal papers dealing with our land grants. We'd like to know where this land lies, and if there's a chance of us ever claiming it."

"I have given you my word that your grants will be honored, once Texas gains its independence from Mexico. As for the location, I've read some law in my time, and I can probably help you with that," said Houston. "Perhaps I can do that tomorrow, while it's daylight."

"We have another decision ahead of us," Creeker said. "We've already decided that we can't claim our grants, as long as there's trouble with Mexico, and it could be years before that's behind us. All the way from St. Louis, we've struggled in and out of wagons, trying to stay dry while we ate and slept, and not successfully doin' either. I reckon I'm speaking for every man and woman here, when I say we got to have better quarters. Me, I don't even have a wagon."

There was a thunderous roar of agreement from all those who had come down the trail from St. Louis.

"I have a suggestion," Houston said. "We built this fort with the intention of it one day becoming a town. It's crude in the extreme, and if it was four times as large, it still wouldn't be decent accommodations for us all. I believe until this fight for independence is over, we should build cabins, grouped together for defense. They can be built of logs, two dwellings side by side. A connecting shelter in between can be used for cooking by both families in wet weather. You'll need many logs, but all of you have wagons and teams."

"I like the idea," said McQuade, "but that's goin' to involve an almighty lot of cabins. We'd be strung out for a mile or more, like we were in the wagons, while we were on the trail. I realize we can't all crowd into the fort, but we must be near enough to help one another in a time of need. Those farthest from the fort could be scalped by Comanches or gunned down by Mexicans before the rest of us could get to them."

"The kind of shelter you agree upon, you will have to build," Houston said, "and I am not going to interfere. My only concern is that your eventual decision be based upon what is best for our mutual defense. As Mr. McQuade has pointed out, we dare not separate ourselves to the extent that we can be murdered a few at a time. Perhaps we should ask for suggestions, accepting the most practical one."

"What about it?" McQuade asked. "We won't have room for much more than a roof over our heads, if we're grouped near enough to the fort for common defense."

"Then we need to put as many of us under one roof as we can," said Will Haymes, "and still have a bit of privacy."

"It won't be all that bad," Maggie said, "if we're only buildin' sleeping rooms. Can't two, three, or four families have a common cook fire, like we did on the trail?"

"Perhaps Maggie's on to something," said Doctor

Puckett. "It's the building of single-family houses, with fireplace and chimney, that will take time. Even if it wasn't going to separate us, we're talking about a massive amount of work for temporary shelter."

"Suppose we built large cabins, each with sleeping quarters for four families?" Gunter Warnell suggested.

"Still too many separate cabins," said McQuade. "If we're going to put up cabins large enough to house four families, why not build a second floor and house eight? With eight families working on a single cabin, we could have roofs over our heads in a few days."

"We could still have a cooking shelter on the bottom level, with all eight families sharing the cooking," Maggie said.

"It'll be better than livin' out of a wagon," said Eli Bibb, "but who gets the top floors and who gets the bottom floors?"

"We can draw lots," Creeker said, "but if you take the top, you'll have a wood floor. On the bottom, it'll be dirt."

"I want a wood floor," half a dozen women shouted in a single voice.

There was an immediate uproar, everybody trying to be heard above everybody else.

"Quiet, damn it." McQuade drew his revolver and fired a shot in the air. It had the desired effect, getting their attention.

"Hell, if we can't settle this without a fight," said Joel Hanby, "let's just scrap the whole thing and live out of our wagons."

"You've all heard Joel's suggestion," McQuade said, "and it makes sense. If we can't reach some agreement, we can leave things as they are until we win our independence from Mexico. Now what's it gonna be?"

"I want somethin' over my head besides wagon canvas," said Maggie. "I want a cabin, if it's just one room. The rest of you, don't just set there like knots on a log. Speak up for the cabins."

Maggie was well-liked, and her plea got results. One after another, women raised their hands, favoring the cabins. All eyes were on McQuade, and he spoke.

"I reckon we'll be building cabins," said McQuade. "Now it's time to take a common sense look at what we aim to build. The single cabin built on two levels, with quarters for four families on each level will get roofs over our heads quickly. Eight families working together will make it easier on us all. Keep in mind this won't be forever. Now is there any one of you opposed to this plan? Raise your hand."

Not a hand was raised.

"Good," said McQuade. "Unless somebody can think of a good reason why we ought not, we'll begin building tomorrow. As for cooking arrangements, I don't see why it can't be grouped among four families or eight, depending on what the families in each of the cabins want. You can build one cooking shelter or two, depending on your needs. Now, are there any questions?"

"Yeah," said Cal Tabor. "Now that we're settlin' down in one place, in what order do you aim for us to stand watch?"

"I believe Mr. Houston is entitled to make that decision," McQuade replied, "since we are becoming part of his forces."

"Your men have become trail-hardened, fighting Indians and outlaws," said Houston, "and I value that experience. Now that we have ammunition, and have eliminated some of Monclova's men, we should be able to reduce the number of sentries and perhaps shorten each man's watch. Men have already been assigned for tonight's watch. Tomorrow, we will meet and work up a new schedule."

As McQuade's outfit soon learned, Houston's fort never slept. At least, not all at the same time. Besides the men on watch, there were fifty or more who would be awake all night. They talked, gambled, and now that they had coffee, couldn't seem to get enough of it. Several owned mouth harps, and the lonesome sound of the instruments could be heard all hours of the day and night. There was one question, being of a sensitive nature, that hadn't come up, but McQuade knew that it must. He just didn't expect it so soon, nor did he expect Doctor Puckett to be the one who would raise it. Puckett came to the wagon and Mary wisely made herself scarce, for when the doctor sought McQuade, he usually wanted to talk.

"I need some advice," said Puckett, "and there's really nobody I can talk to. Frankly, I am ill at ease, talking to you. The cabins you're proposing will be for families, and that, I am assuming, means man and wife. What of the single men and single women? As you well know, the ladies Rufus Hook had intended for his Texas saloon have become attached to some of the teamsters, and however good their intentions, I doubt there is a preacher within five hundred miles."

McQuade laughed, amused at Puckett's nervousness. "And you're wondering if these teamsters and their women will be allowed to live as families, when these cabins are built."

"Yes," said Puckett.

"These are grown men and women, Doc," McQuade said. "If they choose to live as man and wife, who am I to say they can't? This is frontier Texas, and there's not a shred of law, except God's. Selma shared a wagon with Trent Putnam, and since his death, I'm damn sure Luke Burke hasn't missed a night with her. I can't see that it's any worse, the two of them living in a cabin instead of a wagon. Are you opposed to all this?"

"Not really," said Puckett, his eyes on his folded hands. "I'm considering becoming a part of it."

"You?" said McQuade, aghast. "You and . . ."

"Maggie," Puckett said.

"My God, Doc," said McQuade, "Ike hasn't been dead even two weeks."

"I know that," Puckett replied, "as well as I know that back east, both of us would be tarred and feathered and

escorted out of town. But we're not back east, damn it.
Don't you know I'd stand her before a preacher, if I
could?''

"I'm not doubting your good intentions, Doc," said
McQuade, "and I don't intend to judge you, any more
than I intend to judge the others. I hired on as wagon
boss, not as a judge, and certainly not as God. Have you
spoken to Maggie about this?"

"No," Puckett said. "I began considering it, because
Maggie is concerned that, since she's a woman, she won't
be able to do her part in the building of a cabin. She
believes she is about to become a burden, since she has
no man to contribute to the building."

"Oh, for God's sake," said McQuade, "there's not a
man in our outfit who would have a word of complaint,
if some of his labor went into putting a roof over Maggie's head. I hope you know that."

"Of course I know that," Puckett replied. "Maggie's
a proud woman."

"Maybe prouder than you realize," said McQuade. "I
reckon you'd better down some of that medicinal whiskey
and talk this over with her."

Puckett sighed. "I reckon you're right, but I'll pass on
the whiskey. When she's done with me, I may be sick
enough."

He faded into the darkness, his shoulders slumped.
Mary appeared almost immediately and McQuade suspected she might have been listening to the strange conversation.

"He seems disturbed about something," said Mary.

"He is," McQuade replied.

"Are you going to tell me, or do I have to drag it out
of you?"

"No," said McQuade, "I'm not going to tell you.
Damn it, he has problems enough, without becoming the
gossip of the camp."

"You are implying that I am a gossip?"

"I'm not implying anything," McQuade said. "I'm

dealing strictly with facts. You are a woman, and as such, you talk to other women. It's your nature, like a coyote howling at the moon."

"So now I'm a coyote," she snapped.

"A gossipy coyote," McQuade said.

"I'll ask Maggie. She knows all there is to know about him."

"If she doesn't, she soon will," said McQuade. "But I'd suggest you wait a while. He's gone to talk to her, and I doubt you'd be welcome."

"There's something purely wrong with a man who keeps secrets from his wife," she said darkly.

She left him sitting on the tailgate of the wagon, and he hadn't the slightest doubt she would learn Puckett's secret. If not from Maggie, from Puckett himself. Mary had been gone only seconds, when Creeker showed up. Hoisting himself up, he sat beside McQuade on the wagon's tailgate.

"What would you say," Creeker asked, "if I told you I aim to build one of the cabins for Lora and me?"

"I'd say go ahead," said McQuade. "Hell, I'm not your daddy."

Creeker laughed. "Let me put that another way. What do you reckon everybody else will think?"

"No worse than they already think," McQuade replied. "After all the time you spent with her in Doc's wagon, why the sudden attack of conscience?"

"It's not so much me as Lora," said Creeker. "She wants to turn her life around, and, well . . . she believes this is wrong. Hell, she knows Doc and Maggie . . ."

"Doc and Maggie what?" McQuade asked.

"You mean you don't know?" Creeker asked, genuinely surprised.

"How would I know what?" McQuade asked. "Doc and Maggie are as old as I am, and I respect their right to make their own decisions. It's too bad the rest of you can't be as considerate of them."

Creeker laughed. "Every woman in the outfit, includin'

yours, knows that Maggie wants to share a cabin with Doc Puckett, but she don't know how to talk to him about it.''

"I don't want to hear about it," said McQuade. "I'd rather fight Mexico single-handed than get caught up in this."

Creeker departed, and within seconds, Mary returned. She took Creeker's place on the wagon's tailgate. Before she could say anything, McQuade spoke.

"I don't want to hear it."

"How do you know what it is you don't want to hear?" she asked.

"I don't want to hear about Doc and Maggie," said McQuade.

She laughed softly. "So you do know."

"More than I want to know," McQuade said. "I don't care what Doc and Maggie do, and I care even less what the rest of you think of it."

She slid off the wagon's tailgate and left him alone with his thoughts. He missed the days on the trail, when threats from Indians, outlaws, and the elements were all he had to contend with.

The following morning, when the emigrants began making decisions regarding the construction of cabins, McQuade stayed out of it. Instead, he took the briefcase that had belonged to Hedgepith to Sam Houston, and the two of them sat at one of the rough tables in the fort, going through the papers.

"I don't look for these to be of much use," said Houston. "As I understand it, there are two forces within the Mexican government. One of these, the weaker of the two, had plans to colonize Texas, using these land grants as bait. The stronger force, however—and this is headed by Santa Anna—fears colonization by Americans. Santa Anna believes, and correctly so, that this can only lead to an eventual fight for independence."

"Establishing these grants along the Brazos and Colorado Rivers shows sound thinking on somebody's part,"

McQuade said. "Without the harsh winters that plague the territory farther north, a farmer with any ambition could raise two crops a season. That's why most of these folks are holding on to these papers. They want this land along the Rio Colorado."

"No reason they shouldn't have it," said Houston. "When we win our independence, we must colonize the territory, and as I have told you before, those of you who have come to fight for Texas will have first claim."

"As I understand it," McQuade said, "this business with these grants has been going on for more than twenty years. What became of those emigrants who arrived early, taking possession of their grants while Stephen Austin was still in charge?"

"Most of them fell victim to intimidation," said Houston. "Night riders burned some of them out, and others were shot down from ambush. Many of those who remained decided the land wasn't worth it, and returned to the states."

"These men who are with you seem dedicated," McQuade said. "How many are owners of grants who have decided to stay and fight?"

"Of the two hundred, not more than a dozen," said Houston. "They all believe they've got more at stake than just the land, for they lost their women and children to Mexican night riders."

"What about the others?" McQuade asked. "What's their stake in this?"

"I suppose you've heard of the fight at the Alamo, and how we eventually took our revenge at San Jacinto," said Houston.

"Yes," McQuade said.

"Most of these men who have stood by me here were volunteers who remained after our victory at San Jacinto," said Houston.

"Most of the men who died at the Alamo were volunteers, I understand," McQuade replied.

"Yes," said Houston. "Thirty-three of them were from

Tennessee, and Travis, their post commander, was from Alabama. These men, these Americans, are proud of their heritage, and they believe these plains we call Texas are destined for something far greater than high-handed control by a Mexican dictator."

"I share that belief," McQuade said. "Has any move been made toward statehood?"

"In a small way," said Houston. "The congress is controlled by northern industrialists who don't care a fig for anything that doesn't further their own interests. I believed that our victory at San Jacinto would have some impact, but so far it has not."

"So you aim to continue the fight, statehood or not," McQuade said.

"I do," said Houston. "I will fight until we win, or until I am shot dead."

"What becomes of Texas if we win the fight for independence and we're still denied statehood?" McQuade asked.

"This will become the Republic of Texas," said Houston. "If we're strong enough to defeat Santa Anna's forces and win our independence, we'll find a way to override these mule-headed, short-sighted politicians from the north."

McQuade laughed. "I'm beginning to see how you've held your forces together. You've convinced me we can give these Mexicans a good switching and send them running home to mama."

It was Houston's turn to laugh. "I fear it won't be that simple. Santa Anna seems to have a strange hold on Mexico, and I believe there'll be war before he'll leave us be. While we have the spirit, we are lacking the resources. The goods and supplies you brought to us were in answer to a prayer, but over many weeks, months—maybe even years—they'll be exhausted. We had the promise of assistance from sympathizers in St. Louis, our goods to come by steamboat to Little Rock, and the rest of the way by wagon, but nothing ever came."

"Maybe the wagons were intercepted by Comanches, or Mexican forces," McQuade said.

"I'd like to believe that," said Houston, "but I sent an escort all the way to the Red, to within a hundred and thirty miles of Little Rock. These men waited for more than two weeks past the time the wagons should have arrived. I believe there are men in high places who are going to great lengths to sabotage our efforts here."

"But why?" McQuade asked.

"There are some who don't want Texas independence because they believe it will lead to Texas statehood," said Houston, "and somehow they have exerted enough influence to cut off any assistance."

"Maybe there's a way to get around that," McQuade said. "Suppose we got supplies from Mexico City?"

"My God," said Houston, "what are you proposing?"

"Exactly what I said," McQuade replied, "but there is one condition. It all depends on Santa Anna sending a ship with supplies to Matagorda Bay. Remember me suggesting that we sink any incoming Mexican ships?"

"Yes," said Houston. "An excellent proposal."

"Maybe not," McQuade said, "after what you've just told me about your supply line to St. Louis being cut. Suppose, after that ship delivered its supplies to Monclova and sailed back to Mexico City, we attacked Monclova's bunch and took that shipload of supplies for our own use?"

"Yaaahoooo!" Houston shouted, slapping his thigh with his old hat. "That's got to be the wildest, boldest scheme ever concocted, especially allowing the ship to escape. There'll be no reason for 'em not to bring another load of goods, and we can take that, too."

"Maybe," said McQuade. "It'll depend on how strong Monclova is with Santa Anna. If Monclova chooses to send a rider to Mexico City with news we've hijacked his cargo, what will Santa Anna do? Will he dispatch another shipload, knowing we'll grab that, as well?"

"I doubt it," Houston replied, "but suppose we staked

out Monclova's camp and saw to it that his rider never reached Santa Anna?''

McQuade laughed. ''I believe we may have solved one of our problems. At least for a while. Trouble is, we'll be leaving Monclova in a bad position, and he'll be desperate to get word to Santa Anna. Once his outfit gets low on ammunition, we'll have him at our mercy just as he once had you at his. We can wipe him out to the last man.''

''That's a start,'' said Houston, ''but it won't stop Santa Anna from marching men from Matamoros. Once he learns we're hijacking his ships, he can always resort to wagons with an armed escort.''

''When he begins marching in from the south,'' McQuade said, ''that's when we'll have to position men at regular intervals from east to west, to warn us of their coming.''

''Great God,'' said Houston, ''we'd have men strung out for three hundred and fifty miles.''

''Maybe you're right,'' McQuade said. ''That might be stretching us a mite thin. Just how sure are you that soldiers marching overland would come from Matamoros?''

''Because Matamoros is practically on the Gulf,'' said Houston, ''and soldiers could be brought there by sailing ship. If they were to enter Texas farther west, they would have to march a great distance to join Monclova.''

''That could be the answer, then,'' McQuade said. ''Send a couple of men south, with instructions to watch for troop movement or anything suspicious out of Matamoros. They could take grub for two weeks, and they would be relieved by two more men with grub for another two weeks. When there's movement of supplies or soldiers from Matamoros, they can easily warn us, and we can act accordingly.''

''That's so practical,'' said Houston, ''I think we should begin watching Matamoros just as quickly as a pair of riders can get there. Then we'll be protected from the possibility of soldiers showing up unexpectedly by land.''

"That would be a wise move," McQuade said.

"We'll be watching Matagorda Bay and Matamoros," said Houston. "Do you think we should be watching Monclova's camp, as well?"

"Not until after the ship arrives and we hijack its freight," McQuade said. "Then we're facing the possibility that Monclova will send a rider with news of what we've done. Right now, if we're covering Matagorda Bay and Matamoros, I think they'll have trouble taking us by surprise."

"I'll choose two men to ride south to Matamoros immediately," said Houston. "Place all these grant papers back in the briefcase. I can't say for sure that we won't be needing them, but in any case, it'll be a while."

McQuade left the fort elated, believing he had contributed something toward overcoming the many obstacles they would face in a fight for independence. He found many of the emigrant wagons had been unloaded, their contents covered by the wagon canvas. Wagon boxes had been removed, leaving only the running gear and iron cross-frames over which logs might be stacked. There were iron U-rings at either end of the cross-frames, and into these, four-foot lengths of heavy oak were being driven. This prevented the loaded logs from shifting and rolling off to the side. Most of the women seemed excited, for the proposed cabins seemed a little closer to becoming reality.

"Shouldn't we be stripping our wagon down?" Mary asked.

"Not necessarily," said McQuade. "If we're building cabins for eight families, there's no reason to strip down all eight wagons. Some of the longer logs needed for the walls can't be hauled in by wagon. They'll have to be snaked in by mules, one at a time. Since there's goin' to be eight of us sharing a cabin, have you given any thought to who we'll be living and eating with?"

"Yes," Mary said. "Doc and Maggie, Gunter and Ellen Warnell, Eli and Odessa Bibb, Cal and Lucy Tabor, Will and Minerva Haymes, Creeker and Lora, and Joel and Mamie Hanby.''

''Good,'' said McQuade. ''I'm glad you settled that.''

CHAPTER 21

❧

*F*or a week, McQuade did his share, felling trees for the proposed cabins. Creeker and Doctor Puckett worked beside him. Sam Houston had laid out a schedule for sentry duty, and with more than three hundred men, each of them drew it once a week. There had been no sign of Monclova's forces since the arrival of the emigrants until one afternoon Creeker and McQuade had paused to catch their wind and wipe the sweat from their eyes.

"Somebody's watchin' us," Creeker said. "The sun reflected off somethin' over yonder to the east. They're usin' a spy glass, I reckon."

Without seeming to, the two men watched for the telltale flash again, and it was a few minutes before it came. This time, McQuade saw it.

"Well," said McQuade, "they know we're here, and that we're aimin' to stay. I reckon the next play is theirs. We'd better tell Houston about this."

Upon returning to the fort, McQuade and Creeker sought out Houston before supper, telling him what they had seen and what they suspected.

"No doubt they've already seen the many wagons near the fort," Houston said, "and now they're watching you men at work, getting some idea as to our strength. Even with their reinforcements, we still outnumber them three to one.''

"There's a possibility they may send a rider to Mata-moros, with word to Santa Anna,'' said McQuade. ''More men could hurt our chances of taking the ship's cargo. I reckon if they can watch our camp, we can watch theirs.''

"I have two good men I can send to keep them under surveillance,'' Houston replied.

"I believe we should find their camp and stake it out tonight,'' said McQuade. ''We've got them worried, and I can't believe they won't make some move to warn Santa Anna of our increased strength. I'd like to ride with those men you have in mind, so I'll know just where their camp is, in relation to our own.''

"I'd like to ride along with you,'' Creeker said.

"See me after supper,'' said Houston, ''and be ready to ride.''

McQuade and Creeker had told nobody except Houston of their suspicions, and it came as a surprise to Mary when McQuade prepared to ride out.

"I can understand Mr. Houston wanting Monclova's movements watched,'' said Mary, ''but if he's sending men, why are you going?''

"Because I want to know where the camp is,'' Mc-Quade said. ''I'll return tonight.''

McQuade and Creeker still hadn't met all of Houston's men, and Houston handled the introductions.

Mr. Creeker, Mr. McQuade, this is Elgin Summerfield and Shanghai McLean. They're from Mississippi.''

"*Southern* Mississippi,'' said Summerfield, offering his hand.

Houston laughed as the four men shook hands. They mounted their horses, and with Summerfield and McLean taking the lead, they rode downriver. Sundown had painted the western horizon with a glorious array of pink, rose, and red. Darkness was only a few minutes away. Summerfield and McLean had nothing to say until they all stopped to rest their horses, and it was McLean who spoke.

"I reckon old Sam's thanked you proper for throwin' in with us, but I'm addin' my own thanks to his. You brung us grub, powder, an' shot, so's we can stay here and fight."

"That goes fer me, as well," said Summerfield. "While Shanghai and me wants Texas cut loose from Mexico, we got a bigger stake. Them Mex varmints burnt us out, killin' our young and our womenfolk."

"They ain't hurt us quite that bad," Creeker said, "but we just got here. I promise you, we'll do our damndest to see they get what's coming to 'em."

"I think we'll have some painful surprises in store for them," said McQuade. "For that reason, it's important that we know when this bunch of jaybirds make a move."

"You can count on me and Shanghai," Summerfield said. "All we ask is that when the deal goes down, we're in the midst of the fight. We owe them varmints, an' we pay our debts."

After resting their horses, they rode on, and when Summerfield and McLean reined up, it was McLean who spoke.

"They're likely camped along the river. We'd best ride north a ways, else we're likely to run right into 'em. With the wind at our backs, they'll hear us comin' a mile off. But we'll turn it around to our advantage. We'll go on well beyond their camp, and when we ride back, we'll be downwind. Another ten mile, Elgin?"

"I'd double that," said Summerfield. "After the thrashin' we give 'em, I doubt they'll make camp any closer."

Eventually they swung back toward the river, and riding into the wind, they smelled wood smoke. Of one mind, they reined up and dismounted. While they were downwind, one of their own mounts might nicker and give them away. They crept along, stooping to avoid low-

hanging branches, tearing free of briars that reached out
to claw at them. Their supper fires had burned down almost to coals, but there was a crackle as a piece of wood
shifted, and the night wind caught up a flurry of sparks.
There was occasional laughter, and men spoke in soft
Spanish, not loud enough to be overheard.

"We got 'em pegged," said Summerfield. "Let's git
back to the hosses."

Nothing more was said until they reached their horses,
and then it was McQuade who spoke.

"We'll be counting on you gents. When are you to be
relieved?"

"Sam said in a week," McLean replied. "It's almighty
dull, settin' on your hunkers an' waitin' fer somethin' to
happen."

"You may not have to wait that long," said McQuade.
"Some of this bunch was looking at us through a spy
glass today. They're up to something."

"Good," Summerfield said. "I'm ready to kill these
varmints, so Santa Anna can run in a new bunch."

McQuade and Creeker rode back upriver, and only
when they were miles beyond the Monclova camp did
Creeker speak.

"If the rest of Houston's bunch is as dedicated as them
two, I got no doubts about the success of this fight for
independence."

"I don't see how Monclova can sneak anything past
us," said McQuade. "I'm of the same mind as Summerfield and McLean. I'd like to get into this fight and be
done with it."

"On the other hand," Creeker replied, "if they'll hold
off a little longer, we'll have our cabins done. When the
fightin' starts, we may not have time for anything else."

Reaching the fort, they reported their success to Houston.

"Most gratifying," said Houston. "Their spying on us
leads me to believe they're up to something. I am wondering if perhaps those reinforcements didn't bring Mon-

clova orders from Santa Anna, which could account for this activity.''

''Maybe,'' McQuade said, ''but they have to know we outnumber them, and for that reason, I can't believe they're planning to attack.''

''Nor can I,'' said Houston. ''I feel better knowing we're in a position to be aware of any movement of men or supplies affecting Monclova.''

When McQuade reached the wagon, Mary wasn't there. He removed his hat, tugged off his boots, and let down the wagon's tailgate. He sat there, alone with his thoughts, and when Mary suddenly appeared, he dropped his hand to the butt of his revolver.

''I need to talk to you,'' she said.

''Talk,'' he replied.

''You won't want to hear this,'' said Mary, ''but . . .''

''You're right,'' McQuade interrupted, ''I don't want to hear it.''

''We have a problem,'' she continued, undaunted, ''because some of these people will end up in a building with certain other people they don't like.''

''And you're expecting me to have an answer to that? Hell, my name's McQuade, not Solomon.''

''Well,'' she said, ''something must be done. We might get around that, if it wasn't for the common cook fires.''

''Far as I'm concerned,'' said McQuade, ''those who don't fit into the cabins will have to make other arrangements. I hired on as wagon boss from St. Louis to the Rio Colorado and we're here. Damn it, am I supposed to wet-nurse these people for the rest of their lives?''

''You don't have to shout at me,'' Mary said. ''I'm only trying to help.''

''I believe in helping when and where I can,'' said McQuade, as patiently as he could, ''but I can't force people to accept other people, and neither can you. These people all must be responsible for themselves. There's evidence Monclova's bunch is up to something, and this is no time for us to bicker among ourselves. I'm sorry I ever said anything in favor of these damn cabins, and I'd favor scrapping them, before this goes any farther.''

She had never seen him in such a mood, and she left him there. He put on his hat, stomped into his boots, and went looking for Doctor Puckett. Not that Puckett would have any answers, but he felt the need to talk to somebody who didn't expect him to walk on water. Surprisingly, Maggie was alone at her wagon.

''Where's Doc?'' McQuade asked.

''Involved in talk about those blessed cabins,'' said Maggie. ''I swear, I believe we'd all been better off, just to go on livin' out of our wagons.''

''I feel the same way,'' McQuade said. ''Mary and me are having hard words.''

''Don't let it come to that,'' said Maggie. ''I've already told Horace . . . Doctor Puckett . . . that I'll withdraw my request for a cabin, if that's what it takes to settle everybody down.''

''I reckon I'll track him down and see what's going on,'' McQuade said gloomily.

McQuade found Puckett, Creeker, Gunter Warnell, Eli Bibb, Cal Tabor, Will Haymes, and a host of others in the fort, seated at the crude tables. Obviously the women had been barred from the discussion, for none were present. McQuade took a seat at the very end of one of the tables, listening.

''My wife's hell-bent on havin' a cabin,'' said Will Haymes.

''Mine too,'' Joel Hanby said.

''Ellen's of the same mind,'' said Gunter Warnell. ''How do you feel, Doc?''

''I feel like this whole thing is a bad idea,'' Puckett said, ''because it's divided us, and I fear we're about to lose sight of our reason for being here. Maggie says she's withdrawing her bid for a cabin, that she'll just go on living out of her wagon.''

Tobe Rutledge laughed. ''Easy for her to say, but I hear it ain't goin' to be just her that's scrunched up in the wagon.''

"If that's what she wants, we'll manage," said Puckett, his eyes on Tobe.

The laughter Tobe had prompted died away to an uneasy titter, and Creeker took over the conversation.

"I don't even have a wagon," Creeker said, "but if we're up against something that's bigger than all of us, then let's put it down and leave it be. If we're to have homes here in Texas, then let's keep our eyes on those we'll build on our land grants, and we can't look toward them until we've won this fight for independence."

"I'll be sharing Maggie's wagon, Creeker," said Puckett. "You and Lora are welcome to mine. I'm sure we can find room here in the fort for the extra weapons, black powder, and such that we took from the Sutton gang."

"You been cuttin' logs for a cabin, McQuade," Isaac McDaniel said. "How do you feel about all this?"

"Cut into shorter lengths and split, those logs will make firewood," McQuade replied, "and so will yours." He got up and departed, before further questions could be directed at him. Before he reached his and Mary's wagon, he could hear voices, and some of them were angry. Determined not to be intimidated, he went on, and when he reached the wagon he found most of the wives of the men who were arguing in the fort. Maggie was there, and she was being drowned out by most of the other women talking at the same time. The moon was bright, and when they saw McQuade, they quickly became silent. It was Maggie who finally spoke.

"I've tried to talk sense to 'em, McQuade. Why don't you tell 'em where you stand?"

"I'll tell all of you the same thing I just told your men in the fort," said McQuade. "I have been cutting logs along with them, and I don't aim for my work to be for nothing. I reckon I'll just convert all my logs to firewood."

Maggie laughed, but none of the others did. They turned away, leaving Maggie, Mary, and McQuade. It was Mary who spoke.

"You're right again, you and Maggie. We've lost that unselfishness that served us so well all the way from St. Louis, and I just want to cry."

"Won't help," said Maggie. "Remember that piece in the bible where the Apostle Peter, walkin' on the water, went to meet Jesus? When he took his eyes off Jesus, he began to sink. Well, we took our eyes off our reason for bein' here, and we're all sinkin' into the waters of selfishness and unneighborly conduct."

"Amen," McQuade said.

"I just want us to be like we were before," said Mary. "What can we do?"

"Nothing," McQuade said. "The rest of these people are going to have to see this just as Maggie explained it. It's a personal thing, like salvation, and those who are blind to it will stumble on to Judgment Day. Nothing matters to them except what they want. There's evidence that Monclova's bunch is about to make a move that will affect all of us. Maybe that will pull us all together and remind us of our true purpose for being here."

McQuade slept little that night, spending some time with the men who had come down the trail with him from St. Louis. To his satisfaction, most of them agreed with him, even the Burkes. The teamsters—most of whose wagons were still loaded—had a request.

"See can we unload these wagons, movin' the goods into the fort," said Slaughter. "I can live in my wagon as long as I have to, but not with it full to the bows. I slept on the ground all the way from St. Louis."

"I'll talk to Houston about it," McQuade said. "It's not an unreasonable request."

The rest of the teamsters—especially those who had women—expressed their approval of making temporary homes in their wagons by removing their goods into the fort. Before breakfast the next morning, McQuade spoke to Houston.

"By all means, all supplies should be moved into the fort. I regret that your plans for the cabins proved unworkable, but I believe you're doing the right thing. We must settle this question of independence, making do with our circumstances.''

Summerfield and McLean rode in at noon. Without a word to anyone, they reported to Sam Houston, and within minutes, Houston had called a meeting that included everybody except the men on watch.

''Summerfield and McLean have brought the information I have been expecting,'' said Houston. ''Monclova and his entire command is traveling downriver, and I suspect they're bound for Matagorda Bay. There is a strong possibility they're meeting an incoming sailing ship from Mexico City, with food, medical supplies, and ammunition. It is our intention, if indeed such a vessel arrives, to confiscate its cargo, once it has been unloaded.''

Thunderous shouts interrupted him, for those assembled were hearing of the bold plan for the first time. Houston held up his hand for silence, and when they quieted, continued.

''As some of you may know, we have men watching Matagorda Bay, and at the first sign of an approaching Mexican sailing ship, they will warn us. We will then have plenty of time to get our own forces into position, for we want the ship to depart before we attack Monclova and seize the cargo.''

''Count me in,'' a man shouted.

''Me,'' a hundred more shouted, virtually in a single voice.

''I will prepare a list and post it,'' said Houston. ''There is no hurry. We won't ride out until we receive word a ship has been sighted.''

Men surrounded Houston, and it was a while before McQuade could talk to him.

''I'd like some of my emigrants, including myself, to be part of that attacking force you'll be sending to Matagorda Bay,'' McQuade said. ''Some of us need to redefine our purpose for being here.''

''I understand the need for that,'' said Houston. ''I will

choose a hundred of these men from my original force, and fifty from yours. Since you are familiar with your men, I will accept your recommendations.''

''You'll have them,'' McQuade said.

Most of McQuade's party had seen him talking to Houston, and guessing his purpose, besieged him with questions. McQuade welcomed their interest, for it seemed the issue that threatened to divide them—the ill-conceived construction of dwellings—had been set aside for this more serious endeavor.

''Houston will take fifty of us as part of the attacking force,'' said McQuade, ''and I'll be talking to all of you during the next several days. While all of us can't go, this is the start of our becoming involved in this fight for independence.''

McQuade spoke to them for more than an hour, and when he was finished, he found Mary in a much better frame of mind.

''This couldn't have come at a better time,'' Mary said. ''While I dread the thought of you and the rest of these men attacking Monclova's forces, we all need to feel like we're in some way helping to gain Texas independence and secure our grants.''

''What about those people who were hell-bent on having living quarters?''

''There's still a few,'' said Mary. ''I'm hoping they'll back off, when they learn the rest of us have given it up.''

''If some of them are so determined, let them go ahead,'' McQuade replied. ''I'm damn tired of trying to talk sense to people who want none of it. How are the rest of the women feeling about living out of the wagons?''

''Most of them have accepted it,'' said Mary, ''and we have Maggie to thank for that. Once she saw how we were becoming divided, she set out to change the minds of all the others.''

The news of an impending attack on Monclova's forces had the desired effect on most of the men in McQuade's party. They gathered, discussing the bold move proposed by Sam Houston, intrigued by the taking of supplies from the Mexicans. The Burkes—Matthew, Mark, and Luke—confronted McQuade with a request.

"We want to be part of that bunch that rides downriver tomorrow," said Mark. "See that you get us included."

"I'll see," McQuade promised. "Before this is done, there'll be plenty of fighting for us all. If you don't go this time, I'll see that you're included the next."

That satisfied them, and McQuade realized he hadn't seen old Andrew Burke since their arrival at Houston's fort. Choosing fifty men to join Houston's forces required some thought, and it was almost supper time before McQuade presented Houston with a list. But the movement of Monclova's forces toward Matagorda Bay was only the start of a series of events that quickly took on ominous overtones. After supper, the men who had been assigned to watch Matamoros arrived on lathered horses. Houston went to meet them, as they all but fell from their horses, and when they spoke, it was loud enough for all to hear.

"Mex soldiers are ridin' north, along the coast. More'n three hunnert of 'em."

"My God," said Houston, "when did they leave Matamoros?"

"Near dawn this mornin'," one of the tired riders said.

Just for a moment, there was a shocked silence, and then all hell broke loose. There were shouts from a hundred men, all demanding to be heard. Somebody drew a pistol and began firing into the air.

"Silence," Houston shouted.

It took a while to restore order. Joshua Hamilton, Stockton Saunders, and Alonzo Holden conferred with Houston, who then beckoned to McQuade. Apparently there was some disagreement among the four men as to the implications of this new development, and it was to McQuade that Houston directed a question.

"We are at odds as to what we should do, regarding these reinforcements. Have you a suggestion?"

"Yes," said McQuade. "With Monclova's bunch headed downriver and with all these reinforcements riding along the coast, I think we'd better prepare ourselves to attack a much larger force."

"I don't see any immediate need for it," Joshua Hamilton said, "unless a Mexican sailing ship arrives, and I now have my doubts about that."

"I reckon you have a reason," said McQuade.

"I do," Hamilton replied, in a manner that rubbed McQuade the wrong way. "There is no reason to believe that Monclova's forces are riding downriver for any purpose other than a rendezvous with the reinforcements from Matamoros."

"I still believe there'll be a Mexican ship sailing in with supplies," said McQuade. "Did you ask these *hombres* that just rode in whether or not these three hundred soldiers have pack mules?"

"Well, no," Hamilton admitted, "but . . ."

"There were no pack mules," said Houston. "I know what Mr. McQuade's getting at, and I quite agree. Santa Anna wouldn't increase Monclova's forces to such an extent, without sending provisions, medical supplies, and ammunition, and what better method than by water?"

"While that may be the case," Stockton Saunders said, "why are Monclova's forces on their way to the coast? Surely all those men won't be needed to unload a supply ship."

"Precisely my point," said Houston. "Santa Anna's no fool. These men are gathering for the purpose of protecting that ship's cargo, to prevent us from successfully accomplishing what we are planning to do."

"Damn right they are," McQuade said, "and if the little schoolin' I've had wasn't all for nothing, they'll have us outnumbered."

"Granted that you're right," said Alonzo Holden.

"What do you propose? That we mount every man we have, and ride in pursuit?"

"Only a damn fool would even consider that," McQuade said, his hard eyes boring into Holden's. "We dare not leave our women, the fort, our wagons, and our supplies at the mercy of the Comanches."

"Well, God be praised," said Holden, "if you have some magic in your hat, perhaps you will share it with us."

Dozens of men had crowded close, seeking to learn what would be done to counter this new threat, and McQuade spoke loudly enough for them all to hear.

"We're not going to fight this battle one-on-one. Too many of us will die. I'm going to ask Mr. Houston, Mr. Hamilton, Mr. Saunders, and Mr. Holden to meet with me in the fort, in private. In addition, I want Riley Creeker, Doctor Puckett, and Will Haymes there. I promise all of you that before we ride out in the morning, each of you will know what I am about to propose. Allow us an hour. Fair enough?"

"Fair enough," they shouted, a hundred strong.

"Very well," said Houston. "Let us retire to the fort and begin."

The eight men made their way into the fort. Houston, Hamilton, Saunders, and Holden took seats on one side of a rough table, while McQuade, Creeker, Puckett, and Haymes seated themselves on the other.

"Begin, Mr. McQuade," Houston said.

"I propose we increase our force another fifty men," said McQuade. "Two hundred. The rest will remain here, securing the fort against possible attack by Comanches."

"I can't agree to that until you explain to my satisfaction how you intend to overcome three hundred and fifty men with a force of two hundred," Joshua Hamilton said.

"For starters," said McQuade, struggling to contain his temper, "we won't ride out in direct confrontation. Are you familiar with the term 'ambush,' Mr. Hamilton?"

"I am," Hamilton gritted, his ruddy face becoming even more ruddy.

"We won't make our move until the ship's cargo has been completely unloaded and the Mexicans have settled in a permanent camp," said McQuade. "Fifty of us will then attack the camp, inviting Monclova's bunch to pursue us. We'll lead them into the guns of the rest of our men. All one hundred and fifty of them. Do I have to ride it on to the end of the trail, or do you understand what I'm proposing?"

"I understand perfectly, McQuade," Hamilton said. "I also understand that you may be sending fifty men to their deaths. Who do you have in mind to lead this suicidal charge?"

"The four of us across the table from you," said McQuade, "and the others will all be volunteers. We can easily draw that many from our emigrants, if you fear for the safety of your men."

Hamilton had a difficult time containing himself, but Sam Houston regarded McQuade with what might have been satisfaction. But McQuade wasn't finished, and spoke as though he wasn't in the least put out by Hamilton's obvious anger.

"As I am sure Mr. Houston recalls," said McQuade, "we have several kegs of black powder and plenty of fuse. This was taken from a band of outlaws, and has nothing to do with the powder for use in our weapons. Tonight, with the help of Creeker, Haymes, and Doc Puckett, I aim to assemble some black-powder bombs. These will be kept handy by the hundred and fifty men waiting in ambush. Throw a few of these, with fifteen-second fuses, and I can promise you Miguel Monclova's bunch will be afoot *pronto*. While we can't cut them all down from ambush, we can be sure that all who escape are without horses. Do any of you have questions?"

"I don't," said Houston. "Joshua? Stockton? Alonzo?"

Not trusting himself to speak, Joshua Hamilton shook his head.

"I'm satisfied," Saunders said. "It's a plan that borders on brilliance."

"It's the least dangerous proposal I've ever heard," said Holden. "Let's go with it."

"It's your plan, Mr. McQuade," Houston said. "I suggest you choose the additional men from within your own ranks, and you are welcome to explain the procedure to all of those who are waiting impatiently outside."

Houston left the fort, and McQuade could hear him addressing the crowd, who wished to know what had been decided. McQuade exited just in time, for Houston had announced that McQuade would explain what had been agreed upon. When Houston left it all up to McQuade, the shouting and questions began. McQuade held up his hand for silence, and when he got it, quickly explained what had been decided within the fort. For a long moment there was silence, and then they all shouted their approval.

"I'm obliged," said McQuade. "Riley Creeker, Will Haymes, Doc Puckett, and me will lead the attack. For the rest of the force, I need forty-six volunteers."

More than a hundred shouting men surged forward.

CHAPTER 22

❧

*B*efore Chance McQuade did anything else, he chose the rest of the men he needed for the initial attack on Monclova's camp. To the surprise of Houston and his lieutenants, men eagerly sought to become part of the force McQuade would lead. Remembering his promise to the Burkes, he included Matthew, Mark, and Luke. Creeker, Haymes, and Doc Puckett had gone for the necessary materials to create the black-powder bombs. Into the fort they brought two kegs of black powder, coils of fuse, and a large wooden box of pint bottles that had once contained whiskey. Many men had gathered around to watch the preparation of the bombs. Somewhere Doc had found a funnel that fitted the necks of the bottles, and began filling them from the kegs.

"We could use some corks," said McQuade, as he dug through the whiskey bottles.

"With some soft pine and a sharp knife, I could make some," Creeker said.

"Some of us can do that," said Matthew Burke. "We'll bring in some pine limbs."

Half a dozen men joined the Burkes, and soon they were all busy fashioning stoppers of wood to fit the necks of the bottles.

"Cut them to fit tight," McQuade said. "Then we'll want to cut away a channel along one side for the fuse."

Puckett had begun helping Creeker fill the pint bottles, and when all had been filled, there were thirty of them. Some of the wooden corks were ready, and using a thickness of fuse as a guide, McQuade whittled a groove down the side of one of the stoppers.

"Groove the rest of them like this one," said McQuade.

With many helping, the task was soon finished. Sam Houston looked on with some appreciation, as McQuade talked to the assembled men about what lay ahead of them.

"I like your plan, us attackin' their camp and leadin' 'em into an ambush," said Elgin Summerfield, "but suppose they don't foller us?"

"It'll be up to us to raise enough hell so they can't resist," McQuade replied. "We'll gun down some of them, and that should be enough to get the rest after us. This will be a hit and run. We'll spread out in a skirmish line like we're about to ride right through the midst of them. Just shy of the camp, before we're in range of their rifles, we'll split our force, half of us riding to either side of their camp. Swingin' in close, we can use our revolvers for greater fire power and accuracy."

Despite his obvious dislike for McQuade, Joshua Hamilton had drifted back to the outer fringes of the group that had gathered.

"The danger will be much greater," Hamilton observed, "for the enemy will also be able to rely on revolvers."

"Hamilton," said McQuade, "from the back of a running horse, accuracy is impossible with a rifle. This will be a surprise attack at dawn, and we don't know that this bunch will be armed with hand guns. Do you buckle a pistol on over your drawers, when you first wake up?"

That drew thunderous laughter, much of it from the women who had gathered around, and Hamilton turned away. But he found himself looking into the stern eyes of Houston.

"Joshua," Houston said, "we have been friends for a long time. Chance McQuade is on our side, yet you obviously do not trust him. May I ask why?"

"He has been here only a few days," said Hamilton stiffly, "yet he has virtually taken over command of this post."

"He has assumed nothing that you or any other man within this command couldn't have," Houston said. "Have you forgotten that it was McQuade and Creeker who alerted us to the possibility of a Mexican sailing ship arriving at Matagorda Bay?"

"No," said Hamilton, "I haven't forgotten, and I presume that you haven't forgotten that no such ship has been sighted."

"Whether the ship arrives or not," Houston replied, "it was an obvious oversight on our part. I believe Mr. McQuade is about to distinguish himself with his planned attack on the Monclova camp."

"As I recall," said Hamilton, "the original purpose of that was to seize the ship's cargo for our own use. If there is no ship, why the attack on Monclova's camp?"

"Joshua, I fear that your dislike for McQuade has overridden your better judgment," Houston said. "You are overlooking or choosing to ignore the ominous fact that the three hundred men riding in from Matamoros will increase Monclova's forces to probably four hundred and fifty. That makes ours the smaller force. Would you suggest that we do nothing, allowing Monclova to attack us?"

"Of course not," said Hamilton. "I would never advocate that."

"I'm sorry," Houston replied, "but I believe you just did. Ship or not, McQuade's surprise attack, followed with an ambush, could virtually wipe out the enemy. It is beyond me how you can find fault with that."

The conversation ended on a sour note, with Joshua Hamilton walking away. Houston stood there, his heart heavy with regret, crumpling his old hat in his big hands.

*   *   *

Monclova's camp was on the south bank of the Rio Colorado, less than a mile from Matagorda Bay. In the distance, the blue of the Gulf of Mexico stretched as far as the eye could see. There was excitement in the camp, as Monclova met with his lieutenants Pedro Mendez, Hidalgo Cortez, and Antonio Hermosillo. Far away, barely visible to the naked eye, was the tip of a sail, first sighted through a spy glass.

"The General Santa Anna, he not forget," Miguel Monclova exulted. "Food, medicine, ammunition, and soldiers."

"*Sí*," Hermosillo said. "*Por dios*, we surprise the *Tejanos*, no?"

"*Sí*," said Monclova. "With the cannon, we knock down the walls of their foolish fort and squash them like mice as they run away."

But several miles north of Monclova's camp, other eyes had observed the distant sail, and men mounted their horses. Sam Houston's suspicions had come to pass, and he must be told.

"Riders comin'," somebody shouted.

By the time the riders had reined up, Houston was there to greet them.

"We seen a sail last night, just 'fore sundown," said one of the men.

"Have any more men ridden up from the south to join Monclova?" Houston asked.

"None that we seen," said one of the men who had just ridden in from Matagorda Bay. "Just the same bunch that rode downriver."

The newly arrived horsemen were now surrounded by many other men, anxious to hear any new developments. Houston spoke loudly enough for all to hear.

"A sail has been sighted off Matagorda Bay, and it has to be the Mexican sailing ship we have been expecting.

The additional men riding in from Matamoros have not arrived."

It was all coming to pass, just as Chance McQuade had predicted, and while many men shouted their excitement, others turned skeptical eyes on Joshua Hamilton. McQuade stood beside Houston, talking to the men who had brought the news. Creeker, Haymes, and Doc Puckett awaited some decision from Houston or McQuade. Houston spoke first.

"Mr. McQuade, I believe we should hold fast another day. We must allow these men riding from Matamoros to join Monclova, give them time to unload the cargo from the ship, and to move it to a permanent camp."

"I agree," said McQuade. "We want the ship unloaded and long gone, before we attack Monclova's camp. We want Santa Anna told that the reinforcements reached Monclova, and that supplies from the ship were safely unloaded."

While none of them relished another day of inactivity, the delay seemed justified, and they prepared to make the best of it. There had been no rain for a while and an increasing cloudiness to the west suggested that a change was in the making. Men patched wagon canvas, stretching it tight over the bows, while women rearranged their belongings to allow room for sleeping. Over a small fire, McQuade had placed an iron pot three-quarters full of hardened paraffin. When it became liquid, using tweezers, McQuade began dipping the prepared loads for his revolver. Other men watched the procedure, and when McQuade had finished, he spoke to them.

"It's a good idea to dip the loads for your revolvers in wax. It keeps the powder dry, and there's rain on the way."

They took turns preparing their ammunition. McQuade used the extra day to speak to the men who would be riding downriver for the fight with Monclova. It seemed much like old times, as the emigrants again depended on their circled wagons. By early afternoon, the big gray thunderheads had swept in from the west, and a rising west wind brought the pungent smell of rain. Canvas shelters had been strung up between wagons, providing dry areas for cooking and eating. The rain began just before dark, driving Houston's men into the fort. On two of the inside walls there was an enormous fireplace a dozen feet wide, for cooking during bad weather. Here, coffee pots bubbled far into the night, for the men were restless, and few of them slept. Sometime before daylight, the rain ceased, and in the predawn darkness, breakfast fires blossomed. As the men prepared to ride, McQuade and Houston made the rounds, seeking to head off any problems. As Houston spoke to the men who would ride with him, McQuade thought it significant that Joshua Hamilton wasn't one of them. McQuade found Doc Puckett at the wagon with Maggie.

"How are you feeling, Doc?"

"Frankly, a little scared," said Puckett. "I've never shot, or shot at, a man before. I'm sure that will take some getting used to."

"You never get used to it," McQuade replied, "and only a damn fool is never afraid."

"Don't let him do anything foolish, McQuade," said Maggie. "I've already lost one man and I'm too old and tired to find and break in a third one."

"Maggie," McQuade said, "you'll never be old. Tired, maybe, but old, never."

McQuade found Riley Creeker and Will Haymes hunkered beside a breakfast fire, having first cups of coffee.

"Suppose we reach Matagorda Bay and those Mexican reinforcements still haven't shown up," Will Haymes said. "Will we wait for them and ambush the lot, or hit Monclova and the smaller force?"

"I'm not opposed to jumping Monclova's bunch and taking the ship's cargo from them," said McQuade, "provided the ship's departed. We want it to take months for word of this to get back to Santa Anna. We can always bushwhack that bunch of soldiers riding in from Matamoros, after we've beaten Monclova and taken the ship's cargo. When we get to Matagorda Bay, we'll change our plans, if need be, but I'm expecting the reinforcements to be there.''

Two hundred strong, they rode downriver an hour after first light. Sam Houston led out, and in a column of fours, the others followed. Directly behind Houston rode Creeker, McQuade, Haymes, and Puckett. They stopped only to rest their horses, and seldom did anybody speak. Near sundown they stopped for the night, eating cold food they carried in their saddlebags. Men stood watch in two-hour shifts, and after a cold breakfast, they rode on. Only once, while they rested their horses, did Houston speak to them as a group.

"At this point, we will ride several miles north of the river, and then eastward, until we sight the Gulf. We don't know that they haven't unloaded the ship, moved inland, and set up camp. If they haven't, when they do, they could hardly miss the tracks of our two hundred horses. We must avoid them until we're ready to attack. If we do not, then the surprise could be ours.''

They rode north of the river a good two miles before again riding eastward. It was a wise move, as they soon learned, for they eventually had an excellent view of the Gulf and Matagorda Bay without being seen. The ship lay anchored a hundred yards from shore, its sails furled. The Mexican flag fluttered from the mast, and as Houston and his forces sat their horses and watched, men poled a raft toward the anchored craft.

"The boat's still here," said Elgin Summerfield, "but we don't know if the soldiers have rode in.''

"We'll know tonight," Houston replied. "Soon as it's dark, some of us will take their measure. I'd say the soldiers are here, and that they haven't chosen to help unload the ship's cargo.''

They watched the men pole the raft alongside the ship. To their surprise, men on deck removed a canvas, revealing a loaded wagon. Secured by ropes or chains to a hoist, it was swung over the side of the craft and slowly lowered to the waiting raft. Once the raft had been poled to shore, horses were hitched to the wagon. The raft was then poled back to the ship and another loaded wagon was lowered over the side.

"Well, by God," said Shanghai McLean, "I been wonderin' how we was goin' to move all them goods back to the fort. They done made it easy on us."

After a third wagon had been brought to shore, the raft didn't return to the ship. It appeared all the cargo had been unloaded.

"Now," Will Haymes said, "if that ship will hoist anchor and sail, we can get down to the business of claiming that cargo."

There was some activity on deck, and it soon became evident that the vessel was preparing to sail. The anchor was raised and slowly the sails were unfurled.

"We saw only three wagons unloaded," said McQuade, "but there has to be more than that. The ship must have dropped anchor early yesterday morning."

They watched the ship sail away, and only when it had been swallowed by distance did Houston speak.

"There is no reason why Monclova shouldn't be moving farther inland. I believe it is time we learned how many of those wagons were unloaded, and whether or not those men riding from Matamoros have arrived. Mr. McQuade, will you choose a man to ride with you, and report to us their activities?"

"Yes," said McQuade. "Come on, Creeker."

Slowly they rode toward the river, knowing they must soon dismount and continue on foot. When McQuade estimated they had ridden a mile, he reined up.

"We'd better leave the horses here," he said.

They dismounted and continued on foot, and they soon heard the rattle of wagons. A thicket offered cover, and they crept closer, until they could see a clear stretch along the river. There were a dozen wagons, and beyond a doubt the reinforcements had arrived, for they rode in a column of fours, stretching back farther than McQuade and Creeker could see. When the caravan had finally passed, McQuade nudged Creeker. They got to their feet and returned to their horses. Their comrades saw them coming, and by the time they had dismounted, they were surrounded.

"The reinforcements are here," said McQuade, "and there are twelve wagons."

"Then we need only wait for dark," Houston said. "Then we can find their camp and lay our plans accordingly."

"After they settle down somewhere," said McQuade, "we'll need some daylight to plan an ambush. We must choose a location where there is cover for us, and little or none for them. Most important, our trap must be near enough so that they don't give up chasing us before we lure them into it."

"You speak with the voice of experience," Houston replied. "I'd consider it a favor if you will choose the place for the ambush. It will be you and the men riding with you who will be in the most danger. Therefore, you should lay the ambush as near as possible to the Mexican camp. Allow us to take up the fight."

"We must have good cover for the ambush," said McQuade, "regardless of how far we must ride to lure them into it. The greatest risk for us will be at the time of our attack. Once they're in pursuit of us, shooting from the back of a running horse, we won't be in that much danger."

"We're likely to be a while settin' up this ambush," said Summerfield. "I can see the need for some daylight in choosin' a place with cover, but this bunch could just ramble on, havin' a new camp ever' night."

"Maybe," McQuade said, "but I don't think so. They have enough men and supplies to justify a permanent camp. If they don't set up one today, they will tomorrow."

"There's little we can do, then," said Houston, "until

we know they've established a permanent camp. You are aware of where Monclova's old camp was?''

"Yes," McQuade said, "and if that's their destination, they should reach it sometime the day after tomorrow. After dark, Creeker and me will look in on their camp, but we're still a day away from our ambush, I think.''

Being downwind from their adversaries, it was safe to have a supper fire. Houston ordered the fire doused well before dark. McQuade and Creeker rode upstream, believing a light west wind would bring them sounds from Monclova's camp before they rode into it. A distinctive smell of wood smoke was sufficient warning, and they dismounted.

"We'll continue on foot," said McQuade. "I doubt this will be more than an overnight camp, but we must be sure.''

They crept close enough to see, and there was no look of permanence. The river bank was much too high, even to water the horses, and the animals would have to be led to and from water. There also was too much cover for potential enemies. McQuade and Creeker returned to their horses and rode downriver, reporting to Houston what they had seen.

Houston sighed. "Then we'll just have to wait. I can't imagine why they chose such a place for a camp, even overnight.''

"Monclova's feelin' his oats," said McQuade, "and on the frontier, over-confidence can become fatal.''

"Well, hell," Elgin Summerfield said, "if there's plenty of cover, we could surround the varmints in the dark and cut 'em down.''

"We could try," said McQuade, "but after the first volley they'd be shooting at our muzzle flashes, and some of us would be cut down. More than half of them would escape, and there would be a running battle for God knows how long. The only sensible way is for us to do exactly what we've planned to do. What you're proposing is too much a military maneuver, where they expect to lose some men. I don't expect to lose any. If all of you will stick to our plans, we'll come out of this alive.''

It was a telling argument, and McQuade could see acceptance in their eyes. Impatient though they were, he was talking sense, and they knew it.

Houston again ordered a breakfast fire, and they took their time, eating leisurely. The Mexican forces—if they were bound for Monclova's original camp—would reach their destination sometime in the early afternoon. McQuade was hunkered down, enjoying a last cup of coffee, when Houston joined him.

"The rest of us will remain here," said Houston, "while you and Creeker ride ahead. I see no reason for all of us advancing, until we're ready to lay an ambush and launch our dawn attack."

"That's wise," McQuade replied. "If they do reach Monclova's old camp, and we're sure they intend to remain there, I think we'll have a look at the country to the south of the river. We'll begin looking for a likely place to spring the ambush."

"I can see the need for luring them south," said Houston, "with them strung out along the river. That means your attack will have to come from up- or downriver, unless you intend to attack from across the river."

"Creeker and me will split our forces," McQuade said, "and we'll hit them from east and west. We'll fan out in a line, gun down as many as we can, and then swing south. We won't actually enter their camp. When we're beyond it, we'll come together and ride a slow gallop toward the ambush, where you and the rest of our forces will be waiting."

"A brilliant maneuver," said Houston. "I'm feeling better about this all the time. Just keep far enough ahead of them so they can't reach you from behind."

"We will," McQuade replied, "but we don't want to lose them. Once we know they're coming, with the intention of following us into the canyon, we'll ride like hell toward the box end. There we'll dismount, and those who survive the ambush will have to face us.''

McQuade and Creeker waited until noon before they rode out, allowing Monclova's forces time to reach the old camp, if that was their destination. They followed the river, for again the light west wind was in their faces. There would be ample warning before they were near enough to risk discovery. Again campfire smoke alerted them, and they reined up.

"On foot from here," said McQuade.

The camp was situated in a long clearing along the river, with virtually no cover for potential enemies, so McQuade and Creeker had to circle to the south. Their eventual view of the camp, however, told them what they needed to know.

"It's near noon," McQuade observed, "and there's a coffee pot hung over a cook fire."

"Yeah," said Creeker, "and there's two tents next to the river."

Teams had been unhitched from the wagons, and horses grazed nearby. Men relaxed, heads on their saddles, tall-crowned, wide-brimmed sombreros tipped over their eyes.

"Let's get back to our horses," McQuade said. "It's time to find a place to arrange our ambush."

Well out of sight of the river, they rode south, and not more than two miles distant, they found exactly what McQuade was looking for. The canyon began shallow, growing wider and deeper. There was a seep, allowing for lush vegetation and a strung-out stand of willows. Along the length of the canyon there was enough cover to hide an army, and at the farthest end, a wall twenty feet high.

"This ambush had better work," said Creeker, "or we're gonna be a flock of dead peckerwoods, when we run headlong into this box end. Are you gonna tell the others of this, before we ride?"

"Yes," McQuade replied. "I won't ask a man to gamble, without telling him what the odds are."

Reaching Houston's camp, they dismounted.

"They've dug in at Monclova's old camp," said McQuade, "and we're ready to attack tomorrow at dawn. We went ahead and found a place for the ambush."

With some help from Creeker, McQuade told them of the box canyon, of the risk.

"This attack may be even more dangerous than we thought," said Houston.

"It could be, if anything goes wrong with the ambush," McQuade admitted. "For that reason, I'm not holding any of you to your commitment, if you don't like the looks of it. Just remember, if you ride with me, our lives will be in the hands of these men led by Mr. Houston. If you have doubts, I won't think unkindly of you if you speak up. Silence honors your commitment."

Not a man spoke.

"It's settled, then," said McQuade. "We'll ride to the canyon tomorrow morning, well before first light. Those of you who will man the ambush will have to take your horses to the nearest cover, returning to the canyon on foot. Are there any questions?"

Again there was silence, and McQuade sighed with satisfaction. They now had only to wait for the dawn, and whatever destiny held in store.

Reaching the shallow end of the canyon, McQuade and Creeker reined up. Houston and the hundred and fifty men who would wait in ambush veered away, toward the south. They would conceal their horses, returning to the canyon afoot. They had been gone not more than a quarter of an hour, when they returned, moving quietly through the predawn darkness.

"Good luck," said Houston quietly, as he led his men into the canyon.

McQuade waited another quarter hour before lifting his hand as a signal to ride. The riders divided, half of them going with Creeker, the others with McQuade. Creeker and his force rode eastward, while McQuade's men rode west. They would sweep in along the river bank, attacking the camp from two sides. Beyond it, they would then come together, riding toward the canyon and the deadly ambush. Reaching their position to the west, McQuade's men fanned out in a skirmish line, awaiting a signal from Creeker. And Creeker wasted no time. There was a fearful screech that would have made a Comanche envious, and before it died away, the rattle of gunfire. McQuade and his men thundered in from the west, their revolvers roaring. Men shouted and cursed, firing a few retaliatory shots, but the surprise was total. Twenty, thirty, forty men were down, dead or dying.

"*Sangre de Cristo,*" Miguel Monclova bawled, "to your horses! Kill them!"

With no time for saddles, the defenders leaped on their horses and galloped in pursuit of the attackers. As McQuade had instructed, his men slowed their mounts almost to a walk, allowing Monclova's defenders to gain on them. Monclova himself, seizing a rifle, ran to a horse, mounted, and galloped madly after his soldiers. Reaching the shallow end of the canyon, McQuade and his followers kicked their horses into a fast gallop. Reaching the box end of the canyon, they swung out of their saddles and sought cover, preparing to fight for their lives. Houston and his men waited as long as they dared, until the vengeful riders were all within gun range.

"Fire!" Houston shouted.

There was a thunder of guns that sounded like a single shot, echoed many times. One of the first to die was Monclova himself, and seeing their leader fall, his men had only one thought, and that was to save themselves. But the jaws of the ambush had closed on them, and there was no retreat. They galloped on, only to run headlong into a wall of lead from McQuade and his men. When it finally ended, the silence seemed all the more profound, as Houston's forces came together.

"Anybody hit?" McQuade asked of his men.

There was only silence, and McQuade could hear Houston asking the same question. Again there was only silence, but only for a moment. Men shouted, waving their hats, and above it all came the bull voice of Sam Houston.

"God be praised, it is a miracle."

"It's all of that, and then some," Doctor Puckett observed. "We wiped them out, and we didn't lose a man."

"No," said McQuade, "we didn't wipe them out. Some escaped, but I doubt they'll stop short of Matamoros. We won this time, but it's only the start of something bigger than all of us."

"I'm goin' to take some men and round up some extra horses," Creeker said. "We'll be needin' them to haul our wagonloads of supplies back to the fort."

"By God," said Elgin Summerfield, "after all that work makin' black-powder bombs, we didn't use a one. Mine's still in my saddlebag."

"There'll be need for them later on," McQuade said. "Our victory couldn't have been more complete."

Triumphant, they returned to Houston's fort. Texans all, Santa Anna's soldiers referred to them as *los Diablos Tejanos*, the Texas Devils. In a fight that Sam Houston led to the finish, they saw the Stars and Stripes raised as Texas achieved statehood, and when the dust finally settled over the bloody plains of south Texas, they claimed their land grants along the Rio Colorado . . .

EPILOGUE

⌀

*T*he Texas Colony, founded in 1822 by Stephen Austin, fell on hard times after Steve Austin's death in 1836. After the bloody disaster at the Alamo in 1836, and the victorious retaliation by Texans at San Jacinto, Mexican-American relations went from bad to worse.

Samuel Houston was born in Rockbridge County, Virginia, on March 2, 1793. After distinguished service in the United States Army, Houston resigned in 1818 to study law. He opened a law office in Lebanon, Tennessee, and in the years to follow, he served in a variety of elected offices, including two terms in Congress and as governor of the state of Tennessee. Houston made his first trip to Texas in 1832, to report on Indian affairs to his old friend, Andrew Jackson. While he was in Texas largely as an Indian agent, Houston was caught up in the rising storm of opposition to Mexico. As the threat of conflict grew stronger, Houston—with a commanding presence and an ability to raise confidence and enthusiasm—quickly rose to prominence.

In the years that followed, Sam Houston twice served as governor of the Republic of Texas. On February 19, 1846, the Lone Star flag of the Republic of Texas was lowered for the last time, and in its place flew the stars and stripes. On February 21, the Texas Legislature elected Sam Houston to the United States Senate, where he represented Texas for fourteen years. Houston was inaugurated governor of Texas on December 21, 1859, but in 1861—opposing secession—he was forced out of office.

Between 1833 and 1855, Santa Anna became dictator of Mexico three different times.

THE TRAIL DRIVE SERIES
by Ralph Compton

From St. Martin's Paperbacks

The only riches Texas had left after the Civil War were five million maverick longhorns and the brains, brawn and boldness to drive them north to where the money was. Now, Ralph Compton brings this violent and magnificent time to life in an extraordinary epic series based on the history-blazing trail drives.

THE GOODNIGHT TRAIL (BOOK 1)
_____ 92815-7 $5.99 U.S./$7.99 Can.
THE WESTERN TRAIL (BOOK 2)
_____ 92901-3 $5.99 U.S./$7.99 Can.
THE CHISOLM TRAIL (BOOK 3)
_____ 92953-6 $5.99 U.S./$7.99 Can.
THE BANDERA TRAIL (BOOK 4)
_____ 95143-4 $5.99 U.S./$7.99 Can.
THE CALIFORNIA TRAIL (BOOK 5)
_____ 95169-8 $5.99 U.S./$7.99 Can.
THE SHAWNEE TRAIL (BOOK 6)
_____ 95241-4 $5.99 U.S./$7.99 Can.
THE VIRGINIA CITY TRAIL (BOOK 7)
_____ 95306-2 $5.99 U.S./$7.99 Can.
THE DODGE CITY TRAIL (BOOK 8)
_____ 95380-1 $5.99 U.S./$7.99 Can.
THE OREGON TRAIL (BOOK 9)
_____ 95547-2 $5.99 U.S./$7.99 Can.
THE SANTA FE TRAIL (BOOK 10)
_____ 96296-7 $5.99 U.S./$7.99 Can.
THE OLD SPANISH TRAIL (BOOK 11)
_____ 96408-0 $5.99 U.S./$7.99 Can.

Publishers Book and Audio Mailing Service
P.O. Box 070059, Staten Island, NY 10307
Please send me the book(s) I have checked above. I am enclosing $_____ (please add $1.50 for the first book, and $.50 for each additional book to cover postage and handling. Send check or money order only—no CODs) or charge my VISA, MASTERCARD, DISCOVER or AMERICAN EXPRESS card.

Card Number_____

Expiration date_____Signature_____

Name_____

Address_____

City_____State/Zip _____
Please allow six weeks for delivery. Prices subject to change without notice. Payment in U.S. funds only. New York residents add applicable sales tax.   TD 4/98